THE
DIVINER

DAW Books Presents

the Finest in Fantasy by

MELANIE RAWN

Exiles
THE RUINS OF AMBRAI
THE MAGEBORN TRAITOR

Dragon Prince
DRAGON PRINCE
THE STAR SCROLL
SUNRUNNER'S FIRE

Dragon Star
STRONGHOLD
THE DRAGON TOKEN
SKYBOWL

The Golden Key Universe
THE GOLDEN KEY
(with Jennifer Roberson and Kate Elliott)
THE DIVINER

MELANIE RAWN
THE
DIVINER

DAW BOOKS, INC.

DONALD A. WOLLHEIM, FOUNDER

375 Hudson Street, New York, NY 10014

ELIZABETH R. WOLLHEIM

SHEILA E. GILBERT

PUBLISHERS

http://www.dawbooks.com

First Printing, August 2011
2 3 4 5 6 7 8 9

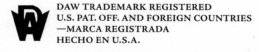

DAW TRADEMARK REGISTERED
U.S. PAT. OFF. AND FOREIGN COUNTRIES
—MARCA REGISTRADA
HECHO EN U.S.A.

PRINTED IN THE U.S.A.

For
Jennifer Roberson
and
Kate Elliott
(and her evil twin, Alis Rasmussen)

This novel is a prequel to *The Golden Key*. Although it helps to have read that one before reading this one, it's not necessary; I hope that I wrote *The Diviner* in such a way that it makes sense all by itself. If it doesn't, I have every confidence that you'll let me know.

In the barbarian land to the north, the Grijalvas believe that the smearing of paint on canvas is more powerful than the writing of words. In Tza'ab Rih, we of the Shagara know that this is not so.

— ZEIF SHAGARA, *Commentaries on the Al-Fansihirro, 1236*

Il-Kadiri

611-630

Let me tell you of him.

Those of you who know of him only from the words of others, you may not believe what I will write. But I heard it from his own lips, and if you think disrespectful some of the things I reveal, be assured that when he spoke to me of his life, he enjoined me to honesty equal to his own whenever I should repeat his tale. Thus I shall spare him as little as he spared himself, and this shall be a faithful telling.

By Acuyib, the Wonderful and Strange, that which follows is the truth.

— FERRHAN MUALEEF, *Deeds of Il-Kadiri*, 654

1

The city of Dayira Azreyq breathed softly that night. No one wished to be caught inhaling a particle of the Sheyqa's air more than was strictly required for survival. Within the shops and houses served by the great reservoir that gave the city its name—Circle of Blue—lovers muffled their sighs, fretful babies were swiftly hushed by nervous fathers, murmurs became whispers as shadows deepened. Those few persons out on the streets walked furtively and said nothing. Those brave enough to speak aloud did so only in their own homes, with faces lowered and eyes downcast. *Do not notice me, I am of no importance, I do not exist*—and one more night of reprieve was begun.

But the city was not entirely quiet, at least not in the precincts of the palace. The Sheyqa was in a mood for celebrating, and her guests acceded to the royal requirement for music and laughter and merriment of all kinds.

Preparations had begun early that morning. In the banqueting hall, with its splendid domed-and-tiled ceiling, white draperies were taken from red silken couches, and massive trays of beaten gold were set on tripods. In the east wing, with its floor-to-ceiling windows shuttered against the scorching sun, musicians tuned their instruments, and dancers were instructed regarding the Sheyqa's preferences for the evening. In the kitchen, with its vast hearths and staggering array of copper pots, cooks sweated and swore, cajoling the roasts to cook and the breads to rise. In the cellar, with its low stone archways and maze of shelves and cabinets, stewards selected the wines, and servants polished the priceless blue glassware seized more than a century ago from barbarian invaders by the armies of Rimmal Madar. If anyone remembered that those armies had been under the personal command not of Sheyqa Ammara Izzad, the present ruler's great-grandmother, but of an al-Ma'aliq, no one mentioned it. Ever.

By sundown the guests had arrived, and the palace echoed with laughter and music. For all that the city breathed softly, carefully, the Sheyqa was in an excellent mood. Her guests—every adult male of the al-Ma'aliq line— were enjoying themselves. She was enjoying their delusions. She smiled when yet another toast was proclaimed to the power of her eldest son's loins. Today Acuyib had shown him to be doubly blessed: his sixth wife, Ammineh, and his seventeenth concubine (whose name the Sheyqa could never quite remember) had each given birth, bringing the total number of her children and grandchildren to fifty, her own exact age.

Her smile didn't waver as one of the al-Ma'aliq raised his wine cup high in salute to his own daughter, Ammineh, mother of the fiftieth. Sheyqa Nizzira joined in the toast and beamed at the girl's father as if genuinely celebrating the triumph. After a swallow of sharp dry wine—she loathed this too-strong varietal, but serving it was necessary tonight—she soothed the bitterness from her mouth with a confection of chopped dates, honey, and candied rose petals. She sucked stickiness from her fingers, delicately dipping them in a bowl of scented water before reaching again for the sweets.

Manners. Elegance. Refinement. These her father had drilled into her from babyhood. "*Make as much war as you wish, Nizzira my daughter—you will be Sheyqa, and it is your right and your duty. But recall that the warrior who is also cultivated and civilized gains not only the respect but the regard of her people.*" He'd been a wise man, her father, never doubting that his only child would emerge victorious in the exquisitely brutal struggle for the Moonrise Throne. Sheyqa Nizzira missed him terribly, and in his memory took every opportunity to show that she was not only a mighty ruler but polished in her person.

But her father had been wrong about one thing. The objective of a warrior was to gain not respect but fear. This she had done and would continue to do so long as the northern borders of Rimmal Madar were beset by barbarian tribes—with whom the al-Ma'aliq were conspiring. They would deny it if confronted, but Nizzira knew their protestations would be lies. Had she been in their position—formerly powerful, loathing her, and taxed so heavily that they had not the wherewithal to make war unless allied to others—she would have collaborated with the Dread and Mighty Chaydann Il-Mamnoua'a Himself.

As Nizzira rinsed her fingers yet again, from the corner of her eye she caught an al-Ma'aliq curling his lip. This was one of Ammineh's brothers, who doubtless had heard her incessant complaints in excruciating detail. The whole family maddened the Sheyqa beyond endurance. Even their name was an arrogance, as if the head of their family—a doddering old imbecile currently lolling on plump cushions and using a dancer's transparent silk scarf as a bib—could still call himself "king." The al-Ma'aliq had anciently held a large portion of Rimmal Madar. Ammineh, Nizzira's eldest son's sixth wife, not a mere concubine—and she cursed the boy for agreeing to a wedding when a bedding was all he was after—prated endlessly about her ancestry, constantly reminding everyone that her forefathers had been kings back in the days when the title had meant something, when the natural order of women owning and ruling land had been for a shameful time overset by the influence of the western barbarians. To Acuyib's Glory, that situation had been righted. Men worked, soldiered, farmed, sailed the ships, commanded the caravans, and crafted the goods for which Rimmal Madar was justly famous—but women's wisdom and women's logic determined the manner in which such things were done. Women controlled the wealth of the family. And one woman presided over all.

In a way, the Sheyqa reflected, it was a pity that one or two of the abandoned customs did not still obtain. It would be a lovely thing to relegate the wives and concubines—and even those of her daughters and granddaughters she didn't much like—to the strictures of the arrareem as it used to be in the old, uncivilized days. Locked away, Ammineh and her ceaseless carping could no longer offend the Sheyqa's eyes and ears.

The al-Ma'aliq still ruled their cities and fields and mountain castle like the kings they hadn't been for generations. They behaved as if Nizzira's own great-grandmother hadn't fielded the army that turned back the western barbarians. Her ancestor had safeguarded the al-Ma'aliq and everyone else in a thousand-mile march from the slaughters that ensued when Believers in Acuyib's Glory refused to accept that outrageous Mother-and-Son religion. But the trouble Sheyqa Ammara Izzad encountered in expelling the invaders was but a prelude to getting the pretentious, condescending, deceiving al-Ma'aliq to own up to their agreement: fealty in exchange for protection.

Aware that she was frowning, the Sheyqa smoothed her expression and scooped up a handful of candied rose petals. The sugary crunch was satisfying and soothed her as if she were still a child—and she was reminded yet again of her father, and how he had doled out candies to munch on when her multitude of half-sisters and cousins had been plotting against her. When she was a child, the sweets had comforted her; when she grew older, reaching for candies had kept her hand from her knife on more than one occasion, and occupying her mouth with chewing had kept her lips from forming regrettable and possibly fatal words.

Ayia, but she had out-plotted them all. Her mother's five other husbands and their vile offspring were either dead or rendered so insignificant as to be effectively dead. This was the truest test of a sheyqa: that she should prevail in the end over every other female of her bloodline with any claim to the throne—for what use was a ruler against outside enemies if she could not defeat those inside her own palace? It was a father's job to keep his daughters safe until they were old enough to put to good use his advice and his years of subtle scheming and the alliances he had carefully nurtured. Nizzira's father had been a brilliant man, but she had also been a genuinely gifted student. Proof: She was Sheyqa of Rimmal Madar. In her hands was all the power—and all the attendant worries. Most of these worries were named al-Ma'aliq.

Nizzira's great-grandmother had personally assembled the troops that had subdued the al-Ma'aliq after the invaders were expelled; her grandfather, acting on behalf of his elderly mother, had been compelled to do it again; Nizzira's mother had been criminally remiss in not setting them back on their silk-covered asses for good and all. Now one of their arrogant, chattering daughters had given Nizzira her fiftieth descendant, and for this she was supposed to be grateful. All the indolent girl had to do was sit around sipping mint tea and gossiping while she swelled up like a hippopotamus and eventually, after a few grunts and groans and a disgusting bloody mess, push out an infant—while all the time Nizzira was managing the dauntingly varied affairs of an entire nation.

And now Ammineh's male relations lounged near the Sheyqa's couch, eating the Sheyqa's food and drinking the Sheyqa's wine, as if the new baby were in any way of their form or making. The infant looked nothing like the al-Ma'aliq. She had Nizzira's luxuriant black hair, her long-lidded dark eyes, her noble nose, her clever mouth. The only contamination was in the chin—square and stubborn like Ammineh's, not rounded and cleft like the Sheyqa's own. But perhaps that would change in time.

Even if it didn't, there would be nobody around to compare the child to. The al-Ma'aliq were attending their final banquet, down to the last man. As for their complacent wives . . . and as for their other pestilential daughters . . . and as for every one of their unruly little brats . . .

They would be taken care of, too.

The Sheyqa dipped her fingertips in the bowl of scented water and smiled. Yes, she was in a mood for celebrating, and the proud, stupid al-Ma'aliq were happy to oblige.

Why, Azzad al-Ma'aliq asked himself for the thousandth time, were women so expensive? And not just in the cost of trinkets, either. They demanded a man's time and exhausted his patience, not to mention his energy. They required so much attention. And thoughtfulness. And conversation.

And money, he thought ruefully, patting the folds of green and gold silk wound around his waist, where until an hour ago a fabulous pearl necklace had been concealed. It was now somewhere in the rubbish heap behind Ashiyah's house. Instead of squealing with delight at the gift, she'd thrown it out her bedroom window.

The idea had been for Ashiyah to undress him—slowly if she liked, quickly if that was her mood; he was always generous and accommodating, wasn't he?—and discover his latest gift, and then—

But that hadn't happened. She'd come at him spitting and clawing, furious that he was late. A hundred women in Rimmal Madar would have waited years just for a smile from the latest handsome al-Ma'aliq male in a long line of handsome al-Ma'aliq males, and yet Ashiyah had behaved as if a paltry couple of hours was sufficient reason to rip his face to shreds.

He'd backed off, desperately groping for the pearls hidden in his gold-and-green striped sash. For just an instant the ploy succeeded; covetous joy sparked hotter than anger in her magnificent eyes when she saw the jewels.

Then she seized the necklace and tried to strangle him with it.

Between his knees, Khamsin heaved an almost human sigh. Azzad patted the stallion's arching black neck. "Do you think you need to tell me I'm a fool? Believe me, it's nothing I haven't told myself a thousand times. But she *is* spectacularly beautiful. And it would infuriate her husband spectacularly if he ever caught us!"

The vexing Ozmin had in recent months been Azzad's guide through the bureaucratic snarl of the Sheyqa's tax collectors. It was the al-Ma'aliq's contention that their lands were being singled out for heavier tribute than usual, and Za'avedra el-Ibrafidia al-Ma'aliq—in futile hopes of rousing her second son to anything even vaguely resembling familial responsibility—assigned Azzad the disagreeable duty of untangling (which meant bribing) enough functionaries to support a protest in the law courts. Absurd, of course; everyone knew it was the Sheyqa who had ordered the extra taxes, and only the Sheyqa would have any say in easing them. Not for the first time, Azzad joined his relations in cursing the ancestor who had thought it expedient to make a bond of defense with a woman everyone had fully expected to die in battle against the heathen—or to be murdered by one of her own lethal siblings in their quest for family dominance.

But Sheyqa Nizzira's great-grandmother had not died, and the oath remained binding, and here they all were: sworn to the descendant of an arrogant bitch from some obscure southern tribe whom Acuyib had inexplicably blessed in war.

"At least I don't have it as bad as Ammineh," he muttered. The stallion's ears twitched, but Azzad's tone indicated nothing more than the usual complaining, so Khamsin ignored him. "She has to *sleep* with the son of that miserable barghoutz. For a little while, *I* slept with Ashiyah."

Not that Ashiyah's whisperings on his behalf when she summoned her husband to share her pillows had done the al-Ma'aliq any good. Azzad hadn't courted Ashiyah only for her usefulness—though had she been skinny and plain instead of sumptuously beautiful, he simply would have closed his eyes or told her that making love in the dark was so much more sensuous. Ayia, memories of her bed would have to sustain him until the next luscious lady presented herself to his fastidious notice. He wondered with a sudden grin who he could bestow his favors on to infuriate Ashiyah most when she heard of it.

He rode through the dark streets toward home, paying no attention to his surroundings. He didn't need to; Khamsin was familiar with this route. Azzad's nose identified the streets for him without his being fully aware of it. The stench of tanneries and butcher shops. The softly tantalizing scents from bakeries in Ayyash Sharyah. The tang of dinner spices wafting silently down from upstairs living quarters in Zoqalo Zaffiha, where from dawn until dark the hammers of brass and bronze and tin workers clanged. The long narrow alley where the stink of dye vats and wet wool was bearable only by daylight, and only because of the eyes' delight in the rainbow shanks hung from balcony to balcony overhead to dry. All workshops were shut up tight now, all streets and squares deserted. No one called out invitations to see or sample various wares, so Azzad was left alone with his thoughts.

Khamsin picked his way along the dirt and cobbles toward home while Azzad dreamed of Beit Ma'aliq's cool fountains, and fruits plucked ripe from the trees, and an evening spent listening to his sisters sing. The girls were of an age now to be of use to an older brother. Perhaps, he mused, fingers toying with the fine bronze wire tassels on the reins, now that they were almost marriageable, some of their prettier friends might be amenable to a dalliance. . . .

He could see his mother's face even now: stern, implacable, her dark eyes knowing every wayward thought in his head, and a single word on her lips as sharp as the silver needle that was her family's name and crest: *No*. Whatever women he amused himself with, none of them could be of rank or wealth.

Then again, Za'avedra el-Ibrafidia might turn a blind eye to such an association, in the way of mothers who knew their sons. If he compromised a nobleman's daughter, he would be forced to wed her. The very thought made him shudder. Getting married. Fathering children. Living a settled life. Doing something useful for the family—something unutterably boring. Staying with one woman for the rest of his life, or at least until her parents were dead. No, when he married—*if* he married—it would be to a girl with no relations whatsoever, not a single woman or man of her family alive anywhere to trouble him on her behalf when he wanted a little variety in his bed. Azzad considered it grossly unfair that only a sheyqa and her immediate family were permitted more than one spouse, the justification being that from them sprang the strength of the nation in the form of strong daughters and sons.

He snorted. Of all the descendants that Sheyqa Nizzira and her sons and daughters had produced so far, Azzad had heard very little to recommend any of them. Fifty of them now; he'd heard this morning that his cousin Ammineh had given birth to a daughter, and—

"Fifty! Acuyib save me! The celebration feast!"

Khamsin didn't bother to swing an ear around this time, but when Azzad hauled back on the reins, the stallion snorted and pranced a few steps in protest. He wanted his stall and his evening feed, Azzad knew—but all the al-Ma'aliq had been invited to the palace tonight to celebrate Ammineh's little girl, and in anticipating an evening with Ashiyah, the royal command had completely slipped his mind.

With a groan—he'd never get there in time and would have to think up some plausible excuse for his tardiness—he turned Khamsin toward the palace. A brisk trot and a shortcut or two, and maybe he'd arrive during the dancing or while an especially incredible creation of the Sheyqa's kitchen staff was being presented, or—well, he'd spent all his twenty years being lucky, and there was no reason to think tonight would be any different.

"Esteemed Majesty," the eunuch whispered at Sheyqa Nizzira's shoulder, "not all of them drink enough."

The Sheyqa smiled, clapping her hands in time to a spirited tune, following the dancers' swirling silks and exposed flesh with her gaze. The youth on the far left, the one who was dark and muscular and half-naked, he might do for later tonight. She kept her eyes on him, annoyed by the interruption, knowing it was necessary to reply. Without moving her lips, she said, "I never meant them to."

"But—Revered Majesty—your kinsmen from beyond The Steeps said—"

She saw the concertmaster watching her and gave him the signal that indicated her choice of the beautiful dark boy. He nodded once and turned to give his own instructions. To the eunuch, the Sheyqa said, "All that is required is that most of them are drunk. Go away. All will be as it should."

"You have commanded it, Exalted One." Bowing low, he melted away into the shadows.

She returned her attention to the boy, whose new role in the dance now required him to shed almost all his clothes. He was the coveted one, the desired one; all the other young men faded into the corners of the room while concubines belonging to Nizzira's sons danced to tempt him.

"No difficulties, I trust, Highness?" asked the al-Ma'aliq seated nearest her—father of Ammineh, smug enough to make Nizzira's palm itch for her knife.

Instead she waved a well-manicured hand, rings sparking a dozen colors by lamplight. "That silly eunuch frets as if he truly were a woman, instead of merely not a man. Do you enjoy yourself, my friend?"

"Truly, Highness, it is a night for jubilation at Acuyib's great generosity to both our houses. For is it not said," he added, his smile dazzlingly white below a luxuriant black mustache, "that the fiftieth of a sheyqa's descendants shall be the joy of her age? My own father finds it so." He directed a fond glance at the drooling ninety-year-old moron who, determined not to wait for grandchildren to fulfill his ambition, had killed seven successive wives in the getting of his first forty-nine offspring. The fiftieth, sole product of the eighth and final wife, attended the old man so devotedly that he practically chewed his food for him. The Sheyqa found this utterly disgusting, but what offended her more deeply was the reference yet again to the long-gone al-Ma'aliq power. That senile, toothless old man ruling Rimmal Madar? It didn't bear contemplation.

What she said, in a mild tone, was, "I hope your daughter has given me a child just as fine for my fiftieth."

"I am confident that she has, Highness." Another raising of the wine to his daughter's accomplishment.

The Sheyqa nodded, smiled, and drank. The exquisite young boy had spurned the attentions of all the girls, no matter what they did to entice him; it was his role to reject them and eventually to prostrate himself at the Sheyqa's feet. She watched as he began the moves that culminated the dance, reflecting that it really was a fine thing to be past the age of childbearing and not have to limit herself to those men she had married for money or land or political alliance. Carelessness in this regard had been her own mother's downfall—one did not bear the child of a Hrumman servant, no matter how tempting his golden looks might be, not when there had never been an al-Ammarizzad born with blond hair. Husbands were tedious at times, but not even a sheyqa could mortify them in such fashion. It was said she had died of a fever, and all her husbands were seen to mourn her—none of them less sincerely than Nizzira's father, who had administered the "fever" in a cup of wine. The act had sealed Nizzira's accession to the Moonrise Throne, for not only had her father taken on the task and thus the responsibility if caught, but he had *not* been caught—and that was warning enough. No one in the palace wished to be similarly administered to. The other husbands had been dealt with in Nizzira's own time, and their offspring as well, and now all of her own husbands were either dead or divorced.

So she could have anyone she wished these days. Truly, it was most liberating. When the boy began his approach, she forgot to wonder whether what was between his thighs was natural or cleverly provoked by drugs. The latter, she thought, rightly judging the glaze in his eyes. But it mattered for nothing; he really was quite the loveliest thing she'd ever seen.

She was just beginning to plan the end of her evening when the first al-Ma'aliq began to vomit.

No one was on the last mile of the palace road. Azzad cursed. No other late arrivals with whom to slide, practically unnoticed, inside the gates. He couldn't even pretend he'd been there all along, caught up in greeting friends or seeing to the comfort of his older relations. His esteemed father would see through that in a twitch of a lamb's ear.

Khamsin suddenly froze—ears pricked, head thrown back, the whites showing in his black eyes. Azzad frowned. Usually he had his hands full preventing the stallion from challenging every other stallion on the palace road, for which the Qoundi Ammar on their grand white horses did not thank him.

But there were no Qoundi Ammar lining the palace road tonight.

He was alone.

And on the soft evening breeze his inferior senses finally recognized what Khamsin's nose had already warned of: fire.

One hundred twenty-six of the almost four hundred al-Ma'aliq had to be helped from the banqueting hall to the outer courtyard, robes stained and bellies churning. The Sheyqa waved aside the mortified apologies of Ammineh's father.

"Young men *will* overindulge, you know it is so," she said as servants hurriedly cleaned up the messes. "Think no more on it, my friend. Come, let's not ruin the celebration."

On the expert advice of distant relations whose help she'd sought for this purpose, she'd made sure that all of the "drunks" would be young men, easily excused in their excesses. For their elders, she had something else in mind.

The eunuch approached right on time, bowing, begging Her Glorious Majesty to accede to the Qoundi Ammar's request that they might demonstrate their joy in her fiftieth descendant. The Sheyqa smiled. "Very thoughtful. My thanks and compliments to the qabda'an, but it can wait until tomorrow. I shall even bring along my little Sayyida to see the salute in her honor."

"Highness," said Sayyida's grandfather, "the disgraceful actions of my kinsmen have soured the atmosphere within. The fresh air of the courtyard would be most welcome, would it not?"

Naturally the al-Ma'aliq would wish to revel in a show of military precision by the elite guard. They thought it a tribute to them. Fifty years ago—at
about the time of Nizzira's birth, in fact—a renegade faction of al-Ma'aliq
had been the only troops ever to defeat the proud, invincible Qoundi Ammar.
The doddering old fool down the table from Nizzira had been the one to
punish his wayward kinsmen, thereby gaining for himself royal assistance in
his claim to leadership of the family. But the necessity still galled, all these
years later. Had things been just slightly different, one of the al-Ma'aliq
women would now occupy the Moonrise Throne. *"Never trust them, my
daughter—never, never. They were kings once and would be again if they could.
Keep them under your eye always."*

Ayia, not her eye—her heel. And even that had not been enough. Who
knew but that Ammineh had been dangled before her fool of a son in hopes
of precisely these circumstances: an al-Ammarizzad with al-Ma'aliq blood,
who one day would seize the throne? Restored to its former glory, the family
would make certain that all the mighty deeds of Nizzira's own forebears were
appropriated to *their* renown.

Never. Never. There were, among her forty-nine other strong, clever,
ambitious sons and daughters and grandsons and granddaughters, many
now at an age to begin vying for precedence in the succession, which amused
her. She intended to live to be at least eighty years old and die in bed with a
beautiful boy in her arms—not with a knife in the spine as her grandmother
had done. (Not Nizzira's knife, to be sure, though she had hated the old
woman, and she had enjoyed tremendously the execution of the cousin who
had done it.) Her plans for the al-Ma'aliq tonight were in part to warn her
own offspring that such could just as easily happen to any of them, should
she become displeased. Another lesson learned from her esteemed father.

But not a flicker of these thoughts showed in the Sheyqa's face. She
chewed another candy, pretending to consider, then nodded. "Very well. Let
us go outside and see what the qabda'an has arranged for our amazement
tonight. Something spectacular, I hope, with lots of pretty riding, and that
trick they do with their swords and axes. Have you ever seen it? Truly extraordinary."

Azzad urged Khamsin back toward the city, and the closer he got to
home the brighter the sky became. The breeze had died, and smoke billowed straight up into the heavens. Smuts of soot began to drift down

onto his blue cloak. People in outlying districts leaned out windows or stood atop the flat roofs of their houses to get a better view, but as he neared home, he had to slow the big stallion to avoid the milling crowd. Only when he turned onto Sharyah Ammar Zaqaf—the Street of the Red Roofs—did he realize that there was no rush toward the flames with buckets of water to fight the fire. The faces he saw, lit crimson by fire glow, were curious and apprehensive at the same time—like dogs confronted by poisonous snakes.

Abruptly furious, he dug his heels into Khamsin, caring nothing for whoever might get in the way. Down the wide avenue he galloped, past shops crammed with silk and silver where his five sisters loved to dawdle of a morning before the heat grew oppressive. At the very end of the double rows of plane trees was the walled magnificence of Beit Ma'aliq, the house of his family. The gate was high and narrow and closely woven, all fanciful curves and bright flowers, like a woman's embroidered shawl draped shoulder-to-shoulder across her slender back—only this embroidery was of iron. Tonight the vivid colors of the painted metal were black against a background of flames.

Someone grabbed at Khamsin's bridle, a mistake that nearly cost him a hunk of shoulder as the stallion snapped angrily. Azzad kicked the man and wheeled Khamsin around toward the back entrance. The surrounding wall was much too high for him to see over, but through small, iron-barred apertures cut into white-plastered brick he caught glimpses of the blaze. And no people. Not one single person was outside in any of the courtyards.

When he got to the rear gate, he understood why. Through the twisting painted iron he could see the sprawl of the main house and the doors leading out to the stable yard—and the stout planks nailing them shut.

There was yet one more way to get in. Frantic now, he turned Khamsin to the alleyway behind the stables and fumbled in his green and gold sash for the key. The postern gate into the gardens was made of wood. Even as he turned the corner, he saw that it too was ablaze, and as he neared, he smelled the stench of rancid oil.

Beyond the high walls spread the garden with its languid flowers and many fountains. Above was the two-story arrareem, the women's private chambers that no man dared enter without Za'avedra's invitation. Azzad coaxed Khamsin nearer, fighting the horse's terror of fire, standing in his stirrups to see over the wall. All the windows spewed fire through ornamental wooden grilles out onto balconies. Behind those windows lived his mother, sisters, aunts, cousins, the wives and daughters and infant sons. And from within he heard screaming.

He swung one leg over Khamsin's neck, preparing to dismount. The stallion, wiser than he, sidled away from the postern gate toward the opposite wall. Azzad was too fine a rider to lose his balance, yet neither could he leap down, for Khamsin had trapped his other leg against the bricks. And the instant his rump connected with the saddle again, the horse pivoted neatly on his hind hooves and galloped down the alley.

He could not turn Khamsin back to Beit Ma'aliq. The stallion had had enough of fire and smoke and did not intend to allow his chosen master to commit suicide. Cursing, Azzad lifted his head into the wind of Khamsin's gallop, feeling the tears dry on his cheeks.

Blazing windows, barred doors, oil-soaked wood—all the women and children of his family would die tonight in an inferno of the Sheyqa's making. Azzad knew he would hear their screams the rest of his life.

Khamsin finally slowed at the outskirts of the city. Azzad had no notion of where they were or how many people had been trampled to get them there. He understood one thing only: the Sheyqa had murdered helpless women and children in their beds, and she would have no qualms about murdering every man of the al-Ma'aliq at the palace tonight.

His cousin Ammineh too would die and her baby with her—no, Sayyida was the granddaughter of the Sheyqa, she would be spared. And she would be the only al-Ma'aliq left.

Unless Azzad could get to the palace in time.

The Sheyqa's servants delicately, unobtrusively guided the men in bronze silk robes to walk through the hammered silver doors of the banqueting hall together, and to file into the courtyard together, and to sit on the front two rows of benches together. The al-Ma'aliq were too flush with drink to notice that some of these servants had never been seen before in the palace—indeed, not in Dayira Azreyq, nor even in Rimmal Madar. And after tonight, they would never be seen within the country's borders again.

The Sheyqa had her own separate platform, with a canopy of crimson. Torches blazed in the courtyard, lighting the vast expanse of hardened earth where every day the Qoundi Ammar practiced drills, most of them showy and all of them lethal. After two hundred and seventy al-Ma'aliq had settled their smugly drunken selves on tapestry cushions, Sheyqa Nizzira signaled for the tribute to begin.

An intricate pattern woven in sleek white horses and crimson tunics and flashing silver trappings delighted the eye, even as the ear marveled at the precision of hooves—one hundred horses moving as one, without a single doubled beat. No horse stepped out of sequence with another. The Sheyqa nodded satisfaction at the preservation of tradition: thus had the Qoundi Ammar fooled barbarian invaders in a famous battle, making them think that a single horse approached through a twisting ravine. The foreigners' leader was slaughtered, and five hundred soldiers besides, by one hundred men on horseback who sounded like a single rider. At the end of the drill, the audience cheered and whistled. The Sheyqa saw the eunuch Arrif nod to the qabda'an, and she hid a smile.

Turning smartly, the hundred rode back to the other end of the court-yard. At the faint hiss of steel and the sword flashes by torchlight, the Sheyqa leaned back in her throne, eyes narrowed. Slowly, then with increasing speed, long swords circled over the riders' heads until it seemed each sat beneath a silver whirlwind. Then an ax appeared beside each man, a smaller but even brighter counterpoint to the brilliant spinning cyclones of steel. Light blazed, and the audience gasped, then cheered.

Suddenly one hundred white horses thundered forward shoulder-to-shoulder at a dead gallop, their riders roaring the Sheyqa's name. A scant armlength from the seats, the horses skidded to a halt, the riders bellowed the Sheyqa's name once more, and the flame-burnished whirlwinds of swords and axes flew straight into the hearts of the al-Ma'aliq.

Cheeks soot-streaked and eyes frenzied, his fine blue cloak singed, Azzad was unrecognizable as his family's most elegant wastrel. Riding along the avenue of plane trees and oleander hedges that led to the reservoir and the Qoundi Ammar barracks that guarded it, he saw in the near distance a small troop on horseback. Melting into the shadows, whispering a silencing word to Khamsin, he waited for them to pass.

There were fifteen of them, all in dark crimson tunics, riding the white stallions of the Qoundi Ammar that looked like ghost horses by moonlight. One of the men wore a gold-and-ruby armband. Another repeatedly tossed into the air a long dagger, catching it neatly by the jewel-studded hilt. A third flourished a white silk cloak, embroidered around the edges with autumn-bronze leaves.

The armband belonged to his uncle and the dagger to his older brother. And the cloak—he'd watched his sisters stitch the complicated patterns on the great frame in their workroom, hurrying to finish it in time for their father's birthday.

"Do you realize what the launderers will charge to get the vomit out of this?" complained the man wearing the cloak.

"Puke soaks out," said another man, who had a length of bronze silk draped across his saddle. "This one will have a bloodstain even if it's washed a hundred times!"

"At least we got the best pickings," advised the one wearing the armband. "Pity the poor menials who'll have to clean up half the palace, with not even a ring left on any of the bodies! Poisoned vomit on the banqueting floor, blood flowing all over the courtyard, every cushion ruined—"

His companions jeered at him for worrying like a house-proud eunuch. Then they rode past the place where Azzad sat trembling in his saddle, and he could hear their voices no more.

"Eminent Majesty," said the eunuch, concluding his report, "Beit Ma'aliq will be gutted by morning. All within the house are dead. Regrettably—"

"What?" snapped the Sheyqa, glancing up from cooing to newborn Sayyida, who lay sleeping on her knees. She truly was a pretty little thing, and looked just like her grandmother—but for the unfortunate chin.

"Regret, Esteemed Lady, for the houses nearby that caught fire," he said quickly. "Eleven, before those flames were extinguished."

"And how did this happen?"

"Unknown, Majesty. But may I humbly suggest that part of the confiscated funds be used to rebuild those houses and repair damage to the others? After all, it was an al-Ma'aliq servant who tipped over a lamp and started the fire." An unnecessary reminder of the official reason for the conflagration; the explanation would fool no one and was not intended to do so. "Thus it would be a magnanimous gesture on Your Illustrious Majesty's part—"

"How much will it cost me to be magnanimous?"

"Not more than a tenth part of the whole, Beloved Lady."

"Oh, very well. It seems I can afford it. What else? It grows late, and my darling little girl wants her nurse." She glanced over to the bronze-draped bed, where a beautiful young woman lay in the tangle of her hip-length black hair. She was perfectly still and perfectly silent. At long last, silent.

"I expect word by tomorrow evening of the extermination of everyone at the other al-Ma'aliq holdings by the . . ." He paused delicately. ". . . the relatives of Your Exaltedness."

"My orders were clear—spare no one, not even the lowliest kitchen boy."

"So it shall be, Majesty," Arrif replied with a bow. "I have prepared a list of candidates to replace the managers and most skilled crafters at all the estates." After a thoughtful pause, he continued, "The fallahin in their villages will also be killed. I surmised that Your Majesty would not wish any al-Ma'aliq supporters to survive. Listeners in the city will inform us of who expresses sympathy here."

"Do what you must," Sheyqa Nizzira replied. "Just so the castle is kept in perfect order for someone to inherit one day. I think it shall be Reihan. For all he is but seven years old, he pleases me more every day. So manly, so clever!"

"As Your Exaltedness wishes, so shall it be done."

The Sheyqa looked up when the eunuch didn't leave. "Ayia, what else?"

"Only one thing, Majesty," Arrif admitted reluctantly. "The count has been made five times. One hundred twenty-six dead of poison, two hundred sixty-nine of sword or axe."

The Sheyqa swore luridly. The baby started to cry.

"A total," Arrif concluded, staring at the carpet, "of three hundred ninety-five. One is missing."

"Which?"

"The qabda'an believes it is the young man who had the temerity to apply to the Qoundi Ammar. Azzad, younger son of Yuzuf."

"Cease this uproar at once!" the Sheyqa ordered Sayyida, who only bawled more lustily.

"A voice to be heard commanding a battle, Majesty," Arrif observed.

"Are you trying to be funny? Call a servant and get this brat out of here. My sweet little Reihan never screamed so. I vow to Acuyib, if Sayyida is as noisy as her mother, she'll end up silenced the same way."

He summoned the nurse, who was so terrified she actually cast a glance at the bed rather than keeping her eyes strictly on her charge. The Sheyqa glanced at the eunuch, who nodded; a new nurse would be found by morning.

When they were alone with Ammineh's corpse, Nizzira said quietly, "Find Azzad. Find him, and kill him."

"As Your Glorious Majesty wills it, so shall it be done."

He could stay, and die. He could flee, and live.

If he stayed, he could accuse the Sheyqa in public and have all know what had been done to the al-Ma'aliq.

Which everybody would know anyway. And nothing would be done about it. The Sheyqa was the Sheyqa.

If he fled, he could establish himself—somewhere, somehow—and one day take his vengeance.

Which was precisely what the Sheyqa feared and why he would be hunted.

He had nothing. With the deaths of the al-Ma'aliq, he *was* nothing.

But the thought of Nizzira wondering—wondering for years, never safe, never at rest, always wondering when and where and how Azzad al-Ma'aliq would strike—filled him with hot, vicious glee. He must survive.

Khamsin snorted softly, as if to remind him that they were still in the capital city of Rimmal Madar and within easy reach of the Sheyqa. Revenge was for the future—if Azzad lived that long.

And if living required money, vengeance required a fortune.

In pearls, perhaps?

Two hours later, so covered in midden filth that Khamsin's nostrils flared in disgust, Azzad had the pearl necklace tucked once more in his sash.

It lacked several hours till dawn, and in those hours he could be halfway to the western coast. Instead, he turned south. South, to The Steeps that marked the border of Rimmal Madar and the Gabannah Chaydann—the Devil's Graveyard. No one would ever look for him there.

In the city of Dayira Azreyq, dawn was stained red-brown. All that morning people muffled their coughing, shuttered windows in vain against thick drifting smoke, and thanked Acuyib that the only fires in their own homes were in ovens and lamps. Anyone who had cut himself anytime in the past week sent up similar praise that the wound was not a sword or an axe through the chest. And those with sicknesses of the belly or bowels paused in their misery to be grateful that only spoiled meat or too much wine afflicted them, and not the Sheyqa's poison.

In the way of great cities, small words traveled quickly. A servant, a day laborer, a lover sneaking out a back door, a cook venturing early to the markets—small words, they were, *fire* and *swords* and *poison*, connected to the once-great name of al-Ma'aliq.

Dayira Azreyq came alive more slowly than usual, but it did come alive; and for all that nearly a thousand al-Ma'aliq had died the night before, it was a day like any other—all its inhabitants furtively thankful for another day of life.

Thus the evil was accomplished. For a jealous Sheyqa's obsession, the al-Ma'aliq were exterminated, from the aged patriarch Kallad to the real ruler of the family, Za'avedra el-Ibrafidia, to Kallad's infant great-great granddaughter, only five days old.

The el-Ma'aliq who had married outside the family were also killed, and their children with them, and their husbands as well for safety's sake. From the mountain castle's fastness to the broad estates in the lowlands, from Beit Ma'aliq's splendor to the small stone huts of the workers, those connected to the al-Ma'aliq by blood or loyalty or employment were obliterated. Within a handful of days, the dead numbered more than four thousand. No one spoke a word against the slaughter.

The Sheyqa's servants who were not the Sheyqa's servants vanished hence they had come, with no one the wiser to their true identities.

Yet for all her triumph, Sheyqa Nizzira al-Ammarizzad could not rest.

Azzad al-Ma'aliq yet lived.

— FERRHAN MUALEEF, *Deeds of Il-Kadiri*, 654

2

Upon reflection, the Gabannah Chaydann had probably been a stupid idea.

The heat was punishing by day, and it seemed that winter reached out early and greedy this year to grip the night. Azzad traveled from dusk to dawn, shivering; from daybreak to nightfall he sweated in the sparse shade of the rocks, having ejected those with prior claim: snakes, lizards, gazelles, and—once—a sand-tiger, the formidable rimmal nimir. He'd have scars on his thigh for life from that encounter.

The pearls seemed to grow heavier as he traveled. Ridiculous notion, going after jewels to buy food and water in a place that had no food or water, let alone anywhere to buy them. He'd filled his waterskin and his belly at one of the rivulets outside the city that fed the reservoir, and left a pearl in payment for the bread and haunch he stole from an outlying village. But a mere three days into his journey to nowhere, the heat was melting the flesh from his bones. The third night, after the water ran out, he walked beside his tired horse, both of them stumbling with fatigue and thirst across hard, stony ground.

And this wasn't even the worst of the desert. That lay beyond The Steeps, with only one negotiable pass where caravans plodded from late autumn to early spring. Azzad hoped the first of them was even now crossing the western lands beyond the desert, bound for Rimmal Madar. If he encountered them in the pass and asked nicely enough, they might part with some food and water for another of the pearls.

The fourth evening he was lucky.

So hungry and weary that only instinct and long training kept him in the saddle, he nearly fell out of it when he heard the screeching of a hawk. Within ten paces, as he was still trying to calm his racing heartbeats, came the clattering of stones and a pitiable scream of a different kind. He froze, at first fearing the Qoundi Ammar, then cursed himself for a fool. If they were near, there would be no noise; all he would have heard was his own death rattle.

Trailing the rattle of stones, he soon saw that Acuyib had sent a rock-slide to trap a gazelle near a hidden pool of brackish water, breaking its leg and leaving it to a slow death. Azzad gave profound thanks for the gazelle and the water as he killed the suffering animal. Long experience of the ritual hunt at the mountain castle of the al-Ma'aliq made him swift and sure in slicing up the meat, but as he worked, he fought back renewed grief. He would never again ride out with his father and uncles, brother and cousins, on the annual parody of a barbarian festival of long ago. The leaving of the castle and the returning to it three days later were always comical events, with the men strutting and the women fluttering and everyone giggling as the women pretended to scream in horror at all the trophy heads. His mother was particularly adept at miming a gracefully ornamental faint, right into his father's waiting arms.

Azzad's movements were vicious as he stabbed chunks of meat onto a stick for roasting. *Never again, never again.* He kept telling himself how lucky he was to be alive, but as the tiny fire died out and he stared up at the stars, he wondered if sparing his life had been a mercy or a prank. He had nothing; he *was* nothing. The wealth and position—and the brilliance and laughter—of the proud al-Ma'aliq were no more.

At dawn of the sixth day he emerged from the pass, and immediately turned Khamsin around again to take shelter in an outcropping of rock, cursing himself yet again for a fool. Down below The Steeps were tents of crimson—the color of the Sheyqa—decorated with a pattern of swords and axes embroidered in white wool. This was the camp of the Ammarad, the tribe from which Sheyqa Nizzira's line had sprung. He could not elude them. The Ammarad were camped here for the season, exacting the Sheyqa's taxes and tribute of their own from every caravan. He could hide the ring marking him as al-Ma'aliq, he could tear off every bronze tassel from Khamsin's bridle and saddle, he could claim any other name in the world—and he might get away with it. But once they learned, as they inevitably would, that their kins-woman Nizzira wanted him dead, they would remember that a stranger had passed by in the wrong direction for this time of year—toward the desert, not toward Dayira Azreyq—and come after him. Their expertise in tracking a man through trackless wastes was legendary.

Hiding himself and his horse as best he could, he spent the day wondering what to do. Fitful sleep was interrupted by visions of axes descending on his neck, of Khamsin disemboweled by gleaming swords, of the Sheyqa's laughing face, all shaded in crimson. And it seemed that every few moments he was jerked awake by the shrieking of a hawk. At dusk he rose, nervous and unrefreshed, and turned Khamsin onto a narrow side trail that took them higher and farther from the pass. He had no idea where he was or where he was going. He only knew he could not descend from The Steeps anywhere near the Ammarad.

Acuyib smiled on Azzad once more, for just as the moon rose to light the rugged rocks, he came upon two bodies: hunters, nondescript in their clothing and wearing no distinguishing jewelry. Identification at this point would have defeated their own mothers; desiccating sun and scavenging animals had obliterated features and flesh. One of the men was a fair match for Azzad in height. Staring down at the corpses, wondering how they had died, he pondered many alternatives before deciding that the thing could be done.

Intending to heft the taller man across Khamsin's saddle and go stage his scene closer to the main road where it would be more readily discovered, he grappled with the limp body for a moment, then blurted in surprise as he learned rather abruptly what had caused the man's death. There was a knife stuck in his lower back. Azzad turned the second man over and found that a smaller knife had ripped through his belly. Crouching beside the corpse, wincing at the still painful wound in his thigh, he pondered for a time, then nodded. Definitely the thing could be done.

By sunrise the depiction of his own murder was complete. The taller man was dressed in Azzad's clothes, the knife stuck through them. Realism demanded bloodstains on the garments; Azzad unwrapped the bandage from his thigh and carefully coaxed fresh blood from the wound. That it was alarmingly easy to do so worried him for only a moment. He'd concern himself with healing later.

"His" corpse also wore a silver armband regretfully donated to the ruse. The golden key of the postern gate lock was tucked into the sash. But a gold ring set with a dark topaz Azzad would not relinquish; carved with the leaf symbol of the al-Ma'aliq, it was a present from his mother. The second man lay on his back this time instead of his belly, with Azzad's own eminently identifiable knife thrust into his gut.

As dawn glimmered through the deep canyons of The Steeps, the last of the al-Maʿaliq sat in the dust, patiently unknotting the pearls. He stashed most of them in his belt, intending to sacrifice ten to the embellishment of the murder. Cradling them and the flower-petal clasp in his palm, he looked from one body to the other and decided that "his" corpse was the better choice. Accordingly, he dropped the pearls and the clasp near one lifeless hand and then limped back from the scene to evaluate his work.

If the Qoundi Ammar indeed followed him, and he had every reason to think that they would, they would discover the half-eaten corpses. With luck, they would soon identify the personal items—the armband, the key, the knife—and return to tell the Sheyqa that Azzad al-Maʿaliq was dead. They would go no farther; they would not reach the crimson tents and ask about a lone traveler. Azzad would be free to descend, claim the rights of hospitality, and depart for the western desert, knowing no one would ever come after him. They would never know who he was.

But even if a caravan or other hunters found the bodies, it was of no real consequence; when armband and knife were taken to be sold and the key taken to be melted down, someone among the city's merchants would know. He was—*had been,* he reminded himself—popular among the crafters of Dayira Azreyq, lavish in his spending on trinkets for himself and his mistresses. The clasp in particular was unique to a certain jeweler, who would certainly remember Azzad. And if there weren't enough pearls left to make the necklace the clasp had originally adorned—well, it was dusty here, and windy, and there were excuses enough for their absence. There was the key, as well: the most identifiable item of all, for its design incorporated the graceful leaf of the al-Maʿaliq. Someone would recognize it. He was certain.

It seemed his dissolute ways, deplored by his family, might save his life twice. Visiting one woman had spared him on the night of the massacre, and giving jewels to the others could confirm his death. Never had he been so glad—or so ashamed—of his misspent youth.

And how odd it was, he reflected, that at twenty years old, he considered youth irretrievably gone.

Khamsin's hoofprints to and from this place would lead riders off the main road to discovery of the scene. As he rode away wearing the dead hunter's clothes, bow and quiver on his shoulder, he apologized to his horse. "I know you'd never leave me, not even if I really was lying there dead. But we have to make it look as if you did."

And then it occurred to him that the horse was more loyal to him than he had been to his family.

Ayia, what good would it serve if he too had died? Who would be left to avenge the al-Ma'aliq? The new granddaughter? Not even if Nizzira allowed her to live. Indoctrinated from her first breath, taught to despise half her heritage—

No. Azzad had been spared for a reason. And as he rode brashly through the pass in the gathering heat of the day, he thought of his family for what he swore must be the last time until he was ready to exact retribution for their deaths. When word filtered through the city that he was dead, there would be no one to mourn. Never again would he watch with hawk's eyes as his friends blushed in his sisters' silked and scented presence. Never again would he see his mother arch a sardonic brow at his latest exploit or listen to his father and uncles recite *The Lessons of Acuyib* at dawn prayers. And never again would his grandfather peer at him from beneath bristling white brows and bark, "Well, boy? Which pretty charmer have you seduced now? Would I have risked *my* venerable balls for ten minutes alone with her?"—and then laugh until he choked on his glee.

Azzad arrived at the tents of the Ammarad the next day. The vast mass of the encampment was denied him; he was not allowed past the outermost tents, which were reserved for travelers who had no shelter of their own. As the laws of hospitality required, the wound on his thigh was tended by the tribe's chief tabbib, a grizzled old man whose treatment seemed to rely more on incantations and the pattern of thrown stones on a carved wooden plate than on any medicines in his satchel. But the chants did no harm, and the wrappings he used on Azzad's thigh were clean and smelled of a spicy salve. Khamsin was fed and watered, Azzad was shown a corner of a tent to sleep in, and everyone appeared to believe his story of going out to prove his worth to his father by hunting down a sand-tiger—which had so vehemently left its mark on his leg.

It rankled to accept their food and drink, but he did just that for three days. For Khamsin's sake, he told himself. He could guess what lay ahead of them in the desert.

"And where do you go now?" the elderly tabbib asked as he prepared to leave.

"East," Azzad lied.

"I know all the tribes who make their camps in the east, Zaqir." The unspoken question was *From which do you come?*

Azzad had called himself falcon, for he intended to fly as free and swift as a hawk and kill with utter ruthlessness. But he had not mentioned a family name. "I would not disgrace my tribe by naming them," he said slowly. "I failed in my quest."

A shrug of bony shoulders. "That you did not succeed in taking the rimmal nimir's pelt is no dishonor, Zaqir. You have the marks to prove you faced the beast. And I am certain your mother will be just as glad that you lived to tell of it."

Azzad gave a nod and a slight smile of thanks. He thought about the tabbib's words as he rode away to the west. His mother would indeed be glad he had survived, he knew that—but what would she think of his means of survival? He'd paid more heed to an illicit tryst than to a royal command, and then he had run away. Still, he was alive, and to squander that gift would be to dishonor those who had died. Azzad vowed to be worthy of survival— and put back on his finger the al-Ma'aliq ring before turning Khamsin south, to the Devil's Graveyard.

"But who can he be?"

"Besides a fool, you mean?" A clucking of tongue against teeth. "You tell me, Leyliah. What do you learn from looking at him?"

"Rich, of course—"

"His clothes were ragged."

"But the ring—"

"Stolen."

Azzad opened his eyes and denied it strenuously—or thought he did. Leyliah's voice was young; the other woman's was older. Both were lilting, liquid voices, oddly accented around the *r* sounds, but he understood them readily enough.

"The horse was stolen, too?" Leyliah asked shrewdly.

"Sometimes you are my favorite student, and at others you make me despair that you will ever learn how to trim a hangnail! Don't look at the *things*, Leyliah. Look at the *man*."

There was a pause. Azzad called frantically on every muscle in his body. Not a single one responded.

"His hands," Leyliah said at last. "There are no old calluses—only new ones, from recent blisters."

"Very good. What else?"

"His feet are rubbed raw where very soft, very fine boot leather has worn away."

"Therefore . . ."

"Therefore he must be rich, as I said before!"

"Or he stole the boots as well."

Sightless, frustrated in his need to move, he was forced to use his other senses. Scents of dry wool and sensuous spices; taste of skin-stored water flavored with an herb he couldn't identify; and, past the voices of the two women, the faint ring of hammers on metal and a light breeze ruffling wind chimes. Not much information; nothing to comfort him. Except that they hadn't killed him. Yet.

"You were right," the older woman admitted, "but using the wrong evidence. The ring and the horse and the boots could have been stolen. The clothes tell us nothing. The things tell us nothing. But the body, this tells us all. We have here a spoiled, wealthy, feckless young fool who tried to cross the Gabannah. He has paid for it with heat sickness, scorched skin, feet that will not carry him for at least fifteen days, and the festering claw-marks of a rimmal nimir, bandaged by either an ignorant fool or someone who wanted him dead. Now, the next thing we ask ourselves is why he would attempt so dangerous a journey. He was not ill before he began it, so he cannot be one of those who seek our healing. Have you any answers?"

"None, Challa Meryem. Unless he truly is crazy—in which case we'd better tie him to the tent poles to prevent his doing us or himself any damage."

"Pampered men such as this one do not stir themselves to folly without good reason. Deadly reason, I suspect. Even a fool must be aware that the Gabannah is death to those who do not know it intimately. So perhaps there is another death behind him, chasing him—one he feared more than the death that nearly found him here."

Leyliah's voice dropped to a whisper. "Do you think he killed someone?"

"Ayia, more likely someone wants to kill him. And by the look of him, for seducing a wife or daughter or sister."

"I'd wondered if you'd noticed! Long eyelashes, long nose, long legs, long—"

Azzad felt sudden heat in his face; had he been able to, he would have turned away in embarrassment. Not at the words of praise, which he knew he deserved; nor that the words came from a woman, for his mistresses had made similar observations; but that the woman who said these things was unknown to him and had seen him naked.

All at once he wondered if she was pretty.

"Keep your eyes in your head, Leyliah, and your tongue between your teeth—and your fingers inside your qufaz when you salve his skin. Who knows what diseases may slither from him to you at contact with his blood?"

"But the texts all say—"

"The texts are no substitute for practical experience. Now, spoon more medicine down his throat, and we'll leave him to heal."

A gentle finger inside a whisper-thin leather glove parted Azzad's lips. Water slid onto his tongue, tasting sticky-sweet with herbs and honey. Again he tried to move, and again failed. Instinct made him swallow against his conscious will. And within a remarkably short time instinct, consciousness, and will all faded away.

When next he woke, it was to the sound of men's voices. His eyes opened readily enough, and he could shift his muscles, though sluggishly, legacy of whatever the women had given him. It was dim inside the wool tent, and hellishly hot.

"Chal Kabir, he wakes."

Shuffling footsteps crossed thick carpeting, then sudden light flared as the tent flap was shoved aside. Azzad blinked and put a hand over his eyes. His fingers encountered sweat-sticky hair tumbling down his brow. Running his hand down his face, he was appalled to discover a thick beard. How long had he lain here?

"Eleven days," said a young man's voice from an old man's gray-bearded face. Azzad blinked again. "The date is the second of Ta'awil Annam."

He had left Dayira Azreyq nearly sixty days ago. Why did he remember so few of them?

"Bad water," the ancient continued, as if in answer to the unspoken question. He seated himself on a tripod stool beside the heaped carpets that were Azzad's bed. "It takes the belly in sickness, and the memory as well. Ayia, city boys are too stupid not to fill their bellies at Ma'ar Yazhrad. Worse, they water their horses. The beast died, you know."

Azzad's whole body spasmed, and he moaned. "No! Khamsin—!"

Chal Kabir nodded. "You see, Fadhil," he said over his shoulder, "he cares more for the horse than himself. A good sign." Then, to Azzad: "Your Khamsin is safe. I told you otherwise as a test. There will be many more before you are allowed out of this tent."

"Khamsin—?" Azzad managed, relief and suspicion flooding him simultaneously.

"Safe," Chal Kabir repeated, settling his sand-colored robes around him. An unusual ring of braided silver and gold and copper flashed from his left thumb.

"I want to see him."

A black brow arched in a parchment-brittle face. "Truly a lordling, accustomed to command."

"I want to see him! Now!"

It took all his strength to put force into the order—and by the amusement flickering in Chal Kabir's eyes, the old man knew it. He gestured with one gnarled hand to young Fadhil, who disappeared out the tent flap, brushing against wind chimes as he did so. "He will bring the horse around. A splendid animal. We will accept him in payment for your life."

Azzad bit back a hot retort. Fear and relief had followed each other too quickly, leaving him dizzy. He must be cautious. Laws of hospitality aside—those same laws that in theory compelled these people to tend him without requiring recompense—Chal Kabir had mentioned tests. This might be another.

It was.

Chal Kabir snorted a laugh. "Ayia, you can control yourself. Good, good."

Movement in the triangle of light at the tent flap caught Azzad's gaze. Khamsin: whole and sleek and fractious, needing three boys to hang onto his halter. A whistle from Azzad calmed him at once, and he followed the boys decorously enough out of Azzad's sight.

"Interesting," commented Chal Kabir.

"He obeys no one but me," Azzad said, sinking wearily back down onto the pillows. "We have been each other's since the moment of his birth."

"You claim brotherhood with a horse?"

"With this horse, yes."

"And he allows you onto his back?"

Azzad peered up at the old man. "I trained him."

"Is it difficult, this training?"

Outraged: "You don't think I'd hitch him behind a cart or a plow, do you?"

Chal Kabir had a closed countenance behind his gray-streaked beard, but Azzad suddenly knew that this was precisely what horses were used for here. Wherever *here* was.

"We will speak more later, when you are stronger. Sururi zoubh." He touched his fingertips to his brow; Azzad recognized the ancient sign for *I mean this with my thoughts*, and gulped because the hand had not touched the chest. That would have meant *I mean this with my soul*. But what the old man said was harmless enough—a simple wish for sweet sleep.

Azzad watched him limp across the sunlit brilliance of the rugs. "Chal Kabir? If it is permitted, please do me the favor of thanking the ladies Meryem and Leyliah for their good care of me."

Beneath the brown, dusty robe, the bent spine suddenly straightened— and not without pain, to judge by the flinching shoulders. Chal Kabir did not turn as he said flatly, "No women have been inside this tent while you have been within it." And then he was gone, and the flap closed, and heated darkness shut him in once more.

Azzad folded his arms behind his head. The old man had lied to him. Why?

Ayia, it was improper for a woman to be inside a tent with a man not her husband or brother or son or father—even if the man was drugged to the eyes and incapable of lifting a finger, let alone his male member. Having satisfactorily explained Chal Kabir's lie, he began puzzling out the truth.

First, who were these people? The tent proclaimed nomads, yet Chal Kabir had implied that they used horses to plow the ground. No meandering tribe he'd ever heard of cultivated crops. The only water was poisonous—he had hazy memories of the water hole, Ma'ar Yazhrad, the old man had called it, and "bitter drinking" it truly had been. But by then he was too stuporous with heat and hunger to have any idea what he was doing. He recalled very well, however, the forbidding land around him: crystalline salt flats, immense sand dunes, ravines dry for a thousand years and littered with sharp stones. What plow could turn this cracked and tainted soil? And even if it could, what could possibly grow?

In retrospect, the look of the desert surprised him. He'd always thought that across The Steeps lay endless sand dunes of the kind that formed the

borders of Rimmal Madar beyond the mountain stronghold of the al-
Maaliq. Horses could not pull wagons through shifting sand like that, but
they could over the hard-baked, unyielding earth he remembered from the
time before his collapse.

And remember it he suddenly did—the suffocating heat even at night,
the dwindling of his supplies, the pain in his thigh, the blisters suppurating
on his feet. What had made him think he could traverse this waste? Sleeping by day in the scanty shade of rock outcroppings, dreaming of a sand-
tiger stalking patiently behind him and a screaming hawk flying ahead of
him, unsure when he woke which was real, or if either could be real. And
then that last day, the churning in his belly, the agony in his gut, the sparks
and specks before his eyes, the dizzying loom-and-retreat of the bleak landscape. No growl behind him, no shriek in the sky ahead. There had been no
one and nothing in view—or so he'd thought. Where had this tribe come
from?

He knew there were at least seven people here—Chal Kabir, Fadhil,
Meryem, Leyliah, and the three boys who'd brought Khamsin to the tent.
The boys must have parents; the men and women must be married and have
children. At least thirty people, and quite likely thirty more. Water and food
for so many would be difficult to carry from place to place. They would know
the land, of course, and centuries of inbred instinct would detect hidden
springs and secret water holes. They would not be here unless they could
survive, becoming part of the land themselves. But how *did* they survive?
Perhaps they were shepherds? Ridiculous. Where could sheep graze in such
barrenness?

It was a puzzle he wasn't likely to solve until he was up and about. But
had not Chal Kabir said there would be many tests before he was allowed to
leave this tent? Wondering what these tests might be, Azzad shrugged, relaxed into the carpets, and slept.

If there were tests, Azzad was unaware of them. Over the next few days he
saw Fadhil many times, Chal Kabir twice, and no one else at all. The food
was bland but nourishing and plentiful, the water remarkably sweet. He
wondered what herbs they put in their storage jars, or what nearby spring
they drew it from. He asked Fadhil about it, but the young man merely
shrugged and said, "That is women's business, not men's."

Azzad couldn't decide whether he meant that domestic responsibilities were beneath masculine notice or that fresh water was a thing much too important to be left for men to argue about.

Fadhil was politely curious, asking questions in roundabout ways, but communicated little about the tribe. Azzad answered honestly enough, speaking of the great city and the mighty land of his birth. But Fadhil had never heard of Rimmal Madar, much less of Dayira Azreyq. From this, Azzad deduced in some shock that in the days since he'd fled home, he'd somehow managed to travel beyond the routes of even the most adventurous caravans.

Unless the young man was lying, as Chal Kabir had done.

"Is Chal Kabir really your uncle?" Azzad asked one afternoon as he practiced walking on increasingly steady legs and feet that didn't hurt too much anymore. "You don't look very alike."

Fadhil was tidying medicines on a low table. "'Chal' is the title given our healers."

"Ah. Then Lady Meryem is a healer also, for I heard Leyliah call her 'Challa.'"

Fadhil, being even younger than Azzad, was less guarded than Kabir. "You heard nothing of the kind," he snapped, much too quickly. "Neither Meryem nor Leyliah has been in this tent."

Azzad smiled. "Then how do I know their names and the rule of the qufaz?"

Fadhil's dark eyes went wide in his golden-skinned face. After a struggle to speak, he managed, "You—you know nothing of such things. You *may* know nothing. Speak of this to no one else, do you understand?"

"It is forbidden for me to know the ladies' names?"

"*Everything* is forbidden!"

"Ayia," Azzad said cheerfully, seating himself on his bed of carpets, "you'd best tell me all about this 'everything' of yours, so I don't offend again."

Recovering himself, Fadhil stood over Azzad—trying to dominate him physically, which really was rather funny. Even wasted with illness, Azzad was half again the boy's size. Sternly, in obvious imitation of his teacher, Fadhil intoned, "Do you value your life, gharribeh? If so, comport yourself as befits a guest—and one whose bones would be whitening in the sun even now if not for the Shagara."

Azzad considered intimidating the boy—easy, with his greater size and al-Ma'aliq arrogance—but decided that the scornful *gharribeh* indicated Fadhil felt threatened. Not in all the days Azzad had been awake and aware had the boy called him by that term—and with the inflection that meant not just *foreigner* but *unwelcome*. It was a deliberate insult and a warning.

Accordingly, Azzad bowed his head. "My life is yours," he said in the ancient form.

"It is," Fadhil agreed pointedly, and left the tent.

The *Shagara*, were they? The word meant *tree*—a singularly inappropriate name for desert nomads. But upon consideration, Azzad thought he understood. The tree was a sacred thing that meant life and water and growth and greenery, and for people wandering a wasteland, a single tree could mean salvation. By extension, the wounds of the desert could be healed by this Tree of Life.

And they allowed their women to learn the healing arts. That was interesting. In his world, clever highborn women were taught to rule families, not sickrooms. They supervised the concerns of a business or farm, an extended kin network, and sometimes—as in his own mother's case—a whole tribe. Or, as Sheyqa Nizzira did, an entire country. But healing was a traditionally masculine art in Rimmal Madar. Long years of study and training interfered with a woman's real work: to choose a husband and bear the children that would establish her dominance, for many daughters and sons ensured the survival of the family and extension of its influence, while managing the household's wealth. Because the men took care of the children, healing was more naturally their concern.

But that was the world Azzad had left behind, the world he could not think about again until he was ready to exact his revenge.

The next night Fadhil entered the darkened tent just as Azzad was ready to shove the flap aside and go where he pleased, damn the consequences.

"You're out of bed," the young healer observed. "Good. Abb Shagara wishes to speak to you."

"May Acuyib bless him for not coming here to me!" Azzad said, reaching eagerly for the black wool cloak Fadhil had brought. "I was starting to believe there was nothing to the world at all except the inside of this tent!"

"Abb Shagara goes to no one. All come to him."

"I would have it no other way." Wrapping himself in the rough garment against the night chill, Azzad gestured to the tent flap. "Lead me, Fadhil, to Abb Shagara."

He knew why they took him from the tent by darkness. They didn't trust him—especially now that he'd regained most of his strength. He wondered what they thought he'd do: seize one of their maidens, leap onto Khamsin's unsaddled back, and gallop off into the desert?

There certainly weren't any maidens around—nor matrons, nor men, nor children, nor even a stray sheep. A couple of rangy yellow-brown dogs lay beside a tent, gnawing on bones; a cat was teaching her six brindled kittens to hunt, but these were the only living things he saw. Pale tents and glowing fire pits, at least fifty of them, studded the landscape; presumably everyone had been ordered to hide from him. It was confirmed when a tent flap twitched, and a small, round-eyed face peered out, and a women's beringed hand grabbed a braid of black hair and tugged the child back inside.

He knew where Khamsin was by the scent on the wind. Good clean horse-smell; they took care of their animals, at any rate, not allowing them to mill around in their own droppings. There was a difference to the aroma, however—something he could only describe as a *wildness* not found in a civilized stable. Perhaps it was due to diet. He'd demand to see Khamsin tomorrow and get a look at these cart-drawing horses for himself.

Abb Shagara's tent was no larger than the rest, and it was the same pale sandy color. All that distinguished it from the others was the size of the wind chime hanging from a carved pole outside. The breeze toyed with finger-sized brass and tin plaques hammered with designs. Fadhil bent nearly double as he opened the flap, bowing to whoever was inside. Azzad considered it polite to incline his body the precise degree due his own venerable grandfather—but when his eyes adjusted to the brightness of a score of lamps within, he felt his jaw drop. Abb Shagara was no grandfather. He was scarcely old enough to grow a beard.

Was this some sort of joke? Did they mock him by sending him to this stripling youth rather than the true head of the tribe?

The boy—perhaps eighteen, perhaps not—tilted his head to one side, a smile quirking his full lips. Long-limbed, slender beneath flowing silvery-gray robes, he sat erect and casually self-confident on a high-piled rainbow of cushions. His jewelry was all of gold. A broad cuff caught his long black curls at the left shoulder. His left ear was decorated by an earring in the shape of an ibis holding a sapphire in its beak. At his breast rested a small plaque crowded with a whirl of colored gems. He was more regal, Azzad thought suddenly, than Sheyqa Nizzira el-Ammarizzad had ever looked in full regalia on the Moonrise Throne.

Azzad bowed once more, thinking that this must be Abb Shagara's favorite son, or his heir, or something of the sort, that this was a preliminary encounter that would lead to a meeting with the real power in this tribe. Certainly the most important of the Shagara would not receive a stranger alone, with no guards but one skinny apprentice healer who carried only his surgical knives. Chal Kabir had said there would be many tests. Perhaps this was one of politeness.

"I am pleased," the young man said, "to see you recovered."

"By your graciousness," Azzad replied, "and the skill of your healers."

A nod, a graceful gesture to be seated on a plump green pillow. Azzad sat, glancing at Fadhil, who stood with lowered head and folded hands.

"Will you drink?" asked his host. "What is your pleasure? There is wine, qawah, the juice of various fruits. . . ."

"Whatever is most agreeable to yourself."

"Qawah, then." The boy leaned forward and confided with a grin, "I must warn you, I prefer it very strong and very sweet and tinged with cardamom."

Azzad was about to speak a polite lie—that this was how he liked it, too—but what came out of his mouth was, "I am partial to strong qawah but without that flavoring."

"Ayia, but you must try it this way. Most stimulating."

Fadhil busied himself preparing what turned out to be a viscous black fluid that tasted like honeyed tar. Azzad sipped the required three times, sternly controlling his expression. Then, resting one elbow on a drawn-up knee, the rim of the silver cup balanced delicately between his thumb and the tip of his middle finger (his father, a stickler for elegant manners in his children, would have been proud of him), he regarded his host with raised brows.

"Ayia, you have many questions," the boy said. "Before you ask them, I have one of my own. May we know your name?"

He could answer with the "Zaqir" he'd used before, but he suddenly found he had no wish to lie to these people. "Azzad al-Ma'aliq."

The boy seemed to be waiting for something else. An explanation, perhaps. At length he asked, "Why do you say this as if all should know the name?"

"You have not heard of me?" Ayia, that was rude—there was such a thing as too blatant an honesty.

But the young man only laughed softly and sipped qawah, rocking lightly back and forth on his throne of cushions. "You come from some faraway place where your name is renowned. For what reason, I could not say; you may be a famous musician, or a great warlord, or a notorious criminal. You will find, Azzad al-Ma'aliq, that such things as are vitally significant in other lands have less than no meaning here. Where do you come from?"

"My country is called Rimmal Madar. You have never heard of it?"

"Should I have? A land of sand and rain sounds both dangerous and pleasant." After a slight pause: "'King of Lions'—that is your name, yes?"

"My mother's choice," Azzad replied, embarrassed as he had not been since his first days in the play yard of the madraza, when all the other boys had teased him.

"But it is a noble name," came the protest. "Mine, on the other hand—" He laughed once more, light as a starling's flight through clear blue sky. "My own beloved mother afflicted me with—I hope you are ready—'Akkil Akkem Akkim Akkar,' by which one assumes she meant 'intelligent ruler whose wisdom flows like water.'" With a smile, he concluded, "You are invited to laugh, Friend Lion. Luckily, now that I am Abb Shagara, I need hear none of these names anymore—except from my mother when she is furious with me!"

Azzad choked. This *child* really was the leader of his whole tribe?

"No strangers to us believe it," mourned Abb Shagara, correctly reading his expression. "They look at me, then look around for my father or elder brother. But I assure you it is true. Perhaps one day you will come to know why a boy of my scant years rules so many. But for now, I see you grow tired. And, as my mother would say, it is long past my own bedtime!"

"If I grow weary, it is not of Abb Shagara's company." This, too, was the truth.

The boy nodded approvingly. "Wherever you come from, Friend Lion, you were taught manners."

"Thus I have hesitated to ask, but I must. When may I see my horse?"

"Ayia, that spindle-legged stud that causes so much trouble? Tomorrow, I think. Yes. And perhaps you can calm him. None of our boys are able to do more than stare at him—and run very fast when he glares right back!"

"Khamsin frets if I am not close by. I regret any difficulties he has caused. I thank Abb Shagara."

Fadhil came to his side and, after more bowing, they left the tent. When they were inside the healing tent, Fadhil turned a wry look on him.

"I told you that you would go to Abb Shagara. I can't help it if you didn't believe me."

"It's a strange tribe, your Shagara," Azzad retorted. "A youth of no more than eighteen leading all your people, women learning the healing arts—"

The humor died in Fadhil's black eyes. "I also said you were never to speak of that. Do you want to die?"

"It's that forbidden, is it?" He decided to change directions. "Why does Abb Shagara have no guards?"

This restored Fadhil's good humor for reasons Azzad didn't begin to understand. "He needs no guard."

"Everyone needs protection."

"Did I say he had none?"

"But there was no guard," Azzad maintained stubbornly.

"No," Fadhil agreed. "No guard."

"Then how—?"

"He wears the ways of the Abb Shagara at his heart. They are all the protection he needs."

Sheyqa Nizzira sent to the winter camp of her kinsmen, the Ammarad, her two eldest sons, three of the Qoundi Ammar, and a wagon of gifts. But so long ago had her foremothers left the desert that she had no notion of what was valued by the ancestral tribe. The Ammarad stared as the Qoundi Ammar unloaded fine wooden tables inlaid with marble, silken tapestries, and great pottery vessels filled with honey and wine and oil.

Abb Ammarad informed the Sheyqa's sons that the gifts were unnecessary. Azzad al-Ma'aliq would be hunted down and killed for the honor of their tribe. Then he commanded a feast, which was laid out on the tapestries and used up much of the honey and oil and all of the wine. And during the feast, when he admired the fine, fast horses of the Sheyqa, the sons instantly comprehended. Thus it was that one proud sheyqir and three even prouder Qoundi Ammar rode back to Dayira Azreyq on unsaddled brown donkeys.

The Ammarad had use of the Sheyqa's horses for less than a season, and their insistence that the mare ridden by one of her sons be included in the "gift" was a tragic error. Two stallions died in battle over the Ammarad mare, one of the bite of a poisonous snake. Such was the size of the half-Ammarad foal inside her that the mare was ripped apart, and her get died with her.

The soldiers of the Qoundi Ammar—forced by the Sheyqa's sons to ride home on donkeys, deprived of the horses that were more beloved than their wives—never forgave the loss and the insult.

— FERRHAN MUALEEF, *Deeds of Il-Kadiri*, 654

3

The following morning Azzad was allowed outside. He immediately went to see Khamsin. Along the way, he got his first good look at the Shagara. They were a handsome, black-eyed people, slim and long-legged, dressed in various desert shades of fawn and ivory and cream. But not all of them were Shagara by birth, or at least not wholly Shagara; Azzad was able to distinguish outsiders very easily by their skin tone. The merciless sun did not darken the Shagara; they looked as if gilded, and the contrast of black eyes and black hair with golden skin was fascinating.

He seemed to fascinate them as well. Some glanced sidelong, others openly stared, but no one ignored him. When he passed by, children stopped playing, and whispered and giggled and pointed—until the old men watching them scolded their rudeness. The Shagara went about their tasks of fetching water and cooking, braiding new ropes and mending boots and suchlike with quiet efficiency. It was altogether unlike the raucous streets of Dayira Azreyq, where men did nothing without discussion, speculation, argument, and commentary—usually at the top of their lungs.

The one familiarity was unexpected: the sound of hammers working metal, just as in Zoqalo Zaffiha at home. Sure enough, Fadhil led him around a cluster of tents to workshops set up beneath wool awnings. Thirty or so men sat cross-legged in the shade, each whispering under his breath, pounding designs into brass, copper, and tin. Some of the men were as ancient as Chal Kabir; others were Fadhil's age. The polished metal bowls, goblets, plates, armbands, finger rings, earrings, and pendants—dazzling even in the shadows of the awning—made Azzad blink. Nearby, beneath another pale woolen roof, a group of boys about fourteen years old watched a very old woman trace a symbol into a large clay tablet propped on a stand so all could see.

"Here you see the talishann for 'wealth of sheep.' Note its difference from that for 'wealth of sons'—and remember that a man will not be pleased if his ewes bear dozens of woolly lambs when he is expecting his wife to have lots of little boys!"

The children laughed as they copied the device onto their own clay tablets, which were then held up for the mouallima's inspection. After a few corrective comments, she moved on to the next talishann.

As they continued past the school session, Azzad said to Fadhil, "That is the most interesting madraza I've ever seen. They're making good luck charms, I take it?"

"For sale at the zouqs. I should mention that one of the master crafters has expressed an interest in making something for your stallion's saddle."

"That's extremely kind, but I have no means of payment." He thought of the pearls, but they were to provide money for a new start. Come to think of it, he had no idea where the pearls were at the moment, but didn't suspect for even a fraction of an instant that they were anything other than perfectly safe and waiting for him to claim them. Traditions of hospitality aside, the Shagara would never steal anything so useless to them as a few dozen pearls.

"Ayia, no matter," Fadhil was saying. "He wants no payment. He says he's never made anything to protect a riding horse before, and the experience would be worth the work." He sounded as if he truly believed that a piece of brass or tin or copper could give a man many sons—or many sheep. Azzad hid a smile.

Khamsin was alone in a chest-high pen of thorny rails, with scarcely enough room to turn around. No wonder he was fractious, Azzad thought angrily, reaching through dagger-long spikes to offer a caressing hand.

Khamsin snapped at him.

"Well, yes, I know you're unhappy," Azzad soothed. "But I do still have need of those fingers. Fadhil," he said over his shoulder, "he needs exercise. Where's my saddle?"

"So beautiful an animal. Why would you wish to put a seat on him and ride him like a donkey?"

"Donkey!" Only children rode donkeys, and then only for their first riding lessons. The picture of a grown man with his legs dangling to the ground was too insulting to contemplate. But he realized something about the Shagara then and perhaps about the rest of the people in this strange country that as yet had no name—and in truth seemed not to be a country at all. Horses were for hauling and donkeys were for riding, no matter how ridiculous one looked. There was an idea in there somewhere, if he could but find it.

Fadhil was eyeing Khamsin warily. "He's so tall! A donkey is close to the ground, with nowhere much to go if you fall off. Of course, your Khamsin is not so big as our own horses, but still—"

"Show them to me," Azzad said. When the young man arched a satirical eyebrow, he recognized the peremptory tone—for the first time in his life, it must be said—and added rather gracelessly, "Please."

A long walk around the perimeter of the camp—much larger than he'd thought, more than a hundred tents—led them to the thorn-guarded pen for the Shagara horses. Azzad saw immediately why no one rode these monstrous beasts. Half again Khamsin's bulk, at least two hands taller at the shoulder, with backs wide enough for a man to sleep on and legs the size of young tree trunks—he gaped at dozens of mares, colts, and fillies whose muscles shifted powerfully beneath glossy hides. The colors of sand and clouds, they were, with thick white manes and tails. Their eyes, huge and dark with lashes long as a man's thumb, held a warning glint of dangerous temper. Azzad had to admit these horses were beautiful in their massive way, but his thighs ached at the very thought of riding one.

Again the half-formed idea teased at him. Again Fadhil interrupted his thoughts. "The stallions are kept apart, as Khamsin is. Our wallad izzahni are careful about bloodlines."

"The boys who tend your horses are to be commended," Azzad replied, frowning. A good thing this pen was downwind from Khamsin; several of the mares were ready to be bred.

"Perhaps if your stallion requires exercise, you can do as we do—run him at the end of a long rope."

Khamsin wouldn't like it—he'd graduated from that training exercise years ago—but it was better than nothing. The rest of the morning was spent thus, with Khamsin galloping in circles and every so often testing the rope's strength with a lunge. At the end of the exercise session the muscles of Azzad's back were stretched to breaking, and his arms felt ready to pop out of their shoulder sockets. But he walked Khamsin until the horse cooled, then rubbed him down with handfuls of dry fodder.

On the way back to the dawa'an sheymma, they passed a tent where a very young man dressed for travel stood among a knot of women. Some of them were crying as the youth embraced and kissed them.

Recalling his own spurious excuse for the welts left by the sand-tiger—completely healed now by the Shagara—Azzad asked, "Is he off to prove his manhood?"

"To do *what?*" Fadhil blinked.

"With a dangerous hunt, or a journey through perilous territory, or something of the sort," Azzad explained, wondering why he had to clarify. All the wilderness tribes he'd ever heard tales of required some sort of test to initiate a boy into full male status within the group. All the northern tribes, anyway. "Proving his courage and resourcefulness, his ability to survive."

"We need no such proof that a boy has become a man. Except," Fadhil added with a shrug, "fathering a child. No, he will marry next month, and today goes to join his wife's tribe. We keep our women here."

"And bring husbands from other tribes into the Shagara?" No wonder these people were so poor. With no competition for the smartest, cleverest young girls to marry into a family and become designers and guardians of its wealth—but perhaps such competition occurred over the men instead. In Rimmal Madar, the best of the sons were kept in the family to attract the best of the daughters from other families. One of Za'avedra al-Ibrafidia's main complaints about Azzad had been his spectacular unwillingness to use his looks and his charm to secure in marriage a brilliant girl who might eventually take her place. The Shagara did things backward, it seemed to Azzad. He worked his mind around this new eccentricity, and at length he asked, "Will you be married outside the Shagara one day?"

"No."

"Why not?" He paused, then added, "If I may ask."

"A student of Chal Kabir is of more value than he would bring in a husband-price."

At least this began to make sense. Of a Shagara kind, anyway. "The other tribes pay to marry your men?"

"Of course. We are Shagara." As if that explained everything.

The midday meal was waiting. Azzad fell on the food, and when his hunger was satisfied, he returned to his questioning. Fadhil sighed quietly and answered as best he could.

"Will that young man go to his wife's tribe alone? No servants, no friends?"

"He will go with one of his brothers, who will stay until the wedding—and perhaps longer, if one of the maidens finds him pleasing. There are few tribes who can boast Shagara husbands. The Tallib, the Tariq, the Azwadh, the Tabbor, the Harirri, the Ammal—these are the Za'aba Izim, the Seven Names, the people we marry. There are other tribes—the al-Kassira, who rule that city, for instance—but we do not marry them. They are not allied to us in peace and war."

"War? Over what?" He gestured to the stony desert beyond the open tent flap.

Fadhil mimicked his outswept arm. "Water."

"Of course. That was stupid of me. My people make war over other things." He considered Sheyqa Nizzira. "Power. Envy. Money. Land. Greed."

"Here, water is all. It is power over death. I can understand envy," he mused, "for those who have little water must desire more. Money I do not understand, and land even less so."

"Money to buy people—and land to feed them."

"Every man has his price, but a man who can be bought for mere money is no man at all."

"There we agree perfectly," Azzad smiled.

"But who can own the land?"

"If it's got your troops all over it—"

"That is not ownership," Fadhil said severely. "That is occupancy. Greed—do you mean in the way a child is greedy for sweets?"

"Very like that, yes."

"But what use is more of everything beyond the sufficiency for living?"

"What use, indeed," Azzad sighed.

"Did you leave your country—this Rimmal Madar—because you tired of war?"

"No. It would take too long to explain." And because Fadhil was obviously about to ask him for that explanation, he said, "Did you never go to war with the barbarians?"

"Forgive me, but everyone not Shagara is a barbarian." Fadhil laughed suddenly. "But you have the makings of a civilized man—if you try very hard."

"My thanks, Fadhil! I meant the barbarians who believe in a Mother and a Son as their deities. They invade and demand that the people abandon Acuyib and swear to their faith."

"Oh, them." Fadhil sounded bored. "There are stories of their coming in great carts that floated on the sea. They were stopped at the fishing villages on the coast. It was a long time ago, and nothing to do with us." He paused, then added thoughtfully, "They rode astride their horses, as well. Is this something your people learned from them?"

"Certainly not!" Azzad had studied history and tactics in futile preparation for joining the Qoundi Ammar—though, in truth, he had been more interested in how fine a figure he would cut in the elegant robes, riding a gorgeous white horse. That had been before Khamsin, naturally. But he recalled the treatises very well, and said, "Their horses weren't as good as Khamsin. One reason they invaded Rimmal Madar was to steal our horses to improve their own cavalry—troops of riders," he explained when Fadhil looked blank. "With swords and axes and—"

"What matter this 'cavalry' against the Shagara?"

"You mean your good luck charms?" Azzad laughed. He stopped laughing when Fadhil gave him a sidelong look.

"I have discovered," the boy said, "that you often speak at great length of things you know nothing about. Now I believe you should sleep. You are not accustomed to such exercise. Chal Kabir will not thank me for allowing you to lose what strength you have regained."

Azzad had to agree with him, and lay back on his carpets. He dreamed of the al-Ma'aliq castle in the northern mountains, where hundreds of swift, long-limbed horses galloped free through the pastures. He woke, hot and sweating, with a curse on his lips for the magnificent animals that now belonged to Sheyqa Nizzira.

Idling around these tents set his feet not one step on his path to revenge. There was no money to be made here, no influence to be gained. Two days, three at the most, and he would thank the Shagara as profoundly as he knew how, ask directions to the nearest substantial town, and leave.

That evening Chal Kabir and Fadhil came in supporting a limp, travel-worn man. Azzad watched in fascination as the man was stripped, washed, and examined, for it was his first chance to observe the brisk efficiency of the Shagara healers.

"What's wrong with him?"

His question was ignored. Azzad hoped the man had nothing infectious. He wasn't a Shagara; his skin was darkly tanned, his hair was straight and brown with a reddish sheen by lamplight, and his filthy robe might once have been red.

Kabir mumbled irritably to himself, then sent Fadhil out of the tent.

The boy returned a little while later with two clay jugs. One of them he placed on the low table near the sick man's bedding, and the other he gave to Azzad.

"Qawah?" Azzad asked, trying not to sound dismayed.

"Wine, to strengthen the blood."

As Kabir and Fadhil bent over the new arrival, Azzad leaned back into his pillows and drank. It was surprisingly good, sharp and dry just as he liked it, with a hint of berries.

In the middle of his dreaming he remembered that he didn't remember falling asleep. He couldn't move, not even in his dream. But he could hear, and the voices were feminine and familiar. *Something in the wine*, he thought, and knew he wasn't dreaming at all.

"And so, Leyliah, what is your judgment of this man's sickness?"

"It is of the circulation of the blood," the younger woman replied with confidence.

"Exactly," said Challa Meryem. "Very good. Were we to look inside, we would find his blood paths thickened and in some places nearly shut. Now, what is the appropriate treatment for his condition?"

Azzad listened, immobile and mute with the drugged wine. Women as healers. And the Shagara didn't want him to know. Fadhil had thus far protected him. But if the others thought he knew, they would never let him leave. They would kill him.

There was something basically illogical about that: Why heal a man only to kill him if he discovered the tribe's secret? Then he thought about the women and how valuable they were. A woman with skill beyond a male physician's would be well worth abducting. Shocking, this thought, but if the Shagara did not allow their women to marry outside the tribe—and Meryem had said that people came to the Shagara for healing. Wherever they made camp, people would come from great distances. Those thorn fences were not portable, so there must be others well-established in other places. Azzad wondered how many and where.

"I approve the treatment, Leyliah," said Challa Meryem. "Write it down for Kabir and Fadhil and then go to bed."

One set of soft footsteps left the tent. Then he heard Meryem's voice directly over his head—so startling that if he'd been able to move, he would have leaped right out of his skin.

"As well you will be leaving us soon, Azzad al-Ma'aliq," she murmured.

"I do not trust you, nor the looks Leyliah gives you—though one cannot blame her for them."

He wondered once more whether Leyliah was beautiful. If Grandfather would find her worth the trouble . . . .

Azzad woke suddenly some hours later, wondering what had disturbed him. The eastern wall of the tent was pale, hinting of dawn. Lying on his side, keeping his body still and his breathing soft and regular, he listened carefully.

And heard the barest whisper of a footstep on the floor.

Kabir or Fadhil would simply have walked across the carpets. Meryem or Leyliah would be quieter, lighter, but not stealthy. Not like this.

Another step. Azzad risked slitting one eyelid open, peering through the spider-legs of his lashes. The "sick" man was moving with exquisite slowness toward him. And even in the feeble light the sheen of steel was unmistakable.

Thanks be to Acuyib, the wine had worn off. He tensed and relaxed all his muscles in turn. His hearing was acute, his head clear. He tried to guess: heart or throat? Quiet demanded the latter. It was the more difficult attack—not a straight knife-thrust between the ribs but a grab of the hair and a slice from ear to ear, to make sure the windpipe was severed and no sound could be made, or a brutal thrust right into the throat. A chest was a much larger target. He shut his eyelid, risked giving a sigh and a snort as a sleeping man might, and shifted as if in a dream.

A long silence. Then another step, and another. The man was good at his trade. Azzad again wondered what had awakened him earlier. It did not matter. His shifting had let him place one hand on his chest to block a knife and the other on his belly to strike at the man's ribs; his right leg sprawled to the side, ready to dig into the bedding for leverage.

Another step. He could hear the man's breathing.

And then the whisper: "For the honor of the al-Ammarizzad—*die*, al-Ma'aliq—"

The hiss of the blade, the fingers snarling in his hair—the sinewy wrist in his grip, the crunch of his fist against bone—and they were on the floor, rolling, tangled and tumbling like a rapist and a furious virgin, all in silence. It was not a knife the assassin wielded but an axe that skittered away, ringing as it hit a brass tub in the corner. Azzad kicked and struck, overturning a table, and felt liquid splash on his face as a pitcher went flying. He heard clay crack against the central tent pole and shatter. Shaking his eyes clear, he grunted as a knee drove into his belly and knocked the wind from his lungs.

Desperately, Azzad pushed off with a foot and rolled the pair of them over and over again until his ribs hit the tent pole.

Suddenly the hands were gone from his throat. Gasping for breath, he staggered to his feet. The man's lips were parted in a soundless cry, his eyes gaping wide with astonishment, his hands twitching limply—and his legs moved not at all. Azzad kicked him onto his side and saw a thick shard of the pitcher's broken handle protruding from his spine and a small spreading bloodstain on his white bedshirt.

Not in all his time here had Azzad ever sensed that the tent was guarded by night. He'd been a fool to think otherwise, he realized, when a golden-skinned face appeared at the tent flap, wide-eyed. Azzad waved a casual hand at him to indicate he was unharmed, and the boy vanished.

Wearily, he sat on his carpets and worked on catching his breath. It seemed he wasn't quite as recovered as he'd thought. He kept an eye on his assailant, curious about how long it would take him to die.

A little while later, Fadhil came into the tent at a run. "Azzad! What happened?"

"As you see," he managed, irked that he was still so exhausted. After this paltry exertion, he was as wrung out and sore as if he were a rug and a servant had just washed and beaten him. He wondered how long the Shagara would give him to sleep it off before they sent him on his way.

"Who is this man?" Fadhil demanded.

"Your other patient. Not just that, of course." He watched as Fadhil finally noticed the shard sticking out of the man's spine. "Perhaps Chal Kabir is needed," he suggested mildly.

"I—yes, of course, you're right," the young man stammered. "I'll find him at once." He cast one last appalled look at the dying man and fled the tent.

A little while later he was back, with Kabir and two women who could only be Challa Meryem and young Leyliah (both were beautiful, Azzad noted). They scarcely had time to exclaim in horror when Abb Shagara himself burst in.

"What has been done here?" Meryem demanded.

"Ask him," Azzad advised. "If he can still talk."

She knelt to examine the wound, the breath hissing in her teeth. "He will live a cripple—"

"*If* we allow him to live," said Abb Shagara. Drawing a loose white robe more closely around him, he went on, "Azzad, tell me what happened."

"He tried to kill me." He nodded toward the corner. "His axe is right over there."

Kabir went to pick it up, turning it over and over in his hands before giving it to Abb Shagara with a significant arch of his brows. They all looked grim-faced at the gleaming steel blade set in a haft of carved bone.

"I wish to know," Akkil Akkem Akkim Akkar intoned, "how did this man enter the dawa'an sheymma with this in his possession? How did a man who is not sick feign illness so well as to fool the most accomplished of the Challi Dawa'an? How did this man outrage our tents by attempting the life of my friend Azzad? And how," he finished harshly, "did a Geysh Dushann come into the camp of the Shagara undetected?"

"Well?" Meryem asked, slapping the agonized face below her. "Speak!" As his lips drew back in a ghastly grin, she slapped him again. "Speak, and I promise I'll kill you quickly." When there was no response, she leaned closer and said with gentle ferocity, "I can make you live. But you will never again walk, never again have strength in your hands, never again enjoy a woman. Speak and die quickly—or stay silent and live to be very, *very* old."

Azzad gulped, and blinked, and was very, *very* glad Abb Shagara liked him.

"This al-Ma'aliq—his death is my honor," the man rasped. "He lives. I have no honor. Kill me."

"Why must he die for your honor?" Abb Shagara asked.

"The Sheyqa our sister—" He coughed, and the spasm widened his eyes with fresh agony.

"I know the rest," Azzad said. "I had better tell you. Sheyqa Nizzira of Rimmal Madar obliterated all my family in a single night. There was a banquet at her palace. The al-Ma'aliq men not killed by poison were slain by sword and axe. As for the women and children—they were burned alive inside Beit Ma'aliq. To my shame and sorrow, I escaped—through no cunning of my own. But now I am the only one left." He glared at the assassin. "And I *will* be avenged."

Kabir caught his breath. "This Sheyqa of your country—she is Geysh Dushann?"

"I've never heard 'dushann' refer to anything but the smoke from a fire. As for a 'geysh,' an army—I can tell you only what I know. Her ancestor came from a tribe called Ammarad and termed herself Ammara Izzad." He shrugged. "A reminder of the crimson harvest of barbarian blood."

"The Geysh Dushann," Kabir said heavily, "are all of the Ammarad."

Azzad rubbed an aching shoulder and said nothing.

"What did your family do, to incur the wrath of this Sheyqa?" asked Abb Shagara.

Softly, Fadhil said, "Power, envy, money, land, greed."

Azzad nodded.

"But to murder a whole tribe—" Abb Shagara shook his head. "To poison men inside her own tent, to slay them with swords and axes, to burn women and children in their home—this Sheyqa is a monster." Pausing, he bowed slightly to Azzad. "I am honored, Azzad al-Ma'aliq, that our enemy is also your enemy. I now accept this Sheyqa Nizzira as the enemy of the Shagara."

Azzad knew the enormity of this declaration in his own country. It sounded very much as if things were the same here. And he knew what was required of him in return. Rising unsteadily to his feet, he said the words gladly. "I am honored, Abb Shagara, that my enemy is also your enemy. I now accept your enemies as mine own, forever."

"Wait." Meryem rose lithely to her feet. "I shall have something to say about this. Or does the Abb Shagara think he rules this tribe alone?"

"Mother—" the boy began.

Azzad stared, but he managed to keep his astonishment unspoken.

"My son, if Azzad has made an enemy of this woman, and if this woman is of the Ammarad, and if we accept *all* of them as our enemies, and if—"

"Mother! Do you question the righteousness of—"

"And *if*," she repeated undaunted, "we all wish to live our lives without constantly looking over our shoulders, then we had best think hard and talk harder about this matter. We Shagara heal anyone who comes to us. We have never denied the dawa'an sheymma to anyone, not even the Geysh Dushann. If you declare the whole of the Ammarad enemy, my son, and not just the Geysh Dushann, you will tear the desert apart."

"But Ammarad *beget* Geysh Dushann!"

"Yes, and train them to come and work their evil and then drift away like the smoke they are named for. If it becomes known that we refuse an entire tribe our healing, one of two things will happen: either the Za'aba Izim will accept the Ammarad as *their* enemies and make war upon them, or they will fear that one day we will deny *them*, so they will make war upon us."

"Never," Kabir stated. "We are their protection."

"And if they do battle with us wearing our protections around their necks and on their arms and beaten into the grips of their swords?"

The old man shrugged. "Ayia, other tribes will come to our defense."

"And thus, as I have said, tear the desert apart." Meryem folded her arms. "Now, should this happen, and I believe it could, think of this Sheyqa who is a sister to the Ammarad. There is a whole nation behind her, not just a tribe. She ordered the butchery of an entire family, and it was done. How many al-Ma'aliq died, Azzad? Hundreds? Thousands? And yet there was no outcry from the people?"

"None."

"Ayia," Meryem said heavily, "they did not protest the injustice. They do as they are told. My son, could we withstand a whole nation? Could any of the Za'aba Izim?"

"The Geysh Dushann are our enemies," Abb Shagara said stubbornly.

"They are *everyone's* enemies. Restrict your rejection to them. No one will question it. They are too much hated by all decent people. After word of this night is spread—*without* reference to Azzad al-Ma'aliq—all will call the decision righteous."

Azzad breathed a sigh of relief. To attach his name to this would confirm his continued existence. Better to keep Nizzira guessing a little while longer.

If, after this, it was at all in doubt that he lived. It was clear to him now that the hunter's corpse in The Steeps had not convinced them. Ayia, and he'd thought himself so clever, giving up the armband and the pearls and the key! It was the ring that had done it, he told himself with a sigh, the ring he could not bear to give up. And it would be a lesson to him, he vowed, a warning that he must be prepared to do anything, give anything, in seeking his just vengeance.

Nizzira would never sleep soundly until Azzad was proven dead—but neither would Azzad sleep in peace until he had his revenge upon Nizzira. And he didn't know what form this could take that would not bring the armies of Rimmal Madar down onto this desert country. It must be something subtle, a mortal wound to the Sheyqa and yet containing a warning that retaliation was useless. He owed the Shagara his life. Nizzira could not be allowed to exterminate them as she had the al-Ma'aliq. By accepting Azzad's enemies as their own, the Shagara were—as Meryem pointed out—receiving much the worst end of the bargain.

Abb Shagara regarded his mother narrowly for a time. Then: "Very well. The Geysh Dushann only. But I *shall* accept Azzad as our kin."

"When did you hear me object? You do not listen, my son. Azzad al-Ma'aliq is indeed kin-worthy. He is civilized and honorable—for a barbarian."

"And therefore," Abb Shagara said, "he will be treated as Shagara. In all things."

There was some significance to this that Azzad didn't understand, but by now bruises and welts and exhaustion were making his head reel. It must have shown in his face or his eyes, for Leyliah was instantly at his side, helping him to lie down.

"No more drugged wine, I beg of you," he muttered.

"You'll sleep the day through without it," she assured him with a smile in her voice, and added, "Aqq Azzad," becoming the first of the Shagara to call him *brother*.

He opened his eyes. She was indeed lovely, with eyes like a fawn and skin like sage honey. "You are Oushta Leyliah now to me, yes?"

"Challa, one day soon."

"I prefer 'oushta.' All my sisters were as beautiful as you—and all my aunts were a million years old." His eyes squeezed shut, and weakness threatened tears.

"How did you escape death? Ah, I can guess—a woman warned you."

"No. But it did have to do with a woman."

"This much is obvious. Sleep now, Aqq Azzad. We will see to everything."

It so happened that when representatives of the Ammarad came to Dayira Azreyq to admit failure, the enraged Sheyqa Nizzira was unable to ride out at the head of her own army to seek Azzad, for the fierce tribes of the mountainous north threatened Rimmal Madar. A century and more of peace, founded on honor pledges with the al-Ma'aliq, had shattered now that the al-Ma'aliq were no more. The Sheyqa needed all her warriors to defend the northern border, a task that would occupy her for many years. She knew victories and losses, and even a wound to her own exalted person when a stray arrow nicked her in the leg. But the injury that festered was the knowledge that there yet lived an al-Ma'aliq.

Her chief eunuch tried to console her by saying that whether or not Azzad lived was of no consequence. Alone in a barren land, surely the idle wastrel Azzad would soon be dead.

Nizzira was not consoled. But with war raging in the north, and not a man to spare from battle, she could only rely on her cousins the Ammarad to honor their promise to kill the last al-Ma'aliq.

— FERRHAN MUALEEF, *Deeds of Il-Kadiri*, 654

4

Azzad never found out just how Meryem killed the Geysh Dushann—but that it was Meryem who killed him he had no doubt. Neither did he doubt that her son watched while she did it. When next he saw the two of them, there was something different about the boy's eyes; he was becoming a man who understood the burdens of responsibility. Za'avedra el-Ibrafidia would have thanked Acuyib on her knees to see such signs in her son Azzad.

A day later, he was invited to Abb Shagara's tent for the evening meal. The first thing Meryem said was, "I have realized, Aqq Azzad, that it was by my fault that you were attacked. I ask you to forgive me. It was I who spoke your name that night."

He shrugged away the apology. "You thought him sleeping from the potion given him. There can be no blame upon you, Challa Meryem."

Fadhil bowed his head. "I must have mixed it wrong." Then, after a slight hesitation, he added, "I have told them what you know."

"What I guessed," Azzad corrected politely.

Meryem shook her head. "No, I have grown careless. And you are not to blame for the potion, Fadhil. I have long worried about the strength of this drug, and lately I have been using less in the mixture for fear of its power. But from now on, it will be as strong as before."

"I beg you, do not test it on me!" Azzad's plea won a smile from her at last.

"I regret to say that is impossible," she replied. "You must leave us tomorrow."

Ayia, so soon? He had been so anxious to get moving, get on with his life and his vengeance—yet now he was reluctant to abandon these people who had become friends.

"We will give you water and food to last five days," Abb Shagara said. "The provisions will take you to the first village northwest of here. Continue due north to the coast, and the way will be easy to any number of cities."

"Which is precisely where the Sheyqa will be looking for me," Azzad pointed out.

"Have no worries about this Sheyqa. We will give you many protections."

The charms he'd seen the men making? He tried very hard not to look skeptical. They believed in the power of the tokens, and he could not insult his friends with open doubt. So he asked, "Is there no way to travel directly west? I have seen trade items from that country, brought by caravan and ship to Rimmal Madar." Not terribly impressive items—blankets and a few spices—but it was trade he could understand and use to his advantage.

"Ayia, north, west, there's not that much difference," said Abb Shagara with a shrug. "They are all barbarians, but I thought to spare you the worst of them."

"In the north," Meryem explained, "people live in cities that are neither clean nor comfortable, but at least one may walk unhindered by towering walls."

"In the west," her son continued, "they live either in small villages perched on mountainsides—and, to my eye, likely to fall off at any minute!—or in huge fortifications with walls that go on forever."

"The northern cities have walls, do they not?" Azzad had never heard of a city that didn't. The invaders with their Mother and Son religion had made walls necessary.

Abb Shagara made a dismissive gesture. "Boundary markers, nothing more imposing. There is no need. They are the friends of the Shagara."

As was Azzad—and they were still speaking of defending his life with a few weights of beaten brass and tin. Acuyib help him.

"But you must go where you wish, of course," finished Abb Shagara. "Five days will take you to the western villages. Whichever direction you take, you will be protected." He turned to his mother. "There should be such protections at the dawa'an sheymma, to preclude any more incidents."

"Abominable," she muttered. "That the very sanctuary of healing must be defended against malefactors."

Azzad tried to keep his expression pleasantly neutral. When he saw Fadhil and Leyliah exchanging amused glances, he knew that his face had betrayed him.

The girl said, "Aqq Azzad does not believe."

"Perhaps he requires a demonstration," Fadhil suggested.

Abb Shagara sprang to his feet from piled pillows. "Wonderful! Fadhil, attack me!"

"Akkil Akkem Akkim Akkar!" exclaimed Meryem, in the manner of all mothers who desire their offspring's complete attention.

And, in the manner of all children whose mothers propose to spoil their fun, Abb Shagara pouted. "But Azzad needs to be shown—"

"Don't be absurd."

"I believe implicitly," Azzad told them.

Leyliah knew he lied. "Fadhil?" she said, catching the young man's eye. And swift as summer lightning the eating-knife in her hand flew across the platters of food, directly at Fadhil's chest.

He did nothing. The knife struck his bleached wool shirt and tumbled harmlessly to his lap. Then he reached inside his clothing to bring out a silvery rectangular plaque about the size of his thumb. On it were inscribed symbols such as Azzad had seen the boys practicing with the mouallima.

"This means 'defense,'" he said, pointing to one of the figures—talishann, Azzad recalled. "This is for safety, and this negates iron's anger."

"But she wasn't truly angry with you," Abb Shagara teased merrily. "How could she be, when—"

"Enough!" snapped Meryem. Fadhil and Leyliah were blushing. "It matters nothing if Azzad believes or does not believe. The fact is that what we shall give him—added to what has been made for his horse—will keep him safe."

"Can't I show him?" Abb Shagara begged. "Please, Mother?"

"No. And don't sulk."

A look of mischievous cunning appeared on his face. "Surely a very little demonstration will suffice." And he reached over to a tray, taking a silver cup such as Azzad had used the first time he'd sat in this tent. He tossed it at Azzad, who caught it easily. "Lie to me."

"Your pardon, Abb Shagara?"

"Tell me a lie. Anything will do. I'll ask a question, shall I? What is the name of your horse?"

Hiding a smile—and perhaps a tolerant sigh—Azzad opened his mouth to say *Barghoutz*, silently begging the stallion's pardon for the insult of calling him a flea.

What came out of his mouth was, "Khamsin."

Abb Shagara crowed with laughter at the surprise Azzad could feel scrawled all over his face. "You see? You remember the first time we drank qawah together here? You held that cup, and you told no lies."

"I—" He thought he might say something polite. Instead: "I don't believe it."

"I know you don't," said Meryem. She rose and took the cup from his hand. "Now that you've had your little game, my son, please allow Azzad to get some sleep. He has an early start in the morning."

"Another few questions, and he would have believed," the boy complained.

"Enough!" Meryem ordered, and he subsided.

The next morning Azzad went on his way, with the whole tribe to watch. Only Abb Shagara, Meryem, Kabir, Fadhil, and Leyliah spoke to him in farewell, but he saw the smiles and sensed the goodwill—and their chagrin that while in their care he had nearly been assassinated. Curiously, there was no resentment that now, because of him, a stranger, the fearsome Geysh Dushann were their openly declared enemies. Truly, Acuyib had made their hearts more open and generous than the hearts of his own people, whom he had known to betray friends for the price of a basket of bread.

He saddled Khamsin—who behaved himself although he was plainly eager for a long gallop—and took a moment to inspect the new decorations on the saddle. Fadhil stood stroking the stallion's neck, watching Azzad finger each of thirteen palm-sized tin disks.

"One for each moon of the year," Fadhil explained. "It is traditional with our own horses. Abb Shagara says we cannot tell you what each means, or you will trust in them too much and not have a care to yourself."

"I see. If I knew that arrows would glance off Khamsin's hide, I'd ride right into an army of archers?"

"Something like that. Not even the Shagara can protect against stupidity."

"I've never had a reputation for being wise, but I promise I'll try not to be foolish." He smiled and grasped the young man's arm. "You've been a good friend to me, Fadhil, and because we are friends, I'd like to give you some advice. Marry Leyliah."

His skin paled beneath its golden sheen, and his eyes went wide. "*Marry—?*"

"Yes. You're both healers, you have an eye for each other—and no wonder, you're handsome and she's exquisite—"

"I cannot," he whispered, glancing away.

"Whyever not? Surely sometimes you marry within the tribe. You're not close cousins, are you?"

"In the sixth degree."

"Well, then—"

"She—will find a husband from another tribe."

"I tell you she wants you. I've seen that look in a woman's eye often enough to know what it means. It would do my heart good to think of you married and—"

"I cannot. Please do not speak of it ever again." Fadhil gave him an anguished look, gripped both Azzad's hands for an instant, and hurried away.

Chal Kabir came forward, clasped his hands briefly, and advised him to be careful. Then Meryem and Abb Shagara approached, the latter with a look of longing in his eyes as he regarded Khamsin—like a little boy who desperately desires to climb a date palm, yet fears that he might fall.

"When I return," Azzad said, "I'll teach you to ride him."

"Me?" The big eyes blinked. "On his back?"

"It's easy, once you learn how." Turning to Meryem, he bowed. "Lady, I thank you."

"Travel safely." That was all she said before leaving her son alone with Azzad.

"You would truly teach me how to ride?" the young man asked.

"Truly. When there is more time. Abb Shagara—"

"Aqq Akkil. Or Akkem, or whichever of my other names you prefer!"

"Aqq Akkim, then, for I have learned that you are indeed wise." He hesitated, then said softly, "Teach some of this wisdom to Fadhil, so that he'll have the courage to ask to marry Leyliah."

"Marry?" he exclaimed with astonishment identical to Fadhil's. And his reply was the same, too: "He cannot."

When a man and woman cared for each other, and there was no impediment in bloodline or wealth or status, why not get married? He frowned at Abb Shagara. "But they obviously—"

The father of his people shook his head. "It is not spoken of. Not even to you, who know some of our secrets. You have the map of where we will be from season to season?"

"Folded in my memory."

"Good." Drawing himself up, Abb Shagara said for everyone else to hear, "Acuyib's blessings upon you and all that you think, all that you say, and all that you do."

"Acuyib's Glory be with you and all Shagara forever. And I promise that I'll be back with wondrous gifts to thank you for my life." Low-voiced, he added with a wink, "And to teach you how to ride."

They exchanged bows, and as Azzad straightened up, Abb Shagara placed a chain around his neck. A finger-length brass plaque set with several gemstones rested at the center of his breast.

"This will protect you, so that you return to us."

Azzad bowed his thanks and told himself that when he ran out of pearls, he'd still have something to sell to keep himself and Khamsin fed. So perhaps the gift was protection of a sort after all.

As the whole tribe called out farewells, he put out a hand to soothe the stallion. He needn't have bothered: Khamsin thought the praise was for him. He arched his neck and pranced after Azzad mounted, and without being signaled to do so reared to show off the thin streak of white on his belly.

"Flaunt it for the mares some other time," Azzad advised him, waved to the crowd, and rode away.

It wasn't until that evening, when he unsaddled Khamsin, that he realized the charms were not tin but silver, and the pectoral about his own neck was not polished brass but solid gold.

The next five days passed placidly enough. There was a trail and a rock shelter the first night, and more trail and a fencing of thorns on the second. The Shagara had even taken into account the time he would make riding a horse rather than sitting in a wagon.

The trail he followed was a double rut in the rocky desert, distinguishable as a trail only because it had slightly fewer stones than the surrounding wasteland. The third night he reached the skirts of some low mountains and camped beside a trickle of water below a cliff, staring up at the extravagant stars. He missed the soft sounds of the Shagara camp, the gentle music of the wind chimes. But on the fourth day, even with the silver on Khamsin's saddle and the gold on his own breast to remind him, the time spent with the Shagara began to seem dreamlike. An eighteen-year-old boy called "Father" who ruled a whole tribe. Trinkets guaranteed to turn aside arrows and swords.

Absurd.

On the fifth afternoon he caught up with a family returning from a visit to their nomadic relations. Parents, two sons and their wives, an unwed daughter, and six squalling toddlers were all happy to be going home to civilization.

"Bayyid Qarhia is not a great city, not like Beit Za'ara," said the father, "but it's certainly better than the squalor of my uncle's tents! Of course," he laughed, "my uncle would slit his own throat before he'd set foot in any town."

Azzad surmised that this Beit Za'ara was the largest community in this man's experience. Two hundred inhabitants at the most, he decided. In Dayira Azreyq there lived two hundred times that number.

But where there was a town, there was money. Probably not a lot of money, but enough to get him started. Precisely what he intended to start was as yet unclear. But from the way the young men eyed Khamsin with that combination of fascination and wariness that Azzad was coming to expect, it would have something to do with the stallion.

The women and children rode in a large wagon drawn by two of those monstrous horses. Azzad could not believe that there was so little contact with eastern lands that Khamsin's breed was unknown to them. But the Shagara had never heard of Rimmal Madar, just as Azzad had never heard of the Shagara. Though nothing more formidable than The Steeps lay between the two lands, he had begun to think that there were reasons why the peoples had never mingled. These possible reasons occupied his thoughts for long stretches of the road, and eventually he thought he might have an answer. If the sheyqas had an agreement with their desert-dwelling cousins that The Steeps were the border, none would pass through that were not approved. The Ammarad would keep to their side out of habit, preference, and understanding with their royal kin. And they would keep everyone else out of Rimmal Madar, as well.

Further, Azzad speculated, the sheyqas would not wish the Geysh Dushann generally known—or, indeed, known at all. What better assassins than one's own blood relations, whom nobody had ever even heard of? And Azzad was abruptly, bitterly certain that just such assassins had advised Nizzira on which poison to use on the al-Ma'aliq men and where to set the fires at Beit Ma'aliq.

Dragging his mind from the past, he patted Khamsin's neck and compared him point by point with the huge desert horses. They were taller, broader, tougher, stronger. Logic dictated that they must be able to survive long periods without much food or water. Yet when they did feed, they must devour half a man's monthly earnings. They were hardier than Khamsin, but slower; more powerful, but more expensive; and the evil gleam in their eyes boded ill for those who trained them.

Old ways died hard; even if lighter, swifter, sweeter-tempered horses were available, few would wish to exchange the wagon for the saddle. A horse that could not be placed between shafts was no good as a horse. The idea that Azzad could convince them otherwise was ludicrous, and he knew it. Expert rider though he was, he wouldn't have tried to sit one of these monsters if his life depended on it. *Only think*, he told himself wryly, *of the insult to Khamsin!* And yet he wondered, watching the men watch Khamsin, if he was in danger of losing his only asset to thieves in the night.

The family was not wealthy. They rented a stall in Bayyid Qarhia's zouq, selling blankets and cloaks woven by their tribal relatives. But something else besides gathering new goods had happened on this trip. To judge by the red-rimmed eyes of the daughter and her mother's black anger whenever she addressed her—as "La'a-tzawaq," unwed—there had been an unsuccessful attempt to find her a husband. To Azzad's exacting eye, the girl's looks were minimal, her feminine allure negligible, and her intelligence doubtful. Possessing one of these three she might have made a match, even at her age—at least nineteen—but lacking any, her prospects were not good.

That evening they made camp, and from his provisions Azzad shared spices to enliven a bland stew. Afterward they all sat around the fire listening to the young wives sing. Their voices were high and sweet, putting him in mind of his sisters. Half-closing his eyes, he could almost imagine himself back at home . . .

. . . *upstairs in the arrareem, lazing on silken cushions and sipping cool fruit drinks after the evening meal. A breeze blew in from the hadiqqa ma'aliqa, scented with citrus and flowers. Alessir—twenty-two, eager to be married, and on the verge of settling things with a beauteous and wealthy girl—blushed furiously as they all teased him without mercy. Grandfather threatened again to marry the girl himself if Alessir didn't get on with it. Omma, not quite sixteen, played the harp and sang languishing love songs; she looked forward to choosing among dozens of handsome, adoring young men when Mother let it be known that her eldest daughter was ready for marriage. Mairid, a year younger, sighed her envy. Ra'abi and Yasimine, still little girls, tended their menagerie of birds and rabbits*

and kittens, begging at intervals to ride the big horses like their sisters and broth-
ers. Mother, glancing up from her tallying books, told them yet again that when
they were big enough to saddle one, they were big enough to ride one, but until
then they must make do with their half-breed ponies. . . .

Azzad rose abruptly to his feet, unable to bear the music any longer. He
paced to the rocks where he'd tethered Khamsin, buried his face in the satin-
soft neck, and, for the first time since that terrible night in Rimmal Madar,
wept.

Late that night, snug in a blanket near the glowing embers of the fire, he
woke abruptly, his heart pounding. No dream lingered to disturb his mind,
but neither was there any sound in the starlit darkness to alert his ears. A
year ago he would have considered it tiresome, all this jolting awake in the
middle of the night. But other times he'd woken thus he'd either learned
something useful or saved his own life. He paid heed to the night and the
desert around him, listening intently and slitting his eyes open.

The mother, father, daughter, wives, and children occupied the wagon;
the two sons had curled up in blankets near Azzad by the fire. These blankets
were now empty. Azzad eased over onto his back, raising his head slightly.
The wagon was still here.

Was Khamsin? The stallion would scream his outrage if anyone came
near. But suddenly Azzad could not get it out of his mind that something
threatened their freedom.

About to rise and investigate, he suddenly heard what must have awakened him: a feminine giggle, muffled as if in a man's shoulder. Azzad grinned
at his own foolishness and relaxed. Of course; the brothers had gone off with
their wives for a little midnight gratification.

A few moments later he heard a soft footstep. Scarce had he opened his
eyes when a woman's voice whispered, "Lie still—I mean you no harm."

The plain, dull-witted, unalluring daughter nudged aside Azzad's blanket and slithered down beside him. She was clad only in her waist-length
black hair. He scrambled away from her, throwing the wool blanket over her
body.

"Lady, what are you doing?" He kept his voice low; if her father and
brothers caught them here, he'd be dead.

Or married.

Which, he realized as she smiled nervously up at him, was precisely her
intention. He was young, handsome, and though he had no family they knew

of and no prospects they could see, any husband was better than no husband. A threat to his freedom, indeed. No wonder the other blankets around the fire were empty.

"Make a baby for me," she breathed.

Acuyib help him! "Lady," he said with careful courtesy, "this is wrong, I will not despoil you—"

"Oh, that's already been done." She sat up, letting the blanket fall from her shoulders. She had very pretty breasts. "One of my cousins did it, but it was not my time to conceive. If you make a baby for me tonight, then I can say it's his, and he'll have to marry me."

Women! What mere man could comprehend them? It occurred to him to be insulted that her object was not marriage with *him*—young, handsome, wealthy Azzad al-Ma'aliq. Young and handsome still but wealthy no longer. He really would have to start remembering that.

It was a measure of Azzad's first twenty years of life that he actually considered her proposal. He'd gone without a woman since early autumn— and it was now full winter. And she did have very pretty breasts. . . .

But it was equally a measure of what had happened to Azzad since the autumn that he shook his head. "Believe me, lady, you are lovely and gracious, and it would be any man's honor and pleasure to be your husband. But I cannot."

She was not fooled by the flattery. Her mirror had schooled her to realism. "Cannot, or will not?"

"Both," he answered honestly. "Any children I father, I will raise and teach." Raised in full knowledge of their noble heritage as al-Ma'aliq and taught to hate Nizzira al-Ammarizzad. Abruptly he wanted such children with all his heart.

"You will not do this small thing for me?"

"It is a very great thing, and I'm sure you can find a man more worthy than I."

She sighed. "But it must be tonight. If I wait another moon, I will not be believed." She reached for his groin with all the seductiveness of a gardener reaching to cull spoiled fruit. "You are a man. I am a woman. Do this for me."

"No." He gently took her hand from his body. She examined his face narrowly in the dim light and drew in a long breath as if to sigh once more— but Azzad knew what was coming. He clapped a hand over her mouth and pulled her against his chest. "None of that, now," he murmured into her lank black hair as she struggled against him. "I will not father your baby, and I will not marry you. But I will tell you how to marry the cousin you love."

She tensed in his arms, but stopped fighting him.

"Very good. The way to do it is this. Hide your moon-cloths from everyone, especially your mother. This is possible?"

She nodded. In Beit Ma'aliq, with servants everywhere, it would have been hopeless. But this girl probably had to wash all her own clothes.

"Run weeping to your parents and say that you fear you are ill, because your moon-days have not come since you journeyed to your uncle's tents. When they ask if you were alone with any man, deny it—and then weep harder than ever and let slip your cousin's name. I guarantee that you and he will be married. When next you bleed, it will be thought that you miscarried of the child. But by then you'll be married, with plenty of chances for another baby. Do you understand?"

Again she nodded. Azzad cautiously took his hand from her mouth. She stayed quiet, so he let her go.

"I hope you'll be very happy," he told her. "Now go back to your bed, and start planning what a fine life you will have with the true father of your children."

She slipped away without a word of thanks for his clever solution to her problem. Women! Azzad lay back, exhaling to the bottom of his lungs and blessing his luck.

The next day he rode on. Quickly, and alone.

The landscape changed subtly. Azzad paid so little attention, trusting Khamsin and involved in his own thoughts, that before he knew it, he was riding up toward a forest. Above were truly formidable peaks, hidden until now by the clouds wreathing their heights. Azzad reined in, contemplating the magnificence with pleasure—until he realized he would probably have to cross these mountains. By comparison, the castle of the al-Ma'aliq stood on flat ground. Nothing in those hills had prepared him for the summits looming above him now. At least the puzzle of why Rimmal Madar knew nothing of this distant land was solved—for who would dare these peaks and cross the desert unless absolutely necessary?

"Ayia," he muttered to Khamsin, "we've come this far—Acuyib won't let us die now."

There was good hunting and forage and plentiful water. Yet as the cold sank into his bones every night, more cruel than the dry chill of the desert, he huddled in his cloak and wished that he believed in the Shagara spells and that such spells included one of warmth. He should have gone to the seacoast after all.

At noon one day he emerged from a narrow tree-lined defile into a bowl-shaped valley. The creek ran full, and the grains and grasses were lush, even in early winter, and the grazing land was strewn with fat brown sheep. A road snaked up the hillside, and stone houses perched along it at intervals. Azzad counted thirty individual structures and a cluster of buildings about halfway up the road—probably markets and workshops. *Bayyid Qarhia?* he wondered. If so, he'd best stay only tonight and then move on, before his would-be mistress and her family arrived home.

Staying even one night was, however, out of the question. He had barely emerged from the trees when a shepherd whistled shrilly. Within moments a contingent of fiercely bearded men were marching down the road, carrying scythes and axes and other instruments of peaceful agriculture easily turned to murderous intent. The laws of hospitality quite obviously did not apply in this country. Azzad hastily weighed his chances of proving himself harmless to man, woman, and sheep—and pulled Khamsin's head around.

"Hold!"

A shepherd blocked the path. It would be simple enough to run him down, but for the fact that he held a massive bow with an iron-tipped shaft nocked, aimed, and ready to loose. Azzad sighed, dropped the reins, and held both hands open and away from his body.

"I mean you no wrong," he said. "I am but a traveler, alone and unarmed."

He heard the men approach behind him. Pressure of one heel turned Khamsin once more to face them. Too late, he remembered the tempting glint of silver on the stallion's saddle and gold from the necklace on his own chest.

"Who are you?" the eldest of the men demanded, teeth showing yellow, like an aged wolf's, through his thick white beard. "Why are you here?"

"My name is Azzad. I am from a faraway land and seek only to pass through your mountains."

This did not impress. The elder came forward, leather boots soundless on the gravelly road, his iron-headed staff poised. When he was within three paces of Khamsin, the stallion took advantage of the lax reins and stretched his head forward, teeth bared. The old man stopped and glared, but neither flinched nor retreated.

"I apologize," Azzad said humbly. "He is not kindly disposed to strangers."

After a moment, the man nodded thoughtfully. Over his shoulder he said, "This one is safe. Let him pass."

"But—Abb Sharouf—"

Azzad repressed an untimely impulse to laugh. *Father of Sheep?* Either he had peculiar habits or there was a lack of women—

"I have decided!" snarled the old man. "Further, he may have water for himself and his horse. Further, a loaf of bread and a portion of fresh-cooked meat. Further, a woolen blanket for the nights he will spend in the high country. Further—"

"You are too generous, Abb Sharouf," Azzad said, wishing nothing more than the furtherance of his journey.

The interruption won him another glare. "*Further,* a satchel of herbs to ease his breathing in the heights." He reversed his staff and thunked the metal tip on a rock, striking a spark. Khamsin danced away from it, rolling his eyes. "I have said it, and it will be."

Azzad was escorted silently up the road to the village. The promised water came from a well. The food he ate hurriedly. The blanket was tied to his saddle; Khamsin snorted a little at its powerful stink of sheep. The small leather sack of herbs was given over with a curt admonition to brew it strong every morning. He felt their eyes on his back as he rode up the slope, and as he passed into a stand of trees, he heard them begin to argue behind him.

Expelling a long sigh, he shook his head, thanked Acuyib for the blessing of survival, and followed the narrowing trail up into the mountains.

He did not understand then, of course. He still did not believe.

Thirty days later, he was living in the town of Sihabbah. He found lodging for himself and the noble Khamsin, and employment caring for a rich man's horses and donkeys, having decided to hoard the pearls until he could travel to the great city of Hazganni in the spring.

It was on the thirty-first day, with but three days until the new year of 612, when the young woman and her father and brothers and uncles and cousins came to Sihabbah, that he finally began to comprehend what the friendship and protection of the Shagara truly meant.

— FERRHAN MUALEEF, *Deeds of Il-Kadiri,* 654

5

Angry voices outside in the stable yard made Azzad swing around and squint into the sudden sunlight flooding the stable. Shadows loomed in the doorway, darkening the cobbles and his dazzled eyes. As his vision adjusted, the rake in his hands clattered to the stones.

"He is the one who despoiled my wife's only daughter! Seize him!"

So startled that he didn't even have time to think about running, Azzad found his arms wrenched painfully behind his back. His feet were kicked out from under him and his body unceremoniously lugged out into the stable yard. There they were: the father, the brothers, and eleven other men—five old, six young, all furious, all armed with knives, all righteously intent on shedding his blood over the flagstones he himself kept clean. The girl huddled by the water trough, wearing an ugly brown cloak, weeping.

Azzad was deposited ungently on the ground. He lay there, flat on his back, wondering dazedly how this could have happened. This mountainside town was not Bayyid Qarhia—it was nowhere *near* Bayyid Qarhia. He'd made sure of it before he decided to tarry the winter here. And yet here they were, practically slavering at the mouth now that they'd found him.

The girl had bungled it. He saw it in her reddened eyes when she dared a glance at him. Somehow, despite his excellent instructions, she'd said the wrong thing, and her father had fixed on Azzad as the malefactor. And now Azzad was sprawling in a stable yard like a calf at a gelding party, with all her male relations holding carving knives.

The village elder, Abb Ferrhan, and Azzad's own employer, Bazir al-Gallidh, respectfully invited the father to explain why the peace of Sihabbah had been invaded by knife-wielding strangers. With every word more and more people crowded around; this was the best entertainment since a vagabond troupe of acrobats and mimes had come through at the last harvest festival.

"And then what did she do," cried the father, "when her mother asked if she'd been with him, but weep and cry out that she had not?"

"A woman protecting her lover," said Abb Ferrhan, stroking his scraggly white beard, "as plain as the sun in the sky."

"Or a woman telling the truth," mused Bazir al-Gallidh, whose family was the richest in Sihabbah and whose name was a byword for exquisite manners. "If he were the guilty one and if she wanted him for her husband, would she not admit to his name?"

"It could have been no one else, I tell you!" the father raged, unable in his fury to accord the nobleman proper respect.

"You could wait and see if the child looks like him!" someone in the crowd called out, to general laughter and the wronged family's increased humiliation.

"Better like him than like the mother," muttered Mazzud, one of the stable hands, who had no manners at all and had never seen the need for any that Azzad could tell.

"Ayia, Azzad?" asked Bazir. "Did you sire this woman's child?"

"No!" He struggled to sit up and repeated, "No! By my hope for Acuyib's Light and Glory when I die, I did not."

"Liar!" shrieked her father. He and his kinsmen had to be physically restrained from slicing into Azzad. Some of them had brought *two* knives.

"What's all this?" demanded a new voice. "Brother, what goes on here?"

"Zellim," said Bazir, "you are come at the right moment, as always. We have need of a legal turn of mind."

The situation was explained to the eminent mou'ammi, who practiced law in faraway Hazganni. Zellim al-Gallidh listened, eyed Azzad and then the girl, pursed his lips, and shrugged elegant shoulders beneath a snowy white robe.

The father folded his arms across his chest. "Now that you have heard all, you must agree—they will marry at once!"

The girl burst into renewed tears. Zellim—not quite so polite as his brother—winced at the volume. The father, belatedly realizing the foolishness of annoying the most important people he had ever met, snarled at her to be silent.

"Stop that!" Azzad ordered before he could think about it.

"You see? You see? He protects her! Defends her! He is her lover!"

"What I *see*," said Zellim in forbidding tones that had resounded in the law courts of Hazganni for thirty years, "is a man objecting to abuse of a woman. This is only right and decent." Approaching the girl, he bowed his head as if to a noble lady and said, "What is your claim in this matter, Lady?"

She sobbed louder.

"Azzad, stand up," said Bazir.

He did, with a helping hand from Mazzud, and brushed stable yard debris from his clothing. As he bent to pick straw off his trousers, he reflected sourly that no one would recognize the famously fastidious Azzad al-Ma'aliq in the unkempt, threadbare stable hand he had become. Not only was he reduced to poverty and namelessness, he was about to be forced into marrying a fool of a girl who couldn't even do what all other women did as easily as they breathed: lie about a lover.

"I ask again," Bazir al-Gallidh said. "Did you get this lady with child?"

"No, I did not," he replied, flicking a last bit of goat-dung from his knee. As he straightened, the Shagara charm about his neck swung free of his torn shirt. Bazir's dark eyes narrowed; this was the only reaction Azzad saw. But within moments murmurs circulated through the crowd.

"He tells the truth—"

"He is not the father—"

"There is a liar here, but it is not Azzad—"

Abb Ferrhan held up a quelling hand. Everyone was silent—Azzad most profoundly of all. *He* knew he was telling the truth, but why did *they* think so? They had no reason to believe him—and yet they did.

"I find he speaks truth," said Abb Ferrhan. "He is not the father of the child."

"*What?*" roared the father, rounding on his weeping daughter.

"I tried to tell you!" the girl gasped, flinching back. "It was our cousin, in the tents one night—"

"But how can this be?"

"In the way of a young woman with a young man, I should think," the lawyer Zellim observed dryly. "Azzad, what have you to say of this?"

Bazir al-Gallidh was still looking at him strangely. Azzad addressed his employer with humility, as was fitting. None except Azzad knew that deference for the nobleman was coupled with profound gratitude for the miraculous ways of Acuyib.

And, he was realizing, the Shagara.

"Al-Gallidh," he said, "it is as she states. I was not the one to lie with her.

It was her cousin, whom she loves, and it is my belief that they ought to marry."

"Yes, have the lovers marry!" a sentimental woman called out.

"Let the girl marry the one she loves!"

"He must be more beautiful than the dawn for her to prefer him over Azzad!"

"He must be blind," muttered Azzad's friend Mazzud.

Once more Abb Ferrhan gestured for silence. "Is this your wish, my child?" he asked the girl. When she wiped her nose, sniffled, and nodded, he lifted both hands in the manner of a pronouncement. "Ayia. It is none of our affair, here in Sihabbah, but my advice to you, good man, is to take your daughter to this cousin and celebrate a wedding as soon as may be."

The girl, her father, her brothers, her uncles, and her cousins got back into their wagon. Azzad saw her direct a fulminating look at him—not a featherweight of gratitude in her at all—as the family departed. The crowd dispersed. Abb Ferrhan returned to his forge. After trading an arched brow with his younger brother, Bazir al-Gallidh went back to his library and his account books—for in this land, Azzad had found, it was the men who took care of such things, and it was rare to find a woman who could so much as write her own name. Azzad was left alone in the stable yard with Zellim.

"Shagara," was all the mou'ammi said.

"I had the honor of guesting with that tribe, yes," Azzad replied carefully.

A slow nod, a long sigh—and a sharp, shrewd glance. "Should I ever be so unfortunate as to stand against you in the courts, I will be certain first that you wear nothing of the Shagara." Before Azzad could react to this, Zellim said casually, "My brother and I are the only al-Gallidh now living. But I have a daughter. Gayyid zoubh."

Faint of voice and wide of eye, Azzad returned the wish for a good morning. Then, touching the finger-length gold plaque at his breast, he murmured a line from long-neglected devotions. "The Ways of Acuyib are Wonderful and Strange. Praise the Ways of Acuyib." And for himself he added, "And the Shagara."

Azzad had exactly one marketable skill (success with ladies brought expenditures, not earnings): he could ride as if he and his horse were one being. His expertise had almost gotten him into the elite Qoundi Ammar, but not even his singular way with horses had been enough to negate his al-Ma'aliq origins. At the time of his rejection he'd shrugged, and pretended not to care, and soon thereafter he truly had not, for Khamsin had then been born, and black horses were not allowed in the Qoundi Ammar.

Back in the Gabannah Chaydann, during the earliest days of his exile, he had been confident that his mastery of horsemanship would gain him entry to the first families of any country and yield large sums as he taught the finer points of riding. But that had been before he'd seen these enormous horses that no man in his right mind would dare to saddle. Men rode donkeys. They looked ludicrous, but they rode donkeys. Even the sight of Azzad on Khamsin, galloping through the al-Gallidh meadows, did not inspire them. So much for his grand plan. Throughout the winter he worked in the stables of Bazir al-Gallidh, gnawing on his thwarted vengeance.

It was boring work—mucking out stalls and cleaning harness, feeding and currying. He wished it was boring to pick out those cauldron-wide hooves and scrape the yellow from those tremendous teeth; smashed bones and missing fingers did not figure in any of his plans. But as fields soaked by winter rain dried in spring sun, and the mountain heights slowly shed their cloaks of snow, he had worked out no plan that led to wealth, influence, and the slow, suffering demise of Nizzira al-Ammarizzad.

And then one day, when clouds seemed to hover within arm's reach above Sihabbah, he was summoned to the library of Bazir al-Gallidh. The maqtabba was a large room with a high ceiling, stuffed with leather-bound books of a dozen different sizes and colors, the titles stamped in gold on their spines. The furnishings were both beautiful and comfortable: a couch and chair plump with pillows, a stepladder of dark satinwood inlaid with swirling silver wire, a broad table covered in maps and ledgers, a many-branched bronze lamp with shades of paper-fine alabaster. On a low table was a beautiful chadarang service, the red squares and pieces made of carnelian, the green of jasper.

Bazir al-Gallidh lavished money on his horses and his maqtabba, and that was all. The rest of his house was neither large nor richly decorated, and he dressed more simply than any servant of the al-Ma'aliq, but the stainless purity of his robe made Azzad all too aware of his own threadbare condition—him, the most elegant young blade in Dayira Azreyq.

Ayia, that was another life. He did not regret the clothes or the jewels;

indeed, he had come to appreciate Bazir's quiet elegance. At past fifty years of age, al-Gallidh was a man completely at ease with himself and the little world he ruled, wishing for nothing larger or more powerful or more opulent. Azzad, less that half his age, was yet ambitious—but he had specific uses to which he would put money and influence, should he ever succeed in acquiring them.

Still, from Bazir al-Gallidh he learned that distinction did not require flaunting display. For example, the nobleman wore no jewels but a ring on the first finger of his right hand. Azzad recognized the design from the treasure room back at home: silver clasping a stone, in this case a pearl as white as the snow that was the nobleman's name. The al-Ma'aliq owned several such rings—*had* owned, he corrected himself with a renewed surge of bitterness such as he had not felt all this winter of placid, mindless, boring work.

"My ring interests you," said Bazir al-Gallidh.

Abruptly aware that he was staring—and, considering his thoughts, staring rather fiercely—he smoothed his expression and replied, "Your pardon. I have seen several like it in the past. Taken from the northern barbarians, was it not?"

"Yes." He held out his hand to regard the pearl. "More than a hundred years ago my great-grandfather came down from the mountains—a place much higher than Sihabbah, whence our family's name—and fought the barbarians. Eventually they were expelled from the coast. My ancestor returned, his head golden with glory, as the old saying goes, and richer by nothing more than this ring."

"A truly noble man," Azzad commented.

"Such rings as these are common where you come from?"

"No. But I have seen three or four. The stones were rubies."

"Ayia, then they were from the fingers of their nobles. Something about protection against storms and lightning, the perils of a sea voyage."

"I didn't know that. Is it written in one of these books?" He gestured to the wealth around them.

"In many of them. Those who dwell on the coast suffered greatly when these barbarians came, and tales of those times are of interest to me. From them, I learned that pearls such as this were worn by those pure of heart—the holy ones, the wise ones. Do you take an interest in the past?"

"Only in the future," he said, and was unable to keep a twinge of bitterness from his voice.

"Which appears to you rather limited, here in Sihabbah." Bazir al-Gallidh seated himself on the couch and gestured to the chadarang service. "Do you play?"

"Badly, al-Gallidh. My mother taught me, but despaired of my ever becoming a serious player."

"This is very, very old. My father always said he could imagine that this was the service on which Acuyib and Chaydann Il-Mamnoua'a played to divide up the world into the green lands and the red."

Azzad nodded. "My mother used to say that chadarang was part of her devotions—it's the eternal struggle between the desert and the garden."

Al-Gallidh picked up one of the towers, fingering a broken crenellation on the jasper. "Your mother sounds a wise woman. But I think there are things more subtle here. There are those of us who live in these, safe and stationary—" He set the tower back on its square and touched the carnelian sheyqa's crowned head. "—and those who have not the grandest title but who rule in truth by moving among the people." Sitting back, he regarded Azzad thoughtfully. "I am told that you are a good worker."

"I have tried to be," Azzad replied.

"I am further told that you are clean, conscientious, do not drink or gamble or follow women about in the marketplace, and indeed have been exemplary."

Looking into the older man's eyes, he felt an absurd desire to shuffle his feet and shrug like a little boy.

"How is it then," asked the nobleman, "that this superlative servant has done my house such grievous wrong?"

Azzad blinked. "I don't understand. What wrong have I done?"

"Perhaps I ought to say that the wrong was done not by you but by your horse." Leaning back, he eyed Azzad with a hint of whimsy. "Five of my best mares are with foal by that spindle-legged stallion of yours."

"Five—?"

"Yes. At about the time you arrived here, they were coming into season and had just been separated from the herd. They were to be covered by my new stud, who was taken to them as planned. But I did not know until today that Khamsin had gotten there before him."

"But—how?"

"Our horses do not require high fences," Bazir replied mildly.

It was true. They could sooner fly than jump anything taller than this couch. But Khamsin—faster, lighter—he'd been trying to fly since he'd tottered to his feet and taken his first steps.

"I know," Bazir continued, "because by this time the mares should be much bigger than they are. I was afraid that I was mistaken when I bought the new stud, that he had no vigor. But—five mares, all of the best bloodlines, all bearing runtlings at the same time? Then I happened to catch sight of your Khamsin galloping across the meadow. He leaped the stream merely for the fun of it."

Azzad nodded slowly. "I am sorry, al-Gallidh. What can I do to—"

"—rectify the problem? Nothing. I blame myself, in truth, for not recognizing that he would get to the mares any way he could. We just don't think about horses leaping fences, you see. And so now we have a difficulty."

Azzad tried not to gulp. This was an appalling thing Khamsin had done, potentially disastrous to the al-Gallidh horses' reputation, not to speak of whatever profits had been expected in this year's crop of foals—

But the nobleman did not look angry; indeed, he seemed almost merry. "I need draft animals, not racehorses. What am I to do with these half-breeds?"

Five foals, not as tall or heavy or powerful as their mothers—

"Mazzud says, and I agree, that judging by their smallness inside the womb, they will be much too frail for harnessing."

—but as light and swift as their sire, perfect for—

"And so how can I use them?"

"Riding," he heard himself say, and all at once the blurry idea of what seemed like years ago became as polished crystal in his mind. So did his mother's face. And the estimable Za'avedra el-Ibrafidia stared at him with disgust for his blindness. "Saddle them and ride them," he said, excitement rising in him the way his manhood rose at the sight of a beautiful woman.

"We ride donkeys." A flat statement, admitting no possibility of change.

"And look ridiculous on them!" Azzad exclaimed. "Only see, al-Gallidh, the advantages! They will be bigger than Khamsin, but not so big as your horses. The terrain here demands strength, which they will have—but grace and a sweeter temper as well, and speed—not so fast as he, but much faster than—"

"You speak as if they were already born."

"I *know* how they will be, I can see every one of them!" And somehow he could.

"Along with that truth charm about your neck, did the Shagara give you a spell of foreknowledge as well?"

The crystalline images shattered. "A—a spell?"

"My brother Zellim also has interests," Bazir murmured. "It was he who pointed out to me the charm and deduced its purpose. Through my own reading, I have learned that when our people rode into battle against the barbarians, they wore amulets to protect them—things of gold and silver made by the Shagara."

"I did not know that, either."

"And now that you do know, you do not believe?"

Azzad opened his mouth and found he had no words. In the matter of the pregnant girl, the people of Sihabbah had believed him. So, he realized suddenly, had the shepherds in that village, who had been ready to kill him; but after he had told them he meant no harm, Abb Sharouf, standing close to him, had believed him. Believed, and let him go. For no reason whatsoever.

Except the Shagara gold around his neck.

"Al-Gallidh," he said at last, "I do not know. The Shagara were a peculiarity to me—kind and welcoming, skilled in medicine as everyone knows, but their ways were . . . eccentric."

"So I have heard. So I have *not* read—which is curious, if they were so important in driving out the invaders. Their name is mentioned in the books, and that is all. Nothing of their ways, their lands, their customs. They crafted armbands and rings, a few shields for the nobility, necklaces—and that is all anyone knows."

Azzad had not seen shields being made. Perhaps the Shagara made such things only in times of war. If, as Fadhil had told him, there was no war here—

Bazir sighed and drummed his fingers on a pillow. The pearl glistened with subtle iridescence by lamplight. "We will speak more of the Shagara another time. For now—you know that as owner of the sire, the foals will be half yours."

This time astonishment completely robbed him of speech.

"In the normal course of things, once they are born, each partner has the right to reject any or all and be compensated."

Azzad's mouth was so dry he thought his tongue would stick permanently to his teeth.

"These half-breeds will be of no use to me at the wagon or the plow. One might say that they are worthless, in which case you could buy my share in them for nearly nothing. However, the foals my mares usually produce are worth a great deal indeed, and it would not be unreasonable of me to demand a price from you to match what I lost when your Khamsin leaped that fence."

Acuyib help him—he would be working off the debt for the rest of his life!

"So it seems the only thing to do is saddle them, as you have said, and I will keep my half-interest until it is clear whether or not these horses are of any value." All at once he laughed. "It suits me, Azzad, that you will make right this very interesting wrong. And it amuses me greatly that while everyone was looking sidelong at your handsome face and guarding their wives and daughters, it was your horse that was the true stud, siring offspring on females not his own!"

Azzad rose in the little world of Sihabbah. Rather than the straw-lined cubbyhole that had been his dwelling all winter, he now occupied his own private room above the stable, with a window overlooking the fields, a mattress stuffed with horsehair, a table only a little rickety, a three-legged stool, and a covered earthenware chamber pot. It wasn't opulence—Azzad knew the feel and smell and taste and look of that well enough—but at this point in his life luxury's definition was leaving the pot outside his door each morning for somebody else to empty.

He was also admitted to Bazir al-Gallidh's maqtabba for dinner one evening of every eight or nine. As spring became summer, their dinners together occurred every sixth night, then every fifth. They discussed the mares, of course—how they galloped about the meadows, when usually by this time in pregnancy they would be plodding. They talked about training the foals to the saddle and bridle, with Bazir recoiling in comical horror at the notion that he be the first to learn how to ride. They exchanged ideas as well, speaking over games of chadarang about the differences in language, devotion, and tradition between this land and Rimmal Madar. They told each other their family histories—Azzad decided that in honor he could have no secrets from this kind, wise, generous man.

They shared a bond in that each was nearly kinless. Azzad had a cousin left in little Sayyida—nearly a year old now—Ammineh's daughter; Bazir had his brother and his niece, and that was all. Tragic as the fate of the al-Ma'aliq had been, the al-Gallidh had been afflicted as well. Bazir's father, an only child of an only child, died young in a climbing accident high in the mountains; his mother perished of a fever shortly thereafter; he lost his beloved wife in childbed, and his twin sons as well. Zellim's first wife, Jemilha's mother, was killed by her jealous sister, who poisoned her food; his second wife succumbed to lung-sickness.

"So," Bazir said with a tiny shrug, "as you may surmise, we guard little Jemilha zealously."

It was impolite for a stranger to enquire about a man's female relations, but Azzad knew he was now considered a friend. "How old is she?"

"Fifteen. Zellim trembles at the thought of her marrying and leaving him."

"I don't understand why he doesn't marry again. You might do the same, for that matter." This truly was impolite; he grimaced at his own words and said, "Forgive my presumption."

"I knew perfect happiness," Bazir said softly. "She was the heart of my heart, the light of my eyes." After a moment's pause, he continued, "Zellim had more courage than I. He risked his heart twice. But he cannot do so again."

"Not even for more children?"

"My friend, I excuse your words because you are young and have never loved."

The one topic they never discussed was the Shagara. When Azzad attempted to tell Bazir of the time he'd spent with them, the nobleman shook his head and said, "Another day, my friend, after you have considered what is wise to say."

"But I have no secrets from you. I have told you what happened to my family, and why, and my intentions for the future, and—"

"You have lived with the Shagara. I have only read of them. But those things I do know tell me that they have secrets that are not yours to disclose, even to me."

Azzad thought about it and could not but agree.

After telling Azzad to design everything their horses would require, Bazir set about preparations of his own. Woodsmen felled trees up the mountain to build a new stable. Weavers set to work on beautiful saddle blankets. Tanners prepared suitable hides for bridles and saddles. Abb Ferrhan experimented at his forge with bits, stirrups, and a new, smaller horseshoe. Azzad was amazed by all this; not until the foals grew would he be able to tell just how to size the tack. But gradually he became aware that Bazir's wisdom had led him to involve Sihabbah's people in this curious accidental project. If the five foals were a success, all could take pride in them. And all would eventually profit, for if minds were changed and men began to ride horses instead of donkeys—Azzad hardly dared consider the measuring of his potential wealth.

He acquired a few new things himself. An embroidered cushion appeared one evening on his three-legged stool. Carved shutters of fragrant pine were placed at his window. A new mattress, stuffed with goose feathers, lay under a brightly patterned quilt. When he ventured to thank Bazir for the gifts, the nobleman professed to know nothing of them.

At last, on a morning early in autumn, one of the mares began her labors. She was early, and it happened so quickly and so easily that the first anyone knew of it was the sight of a leggy pewter-gray filly romping about the meadow in the warm afternoon sun. Delivery was just as swift for the other mares, although being forewarned by the first labor, the four were comfortably sheltered in the stable.

"Almost without effort," sighed Bazir happily, resting his arms atop the stall door as he gazed at a coal-black colt with a white blaze down his face. "I've never seen it happen so fast."

"They're small," sniffed Mazzud, eyeing the foal. "Easy it was, al-Gallidh, and quick, but every one of them a runtling."

"They'll be bigger than Khamsin, once they're grown," Azzad countered. "Will you name them, al-Gallidh?"

The three fillies were called Farrasha, Shammarra, and Shouzama, for the markings of white on their gray hides: a butterfly, a candle, and a tulip. The sturdy black colt was named Ibbir, for he was the color of ink. The second colt—mud-gray, scrawny and tentative—Bazir called Haddid, which meant iron and which he hoped would inspire the little horse to strength.

The day after the last was born, the stables received visitors. Everyone in Sihabbah turned out, it seemed, to view the five half-breed foals. Comments ranged from "Beautiful" and "So sweet" to "They'll live two moons" and

"Those skinny legs will snap"—but Azzad took no offense at the criticism until one young girl, who looked about twelve, peered into Ibbir's stall and announced, "That's not a horse, that's a mistake!"

Bazir began to laugh silently. Zellim, inspecting brindle-gray Shouzama, glanced over with a grin. "You must forgive her the insult," he said. "A black horse is a rarity in our land. It is said that in times long past, whenever a black foal was born, it was instantly killed."

"But why?" Azzad was horrified.

"Acuyib in His Wisdom created for the benefit of mankind the brown sheep, the gray goat, the red deer, and the white-spotted cow. Seeing this, Chaydann Il-Mamnoua'a laughed into his beard and created the horse, a vile-tempered and contrary animal, to plague mankind. It is only by the Grace of Acuyib that the horse was tamed. Even now, it serves us reluctantly, and we must always watch for signs of its creator's influence. And a black horse—"

"Azwadhi izzahn, azwadh qalb," the girl announced, tossing a long braid over one skinny shoulder. *Black horse, black heart.*

No wonder everyone looked askance at Khamsin, Azzad thought. "But you see," he said to Zellim, for in this land one did not address a girl without permission from her male relatives, "Ibbir will be just like his sire—sweet-natured and biddable." As if understanding this choice mendacity, and resenting the slander, Khamsin snorted from his nearby stall.

"Huh!" Allowing for the different lengths of their noses, the noise from the girl was a fair match for Khamsin's. "Just wait until you try to hitch him to a wagon or a plow!"

Azzad forgot his manners and glowered. "Not one of these foals—*not a single one!*—will ever—"

"We shall ride them," Bazir interrupted smoothly. "I told you that, qarassia. Azzad will show us how."

"What use is a horse that can't pull something?" Then she laughed, a surprisingly lovely sound, like sunlight sparkling on a mountain stream. "No matter, Chal Bazir! It will be so funny watching him try to train them!"

Azzad gulped. This little pest must be none other than Jemilha al-Gallidh, who would inherit every stick, stitch, and stone of her family's vast holdings. Sheltered in her father's house in Hazganni, educated at her own insistence, she came to Sihabbah rarely. Azzad had in fact never seen her before today; considering his lowly status, this was not surprising. But he would have to get into her good graces, for in a way, she too was his partner in this venture.

Her scorn did not bode well for the future.

By spring, Azzad could see that he had been correct about the advantages of cross-breeding. Many others eyed the five half-breeds with doubt, disgust, or—as in Jemilha's case—amused scorn. How could such small, spindle-legged, scrawny horses ever be of any use? But these foals when fully grown would indeed combine the strength of the native breed with Khamsin's grace and speed. As for temperament—at least, unlike their mothers, they didn't try to kick or bite everyone who came within range.

When the foals were a year old, and four more al-Gallidh mares had delivered Khamsin's get (all fillies), Azzad asked for permission to visit the Shagara.

"I owe them my life, al-Gallidh," he explained to Bazir. "In the two years since I left Rimmal Madar, I have prospered, thanks to—"

"—to Khamsin's efforts!" The older man laughed. "No, I do not devalue your hard work, but were it not for your horse, you would yet be cleaning stalls."

"I know," Azzad admitted. "Having nothing to recommend me, I would probably have starved by now."

"So now you wish to repay your Shagara friends. This is an excellent thing, Azzad. I approve. What will you gift them with?"

"Two of our first horses," he said forthrightly. "I will cede total ownership of two others to you. The fifth will be ours together."

"This is agreeable to me—for you shall also be transporting some small gifts from me to the Shagara. How long will you be gone from Sihabbah? One month? Two?"

"Two, I think, possibly a little longer."

Bazir nodded. "I shall miss you, my friend. Now, tell me, what would the ladies of the Shagara appreciate most from an old man admiring of their beauty?"

And so, nearly two years after Azzad had left Dayira Azreyq, he left Sihabbah of the clouds and descended from the mountains to the wasteland. He rode Khamsin and led two donkeys loaded with gifts. The filly Farrasha lived up to her name by flitting all over the landscape as lightly as if she had wings; Azzad was forever whistling her back from her explorations, and finally had to put her on a lead rein. Her half-brother Haddid, still small but stronger than Azzad had dared to hope, needed no tether and followed placidly in Khamsin's wake. The colt, tranquil of temperament and soft of gait, would be given to Abb Shagara. Azzad wasn't sure who would be able to ride Farrasha, but he was betting on Leyliah.

Confident, eager to see his friends, he rode blithely into the wilderness bearing gifts.

He got lost, of course.

Farrasha, escaping her tether, galloped away into the wilderness and would not return at his whistle. He could not chase her—the donkeys were slow, and heavily laden. He cursed fluently all day long, agreeing at last with Jemilha al-Gallidh that horses were surely the work of Chaydann.

All day he followed puffs of dust raised by Farrasha's hooves, the air black with his mood as he imagined the filly lying helpless, her leg broken, about to be devoured by a rimmal nimir. At length even Khamsin, after so much soft living, was tired. Azzad decided to search one more day, and if he did not find Farrasha, he would continue on to the Shagara without her. The next day brought no sign of her. Worse, he had no idea in which direction the Shagara tents lay.

At dawn the next morning as he saddled Khamsin, a familiar voice asked, "Whatever are you doing way out here?" Azzad laughed—once his heart started beating again after the shock—and embraced Fadhil, asked after all the Shagara, and finally told him what had happened.

Fadhil merely shrugged. "So her name is Farrasha? Fitting. She flew into our camp yesterday and fluttered about until dusk before we caught her. We knew her for Khamsin's, so I came looking for you."

The Shagara had identified the filly as Khamsin's get easily: three of their own mares had birthed foals that looked exactly like her.

— FERRHAN MUALEEF, *Deeds of Il-Kadiri,* 654

6

Farrasha having given early warning of Azzad's arrival, by the time Fadhil led him into the camp, preparations were underway for a feast. Azzad went around to each tent with bags of pine nuts and exotic spices as well as candied fruit for the children—making sure everyone knew that Bazir al-Gallidh was the source of the gifts. His own presents were given in private. For Chal Kabir there was a new scale to weigh medicines and a bag of mountain lavender for sweetening potions; for Meryem and Leyliah, tooled leather purses; for Fadhil, a set of fine surgical knives; for Abb Shagara, the two horses with all their equipment and a pair of tall leather boots. And finally, also for the ladies, long white silk scarves embroidered at either end with silver snowflakes.

"Bazir al-Gallidh," Azzad said, smiling as Meryem and Leyliah exclaimed over the beauty of the work, "has read a little and heard a little more about the Shagara."

"Truly an elegant man," Meryem replied, running the filmy silk through her hands. "But bold, to send presents to women he has never met."

"I am sure," grinned Abb Shagara, "that Azzad spoke so much of you, and in such detail, that the al-Gallidh feels he knows you both!"

"All I ever said was that you were smart and beautiful," Azzad promised them. "Of the rest, he knows nothing."

"I never doubted that you would keep our secrets," Leyliah answered graciously. Swirling the scarf around her shoulders, she admired the snowflakes again while saying, "And I know just when I'll wear this!"

"Leyliah," said Fadhil in a cheerful tone, "is getting married next year."

Before Azzad could find words to express his congratulations, Abb Shagara added, "Her husband is Razhid Harirri, a man of subtle eyes, silken beard, and many fine goats. It's my opinion that she's marrying him for the goats." Leyliah laughed and threw a pillow at him; he tossed it back, grinning. "But they're very *fine* goats!"

"You should know," she retorted. "You bleat like one!"

Turning to Azzad, Abb Shagara asked merrily, "So, have you met any girls?"

"My son," Meryem said mildly, "you pry into thing that do not concern you."

"He's Shagara now, Mother—I can ask him anything I want. Isn't that right, Azzad?"

Still in shock that Leyliah was marrying someone other than Fadhil, Azzad blinked and nodded mindlessly. Summoning his manners, he addressed Leyliah. "Razhid Harirri is a fortunate man—I hope he knows it?"

"Ayia," laughed Abb Shagara, "we made certain of that before we accepted him! Now, Azzad, you cannot mean to say you've left not even one girl sighing for you in this Sihabbah you now live in?"

His thoughts flew at once to the women in a cottage up the mountain, who saw to the needs of Sihabbah's unmarried men—and not a few of the married ones. It was a family business like any other, common in every community of any size from Dayira Azhreq to the Great Western Sea. Despite the differences between these lands and his home—which he was startled to find he had stopped thinking of as *home*—some things didn't change. Still, he had been surprised to find Bindta Feyrah and Bindta Sabbah interesting company as well as skilled practitioners of their art, neither attribute an expected one in so remote a place as Sihabbah. But had he truly visited them only a few times?

Forcing a smile, he said, "I rise at dawn, eat, work until noon, eat, rest for a time, work some more, eat, and fall into bed. When is there time for women?"

This brought a stern lecture on the damage he was doing to his health. He bore it with good humor, hanging his head in pretended shame—which, after all, was not such a pretense. His mother would have sent instantly for the family tabbib; his grandfather, for his own favorite mistress.

"Enough!" Leyliah finally said, scowling at Abb Shagara. "Leave him alone, cousin. I want to hear about Sihabbah and this charming al-Gallidh, who sends such lovely presents. And so appropriate to my husband's name!"

"He of the silken beard," teased Abb Shagara, and Fadhil added slyly,

"And *many* fine goats"—and both yelled as this time she threw pillows at both of them.

That night before the feast, Azzad washed up in Fadhil's tent. His young friend was now Chal Fadhil, a fully trained healer, entitled to his own tent and the triple-braided ring of authority. Azzad congratulated him sincerely on his new status, wondering—but not quite daring to ask—why this high rank had not earned him marriage with Leyliah.

The feasting went on until well after dark and the dancing until midnight—and the drinking until dawn, as far as Azzad knew. Pleading the tiring length of his journey from Sihabbah, he left the celebrations a little after midnight, replete with excellent food, congenial conversation, some very interesting stories, and quite a bit of wine. He made his carefully studied way back to Fadhil's tent, didn't trip on any cats or dogs along the way, and fell onto a pile of carpets in the dark.

The carpets were already occupied.

"Fadhil," he slurred. "Sorry—"

"No man could have had so much wine," said a feminine voice, "that he cannot recognize that a woman is in his bed, not a man. Unless you would prefer Fadhil?"

Scrambling back, he toppled over and lay propped awkwardly on one elbow, trying to see into the blackness. "Leyliah?"

"I admit he is quite handsome, and a wonderful friend, but it seemed to me always that your eyes were for women, not men. I might be wrong, though."

There was the sound of flint and iron, and a candle flame sprang to life. His elbow slipped out from under him with the shock. *"Leyliah?"* he repeated stupidly.

She wore nothing but her curling black hair and the white silk scarf with silver snowflakes, draped lightly about her slender form. "Ayia, Azzad, if my identity is now established, perhaps you would tell me if I am welcome to sleep with you for what remains of the night—or if I should indeed call Fadhil."

Fadhil spent what remained of the night elsewhere.

At dawn, Azzad was twining a lock of Leyliah's hair around one finger, the other hand tickling her breasts with the fringed ends of the scarf. "You still haven't told me why."

"Your health, of course."

"That's not what I meant," he said, trying to be severe—difficult, when she stretched languidly and looked up at him through thick black lashes. "Why you?"

"You would prefer someone else?"

Realizing the implied insult, he quickly—and sincerely—said, "No! But you're to be married—"

"Yet you will have noticed I am not a maiden."

He had. "I don't understand."

"I do as I like, when a man pleases me."

"But—" But it left a sour taste in his mouth, for he was reminded of Sheyqa Nizzira's appetites. Why equivalent behavior should be different for a woman than for a man, he was not entirely sure—had never been entirely sure, in fact, although he trotted out the explanation his mother had given. "When a woman has charge and control of a family's business and fortunes, she owes it to her own honor to be sure her children are her husband's. Also—"

"Do you think me such an idiot that I do not know when I am fertile?"

"Also," he repeated, "it doesn't do, does it, for a woman to admit she made a mistake in her marriage? That she chose the wrong man?" A thing his mother had not done—and was too proud ever to admit if she had. His parents had genuinely loved each other and had been happy. He was certain that Leyliah and Fadhil—

"I have chosen *exactly* the right man!"

"I meant no disrespect or disparagement," he said hastily. "I only meant—" He paused. "I'm not sure what I meant. Leyliah, I'm gratified and I'm honored, but I'm also confused. Why me?"

"Very few have pleased me," she continued. "You, one or two others—"

"Fadhil?"

"He was my first and most cherished—as I was his. You don't know our ways, Azzad. Perhaps one day you will, but for now—"

"Why don't you marry him? You love each other."

"Of course we do."

"Then—"

"Fadhil, Fadhil!" she exclaimed. "Would you rather talk or have love with me again?"

"Both," he said frankly. "But if you're giving me a choice—" And she smiled as he lay beside her again.

All the next day he could barely look at Fadhil.

Waking without a headache, even after the quantities of wine he'd imbibed the night before, Azzad presented himself at Abb Shagara's tent. Fadhil was already there. Together the three young men inspected Khamsin's Shagara foals, a colt and two fillies, all healthy and finely grown. A wallad izzahn came along to record Azzad's advice; full of importance at the privilege, the boy obviously saw himself as the future man-in-charge. Azzad went into great detail for his benefit, quickly boring Abb Shagara.

"But when can I ride one?" he demanded.

"Another year, perhaps a little less. Tomorrow I'll teach you how—on Khamsin."

Fadhil grinned. "My thanks for the warning, Azzad. I'll spend this evening steeping poultices."

Azzad fought a blush. Was this Fadhil's way of telling him he would not be in his own tent, so Leyliah could come in again if she wished?

"Ayia," said Abb Shagara, "if the price of riding is a sore behind, I'll gladly pay."

Azzad clapped him on the shoulder. "You'll be sore in places you never suspected *were* places."

After the noon meal, Azzad had a chat with Khamsin about Abb Shagara's lesson on the morrow. "No tricks, no whims, no wiles, and especially no gait faster than a sedate walk. Disobey me," Azzad told the stallion, looking into one black eye, "and I'll not only tie your tail in knots, I'll think seriously about having you gelded."

Khamsin snorted.

That night, after a dinner with his new student spent discussing the basics of riding, Azzad returned to Fadhil's tent and paced, waiting for Leyliah. She never came.

Instead, Meryem entered, carrying a clay pot of qawah and two silver cups. She sat on a pile of carpets, poured for herself and Azzad, and said pleasantly, "If tomorrow this riding foolishness ends up killing my son, I'll have your tongue, your teeth, your toes, your fingers, and your balls gilded and hung from my tent as wind chimes."

He didn't doubt her for an instant. "I've already discussed it with Khamsin," he assured her. "You have my word that no harm will befall Abb Shagara."

She raised her cup, and he raised his, and they drank to it. The qawah was hot and thick and bitter, with a hint of cinnamon—precisely the way he liked it. He had just taken a large mouthful when Meryem spoke again.

"Do you ever wonder why no more Geysh Dushann have come after you?"

Azzad choked, coughed, and wiped tears from his eyes. He had forgotten them. Truly, he had. He'd been so busy—his days were so full—his nights were spent in exhausted sleep—he had the horses to worry about and so much else besides—

"I see they have escaped your thoughts, much as you have escaped their traps," she went on. "Ayia, you foolish boy—didn't you know?"

Numb, he shook his head.

"We have hosted emissaries from the Ammarad in these last two years. They have been perfectly polite, properly respectful, and preposterously eager to agree that if any harm comes to you, they will forfeit Shagara medicine forever." She paused for a sip of qawah. "Of course, we don't believe them."

"But no Geysh Dushann have attempted my life—"

"—that you know of," she finished for him, nodding to the necklace at his chest. "They've given up the use of knives, axes, poison, and the like in favor of creating circumstances that appear accidental. Have you experienced anything interesting since you went to Sihabbah?"

Acuyib help him, was *that* the reason behind the swarm of snakes in the stables last year? And last summer, the rockslide on a mountain road a few seconds after he passed, and—

She had been watching his face, and now smiled shrewdly. "Doubtless you thought them lucky escapes from random occurrences."

That was precisely what he had thought. "But they were intentional?"

"Of course. The Geysh Dushann accepted Sheyqa Nizzira's commission. Acceptance is never canceled. Never. How it must pain them to have failed so often—like bedding down in nettles." Meyrem's lips twitched at one corner. "Stop looking as if you believe yourself a walking dead man. You've survived thus far, have you not?"

"Yes, but—"

"But nothing. Acuyib has some purpose for you, Azzad—though what it might be I'm sure I can't imagine! He will protect you—with a little help from the Shagara." She paused to pour more qawah. "You are too polite to ask me why Leyliah came to your bed last night."

This time, astonishment nearly made Azzad drop his cup—along with his jaw.

"It is a mystery only to those not Shagara. You are counted a brother, so I will tell you why. It is true she will marry Razhid Harirri of the silken beard and many goats—and the very subtle eyes," she added with a faint smile. "Of all the young men who came to the Zoqalo Tzawaq last year to find wives, he was the best. She has chosen well. But you know she has always had an eye to you, Azzad."

He actually felt himself blush. "I am honored."

"And yet confused. Here is further bewilderment for you. A Shagara woman does not wed until she has proved herself fertile. Yes, Leyliah has a son. A very sweet little boy of four, who has shown himself very bright and clever. He may even become Abb Shagara someday."

"Does—does Harirri know?"

"Of course. When a man weds a Shagara woman, he knows he will become a father." She paused to drink, then said, "It is strange to you, I appreciate this. But you must understand how it is with us."

"Lady," he said carefully, "I don't understand the first thing about the Shagara. But if these are your ways, I accept them."

"How very well-mannered of you," she observed, arching a brow. "Yet still you do not see. Look at what is in front of your eyes, Azzad. We send our men out to make blood-bonds with other tribes of the Za'aba Izim—but only after they have proven they can sire a child."

It hit him then, the way the future of Khamsin's half-breed foals had hit him. And again he could see his mother's face as she looked upon her idiot son. *You have your father's height and your grandfather's nose, and your eyes you inherited from me—but may Acuyib strike me down with a thunderbolt if I know from whom you received your total lack of intelligence!*

"Fadhil—and Abb Shagara—they will never be fathers."

"Now you begin to understand."

Abb Shagara's riding lesson was a success, though for the first little while he sat Khamsin like a sack of grain, reins flapping and boots slipping from the stirrups. Then he straightened his spine, tucked in his elbows, mastered his heels, and kept his backside firmly in the saddle.

"Better than riding a donkey?" Azzad teased. Khamsin had behaved himself perfectly, his steps soft as velvet as he walked at the end of a lead rope.

"Wonderful!" the young man exclaimed, patting Khamsin's neck. "I can see *everything* from up here! How do I look?"

"Like a sheyqir," Fadhil assured him.

As Abb Shagara preened happily, Azzad exhaled a long, satisfied breath. He was going to make a fortune.

"I want to go faster," said Abb Shagara. "How do I make him go faster?"

"You don't." He tried to shorten the lead. Khamsin jerked his head indignantly.

"Azzad, I *will* go faster! There's nothing to this riding—see how well I'm doing?"

"Wonderfully well," Azzad said. "But this is only your first lesson."

"Speaking of which," Fadhil murmured, "I hear Challa Meryem lessoned *you* last night. And you understand a little more about the Shagara."

"Yes, but—" Azzad wrapped the lead around his hand, scowling at Khamsin's answering lunge.

"I want to go *faster!*" cried Abb Shagara, flapping the reins and his heels.

"Stop that!" Azzad exclaimed. "You're not ready!"

"Yes, I am! And so is the noble Khamsin—see?"

Khamsin danced to one side, tossing his head. The lead snapped taut, staggering Azzad forward. Fadhil called out in alarm as Abb Shagara reached into his sash for his knife and slashed the rope from Khamsin's bridle. Free, the stallion snorted and gathered himself to obey the commanding heels. The next instant he was running—straight toward a thorn-studded fence.

Azzad's mouth was so dry he couldn't whistle the order to stop. Abb Shagara was laughing like a maniac as Khamsin cleared the fence with daylight to spare and raced off into the desert.

"Acuyib have mercy!" Azzad watched in horror as his horse galloped away at full speed into a wasteland of rocks and ratholes and scorpions and snakes and Chaydann only knew what all else. "Meryem will kill me!"

"Azzad, calm yourself. All will be well. No snake will harm them." He paused. "Though I've never done anything quite like this before."

Azzad peered into the distance, following the dust raised by Khamsin's hooves, praying that Abb Shagara would stay in the saddle or at least in one relatively uninjured piece, so it took him a minute to grasp Fadhil's words. When he did, he swung around and stared. "Quite like *what?*"

"We had to work fast, but I helped by doing the research—"

"Fadhil, what are you talking about?"

The young man sighed. "Abb Shagara will be protected from all injury— and Khamsin, too. You're worrying for nothing, Azzad. Now, let me see your hand." He inspected the reddening welts across the palm, probed with his fingertips for breaks. "Nothing salve and a wrapping won't cure. But if Abb Shagara hadn't cut the lead—"

"Fadhil!" The breath he drew in hurt his chest. "Do you mean to tell me that—that you trust some *charm* to keep him safe?"

"More than one charm, and we call them hazziri," Fadhil replied. "Yours worked, didn't it?" And he pointed to the plaque around Azzad's neck. "You made a point of thanking Abb Shagara for this when you arrived."

"But—"

"But you didn't mean it? Not seriously?" Fadhil laughed. "Ayia, don't tell him that! It would break his heart!"

His mind swimming, he turned the hazzir to look at it. Gold, set with four kinds of cabochon stone: a central lapis, three speckled bloodstones, two turquoises, a garnet at each corner. On the back was a stylized hawk, wings and claws outspread.

"I used turquoises for Abb Shagara today," Fadhil said. "They bring luck and protect the horse."

When he had held the silver cup in his hand and been unable to tell Abb Shagara a lie, Azzad had not believed.

"We use one jewel for each property we wish to give the hazzir, inscribed on the back with the appropriate symbol, the *talishann*."

When Leyliah had thrown a knife at Fadhil and it glanced harmlessly off his chest, Azzad had not believed.

"The lapis is for truth, acting with the bloodstone that causes belief."

When the shepherds had been ready to kill him despite his protestations, and their leader had come close enough to see the hazzir, Azzad had not believed.

"The four garnets are for Shagara friendship, its power and its constancy, and to protect against wounds."

When the girl's family had come to seize him, and no one in Sihabbah had any reason to trust in his word, and the hazzir had fallen free of his torn shirt, Azzad had perhaps begun to believe.

"Bloodstone also eases wrath, and as a nice addition for one traveling through these lands, protects against attacks by scorpions."

But not until this moment, with Fadhil serenely explaining his art—Acuyib help him, he had not truly believed until now.

"After hearing your story, I decided the hawk would be best for you. It has the qualities of strength, energy, and inspiration, which you will need if you are to fulfill your oath of vengeance. The hawk," he added musingly, "does not rest until his objective is achieved."

Acuyib help him, Azzad believed.

As Khamsin cantered toward them, Abb Shagara still securely in the saddle and even laughing, Fadhil glanced sidelong at Azzad. "Abb Shagara wanted to include wealth and many children, but Meryem said that we must leave you *something* to do on your own."

Still stunned, Azzad saw Abb Shagara wave gaily at them, a new hazzir around his right wrist: gold, set with turquoises and a large bloodstone.

"And Leyliah said this morning that with your face, which is not even to speak of your other attributes, you were perfectly capable of getting more children than you'd know what to do with."

Reminded through his shock of what had transpired with Leyliah, Azzad's head snapped around. "Fadhil—"

"It's all right. I don't mind, not really." He smiled.

Whatever Azzad might have thought to reply was swept away in the wind of Khamsin's arrival. Abb Shagara was as happy as a kitten in a yarn basket.

"That was splendid! May I do it again tomorrow? Will the half-breeds be as swift as Khamsin? It was like flying!"

Azzad looked at Fadhil and swallowed hard. "I apologize," he murmured.

"No need. Enjoy the time you have with her. She is an extraordinary woman."

"Azzad!" Abb Shagara called. "Again tomorrow? Please?"

"Uh—yes, of course," he said, hardly knowing to whom he spoke.

Fadhil added softly, "You shouldn't take Meryem's sternness too much to heart. She and Leyliah drew lots for you."

And, with a wink and a grin, he went to congratulate Abb Shagara on his first riding lesson, leaving Azzad standing there with a broken lead in his hand and an expression of absolute amazement on his face.

By day, Azzad gave riding lessons and advice on horses. In the evenings, he had dinner with Abb Shagara, Chal Kabir, Fadhil, and the other men, discussing those things men discussed everywhere. At night, he slept with Leyliah.

One afternoon, as Azzad sat with Abb Shagara in an awning's shade playing chadarang, a rider on a donkey appeared on the horizon. Instantly the Shagara went within their tents, and the wallad izzahni counted horses and took up guard positions around the thorn fences. Abb Shagara, murmuring an apology to Azzad for abandoning their game, vanished inside his tent. Chal Kabir emerged from the dawa'an sheymma in a fresh robe the color of sand, with Fadhil at his side, to wait for the newcomer.

Azzad, squinting into the distance, thought about joining Abb Shagara, then gave a start as he realized that the man astride the donkey had come from Sihabbah. Bazir al-Gallidh often sent messengers back and forth to his brother in Hazganni; these men dressed in white robes with a thick stripe of black down each sleeve. The visitor wore such a garment. As he neared, Azzad even recognized him: Annif, younger brother of Mazzud who worked with him in the stables.

Striding swiftly to where Chal Kabir and Fadhil stood, Azzad said, "I know this boy. He comes from al-Gallidh, my employer."

Fadhil shook his head. "It can be no good thing that brings him so far."

And so it proved.

"Al-Gallidh is ill. He may be dead even now," Annif reported, gulping water between sentences. "I have had a time of it, probably too long a time, finding you, Azzad—even after Mou'ammi Zellim made a map from what you told him of your route. He sent me to bring you back to Sihabbah."

Azzad sucked in a breath, worry for Bazir clenching his chest. But before he could ask any questions, Chal Kabir spoke.

"What is the nature of his illness?"

Annif shook his head. "The tabbib doesn't know. Al-Gallidh was well in the morning, but by afternoon his breathing was bad and there was pain."

"What kind of pain?"

"In one arm."

Kabir sighed impatiently. "*Which* arm? The left? And *don't* ask if it matters, because it matters a great deal."

Azzad said, "Chal Kabir is more accomplished than any tabbib you've ever heard of, Annif. Now, which arm was it?"

"The left, I think." The boy glanced around the empty camp beyond, his eyes widening. "Is this all there is to the Shagara?"

Kabir ignored him in favor of Azzad. "You have said that Sihabbah is high in the mountains. Has he trouble breathing sometimes? Must he climb stairs slowly or grow dizzy?"

"This I do not know," Azzad admitted. "I have never been above the ground floor of his house."

"Is his bedchamber there?"

"I believe so—yes, right next to his maqtabba."

"He has hundreds of books—" the boy bragged, only to be ignored once again.

"Then on purpose he does not climb stairs. How old is al-Gallidh?"

"About your age." With the customary politeness and respect for the elderly, Azzad lopped ten years off his truest estimate. "Fifty-five or thereabouts."

Kabir's lips thinned—with annoyance, Azzad thought in bewilderment—and Fadhil coughed behind his hand for no reason Azzad could discern.

"It is his heart," announced Kabir. "If you leave at once, you may be in time. I will give you certain things that will help al-Gallidh."

Annif blinked. "You can, when our own tabbib cannot?"

"Your tabbib must be a very great fool not to know the signs," Kabir snapped and turned for the dawa'an sheymma.

When Annif was settled with food and drink in Fadhil's tent, Fadhil drew Azzad aside. "Would you like me to come with you? I could ask Abb Shagara for permission. I might be able to help al-Gallidh."

"I would be very grateful," Azzad said, surprised. "But surely the Shagara do not leave the tribe?"

"There's a first time for everything," the young man said blithely. As they passed Leyliah's tent, Fadhil paused. "Besides, I have a wish to see this place in the clouds."

Abb Shagara gave his consent to the expedition. Khamsin was saddled, and Azzad reasoned that as slim as Fadhil was, Khamsin would not be very much slowed by carrying double. Annif would follow on the donkey, leading the other two donkeys and the Shagara-bred fillies, which Abb Shagara insisted Azzad take.

"Not as payment for Haddid and the charming Farrasha," he said, "but because I have listened to what you've said about breeding. If Khamsin's foals are so much smaller within the mares, it is more than likely that our studs would sire foals too big for his get to carry. The two colts will service our best mares when they're old enough, but I have decided that Farrasha will be my riding horse only and never bred. I am already most passionately in love with her, and it would pierce my heart to lose her."

"In truth," Azzad replied, "that is a wise decision. Only if you were to find another of Khamsin's breed could you be certain that Farrasha would survive. I'll send more saddles back with Fadhil, but you must promise not to ride any of them until they're full grown. And now I think we must leave. Fadhil, are you ready?"

"My things are already in Khamsin's saddlebags." Swallowing the last of his qawah, he rose and said, "I must say farewell to Meryem and Leyliah."

When he was gone, Azzad watched Abb Shagara over the rim of his cup. The fey, expressive golden face was solemn, almost sad, and one could see the old man he would one day be. He reached underneath the piled pillows and brought out a small, thin gold ring set with a chip of green emerald.

"It would please me if you would give this to Fadhil. I cannot do it myself."

Azzad took the ring, knowing enough now to look on the inside, where a tiny swallow and an even smaller butterfly were engraved. "Beautiful. May I ask—?"

"I want him to find a woman he can love," was the forthright reply. "Leyliah is lost to him, but in Sihabbah—you understand, don't you, Aqq Azzad?"

"Yes." At least, he understood that Abb Shagara believed this ring would help Fadhil find a suitable young woman. Fadhil would believe it, too—and perhaps that was all that counted. "I'll tell him I asked you for something of the kind, because he is my friend and I worry about him."

"Thank you. And now I think you must leave us again." His smile returned. "If I am not too much mistaken, your Khamsin has left us with another remembrance or two."

"If I'm not careful, you'll set yourselves up as rivals to my horse-breeding scheme," Azzad teased.

"'Scheme'? I thought it all happened because of a mistake!"

"That's just what Jemilha said," Azzad complained.

"Ayia, so you *have* met a girl!"

Bazir al-Gallidh did not die. Azzad and Fadhil arrived in Sihabbah in time to help the nobleman. Within two handfuls of days, al-
Gallidh was strong enough to stand at his windows to inspect Khamsin's
two Shagara half-breed fillies. At the end of two months, he announced
himself cured.

But Fadhil warned Azzad in private that while Shagara healing
was powerful, it was not invincible. Al-Gallidh was advised to leave the
mountains, where the air was too thin. After much resistance, he went
from Sihabbah to his house in Hazganni. Azzad was charged with
overseeing all the al-Gallidh possessions. Fadhil, who had commanded
himself to resignation regarding Leyliah's marriage to Razhid Harirri,
discovered an alternative: Rather than remain with the Shagara and
witness daily her happiness with another man, he remained with his
friend Azzad.

Every third month they traveled down to Hazganni together, to
visit the al-Gallidh brothers and report on the Sihabbah holdings and
horses. Fadhil was not the first Shagara to visit the great city, but he
was the first to become familiar to its citizens. He gained a reputation
as a noteworthy tabbib, though his healing was of medicine only, for it
would be dangerous to practice the craft of the hazziri outside the secrecy of the Shagara encampment—or the Sihabbah house of al-
Gallidh.

— FERRHAN MUALEEF, *Deeds of Il-Kadiri*, 654

7

Azzad al-Maʿaliq slouched in his chair, glaring at the ledger on his desk. The rulers of Hazganni, that celebrated city on the plain, had managed to kill every single one of the trees he'd sent from Sihabbah. Now they were demanding either repayment or a hundred more trees to replace those dead of their neglect.

"We sent them instructions," Azzad muttered aloud. "We sent them the correct fertilizer. We even sent them hazziri to plant with the trees, Acuyib witness it! Ayia, I want to see these dead trees for myself, to see if they really are dead—and to prove that stupidity killed them."

Fadhil looked up from a book. "So we go to Hazganni again? That's three times in two moons. Perhaps it's not the trees that draw you there."

The entrance of an al-Gallidh servant to light the lamps kept Azzad silent. Bazir's maqtabba gradually began to glow with a golden shimmer, the paper-thin alabaster shades diffusing the tiny flames. When the servant had departed, Azzad said, "It's a pretty journey—as well as much faster, now that you've mastered riding."

"I speak of your eagerness to visit Hazganni, not your enjoyment of the trip."

He shrugged. "I grew up in a large city, so naturally I feel comfortable there. Especially in the zouqs—my aunts and sisters were dedicated shoppers, Acuyib delight their souls!"

"Ah, now we come to it."

"Come to what?"

"It."

Azzad eyed his friend. "Make sense, Fadhil, I beg. What 'it' have we arrived at, and why did I not know we were going there?"

Fadhil grinned over at him. "Women. More particularly, ladies. Most particularly, *one* lady, who if she isn't in your thoughts ought to be."

Azzad searched his mind and memories. In the year and a half since Bazir al-Gallidh and his family had moved permanently to Hazganni, Azzad had visited many lovely ladies, some of them more than once. A few were as beautiful as Ashiyah, but he'd found none he would gift with her pearls. And he'd found none as agreeable in bed—or as interesting to converse with, truth be told—as Bindta Feyrah up on the mountainside.

"Which lady?" he asked Fadhil, genuinely curious.

"If you don't yet know, I'm not going to tell you."

"Ayia, I think perhaps *you* don't like leaving Sihabbah, for the sake of one lady in particular," Azzad teased.

"Not one—four," Fadhil replied serenely.

"Shameless," Azzad intoned, shaking his head, secretly disappointed that the ring had not done its work.

"On the contrary. Each is so thoroughly in love with me that to choose one above the others would break their hearts." He paused, then closed his book and went to the window. "What commotion is this?"

Azzad joined him, peering into the dusky gloom. His jaw dropped open; in the next instant he nearly laughed at himself. Had it been so long since he'd left Rimmal Madar that the sight of four men on horseback shocked him so?

"Acuyib's Glory—that's Challa Meryem!" Fadhil exclaimed, and raced from the maqtabba. Azzad followed, running out into the courtyard where Meryem had dismounted a young mare. She embraced Fadhil, took off her gloves, and regarded Azzad with a whimsical smile.

"As Challi Dawa'an, I prescribe for myself a long, hot bath! You never said riding would be so difficult on the muscles, Azzad!"

"A bath with soothing salts, as hot as you can stand it," Azzad told her. "You are welcome to Sihabbah, in the name of al-Gallidh."

With Meryem had come two young male cousins and Razhid Harirri's uncle—a dignified man of fifty or so who had a tale to tell. When they were all seated in Bazir's maqtabba while baths were prepared, Ba'adem began to speak.

"When it was learned that Challa Leyliah would honor the Harirri with marriage to my nephew, there was great rejoicing in our tents. And, in the way of the desert, word carried to other tribes. One of these was the Ammarad." He scowled, heavy brows darkening his eyes. "They sent four Geysh Dushann! We did not know it at the time, for they presented themselves as members only of their tribe, not of the order to which they belong. They wished to know all about the wedding, and what gifts the Shagara would favor, and suchlike."

"It was their way of conniving an invitation," Meryem said. "Evidently they thought that perhaps you would come to the wedding, Azzad." She gave a shrug. "Perhaps they are more confident, working their wickedness in the desert."

"And so," Ba'adem went on, after taking a long swallow of qawah, "to our shame, we told them of the plans. But my nephew—"

He of the subtle eyes, thought Azzad.

"—did not trust them, having learned from Leyliah the facts of the matter. So he followed them with his brothers and myself, and at the first water outside our camp we overheard their plots. They tended to their knives and their potions for poisoning. We knew them then for Geysh Dushann. And we killed them."

Azzad had the feeling there was much more to the story than this simple statement. "You have courage, Ba'adem Harirri, and I thank you for your good work."

One hand waved dismissively. "It is surprisingly easy to kill men who think they are better at killing than anyone else. We burned them in the desert and took their horses. Razhid had also learned from Leyliah that your Khamsin had sired foals on Shagara mares, and so we bred the stallions to our own mares, just to see what would happen. Five fine colts, which we ask now if we may keep, to breed riding horses for the Harirri."

"He asks," Meryem said, "because Razhid gave the horses to Leyliah as his marriage price, and Leyliah now gives them to you. So the foals are now half yours."

Azzad sat back, stunned. He had fifteen of Khamsin's get here in Sihabbah, and now they were telling him there were five more colts sired by studs other than Khamsin, which meant that in time they could be bred to Khamsin's line—

"We also bred the studs to several of our own mares before we came here," Meryem added. "So you own half of those foals as well."

His brain spun within his skull. And all at once he remembered a conversation with Fadhil, when he had first sojourned with the Shagara: *"Greed—do you mean in the way a child is greedy for sweets? But what use is more of everything beyond the sufficiency for living?"*

To accept all these horses would be sheer greed. It would go a long way toward sinking him to the same level as Sheyqa Nizzira al-Ammarizzad, rapacious and ruthless. So he shook his head. "No. I thank you with all my heart, but the foals are yours. My only caution is that the mares should not be bred to your stallions, for they are too small to carry such large foals. Other than that, all these horses are yours to do with as you please."

"Just make sure the town of Sihabbah gets all the contracts for making saddles and bridles and riding boots," Fadhil added with a smile. "And now I think it's time for those hot baths." When the two young cousins nodded emphatic agreement, he laughed aloud. "I have a thing or two in my medicine case that will help. Come with me."

Ba'adem and the two boys left; Meryem lingered with Azzad. "My son told me you might say something of the kind. He will agree to keep one stallion to breed to Shagara and Harirri mares, but he says that you will take the other stallion and the two mares or he will be extremely angry."

"Challa Meryem—"

"Abb Shagara has said it, and so it shall be." Her lips twitched in a smile. "Relent, Aqq Azzad. Leyliah says she fully expects to see her sons riding horses when they're big enough. And at the rate her first son by Razhid is growing—"

"She has a son?"

"A fine little boy with his father's eyes. His name is Fadhil. And now I will have my bath, if it's convenient."

Azzad called for servants to escort Meryem upstairs to Jemilha's old rooms. He sat a while longer in the maqtabba, planning the next several generations of horses. From Sihabbah to Hazganni and in every town between, people stopped and stared whenever Azzad and Fadhil rode through. In five years he would have horses enough to sell to rich men who wanted to travel swiftly and look like sheyqirs. And then, with the money and the influence . . . he fingered the hazzir at his breast, his thumb caressing the hawk. Retribution. Yes. At last.

Azzad gave Ba'adem Harirri and the Shagara cousins three fat, comfortable donkeys on which to ride home. They had grown familiar enough with horses to be chagrined at the alteration. As they rode away, Azzad hid a smile: they sat the donkeys as they would horses, pretending for their own pride.

Meryem intended to go with Azzad and Fadhil to Hazganni and ride back to the Shagara spring encampment from there. Accordingly, they mounted up, with Meryem on a white stallion Azzad knew could only have belonged to one of the executed Qoundi Ammar. He himself rode Khamsin, as always, and Fadhil spent the first miles out of Sihabbah struggling with one of the new mares.

"How did you ever manage these brutes all that way from the camp?" he asked, sweating as he fought the reins.

In answer, she removed the glove from her right hand and showed him a new ring. "All four of us have one of these, made by Abb Shagara personally."

Turquoise brought luck and protected both horse and rider. Fadhil had been wearing a turquoise armband ever since leaving the Shagara, yet he was having trouble with the mare.

"My son is becoming adept at hazziri for horses and riders," Meryem added.

Fadhil made a face. "He uses the blood of the horses as well as the riders," he accused. "Is that not so? It's the only way he could accomplish it."

"Perhaps. Perhaps not." She smiled sweetly. "But surely you've been riding so long that a little mare like that cannot be too much trouble!"

The residence of the al-Gallidh was in the finest quarter of Hazganni, a district of whitewashed three-story houses and high-walled gardens. Tiled roofs of red and blue and yellow and green—and sometimes wildly patterned with all of these—were shaded by palms and plane trees, and white-flowered oleander bushes that grew almost as tall as the houses. Oranges and lemons were in bloom. Pink and white and scarlet geraniums overflowed window boxes, and jasmine spread fragrance everywhere. Hazganni could almost have been Dayira Azreyq but for two things: There were no horses in the narrow streets, only donkeys; and there was no looming bulk of a palace always on the edge of one's vision.

Meryem so far forgot her habitual poise as to exclaim in amazement at the variety of foliage, the bustle of the streets, the wares in the zouqs, the bright clothes of the citizenry. Azzad grinned to himself and made a mental promise to have Jemilha take Meryem shopping. The girl was nearly as accomplished as Azzad's sisters at picking an entire market clean of bargains.

They were welcomed into the house of al-Gallidh by Bazir himself. When he learned the identity of his feminine visitor, he called for his niece to come and greet her. Jemilha, who had recently celebrated her eighteenth birthday, was as yet unwed and showed no signs of choosing a husband. Azzad worried sometimes that her husband would think breeding horses too risky a venture and convince her not to continue, but because he could do nothing about her choice, he shrugged his concerns away. Besides, with Abb Shagara's gift, Azzad would have enough money to buy out her husband, if it came to it.

Bazir led them into his maqtabba. Meryem's eyes went wide at the sight of so many shelves laden with so many books; seeing this, Bazir offered her anything in his collection. "Azzad has told me the Shagara ladies are learned indeed."

Meryem shook her head, then gestured to the books. "*This* is learning, al-Gallidh. I would welcome your guidance on what would most benefit my studies."

"Tell me your interests, lady, and I will do what I can to advise you. And my daughter will be able to suggest a few books as well. A new shop recently opened, specializing in foreign works. Perhaps you would like to visit this place with her during your stay."

Thus was Meryem Shagara conquered. Azzad hid a grin as he sorted through messages. Bazir kept one basket for him and one for Fadhil; those waiting for the tabbib were from patients, and the notes for Azzad were from various ladies. He excused himself and went upstairs to his room to read them. Remembering Fadhil's teasing about "one lady in particular," he called up faces to go with the names. None stirred his blood beyond a fleeting memory of pleasure, and his heart was completely untouched. Which of them could Fadhil have meant?

The next morning, while Fadhil attended his patients and Jemilha took Meryem shopping, Azzad went to see the dead trees for himself. It had been difficult to convince people that trees were necessary outside the walls. What was obvious to all in Dayira Azreyq had been anything but obvious here. Trees held back the desert. It was that simple. On his first visit to the city,

Azzad had been appalled at the nearness of the dunes that surrounded it. Even worse, every year a little more farmland was lost to the encroaching sand. Only the farmers understood the danger. In Hazganni there was water aplenty from several generous springs that supplied the city in a rather sophisticated plumbing arrangement. Because everyone had water in the home for kitchen and garden and bath, no one thought about water at all. As long as trees grew in their own gardens, who cared?

Every child in Dayira Azreyq knew the story of how the foreign barbarians had burned all the trees around the city, thinking to force it to yield. After the gharribeh had been defeated and expelled from Rimmal Madar, their legacy of scorched earth had resulted in torrents of sand and ash blown in by eastern winds to choke the city. The official story was that back then, the ancestor of Sheyqa Nizzira had commanded every man over the age of fifteen to march into the surrounding hills, uproot a tree, and bring it back to replant the devastated ground. But Azzad knew that it had been his own ancestor who had gone to the al-Ma'aliq lands and brought back the first hundred trees.

In time, the desert had been forced back. Trees, always more trees—added to bushes and succulents and herbs and anything that would root and hold and nourish the soil—these had kept Dayira Azreyq safe from the greedy sands. But Hazganni—

"Fools!" Azzad slid off Khamsin's back and looped the reins around his hand, walking between rows of dead trees. Shameful, a scandal, an affront to Acuyib Himself, who had battled Chaydann Il-Mamnoua'a over a chadarang board to see how much of the land would be green. "I'll replant these with my own hands if need be," he vowed, "and stay with them until they're established—and cut off the fingers, one by one, of anyone who neglects them!"

In his mind he saw a thousand trees, and another thousand, and the desert was forced back, and beneath the trees children played and young people flirted and old people dozed in the shade. There was a reservoir with ditches leading out from it to water the trees, and fountains splashing coolness into the air, and—and—

"And right now," Azzad muttered, "all I've got is a hundred dead trees." Khamsin tossed his head so the silver on his bridle jingled. Azzad faced him, caressing his ears. "But by next spring, Acuyib witness my oath, a hundred *living* trees!"

Swinging up into the saddle, he rode back to the house of al-Gallidh, where he was privileged to see Meryem and Jemilha returning from the zouqs. Behind them, at a respectful remove, was a crowd of young men.

Azzad took the greatest pleasure in greeting the two ladies loudly and familiarly. "So few packages? I would have thought you'd buy out every shop, Meryem!"

"I was tempted," she admitted, and the sparkle in her eyes told him she knew exactly what he was doing.

Azzad glanced at their entourage. Every last one of them showed chagrin that this man could speak freely to such beauties; one or two frowned as if trying desperately to remember if more than a casual acquaintance could be claimed with Azzad. He grinned cheerfully at them, dismounted, and escorted the ladies inside the courtyard.

"How long has *this* been going on?" he asked as he swung the gates closed.

"All morning," Meryem said at the same time Jemilha replied, "Almost three years."

Azzad blinked. Jemilha glared as if daring him to disbelieve, then went into the house, her silks aflutter.

Azzad turned to Meryem. "What did I say?"

"What did you *not* say?" she countered. "And to think my son admires your way with any and every woman!"

"Jemilha isn't *any* woman," he heard himself say. "She's *Jemilha*." Meaning the leggy little scrap of a girl who had insulted Khamsin's foals.

"Ayia? Those men outside have a different opinion." And with that, Meryem followed Jemilha into the house, leaving Azzad to wonder what she meant.

"You did rightly in giving the finest of our donkeys to the esteemed Harirri," said Bazir. "But it seems poor payment for such magnificent horses." He smiled, pouring more qawah for Azzad and another cup of herbal chiy for himself. "Moreover, *white* horses! That will please Jemilha." Sipping, he arched heavy brows in surprise. "What does the Lady Meryem do that this is so much better than what my cook prepares for me?"

"I'm sure she'll share her secret, to please you." He grinned. "Surely you've noticed, al-Gallidh, that you've made a conquest?"

"And it took nothing more than my books, whereas in years past it needed music, recitations of poetry, languishing glances, and an expedient gift of jewelry." He sighed dramatically, dark eyes dancing. "If I'd known in my youth that it was so easy, I would have canceled my elocution lessons—and my account at the gem cutter's."

Azzad laughed and drank more qawah, and they settled to business again. Fields, orchards, horses, donkeys, timber, mining, fishing, trapping—all the varied enterprises of the al-Gallidh estates that Azzad had been managing were discussed in detail. Bazir declared himself satisfied—and then brought up a different subject entirely.

"Azzad, how old are you now?"

"Twenty-four this summer."

"Not so great an age, to one of my years," al-Gallidh sighed. "But to you, it must seem rather advanced."

"Not at all." He had no idea where this conversation might be going. "I believe a man grows wiser as he grows older—for in my former home, those who were unwise did not live long enough grow old."

"What contributes to this wisdom, do you think?"

"Attention to work and responsibility, of course." Azzad thought for a minute. "Learning from friends and superiors. Studying as his interests take him."

"Ayia, I quite agree. But you have forgotten marriage to a clever woman."

"I—I have no opinion on the subject, al-Gallidh." He could now see the destination of this chat, and did not much like the scenery.

Bazir continued with exquisite casualness, "My own opinion is that a man should marry when he is old enough to have established himself in his work but young enough to need a woman's brain to help him, so that he is grateful for her presence as well as her person."

Azzad took a deep breath. "Is it your wish, al-Gallidh, that I look for a wife?"

"By Acuyib's Glory, no!" He laughed, as if at some private joke.

Confused by the change in direction, Azzad frowned. "If not, then—"

"Have you no wish for a house of your own?"

He thought of Beit Ma'aliq, to which no other home could compare—and wondered which of Nizzira's progeny lived in it now. If, indeed, it had been rebuilt at all, or still remained as a burned scar in the city. "No, al-Gallidh. I am content."

"But I am not. It is therefore my intention that you shall live from now on in my house in Sihabbah."

"Al-Gallidh—I am honored, but—I cannot, it would not be right—"

"Nonsense. That great empty house does nothing but gather dust. The servants are idle, and the town is desolate—for as you know, I used to give entertainments. But my home has been silent, and I do not like to think of it that way."

"You—you are very generous, but it is not my house, I am not al-Gallidh—"

"Ayia, there is that, I suppose." The old man eyed him. "But if you became part of my family . . ." He paused.

Azzad abruptly realized that this was all leading to a place he hadn't envisioned.

"Is the idea so displeasing to you?" ask al-Gallidh.

"No—not at all. She is beautiful, and—and—" He gulped for air. "But she—"

"Do not say she is too far above you, al-Ma'aliq descendant of sheyqirs."

"Here, she is infinitely my superior," he said frankly. "Here, I am nothing."

"Nonsense!" Bazir declared once more. "Your 'nothing' is a hundred times any other man's 'something.' You are intelligent, ambitious, clever. You work hard and manage my estates wisely. And through your own efforts—and those of your Khamsin!—you will be a very rich man."

Azzad heard the list of his virtues with no small perplexity of soul. His parents would not have recognized the description of their rascal son; had he changed so much in the nearly four years since he'd escaped the poison and axes and swords?

"Consider it, Azzad," murmured Bazir al-Gallidh. "I ask this most humbly of you, my friend. I want you in my family. I want to know that when my brother and I are dead, Jemilha will have the best husband we could wish for her. I want to know that the houses of the al-Gallidh will be filled with my brother's grandchildren and great-grandchildren, descended from sheyqirs."

"What about Jemilha?" he blurted. "What does she say about—"

Again Bazir laughed, this time until he nearly choked. "Ayia, did you not know? It was she who demanded that I speak to you!"

"She did?"

"She thinks you will make a very good husband."

"She does?"

The old man grinned. "And she likes the way you look on a horse."

"She—" He swallowed the rest. So much for his intelligence and cleverness.

"Go riding, Azzad," al-Gallidh advised kindly. "It always helps you to think."

But even miles away from Hazganni, into fields and orchards not yet threatened by sand, where all was lush green life as Acuyib had intended, he had no clear thought beyond the stupefied realization that he was going to have to marry Jemilha al-Gallidh.

Just why he had to do this was a mystery to be untangled at some later date, when he had his wits about him again. He only knew that marry her he must—and as he rode back to the city through the golden dusky gloom of spring, he decided that perhaps this would not be so bad a thing after all.

"Lady," Azzad said, "your uncle tells me it would not come amiss with you— that you would not object—that you—Chaydann take it, I don't know what to say!"

He glared at his own face in the mirror, disgusted that the glib seducer had turned into a tongue-tied imbecile. He was lamentably out of practice. He could excuse himself with the fact that bedding had always been his goal, not wedding. Besides, Jemilha was a *lady*. He had to find just the right words, just the right tone of voice—

"Lady, it has come to my notice—you have come to my notice—"

Oh, yes, his haughty and august notice, as if he'd inherited all the al-Ma'aliq land and money. He tried again.

"Lady, your uncle and I have spoken, and he says that marriage—"

He stopped when he saw the expression on his face: that of a man about to recite the devotions at his own funeral. He rearranged his features into serious, gentle lines—or so he hoped—and took a breath.

"Lady, it has been suggested that you and I—"

No, that made it sound like a business proposition—which, after all, it was in a way, but it would never do to say such a thing to a young girl.

"Lady—"

"You could try using my name, you know."

He pivoted on one heel, horrified to find Jemilha standing in his doorway. She wore a robe of white silk belted over a long crimson tunic, with embroidered gold slippers and a matching gold scarf tying up her hair.

Abruptly he did not wonder why all those young men had followed her to-day—or why they had been doing so for almost three years. The skinny little girl with the unruly braids had been transformed. But how and when had she become beautiful?

"I'm sorry," he said. "I did not mean you to hear—"

"—until you had perfected your little speech?" She raised a sardonic eyebrow.

Sighing, he rubbed the back of his neck and shrugged. However long she'd been listening, she'd heard more than enough. So he plunged in. "Your uncle and I have spoken of marriage—"

She gave him a sweet smile. "I hope you'll be very happy together."

"Jemilha!"

"Good—my name. Now we make a start." She entered his room, leaving the door open, and sat on the chair beside the window. A breeze through the carved wooden shutters plucked at the scarf and toyed with tendrils of her black hair. "Uncle Bazir told me that you and he talked yesterday. Now you and I will talk. Yes, I have it in mind to marry you. My uncle and my father approve of my choice. I know you do not love me, and neither do I love you—but love is nothing to the point in such matters, don't you think?"

"I—"

"A moment, Azzad, I'm not finished. Uncle Bazir told you why he and Father approve, but I will tell you two other things. I trust in your capacity for friendship—Fadhil and Meryem are devoted to you, and they are both persons of quality, so there must be something substantial to you after all. And the second thing is that I think you and I will make very interesting children." She folded her hands in her lap and looked up at him expectantly. "Ayia, I'm done. Your turn."

His tongue wasn't just tied, it was tethered. "L-Lady—"

"I thought we had decided that I do indeed have a name."

He knew how to accomplish a seduction. The self-possessed girl sitting before him now was, to all appearances, not seducible. *"Rubbish!"* snapped his grandfather's voice. *"Any woman who isn't dead below the neck—"*

But this wasn't *any* woman. This was Jemilha of the tart tongue and untidy hair and—and the huge dark eyes and lithe quick body and—

—and a father and an uncle who would do unspeakable things to him—and very slowly, too—if he hurt her in any way.

"Jemilha," he said at last, "are you certain you want me? You could have any man."

"You are not just any man, Azzad."

He crossed to her, holding out both hands. She allowed him one of hers. It was small and warm and dry, and the pulse in her wrist was perfectly steady. He could hear his grandfather's cackling laughter in the back of his mind: *"You'll soon change that, boy, or you're not my grandson!"*

"Jemilha, it would be a greater honor than I deserve if you would consider taking me for your husband."

She looked up at him through thick, blunt lashes. "Would you consider taking me for your wife?"

"Did I not just say so?"

"No."

Up until now, he'd had the uncomfortable feeling she was secretly laughing at him. The expression on his face evidently made keeping the laughter secret impossible. Hers was not a girl's giggle, but a woman's full-throated chuckle. For a moment he was annoyed. But as her lips parted to reveal dazzlingly white teeth, fine and even but for a bottom front tooth set slightly askew, he found himself thinking two things. First, that he hoped Jemilha laughed at him often, for she had a lovely laugh; and second, that he wanted nothing more in this world right now than to run his tongue over that slightly crooked tooth.

Ruefully, he smiled back. "I wish very much for you to be my wife."

All at once her mirth vanished and she bit her lip. "Azzad—"

"Yes, Jemilha?"

"I risk much in telling you this—you may lose all respect for me—"

"Never."

The dark eyes flashed up at him. "Don't interrupt me when I'm trying to tell you I've thought of nothing but marrying you since I first set eyes on you!"

He gaped at her again. "You have?"

"Yes. And I accept you as my husband." But as he bent to press his lips to her wrist, as a proper lover ought, she drew her hand away. "Now that it's settled, there are other things to discuss. What are your plans for the new horses? And what about all those poor dead trees? And—" Here she fixed him with a pair of suddenly fierce dark eyes. "—and I tell you now, Azzad al-Ma'aliq, that if ever you think to amuse yourself with other women—even

Bindta Feyrah, whom I rather like—I will have your testicles served to you on a golden plate with white wine sauce."

He stared; she really meant it. Wordlessly, he nodded.

"Just so we understand each other. Now, sit down, Azzad—no, not so close to me, we're not yet wed—and tell me about planting trees."

Azzad and Jemilha were wed that summer. By the next summer Azzad greeted his first son, Alessid. In 617 Jemilha bore him a second son, named Bazir for the uncle who—despite all Fadhil's efforts—lived only long enough to learn he had a namesake. Two years later, Kallad was born, and Zellim after him. Next came two daughters, Azzifa and Meryem, and then Yuzuf.

By then Jemilha's father too was dead, and Jemilha inherited all that the al-Gallidh owned. In 621, the year of Zellim al-Gallidh's death, this included 62 half- and quarter-breed horses. By 627, the year of Yuzuf's birth, due to the sale of these and other horses, the total al-Gallidh wealth had tripled.

And yet Azzad is not known as Il-Izzahni, the Bringer of Horses. Instead, history has named him Il-Kadiri: the Bringer of Green. For as his fortune and his influence increased, he used both to purchase land around Hazganni. On this land he planted trees. He did so in other towns as well, and after a time the wisdom of trees was accepted. The forests and groves and orchards everyone now takes for granted are Azzad al-Ma'aliq's enduring legacy.

As he neared his thirty-seventh year, he possessed great riches, magnificent horses, fine houses, a wife he had grown to treasure, and seven children he adored.

What he did not yet have was his vengeance.

— FERRHAN MUALEEF, *Deeds of Il-Kadiri*, 654

8

"Husband," said Jemilha, "I don't like this."

Azzad glanced up from the account books. There were seven large leather-bound volumes, one each for notes and figures on timber, crops, orchards, trapping, mining, fishing, and horses. An eighth book, twice the size of the others, was written in Jemilha's precise and dainty script, recording trade in all these things. Beside the desk was a carved wooden lectern holding a ninth ledger; this was for the yearly total of profits and losses in all endeavors. In the years that Azzad and Jemilha together had managed the al-Gallidh estates, there had been no entries under *Losses*.

Jemilha resettled the matron's silk shawl across her shoulders—a new fashion introduced by traders from Rimmal Madar, with whom Azzad did much business using the al-Gallidh name. At thirty-one, Jemilha was seven times a mother and looked as if she had borne not a single child. Azzad no longer wondered why he had felt compelled to marry her. He would have been a fool not to. She had given him more happiness than he had ever thought to receive and more good advice than he deserved. Something in him that was wiser than his brain had prodded him into marrying her. Now—thirteen years, five strong sons, and two beautiful daughters later—he thanked Acuyib daily for that wordless certainty. She was worthy, and more than worthy, of the pearls he had placed around her slender throat on their wedding day. Back then, the necklace had been his only wealth. But in that instant, his wealth had become Jemilha. He adored her even when she laughed at him . . . but she was not laughing now.

"I don't like this idea of yours," said his wife. "And once more I must warn you against it. The Sheyqa has obviously forgotten all about you—why can't you forget about her?"

Azzad did not tell her the one secret he had kept from her all these years. It would not do to worry her about the Geysh Dushann contrivances he and Fadhil had foiled. Ayia, it had mostly been Fadhil, truth to tell, who was as fiendishly clever as the assassins sent to fulfill the Ammarad contract with Sheyqa Nizzira. Azzad's houses, horses, and person were firmly protected. Though several times there had been near misses—a rockslide when he was up in the mountains inspecting the mines, a new design of fish trap that had almost redesigned Azzad's face, for instance—nothing had so much as caused a stubbed toe.

But he wasn't about to tell Jemilha that.

Azzad leaned back in his chair and sighed. "Do you remember, Jemilha, when your uncle died, and then your father? Do you remember what I said to you then? I had sworn when I was younger that I would not marry unless the girl had no father, uncles, brothers, or cousins to interfere with my freedom. I told you then, wife, when Zellim and Bazir were gone, that I mourned your father and uncle as I mourned my own—and if I could give them back to you, I would gladly give up my freedom and spend the rest of my life in the Sheyqa's darkest prison."

"Nothing will bring any of them back to us," she replied. "You've made a new family, a new life. Is it not good? Are you not happy?" It was as close to a plea as this proud woman would ever utter.

"You know that I am." Rising, he went to where she sat on a tapestry couch, knelt before her, took both her hands. "But Nizzira destroyed my family. All the women, the men, the children, even the babies."

"What about *our* babies?"

Resolutely, he went on, "It was not only those of the al-Ma'aliq name. She massacred our servants, and the fallahin who worked on our lands, *everyone* who had any connection with the al-Ma'aliq. She deserves punishment. Surely you must see that she deserves it. Acuyib in His Wisdom would not have let me live if I were not to be the instrument of that punishment."

Jemilha shook her head. "That is vanity, Azzad, and you know it. It's more reasonable that Acuyib spared you to come here and be my husband, and father my children, and—"

"Qarassia," he said, kissing her wrists, "I believe this, too. But I believe just as strongly that I am meant to make Nizzira pay for the ruin of my family."

"*We* are your family now," she countered stubbornly.

"Our children are al-Ma'aliq," he pointed out.

"Yes, al-Ma'aliq—of Sihabbah and Hazganni," she insisted. "Not of Dayira Azreyq."

He stood, looking down at her with a spark of annoyance. He had heard all this too many times, though the manners instilled in him by his father forbade him to say so. Still, her dark eyes ignited with barely repressed rage as surely as if he'd reprimanded her out loud.

"You know what I think, Azzad, you know how I feel—in every other matter, my thoughts and feelings are important to you. But not in this. In this, I am ignored as if I were any other woman and not your wife!" She took a moment to calm herself, then continued, "Don't you see? If you do this, if you carry through the plans you have been making this last year—ayia, don't think I don't know all about this! If you succeed, the Sheyqa will have no choice but to retaliate. Dearly as I love Fadhil and clever as he is, I don't think even his most powerful hazziri will protect us—or our children."

"I understand your will on this, and will consider it most carefully." It was a standard formula and they both knew it. And because he knew himself to be a breath away from rudeness, he walked out of their maqtabba without speaking another word.

Crossing the courtyard to the stables, he nodded to Mazzud and went to look at the latest foals. As ever, his heart swelled at the sight of them: brown and golden, silvery and white, gray and black, ranging from almost exact copies of Khamsin at that age to the sturdier half-breeds, to quarter-breeds nearly indistinguishable from their purebred cousins. In the years since Khamsin's first get had come as such a surprise, Azzad had learned how to produce foals with exactly the combination of strength and speed he wanted. More importantly, rich men from cities as far away as the coast wanted them, too, and paid vast sums for the privilege of looking like shey-qirs on horseback. Sihabbah had profited as well, for the finest saddles and bridles were made here, along with boots and blankets and everything else necessary to riding. Azzad had done well by his adopted home.

Not only in Sihabbah but in Hazganni and fifty other towns and villages his name was blessed. The destruction wrought by the hideous tza'ab azzif of 623—during which Jemilha had given birth to Azzifa, named for the storm—had finally taught everyone the wisdom of trees. Twelve days of un-relenting wind, like the breath of every damned soul exhaled from hell, had heaped sand and rubble from one end of the land to the other. A whole new industry had sprung up in the five years since, of foresters and gardeners and other experts in horticulture, and when Azzad rode through the land and saw the green, he gave thanks to Acuyib—and to the al-Ma'aliq who had planted the first hundred trees in Dayira Azhreq.

All these things, and the family he had sired, were reasons why he had been spared on that horrible night long ago. Jemilha was correct in this. He had done well and lived well. She did not understand, though, that his life was as yet incomplete. Riches, lands, respect, renown, family, friends—he had everything any man could desire. But, as his wife had told him the day he'd asked for her hand, Azzad was not just any man.

He watched his horses for a time, picking out which would be sold and which he would keep. The more placid ones were easy to sort; those with the finest conformation he kept for breeding. But the others, the ones who raced about the field, kicking and leaping for no reason at all but sheer joy—care must be taken in their training and sale, for to match a spirited horse with an indifferent rider was to hold out one's arms to embrace disaster.

But the rider he had in mind these days was an expert—who had learned, undoubtedly, on al-Ma'aliq horses, and may Acuyib curse him and his forever. Azzad left the paddock and crossed behind the stables to the pasture. Of the more than fifty horses grazing there, he picked out the three-year-old colts that might suit his plans. One was dapple gray, one sandy gold, and the third coal-black with a white blaze on his forehead. Beautiful, long-legged, swift and strong, spirited without the unruly and sometimes thoroughly evil streak that plagued some of the half-breeds—his only problem was to decide which horse to use. Which of them would appeal most to an al-Ammarizzad accustomed by now to the finest horses in the world: the al-Ma'aliq horses seized seventeen years ago this autumn?

Annif, Mazzud's brother, came running up to him from the stables. "Do you have need of anything, al-Ma'aliq?"

"Yes," he muttered. Then, because Annif would not understand his real need, he said, "Qama'ar, Nihazza, and Najjhi—separate them out this evening, please, and put them in the small enclosure. I will train them myself."

"As you wish, al-Ma'aliq. Zellim has his eye on Najjhi, I think. And Bazir's is on Nihazza. They know horseflesh."

Being Azzad's sons, they would.

"Alessid, of course, wants Zaqia."

Azzad laughed. "Does he, by Acuyib's Beard?" Twelve years old, growing fast toward manhood and brash with it, Alessid was Azzad's eldest and favorite son. Jemilha preferred the steady, good-hearted Kallad; everyone adored Bazir's playfulness; earnest Zellim took after his grandfather of the same name, the scholar of the family even at barely six years old; Yuzuf was only a baby with as yet no distinctive personality beyond a winsome smile. Azzad loved them all most devotedly, but in Alessid he saw himself, as most fathers will do with one in particular of their sons.

"He says," Annif went on, "he'll have a pureblood of Khamsin's siring or no horse at all."

Ayia, that was stubborn, proud Alessid, from thick black curls to muddy boots. "If you find him up on Zaqia, blister his bottom for him at once— don't wait for me to do it."

Annif grinned. "As you wish, al-Ma'aliq."

That evening, Azzad went into the stables to view the three selected colts. He would be sorry to lose any of them—but one horse was not so great a sacrifice, considering what he would do to Sheyqa Nizzira. He went into each stall, running his hands over smooth flanks and powerful muscles, confirming that Qama'ar, Nihazza, and Najjhi were the finest half-breeds Khamsin had ever sired: strength without bulk, spirit without intransigence, speed in short runs and endurance over long. He stroked their sleek necks and fed them carrots from his pocket, and smiled.

There was the faintest odor of fresh paint in each stall. Azzad searched briefly and found what he knew he would: Fadhil had heard about his orders to Annif and correctly deduced their meaning. Sometime this afternoon he had painted griffins on the rafters above each door. *Retribution.*

There were similar icons and sigils all over the al-Gallidh houses in Sihabbah and Hazganni. Some were cunningly worked into decorative motifs, others were hidden in out-of-the-way places, and a few were right out in the open for all to see—*if* they understood the language of Shagara magic. No one did. Over the years Azzad had become casual about these protections, for although he believed, his belief made him uncomfortable, and it was easier to forget the talishann symbols were there. For one hazzir, however, he would be eternally grateful: the silver owl clutching an onyx in its claws that perched over Jemilha's birthing bed. It had watched over her during seven labors now, and she had come through each in perfect safety.

"The owl holding the jazah, these will see her through," Fadhil had explained. "All our women have such; it is one of Abb Shagara's primary duties to make them for every woman when she becomes pregnant for the first time."

"I've never seen or heard of one of these before," Azzad had said, stroking the owl's silver feathers.

"We keep them for our women only. But even were she not your wife, and therefore part of the Shagara, I would have made one for her."

"Fadhil," he said, amused, "I believe you are a little bit in love with Jemilha."

"I do love her most sincerely, Azzad, but not in the way you imply." Holding up the hand that wore the emerald ring, he grinned. "And this has nothing to do with it."

"It was kindly meant, by me and Abb Shagara."

"I know. I will tell you something, Azzad, that you must not repeat to anyone. If a person who wears a hazzir knows its meaning, he can resist it if his will is strong enough. Meryem can tell you about a patient of hers, brought to the dawa'an sheymma by his daughters after his wife died. Meryem did all she could, but knowing where he was and what she was trying to do, still he died. He *wanted* to die, you see."

"As you did not wish to fall in love."

"Now you understand."

Gazing at the crimson griffin painted above Nihazza's stall door—crimson paint, crimson blood—Azzad wondered again how much belief and knowledge, or their lack, played a role in Shagara magic. He had not known what his own hazzir meant and had not believed until multiple demonstrations of its power had convinced him. In the healing tent, people would believe they could be healed. But Fadhil knew what the ring was for and resisted it successfully—or so he said.

It was all very confusing. If one did not know, and even if one did not believe, the hazzir could do its work. If one knew and believed but rejected, it could not. He supposed the most beneficial combination was one of knowledge, belief, and acceptance.

But would it work on a horse?

Glancing one last time up at the griffin, he shook his head, laughed a little, and returned to the house.

Trade with Rimmal Madar was highly lucrative that spring of 628. Azzad had planned it that way. He knew his home country. He knew what would sell and what would be of no interest, which level of functionaries to bribe and which to ignore, and who among the merchants dealt fairly and who would swindle given half a chance. He had created several new markets— roasted pine nuts, for instance, beautifully woven cloth, fine timber, and elegant furniture made of that timber—and by now Dayira Azreyq clamored for the products of faraway Hazganni. It mattered nothing that no one had ever heard of the place before; no one really cared, so long as supply of Hazganni's goods was steady and not too expensive.

No one knew who was behind the trade. Azzad had made no secret of his name, not in Sihabbah or Hazganni or any of the other towns where he planted trees. For years now the Geysh Dushann had failed to kill him, but failure was not recognized in their code of honor. They wanted to take his head back to their kinswoman the Sheyqa. His head remained firmly on his shoulders. The hazziri had protected him. His association with the Shagara, and their declared enmity for the Geysh Dushann, had not caused the Ammarad to cancel the assassination, but it had limited their methods. The unambiguous trademark of an ax in the spine was not an option if the Ammarad wished to retain the privilege of Shagara medicine. Abb Shagara had let it be known that Azzad's death would be counted as murder of one of his own tribe. Thus all the attempts had been subtle, seemingly accidents that could have been fatal—but, because of the hazziri, were not.

Fadhil took a sort of solemn delight in practicing his craft, and not only for the safekeeping of the family. One year he made a lampshade for the maqtabba, set with tiny beryls to quicken the intellect; Azzad wasn't sure how well it worked, but it was beautiful nonetheless, with light gleaming sea green from the brass arabesques of the shade. He was convinced, however, that the silver nibs Fadhil had fashioned for the children's pens really had helped. From one day to the next, Alessid went from barely forming the characters of his own name to scribbling words like a chief scribe —with a pen bearing the likeness of an ibis, the bird of writing.

There were the more serious hazziri, too. Bazir al-Gallidh had long ago ordered a workshop built for Fadhil, which Azzad had expanded as his needs grew. The children loved to watch while he set a stone into a ring or armband. They didn't know, of course, what his true craft was; they knew only that sometimes on their birthdays, Chal Fadhil gave them a new piece of jewelry or a wind chime.

He spoiled them, of course. So did Azzad. Discipline came from

Jemilha—not only for the children but for Azzad himself. Which would have had his grandfather demanding that he strip and prove his manly parts were still intact. His mother would merely have nodded with supreme satisfaction, well-pleased with Jemilha's effect on her wayward son. Every time Azzad looked at his wife, he was reminded of his incredible luck in coming to Sihabbah. The wastrel who had shuddered at the thought of marriage and sidestepped responsibility with matchless agility now gazed upon his wife and resolved to redouble his work on her behalf. Occasionally, lying beside her in the dawn light, he wondered why he had ever resisted marriage. Ayia, had he married back in Dayira Azreyq, it would have been to the wrong woman. Jemilha was the right one.

Acuyib had indeed smiled upon him. He had wealth, influence, respect, work he enjoyed, a wife he adored, sons to guide to manhood, daughters to gladden his heart—all that a man could wish. And now at long last it was time to begin the work for which Acuyib had spared him so long ago.

"Reihan," he murmured, staring down at a report recently arrived from his agent in Rimmal Madar. The beryl-and-brass lamp shone down on the page, dappling it in sea-green and golden light. "Sheyqir Reihan al-Ammarizzad. The Sheyqa's favorite, most beloved son . . . ."

His agent sent voluminous letters full of events, rumors, descriptions, and speculations. Nizzira, after long, hard years of fighting the northern tribes made unruly by the demise of the al-Ma'aliq, had finally concluded a peace with them in 624. For the last few years she had been rebuilding an economy ravaged by war. Of this, Azzad had taken full advantage—while praying for Nizzira's continued health. At sixty-seven, she was hale and hearty, though it was reported she was emotionally weary while at the same time restless, which to Azzad meant she was probably bored. Governance was complicated, often tedious, sometimes troublesome; Azzad knew that from ruling his own little realm. That was why he loved to escape the maqtabba, saddle Khamsin, and gallop up into the high hills or down to the fertile valleys. Occasionally he took along Fadhil or his sons for company, but more often he rode alone. The Sheyqa could not do this; there was no escape for her, despite—ayia, because of—all her power. Azzad almost felt sorry for her.

But faint stirrings of pity had not prevented him from laughing when his agent reported that after Sayyida's birth, not a single additional offspring had been born to any of the Sheyqa's children. Not the sons, not the daughters—not even the grandsons and granddaughters. It was whispered that the men of the al-Ammarizzad tribe spent their vigor on the battlefield rather than in bed, and the women in scheming instead of breeding. With the arrogance and contempt of a strong young man who had sired seven children and would likely sire more, Azzad laughed and sent his agent many fine gifts in exchange for this delectable information.

The Sheyqa's only true solace was Reihan. By all accounts beautiful and brilliant, Reihan was more and more at his mother's side these last years, not only as an advisor but as a comfort. He played twelve instruments, sang exquisitely, wrote his own songs and poetry, and yet had also led troops into battle on several occasions, acquitting himself well as a warrior. The perfect son—so perfect that Nizzira was actually thinking of altering law and tradition by naming him to succeed her. But the eldest of Nizzira's daughters had married a man with hundreds of powerful relations—too powerful to insult. There were many children of this marriage, including several daughters ruthless enough to contend for the Moonrise Throne. Azzad's lip curled as he reflected that not even Nizzira would play the assassinate-the-whole-family game more than once. He was willing to bet every foal Khamsin had ever sired that in seventeen years no one had accepted an invitation to the palace without first making peace with Acuyib and downing an antidote to poison—just in case. Against swords and axes there could be no defense, of course. Not without Shagara tokens. So many ways of killing . . . but neither poison nor blade featured in Azzad's own plans.

"Sheyqir Reihan al-Ammarizzad," he murmured again, and with a sigh set himself to reading the sheaf of poetry sent with the report. The young man really was quite good, Azzad thought, and once more was almost moved to compassion for Nizzira.

Almost.

So it happened that Sheyqir Reihan, favorite of Sheyqa Nizzira's sons, received in the winter of 629 a magnificent stallion of a breed never before seen in Rimmal Madar. With the horse came a letter, unsigned, begging the young man to accept Nihazza as thanks for the pleasure his exquisite poetry brought to a faraway admirer.

"But who has sent him?" Reihan asked the boy who held the reins. The child had no answer; he had been paid by an unknown man to bring the horse to the palace and ask for Sheyqir Reihan, and that was all he knew.

As Reihan galloped his new possession around the Qoundi Ammar parade ground, his brothers and nephews and cousins whispered in envy. This was the very exemplar of a warhorse: as swift as their own white stallions but obviously much stronger. To breed this stud to mares formerly belonging to the al-Ma'aliq would produce horses of superb quality. And with enough of them, perhaps the Sheyqa would abandon the shameful compact of peace and ride to war once again and this time fully obliterate the rebellious northern tribes.

But why wait years for more horses to be born and grow? Why not find the man who had sent this one? Where there was one such, there were certainly others. Many, many others.

Though Reihan cared little for war despite his proficiency at it, he agreed that the mystery of this golden horse and its giver must be solved.

After much inquiry, he learned that Nihazza had been sent by ship from a faraway land with which much trade had flourished in the last ten years. And in the spring, despite his mother's unhappiness at losing his company for the duration of such a journey, Reihan, two of his brothers, and seven of their cousins set out across the desert wastes toward a city they knew only as Hazganni, a place of "luck" and "riches."

— FERRHAN MUALEEF, *Deeds of Il-Kadiri*, 654

9

One morning Azzad woke with a great many things on his mind—and no wife lying beside him to tell them to. To hear Jemilha's counsel and conversation while they lazed in their bed was one of the joys of his life—a joy increasingly denied him these days, part of her campaign to make him rethink his plans for Reihan al-Ammarizzad. She knew Azzad very well indeed; she knew she didn't have to be in his presence to be foremost in his thoughts. Indeed, her wisdom was such that her absence was on occasion a more definitive statement than any words she might have spoken.

But this morning he wanted her. Something seethed inside him, perhaps to do with a dream not remembered, perhaps pertaining to the subject he refused to discuss with her. He lay there, listening to the wind chimes hung from the eaves outside the bedroom windows, picking out the different notes sounded by steel and silver and gold, telling himself that he really ought to use up his restlessness in starting the day's work early. Work would tire him, but not satisfy him—and he realized that what he truly needed was to talk with a woman. Lacking his wife, he must find another with the shrewdness only women possessed. He required counsel, and no discussion with a man would suffice.

There was only one place in Sihabbah other than his own house that would provide what he needed, and it would be necessary to ride there—not only because it was up a steep hillside trail but because riding would show respect for the lady he intended to visit. Accordingly, instead of heading for the barns, he turned for the pasture where Khamsin ambled about in honorable retirement from everything but the occasional canter with Azzad on his back—and siring foals, of course. Azzad whistled; Khamsin did nothing more than raise his head from the sweet grass and blink at him, supremely uninterested.

"Look at you, you lazy old barghoutz," he chided. "You're as fat as a eunuch. Get over here. We're going to pay a call on a lady."

Azzad's destination was the little group of cottages where the men of Sihabbah took their ease when they wished to escape their homes—and their wives. The two women Azzad had known during his first years here had retired, giving over the business to their daughters, as happened in any family trade. Azzad had not been their customer since his marriage, but he visited sometimes all the same. Bindta Feyrah in particular was a woman whose acumen he respected.

He knocked politely on the door of the main building and was admitted with cries of welcome. Akkilah, youngest and prettiest of the girls, instantly set about making fresh qawah. Meyza, Yaminna and Lalla made Azzad luxuriously comfortable in a throne of silken pillows.

"Our little brother Dawwad came to see us last week," said Yaminna.

"He is very happy working for you, al-Ma'aliq," said Lalla. "It was good of you to give him employment in your house."

"We have Feyrah's son to do chores and take care of the occasional drunk—"

"—but Dawwad isn't big enough to be a deterrent—"

"—so we're all *very* pleased he's found such a good place with you," finished Yaminna.

"It is entirely my pleasure," Azzad told them. "He's a fine worker."

"You're too good to us, al-Ma'aliq," said Yaminna.

"He's too good to *everyone*," said Lalla.

"That's why I can't understand why those dreadful men keep coming to kill him," said Akkilah, arriving with a pot of steaming qawah.

Yaminna frowned as she poured for Azzad. "That reminds me, al-Ma'aliq—there was another one through here last night—"

"—he was small, though, and younger than the other four we've seen," added Lalla.

"—we searched his clothing while Lalla kept him busy, but there were no swords or axes," said Akkilah.

"—and we were about to send one of the boys down to tell you, only you've come here to us instead!" finished Yaminna.

"Cease this chatter at once," came a scolding voice from the doorway. "By Acuyib, anyone would think you descend from geese!"

Azzad turned and got to his feet with a smile as Feyrah entered the cottage. In days long past, he had divided his favors—and his wages—equally between her and her sister Addah, but Feyrah had been his secret favorite. Perhaps this was because her sharp wits and acidic tones reminded him of Challa Meryem. She ran her family business as acutely as Azzad ran his.

"Greetings and Acuyib's Blessings, Feyrah," he said with a short bow of respect.

"And to you, Azzad."

She was one of the few people in Sihabbah who did not call him *al-Ma'aliq*. A single gesture of elegant fingers scattered her daughters and nieces, and soon she and Azzad were comfortably drinking qawah and nibbling dates stuffed with almonds. According to the traditions of her calling, Feyrah asked no questions and merely waited for Azzad to get around to what was on his mind. For his part, he too adhered to custom and entertained her with a story he knew she would enjoy. And soon indeed he had her giggling at Alessid's latest exploit, a project involving ducks, a belled cat, and the fluttering terror of the waterfowl when a bell rang but no cat appeared.

"Ah, I would have liked the honor of that one's initiation myself," Feyrah said at the conclusion of the tale. "But a boy needs a girl, not an old woman."

"I know you too well to think that I need scoff and compliment," Azzad countered. "That sort of thing is for other men to stammer their way through. What I will say is only this: If you are what old age looks like, then Acuyib have mercy on every girl of nineteen from here to Rimmal Madar."

"Very nicely said," she approved, her eyes dancing. "And just the right age, too. Any older, and I would have been insulted. Any younger, and I would have been so busy being offended by your mockery that I would have missed that lovely piece of exaggeration at the end. But while we are on the subject, I have it in mind to propose Meyza—who really *is* nineteen!—for Alessid. Your opinion?"

He considered, and nodded approval. Thoughtful and playful by turns, Meyza was a lovely girl and an entirely appropriate choice. "Perfect. I tell you without flattery or exaggeration or any other pretty words, Feyrah, that I feel fortunate such fine girls are here to teach my boys what they must know to please a wife. My own father sought all over Dayira Azreyq to find just the right girl for me."

"If she was your first, I will cut off all my hair and go north to the barbarian lands, and live in one of their dreadful walled arrareems." She offered him more qawah. "Now, tell me why you have come to talk to me today."

When he drew in a long breath and let it out in a sigh, she added, "Of course I will have heard none of it, once you set foot outside my door."

He nodded gratefully. "I never thought otherwise. Here, then Feyrah, is my problem."

She listened, asked no questions, and refilled their cups at intervals. At last, when he had finished, she pursed her lips and began toying with the crimson fringe of a pillow.

"Azzad, I see now why you are a rich man."

He blinked his surprise at this observation.

"Had you only yourself to consider, you would have done one of two things long ago: sink into utter obscurity or die of a jealous man's anger when he caught you with his wife. In the first case, you would have discovered that charm and good looks are worth only so much in this life, and in the second, you would have learned that charm and good looks can also be the means of leaving this life. But because you are the last of your blood, except for this cousin you mention in your homeland, you used your charm and your good looks for goals other than your own gratification." She smiled through her lashes. "I approve of this, Azzad. Everyone ought to have an ambition.

"But yours," she went on, serious again, "is very much greater than yourself. You are the least avaricious man I have ever known—and yet you have worked these many years to accumulate riches. I have wondered about that, and now I understand. Your ambition has nothing to do with you, or your family here, or even those who died long ago. It has everything to do with your sense of what is right and what must be punished. Wickedness and waste offend you, someplace deep inside where you might never have looked had not everything else been stripped from you. I believe that in this place you saw something very simple: a disorder of things that must be put right."

"You ascribe to me too much honor," he replied slowly. "All I am after is vengeance."

"That is not true. It is a part, but it is not all. There are people like you in the world, Azzad, very rarely—those whom Acuyib uses. You may believe yourself prompted by personal and even selfish considerations, but there is something more profound at work here. What the Sheyqa did to your family was a very ugly wrong. It is obvious that your task is to right that wrong. But it is for you to decide how ugly you wish the righting to be."

"I want . . . I want her to suffer as my mother and sisters suffered. I want her to know what it is to be helpless. But I do not want her to die. I want very much for her to live—and that makes me worse than she, Feyrah. Much worse." Azzad looked into her large, fine eyes and said, "And perhaps the worst thing of all is that although I know this, *I do not care*."

"Then you will certainly succeed." She regarded him for a long moment. "I have done nothing to ease either your heart or your mind, have I? But ease is not what you were seeking, I think. Nor approval."

He had to shake his head. "Neither one, you are right. I think what I needed was to hear myself say it to someone . . ." He paused, at a loss to explain.

"Someone for whose life you are not responsible," she interpreted, nodding. "Ayia, it has been accomplished, then. I won't ask if it helped."

"But it did. Very much. I'm not sure I agree about any greater purpose, but I do understand more clearly some of the possible consequences."

"Do you?" She rose smoothly to her feet. "I wonder." From a pocket of her robe she took a small brass bell that Fadhil had made for her long ago, and rang it four times. "You have said nothing, I have heard nothing," she told him just before the girls ran lightly back into the cottage.

"We've been petting Khamsin—"

"—I hope it's all right that we gave him carrots—"

"—he nibbles daintily as a lamb!"

Azzad laughed. "He knows to behave himself around ladies." Pushing himself to his feet, he bowed to Feyrah. "My thanks, as always. Perhaps you will agree to advise me on a new type of qawah blend some farmers along the coast have concocted. I shall send a bag up to you, and await your judgment."

Feyrah nodded acceptance of this means of paying her for her time. "I'll look forward to it."

"You're not leaving so soon!" cried Lalla.

Yaminna made a face at her pouting cousin. "Do you really think to tempt al-Ma'aliq?"

Azzad bowed. "I am tempted almost beyond reason every time I visit here."

"A lie!" laughed Meyza. "Everyone knows your eyes are only for your wife!"

He smiled ruefully and shrugged. "Nonetheless, I must abandon the unique fascinations of your company. I have an appointment later today with

Ferrhan Mualeef, who has literary ambitions and seems to think my life makes a good story."

"Ayia, he was here some days ago," Lalla said with a giggle. "What *do* they teach their young men in Hazganni?"

Azzad deduced she had not been impressed and gave thanks he had learned *his* lessons in Dayira Azreyq.

It all seemed a very long time ago. Another life. Another Azzad. As he rode back down to Sihabbah proper, he reflected on how much this land and its peoples had shaped and changed him, had made him their own. His life had been saved by the Shagara, who befriended him and made his enemies theirs. He had married a noblewoman of Sihabbah, who had made him so thoroughly hers that he had not even thought about another woman since his marriage. What had he done in return, for these people and this land? Ayia, the horses and the trees—they were the most obvious—but most important were the children. They belonged here, to a land and a people theirs by right of birth. Azzad had given five sons and two daughters to this place that had become his life. He considered the debt paid.

But the debt to the Shagara, for giving him back the life he had so nearly lost in the wastelands—that could never be repaid. For the wise Feyrah had been correct: It was the loss of everything else that had made him look deeper than he ever would have done, and if she had been mistaken about the nobility of what he'd found there . . . still, it made a pretty wrapping for a thing that would be very ugly indeed.

The Geysh Dushann who had visited the ladies was seen in Sihabbah only once more—when his body was recovered from a streambed that marked the border of Azzad's farthest pasture. The fence he had evidently attempted to climb was studded every few handspans with thorns such as were used in Shagara fencing; perhaps he had pricked a finger and died of the poison, or perhaps he had simply lost his balance. By the time he was found, it was difficult to tell.

A curious thing was found in his possessions, something the ladies had not known to be significant. A small drawstring pouch, stamped on the outside with talishann, hung from a leather thong around his neck. Inside was a chunk of pyrite and a bit of hammered tin with a sign Fadhil did not recognize, packed in amid six different kinds of dried leaves and flowers. Fadhil identified two herbs as moderately curative, but to put them in combination with the others was a waste of a healer's time and effort. Perhaps the blend had been meant merely to provide a pleasing scent—if so, it had long since faded.

The pyrite was of interest for its qualities of practicality, memory, and protection. The Shagara markings on the pouch meant nothing more sinister than success, luck, and knowledge. But when Fadhil detected a trace of rust-colored stain on the tin, he frowned and sorted through the dried herbs again. A tiny clump of leaves and flower petals was stuck together with blood. Shagara blood. Whatever the unfamiliar talishann meant, someone had been serious about this pouch and its contents.

"No match for your skills, certainly," said Azzad, shrugging, and poured more qawah for his wife and Fadhil. "Merely another failed assassin."

Jemilha, watching Fadhil's studied lack of expression, said quietly, "Or the first to be armed with Shagara work. He is the first, is he not?"

"Insofar as I am aware," the healer admitted, uneasiness shifting his shoulders just a little. "I think that he may have obtained these things illicitly—in which case the talishann would not function as well as if they had been made specifically for him."

"Have you ever seen such a collection before, worn in a pouch filled with herbs?" she persisted.

"Ayia, there are certain antiquated customs—"

"Herbs that are mostly useless for healing? Herbs that had lost their fragrance long since?"

Azzad approached and formally presented her with a fresh cup of qawah. "Qarassia, if it will bring peace to your thoughts, I will send to Challa Meryem and ask. But we all know that the Geysh Dushann are forbidden the healing tents of the Shagara, so this man must have stolen these things— hoping in vain that they would protect and aid him. They did not. So ends another Geysh Dushann."

"And this discussion?" she asked, in that silken tone he had come to dread over the years, a tone like a soft fog that wrapped a man's heart in sudden ice.

"If there is nothing else to say, nothing else to learn, and nothing to plan for . . ." He shrugged again.

"And you have far more important plans to make—yes, I know, husband." She set aside her untasted drink and rose. "The children's lessons must be heard. I will leave you to your plans."

Azzad hesitated, then asked, "Once Alessid, Bazir, and Kallad have re-cited to your satisfaction, may I see them afterward?"

Her face tightened like an angry fist. But all she did was nod and stalk out of the room in a swirl of bright silks.

"She isn't happy," Fadhil said mildly.

Azzad cocked a sardonic brow. "I'm sure she was hoping you wouldn't notice."

"She could forbid this, you know. It is well within her rights."

"Happy or unhappy, approving or disapproving—she *understands*. Men simply see a thing and decide one way or another and don't bother much with reasons. Women *think*. And those who think longest understand best. As the writings have it, men's thoughts are the sand, easily scattered by any wind that happens along. But women are the rich earth that grows thoughts and ideas, and from these come understanding."

"And what of you, the one they are calling Il-Kadiri?" Fadhil smiled.

"That silly child, Ferrhan Mualeef, has been reading bits of his work to you, hasn't he?" Azzad sighed. "'Bringer of Green,' indeed! It's only common sense—"

"Sense, Meryem says, is the least common thing of all." He glanced around as Alessid's voice echoed down the stairwell, teasing his brothers into a jumping contest. "Do we tell them everything tonight?"

"Not quite everything. They're good boys, but still only boys, after all. They might say something unawares."

"And we cannot allow a single grain of sand to stray outside Sihabbah, or it will surely stick in the eye of this Sheyqir Reihan. Ayia, when the time comes for them to know everything, I will be ready with something for them." He frowned. "I wish, though, that I knew how the Geysh Dushann came by those Shagara items. And what that strange sign means."

Whatever Azzad would have replied was lost, for Alessid burst into the room, Bazir and Kallad a step behind him, shouting, "I won! I won!"

Azzad hid a smile. Alessid always won.

"They're coming."

Azzad nodded in the twilight gloom. It would be impossible to miss them: the white horses that were the pride of the al-Ammarizzad practically glowed in the dark. The one golden horse, pride of one al-Ammarizzad in particular, shone like the rising of the summer sun.

Mazzud shifted in his saddle and whispered, "We're too close to the city. We should have taken them last night at the watering hole."

Azzad stayed silent, not reminding his old friend that they were so far from Hazganni that none but the owls would hear, and that the stop at the watering hole had been part of his plan. While the group of al-Ammarizzad and their servants slept, foolishly trusting their horses to warn them of approaching danger, Azzad and Fadhil had, with the aid of specially crafted hazziri, slipped into the saddle waterskins a tasteless, odorless drug. Now, almost a whole day later, peering from the shelter of trees and bushes he himself had ordered planted, Azzad saw the sedative taking slow, subtle effect. Ten offspring of Sheyqa Nizzira and the ten men who served them swayed slightly as they rode, drooping forward, jerking upright again as they felt themselves falling asleep.

Azzad glanced at his sons. Alessid grinned back—the typical impudent thirteen-year-old, well aware that full manhood was close upon him. Bazir, almost eleven and tall for his age, nodded solemnly when he saw Azzad looking at him; Kallad, two years younger, smiled. Both boys were nervous, but hiding it well. Alessid, by contrast, looked as if he and his horse awaited the start of a race: eager yet controlled, excited yet utterly confident. Azzad was well pleased. He was determined that his sons participate in this act that would define them as al-Ma'aliq. This was their vengeance as much as his. He only regretted that Zellim and Yuzuf were too young to be here.

The ten sheyqirs lolled drunkenly in their saddles. Azzad knew who they were by name, thanks to his agent in Rimmal Madar, and could not have been better pleased had he given specific instructions to Nizzira about which of her progeny to send. Acuyib was not only smiling, He was laughing in His Beard at the joke shared with Azzad. The Most Noble and Mighty Sheyqirs were all young, all intended for vital marriage bonds with powerful families, to bring a harvest of wealth, alliances, and children.

Azzad lifted a hand in signal to Fadhil, Mazzud, and the three boys. The al-Ammarizzad reined in, their movements sluggish, confusion scrawled on their faces in the sunset as six riders emerged from the trees on either side of the road.

"Who're you?" a bearded sheyqir slurred.

"Azzad al-Ma'aliq."

He laughed a sloppy, drunken laugh. "The al-Ma'aliq're all dead."

Azzad smiled. "Not all." He turned his attention to the rider of the golden stallion. "Nihazza is an impressive horse, is he not, Reihan?"

The young man was indeed exceedingly beautiful, even slack-lipped and bleary-eyed with Fadhil's drugs. He retained enough wits to know this was a trap. He hauled clumsily on the reins—but Alessid leaped lightly from his saddle and gave a soft, melodic whistle between his teeth. Nihazza responded instantly by planting his hooves in the dust and refusing to budge another step. Alessid came forward quite casually and laid a hand on the stallion's bridle; Nihazza snuffled, recognizing him, and nuzzled a pocket for the expected treat.

Reihan's brothers and cousins, belatedly realizing there was danger but not quite believing that danger to their royal persons could come in the form of three men and three boys, attempted to maneuver their horses. But before the al-Ammarizzad and their attendants could do more than fumble at their saddles, bridles were seized and swords were taken and piled on the ground.

"Robbers," one of the sheyqirs announced, as if weeks of heavy thought had led him to this brilliant conclusion.

"Whassa trouble?" another demanded. "Outta way, fallahin—"

"Al-Ma'aliq," Alessid corrected him, almost pleasantly.

"They're all dead," came the reply, with a befuddled snort.

Another, looking to be the youngest, nodded, his head loose on his neck. "Long time ago—orders of the Sheyqa my gran'ma—"

"You," Reihan said, swallowing dry and hard as he peered at Azzad. "You sent him—Nihazza—"

"—knowing you would want more like him," Azzad finished. "I know you, al-Ammarizzad. I know all of your greedy kind. Acquisitive, selfish, arrogant—I knew Nihazza would be the only invitation you'd require. Acuyib meant this to happen."

"It was nothing t'do with me." Reihan shook his head in a vain attempt to clear it. "I—I was no more than a child—"

"So were my sisters," Azzad said. "And all the children your mother ordered burned alive. Innocent children, whose only crime was that they were al-Ma'aliq. Your crime is that you are al-Ammarizzad."

"Brigands," proclaimed the Intellect among them. "Gonna rob an' kill us—"

"Kill us?" a proud sheyqir whined, and a third blustered, "Wuddun' dare—"

"I have no intention of killing you," Azzad said—reluctantly, for this had been a point of contention between him and Fadhil. But this way was better; it would cause Nizzira more anguish. "You will live and return to Rimmal Madar."

Nine of them had gone limp in their saddles—half with relief, half with the powerful sedative. Only Reihan still fought, his fine features tense, his magnificent dark eyes forced wide open by sheer effort of will.

Azzad contemplated him for a moment, then said, "All of you, get off my horses."

"*Your*—?" The Intellect drew himself up with what he probably imagined was dignity.

"Which one are you?" Azzad asked.

"I—Sheyqir—" He listed to the right before lurching back and steadying himself. "Azhim, third son of Sheyqa Nizzira an' fourth huzbin'—I mean, fourth son, seccun' huzbin'—" He frowned his puzzlement that he couldn't quite place himself within the royal hierarchy. At last he simply shrugged, an action that nearly toppled him from his horse, and said, "'M Sheyqir Azhim."

"Sheyqir Azhim," Azzad said pleasantly, "if you open your mouth one more time, I'll cut out your tongue. Now, get off my horses."

After some encouragement at the points of their own swords, they did so, sliding bonelessly to the ground. Bazir, Alessid, and Mazzud swiftly tied up the servants, then hobbled the horses. Kallad and Fadhil placed on each al-Ammarizzad's left thumb a silver ring. Azzad had watched Fadhil craft the rings, set with etched carnelians and inscribed with rows of tiny ants. Azzad had insisted on the insects, enjoying the pun: Ants were a symbol of harvesting, which was the meaning of *izzad*.

One of the brothers squinted at his new jewelry and muttered, "Ugly thing. Wuddun' givvit to a whore."

Another, dimly perceiving that Azzad held all the power here, said, "Issa nice present. C'n we go now, al-Ma'aliq?"

He ignored them. Still astride Khamsin, he nodded to Mazzud, who kindled a fire in the stone circle constructed that afternoon, then said to the al-Ammarizzad, "Remove your sashes."

They grumbled but obeyed, swaying on their feet, fingers awkwardly unwinding the red silk, golden fringes tangling. Bazir and Kallad collected the sashes, then ripped each lengthwise down the middle. Blurts of outrage became gasps as the sheyqirs were knocked off their feet into the dirt. They struggled feebly, but the fear in their brains could not overcome the drug in their bodies. Their hands were bound behind them with their own torn sashes. Azzad watched terror brighten their blurry eyes as the fire lit the clearing in yellow and angry crimson—and showed them the instrument slowly glowing to white heat in the flames.

Anyone who knew anything about horses would recognize such an instrument.

"Bring Nihazza," Azzad commanded.

Mazzud and Alessid held the gray stallion triple-roped. Bazir held Nihazza's head, stony-faced, regretting the horse he had hoped would be his, but knowing the sacrifice to be necessary. Quickly and carefully, Fadhil smoothed a thick, sickly-sweet smelling unguent on and around the testicles. Azzad dismounted and personally gelded the stallion with cauterizing white-hot iron.

Nihazza jerked once, but the salve had deadened pain. Bazir turned his head away. Azzad thought of how he would feel had it been Khamsin.

Turning to the ten offspring of Sheyqa Nizzira, he said, "This also I will do to each of you. But I will allow you to live, which is more than the Sheyqa allowed the al-Ma'aliq."

There were outcries, some of disbelief and some of fear and some of blustering rage. The only one who made no sound, the only one who seemed to understand, even through the drug befuddling his mind, was Reihan. He did not doubt Azzad's word about what was about to occur; he was neither afraid nor angry. He hated. And in the dark loathing that shone from his eyes by firelight, despite the sensitivity of his poetry and the elegance of his beauty, Azzad saw in him a true son of Sheqya Nizzira.

Azzad thrust the gelding shears into the fire, and again, and again, ten times in all. And so he harvested the al-Ammarizzad.

In due course Azzad received a letter from his most trusted agent in Dayira Azreyq. It had been well worth waiting for.

They have returned. They were led into the palace by night, and in secret. No one saw them but the servants who opened the doors. My sources tell me that many tabbibi came in haste that same night and

*departed just before dawn in fear for their lives. What this must mean,
I think you know.*

Of course he knew. Nizzira wished no one to discover that ten of her
progeny were no longer men.

*All Dayira Azreyq holds its breath. The Sheqya has not been seen in
days, and there are dire tidings of her rage. More tabbibi have come and
gone, and my friends among them says that the violence of her grief may
well be the death of the Sheyqa.*

Ayia, Azzad hoped so. Let her feel more anguish than a human heart
could hold. Let her suffer every time she thought of her ten gelded darlings.
Let her scream the name of al-Ma'aliq without ceasing.

*I regret to write that three days ago, the order for Sihabbah timber was
canceled. My friends in the Zoqalo Zhaddim say that orders for certain
other items have also been canceled. What this must mean is confirmed
by the departure of the officials of the provinces held by the al-Akhdir
from court, with no marriage contract regarding Sheyqir Azhim in their
hands.*

Azzad wondered if the al-Akhdiri ambassadors had any idea of why
Azhim would not be getting married to any woman.

*There has been talk about sending an army to Hazganni by sea. It is not
agreed upon, but should this occur, I will give ample warning.*

Very efficient of him, Azzad thought, but unnecessary. The Shagara
hazziri, old as they were by now, that had protected this land from invading
northern barbarians would function just as well against the soldiers of Rimmal Madar. Besides, with the northern tribes formerly allied to the al-Ma'aliq
restless still, Nizzira could not afford to send half her army out of the country.

*Yesterday two of the Qoundi Ammar were dispatched to The Steeps. I
saw them ride out myself. What this must mean, I believe you also
know.*

He would be five times a fool if he didn't. There was more to the letter—inventories, business dealings, the usual—but after a quick perusal Azzad returned to the best news. He read it again and again. The proud sheyqirs slinking into the palace by night. The tabbibi summoned to confirm that the deed was hopeless of remedy—and threatened with death if they spoke of it. The marriage alliance that would not be—all the marriages that would never be. The sending of emissaries to the Geysh Dushann to demand revenge. And especially—ayia, especially!—the helpless rage of Sheyqa Nizzira. Worst of all, her favorite son, her beautiful, poetic Reihan, light of her heart and joy of her old age—

"And so," his wife said, standing in the doorway of the maqtabba. "At last you have your vengeance."

"Yes," he replied with a humming sigh of satisfaction. "I have it."

"Is it sweet to the taste, husband? Does it fill you the way a new child fills me now?"

Azzad sprang to his feet. "Jemilha—!" He rose to embrace and kiss her, but she eluded him, holding out two shiny objects.

"I asked Fadhil to make these. One set for you, and one set each for all of us. Say you will wear them always, and I will never speak of this matter again."

His gaze fell from her adamant face to a pair of wide silver armbands studded with a rainbow of tiny gems. Purple amethyst, blue turquoise, sea-green beryl and spring-green peridot, golden topaz, red-orange carnelian and crimson garnet—a dozen of each, set around complex talishann, and a single owl for watchfulness. He didn't remember all the meanings of all the jewels, but he did recognize one because Fadhil had once said it was extremely rare.

"Peridots. These must have cost as much as Khamsin's best foal." He eyed his wife sidelong. "But a small price to pay for protection against my own folly—is that the way your thoughts run, Jemilha?"

"Will you put these on, Azzad? And never take them off? If you promise, this will be the last you'll ever hear from me about what you did to Nizzira's sons and grandsons."

"I promise." He clasped the silver hazziri onto his arms and again tried to embrace Jemilha. Again she avoided him, turning on the heel of one white velvet slipper. In the whirl of her movement the sleeves of her bedrobe shifted at her wrists, and by the lamplight he saw the bracelets that were a match for the armbands. "Qarassia—"

"Sururi annam, husband," she said over her should as she left the room. And he wondered if she would ever sleep sweetly again.

Ayia, this was all nonsense. Nizzira would know who was responsible, but what could she do about it? Send her army? It would be an invitation to the northern tribes to attack. Send the Geysh Dushann? Likely, but not all that worrying. Azzad glanced around the maqtabba. Shagara safeguards were all over the house in Sihabbah, the house in Hazganni, at the perimeters of all the al-Gallidh holdings. Even if assassins got past these, there were the protections on his person. He held up his arms, admiring the gleam of silver and jewels by lamplight. He and his were safe.

And there would be a new baby in the new year—a sixth son or a third daughter. It would be a daughter, he decided, a sign of Acuyib's approval. He'd name the girl Oannisia, for Acuyib had indeed been merciful to Azzad, and just.

The evening shadows deepened, and Azzad was lighting another lamp so he could read the letter yet again and gloat over it when Fadhil came into the maqtabba. His golden skin looked pallid and fragile, drawn tight across fine bones by worry, lined with sorrow.

"What is it, my friend?" Azzad asked, rising.

"Khamsin," was all Fadhil said.

He would never know how he got to the stables. He only knew that one moment he was surrounded by books and the scent of fragrant lamp oil, and the next he was in Khamsin's stall with the reek of medicine in his nostrils.

"It's no use, al-Ma'aliq," said Mazzud, tears unnoticed on his weathered cheeks. "He is old, and it is his time."

Fadhil crouched beside him. "I've done all I can. Mazzud is right. It's his time."

He knelt there all night, remembering how he had done the same when Khamsin was newborn, so that Azzad would become familiar and beloved. He remembered all the years since—twenty-two of them—that had taken him and Khamsin from the ancestral castle of the al-Ma'aliq to the city streets of Dayira Azreyq, from the brutal climb of The Steeps to the camp of the Ammarad, from the tents of the Shagara to the sweet mountain meadows of Sihabbah.

The stallion's heart stopped just before dawn. There was a final sighing breath, and a slight movement of the head against Azzad's caressing hands, and then the last gleam faded from the huge eyes.

"No," Azzad said, and buried his face in Khamsin's neck and wept.

Despite the commands and the threats of Sheyqa Nizzira that no one—no one—know of the mutilations, rumors spread. What was whispered in the streets about why, and how, and by whom, was voiced aloud in the secure seclusion of private houses—though softly still, and with caution, and only to those one trusted absolutely: "Azzad lives! An al-Ma'aliq yet lives!" And without Azzad's knowing of it, his name became the stuff of ballad and legend.

It also began to be whispered that there yet lived another al-Ma'aliq—if not by name, certainly by blood. Her name came to adorn ballads and legends, too. But, unlike those songs and stories about Azzad, which dealt with past deeds, the name of the young Sayyida el-Ammarizzad was coupled with hope for the future. The daughter of Ammineh al-Ma'aliq listened, and smiled.

— FERRHAN MUALEEF, *Deeds of Il-Kadiri*, 654

10

The Geysh Dushann renewed their attacks. They cared no more for subtlety. For their pride's sake, it no longer mattered to them whether or not the Shagara knew who killed Azzad al-Ma'aliq.

But Azzad was not killed. And if he had had any lingering doubts of the effectiveness of Fadhil's hazziri, he had none at all after one would-be assassin fell from a second-floor balcony and was gutted by his own ax. Viewing broken railings the next morning, Azzad traced with one finger the talishann painted on the wood. For a few moments he debated asking Fadhil to tell him exactly what protections had been added to the house, but two things stopped him. The ways of the hazziri were the deepest secrets of the Shagara, and he didn't want to put his friend in a position where he must refuse to answer. Also, he recalled very well what Fadhil had told him long ago: If one knew the hazzir's precise meaning, too much trust would be placed in it, and the wisdom of ordinary caution would fly away. *"Not even the Shagara can protect against stupidity."* Azzad concluded that whereas belief could increase the power of the magic, one could in fact believe too much.

The Geysh Dushann came, singly and in pairs, openly and in disguise. Every one of them failed. Jemilha was true to her word; no reproach ever passed her lips for the danger. But her eyes grew larger and larger in her weary face with the strain of her fear and the new pregnancy.

Fadhil made new hazziri for her and the children. He repainted the protections in and around the house in his own blood. He sent to Abb Shagara informing him of events, and by way of reply came six young Shagara men, who worked for eight days reinforcing Fadhil's work with their own. A letter from Abb Shagara said that if the noble Lady Jemilha grew bored in Sihabbah, she was very welcome to visit his tents and stay as long as she liked. A note from Meryem was less tactful: She recommended that Fadhil tell Azzad not to be more of a fool than Acuyib had made him and get his wife and children out of Sihabbah at once. Azzad sent a letter back with the six young men, thanking Abb Shagara for his care. But he did not leave Sihabbah.

There were attempts at the house, at the stables, in the town. The Geysh Dushann sabotaged saddles and bridles, poisoned provisions, dusted the insides of gloves with toxic powder, and ignited na'ar al-dushanna that filled rooms with noxious smoke.

A little furry creature, oddly manlike about the hands and eyes and ears, was caught in the kitchen while putting something into the soup. Alessid made a pet of him, teaching him to add sugar to his mother's qawah and training him to do many other tricks. But the animal sickened during the cold weather and died. By then Alessid had a new pet: the deadly snake he found slithering across his room one morning. With its poison sacs removed, it was an oddly affectionate creature, and Alessid's hunting skills grew apace when it turned out the snake preferred succulent pasture-fed mice to the grain-eaters of the barns.

Nothing the Geysh Dushann did could touch Azzad or his family. Yet by midwinter in the new year of 630, the perspective of Sihabbah's people began to change. Outrage at these offenses became annoyance at their continuance—and this was but a step away from anger directed at Azzad. None among them had been injured, but it was hard to live in a place where every stranger must be suspected of intent to commit murder.

Azzad humbly consulted Abb Ferrhan—past eighty and more sternly judgmental than ever—and apologized for the ruination of Sihabbah's peace, promising that when Jemilha was delivered of her child and could safely travel, he would take his family elsewhere.

"But you say she isn't due until spring!" Abb Ferrhan protested.

"I am sorry. But she cannot be taken great distances in her condition."

This was not strictly true. Though this pregnancy was giving her trouble, when none of the others had, still she was perfectly capable of a journey if taken slowly. Azzad simply had no intention of running away. And he trusted to Fadhil's hazziri to continue protecting him and his, as they had through nearly five months of unsuccessful strikes by the Geysh Dushann.

And then the assaults ceased.

Spring came, and Jemilha gave birth to a healthy girl, duly named Oannisia as Azzad had promised to Acuyib. All the children grew and progressed well in their lessons. Kallad, serious and bookish, was obviously destined to become a scholar. Zellim showed an aptitude for music, Bazir for mathematics. Yuzuf was the charmer of the brood, with a pair of huge brown eyes, soft and sweet as a fawn's, that allowed him to escape nearly all punishment for boyish misdeeds. Azzifa and Meryem were lovely, carefree, their father's delight. And Alessid, his firstborn—ayia, Alessid would soon be a man, and a fine one, tall and strong and handsome, who would be sought after as a husband by every girl in every town and village between here and the great northern ocean.

All of Azzad's world was perfectly at peace. Trade was as good as ever, perhaps better; Khamsin's last foals were born and thrived.

But Fadhil, Azzad saw one afternoon in early summer, had become old.

They were on the way to a house outside Sihabbah's boundaries. Fadhil had chosen to walk rather than ride, and Azzad went along with him to carry his satchel of medicines.

"You don't have to act as my apprentice," Fadhil said irritably.

"You were favoring your right shoulder last night," Azzad replied, "and you never walk unless your back is aching so much that you can't ride. I'm not the only one who observes symptoms, Fadhil."

"And pleased with yourself for it, too, Chal Azzad," the Shagara answered with a little smile. "Very well. Yes, my shoulder is troubling me, and I believe I rode too far with the boys the other day, which is why my back hurts."

"Can't you cure yourself?"

"Sometimes it's wiser to allow the pain to work itself out. If it does, good. If it doesn't, there may be something else wrong that curing the first might mask."

"You're the tabbib," Azzad said, shrugging.

"Indeed I am."

Their destination was a cottage just outside town—one of the prettiest properties in all Sihabbah, in fact. Nestled beneath a stand of towering pines, with a view down the whole valley, it was the home built for Feyrah this spring when she had given over the entirety of the family business to her daughters and nieces. She and her sister now lived there, tending for amusement and pleasure a garden of exotic herbs that Azzad had ordered for them from the barbarian lands to the north.

Except for trees, which were the most important of all Acuyib's gifts, plants rather bored Azzad. He appreciated flowers because of Jemilha's delight when he gave her a bouquet; he acknowledged the usefulness of herbs for healing; he had his favorites among the spices that flavored his food; he valued the grains that fed his horses. But all these required constant care and cosseting, season after season. A tree, once established, settled down and went about the business of growing. If not an eternal thing, the way a mountain's bulk or a desert's vastness was eternal, a tree was as permanent as a mere man could wish to see. It simply *was*, and *continued*, and for reasons he didn't understand he found this notion a comfort.

But this garden of Feyrah's interested him, and the interesting thing about it was the fascination it inspired in Alessid. The boy liked nothing better than to ride up here after lessons and help the ladies tend the plants. For someone as physically restive as Alessid, a liking for the gentle occupation of gardening was perhaps the last thing one might expect. Azzad had asked him about it once, and received a muddled sort of reply that boiled down to: *I like to find out the differences and the samenesses.* An interesting boy, to be sure. Azzad sometimes wasn't quite sure what to make of him, but knew he'd enjoy watching what the boy made of himself.

The ladies welcomed their visitors with all the usual warmth, plus that bit extra always reserved for Fadhil. A new harvesting of herbs was produced and exclaimed over; there were significant hopes for a powerful painkiller from an infusion Fadhil spent a great deal of time discussing with Feyrah, and this told Azzad much about the reason for this long walk today.

As qawah was served—outside on the patch of grass, for it was a lovely day—and the newest recipes for smallcakes were sampled, Azzad watched his old friend with worry in his heart. Fadhil moved with a kind of studied grace these days, as if his brain must constantly remind his body what walking and reaching and shrugging looked like to others so that no one would notice his pain. It was only when the younger ladies arrived for their daily visit that Azzad pushed aside his concern and exerted himself to be charming.

They had news for him.

"Yet another one, al-Ma'aliq, we can scarcely credit it!" Yaminna told him as he selected the choicest cakes for her as a gentleman ought. "He wasn't like the one who came this winter—"

"His hair didn't have that reddish cast," Lalla interrupted. "I mean, it did, but it was obviously hennah." She giggled suddenly. "Yaminna, do you remember the time you had a notion to become a redhead—"

"And I had a terrible time correcting the damage," Fadhil said. "Shame upon you, Yaminna, trying to improve on the glory Acuyib gave you."

"I repented, Chal Fadhil," she replied, laughing. "Ayia, how I repented!"

"Something else about this man," Lalla said. "He had dyed his skin as well as his hair. The brown was all over his body, but in a few places not as well applied as in others. If you understand what I mean! But the point is that he was a stranger, though not one of *them*, even though he tried to seem so. His natural skin was golden, like Chal Fadhil's." She sat back on her heels with a *What do you think of that?* look on her face.

Shagara pretending to be Geysh Dushann? Ridiculous. But Azzad was too polite to say so. "I shall watch most carefully for a man with badly hennah'd hair," he assured her.

In the normal course of things, the two men would have whiled away the afternoon most pleasantly. But Azzad, alert to his friend's attempts to hide pain, saw suddenly that he was also attempting to disguise unease. He was halfway through a gallant speech of reluctance to leave the ladies' company when Yaminna leaned closer to Fadhil and whispered something in his ear.

He smiled at her and shook his head. "I thank you, but no. I am too weary to do you justice, I fear."

On the walk back to town through the golden dusk, Azzad confronted him. "Tell me the truth. Are you ill?"

"No."

"You look ill," Azzad said bluntly.

"As you said earlier, *I* am the tabbib."

"Fadhil—"

"I would rather speak of the Shagara who has disguised himself as an al-Ammarad—for can you doubt, from the description, that this is what he is?"

"Fadhil!"

A long, quiet sigh. "Very well. How old are you this year, Azzad?"

"Thirty-nine—and don't remind me! The gray hairs in my head and beard—caused by my children, I swear it by Great Acuyib!—my age sneers at me from every mirror!"

"Would you like some of what I use to hide mine?" Fadhil gave him a sidelong smile. "No danger to one's hair, unlike that awful stuff Yaminna tried—"

"What?" Azzad stared at him. "What are you talking about?"

Fadhil kicked at a stone in the path. "Among the Shagara, such cosmetics are not necessary. We know. We understand. But here—ayia, no one would believe that I am two years your junior if I did not dye my hair and beard. I am afraid, though, that in the last year or two, the lines on my face have betrayed me." He glanced over at Azzad with another tiny smile. "There is no hiding *them*, you know."

"Betrayed you?"

"Yes. They show what I am."

"Everyone knows you're Shagara—"

"There are Shagara and Shagara, as you know. At least, you know a part of it." He held a pine branch out of Azzad's way.

Azzad stopped, staring at his friend. "You mean about not being able to sire children?"

"That is an aspect of it. In the next year, my shoulder and my back will not be my only aches. I am fortunate in that my hands remain strong and free of pain." He let the branch drop, and sighed again. "How old do you think Chal Kabir was when he died in 614?"

Recalling the tabbib's appearance the year before, when Azzad had taken Farrasha and Haddid to the Shagara camp, he said, "More than seventy, less than eighty."

"He was forty-one."

Azzad felt his jaw fall open.

"Forty-one," Fadhil repeated softly. "You have not seen Abb Shagara in many years, Azzad. He is my age—we were born almost on the same day. When I visited last summer, I saw what the cares of being Abb Shagara can do. His hair and beard are now almost completely white."

"Ayia!" Azzad breathed. "Then you—and Abb Shagara, and those like you—"

"Within the tribe, we are called Haddiyat."

"You use yourselves up in service to others," Azzad heard himself say, the words coming from the instinctive place that was wiser than his conscious mind. Grief and guilt crushed his heart. "The cares of caring for us—what you've done for me and mine, especially since last spring—all the hazziri, and your blood in the paints—all the things that keep us safe from the Geysh Dushann—"

"Do not, Aqq Azzad," Fadhil said swiftly, his fine, strong hands clasping Azzad's shoulders. "It would happen wherever I lived, whatever I did. Some of the Haddiyat spend themselves in making hazziri for strangers, in healing strangers. I have been singularly blessed by Acuyib, because my work is done for people I love, for a woman and children I cherish as if they were my own—and a man who is my brother more than any Shagara could have been. How better should I spend myself than for love of you and yours, who are also in some ways mine?"

Azzad had no words now. He embraced Fadhil, remembering at the last moment not to grasp too strongly lest he cause pain. They had been young together, and Azzad had always assumed they would grow old the same way. He could not imagine growing old without Fadhil at his side.

"How long?" Azzad grated. "How long will you—"

Fadhil deliberately misunderstood him. "I will work as long as I can."

"How long?"

This time he did not pretend. He sighed quietly against Azzad's shoulder. "Do not grieve over me yet, my friend. I am alive and as well as any Haddiyat can expect to be at my age. I have never regretted what I am. And Acuyib has favored me beyond human reckoning. I have a good life, and it is not yet over." He drew back a little, to smile into Azzad's stricken face. Lines there were on his golden skin, and the frail dry wrinkles of a man half again his age, and a depth of weariness to him that now frightened Azzad. "Another secret to keep, to be locked away with all the others."

"I won't tell Jemilha," he said thickly, letting Fadhil go. "Or the children."

"I didn't think you would." His gentle smile widened to a grin. "Only please, Azzad, do take that pitiful expression from your face before we get home! Jemilha is no fool—and neither are your children."

"But Sheyqa Nizzira is," another voice said behind them. Both men whirled to confront a man unknown to them: young, perhaps twenty-two years of age, with a scanty beard and a reddish glint to his thick black hair. "You don't recognize me, I suppose, Chal Fadhil. I was only a child when you left the Shagara tents. My name is Haffiz, son of Murrah, and I have come to warn you."

"Warn of what?" Azzad asked warily.

"May we speak of this in a place more private?"

They walked on in silence, to a side path leading to a rocky promontory overlooking the valley. It had been one of Jemilha's favorite sites since childhood; she had herself built the knee-high pebble castle, endearingly lopsided, next to a bench put there for her father and uncle. Azzad sat on the bench now, with a glance for the shadows sliding across the hills. Soon the nightly promise of Acuyib's Glory that was the sunset would paint the land in fabulous colors, intimations of the splendor that awaited the faithful after death. A few hundred feet below, clinging to the side of the mountains, was Sihabbah; below it was the estate still known as the House of al-Gallidh. All at once Azzad felt the threat to its peace deep in his bones, an ache like unto the pain Fadhil had finally admitted today. Fadhil stood behind him, watchful and silent, as Haffiz turned his back on the valley and faced them to tell his tale. He had recently journeyed to the coast, with hazziri for the zouqs in several towns there. In one place, he heard of a party of al-Ammarad merchants, also there for trade, and put himself by way of observing them.

"But if they were merchants," he said flatly, "I am the next Sheyqa of Rimmal Madar."

"Geysh Dushann?" Azzad asked.

Haffiz nodded. "The same. And with much time to spare before their assigned kill, or so I thought, for they were drinking like horses ridden hard for three days. I disguised myself, as you see—" He gestured to his hair. "—and pretended to be an Ammarad trader, long resident in this land. They drank, and I drank, but I was wearing this to protect me from drunkenness." He held up his left first finger, encircled by a silver ring set with an amethyst. "What I heard when we all stumbled back to their lodgings is what I will tell you now."

"Which is?" Fadhil prompted.

"Nizzira is sending an army. Five hundred of the Qoundi Ammar, supported by Acuyib only knows how many foot soldiers. Their orders are to lay waste to all that Azzad al-Ma'aliq possesses."

Azzad shrugged. "Nizzira cannot spare so many from Rimmal Madar and hope to keep the country in her palm. Her soldiers are her fingers, and the northern tribes will take advantage of her loosened hold."

"I know nothing of this," Haffiz replied. "I know only what I heard that night. The failure of the Geysh Dushann weighs heavily upon them—they are to meet this army when it comes ashore and guide it first to Hazganni and then here to Sihabbah. This is why they drank, to drown the voices of reproach in their heads for their failure to kill you all these many years. That night, they were angry. What they will do to the people of this land when they are both angry and sober does not bear considering."

"Is this possible, Azzad?" Fadhil asked quietly, his voice hushed in the deepening shadows. "You know this Sheyqa. Would she do this?"

Azzad rubbed his beard. "The Geysh Dushann have known nothing but failure, as Haffiz has said. Nizzira could be that desperate. If my agent in Dayira Azreyq knows what happened to the sheyqirs, then others must— and such a thing cannot go unavenged."

"As we have seen." Fadhil paced a few steps from behind the bench to the cliff's edge, then turned. "They have been preparing over these last months, then. Gathering themselves elsewhere. That is why there have been no attacks."

Azzad nodded his agreement with this estimation. "And this is what I feared, my friend, when Abb Shagara made my enemies his enemies so many years ago." And still Azzad had taken his vengeance, and still he gloried in it, and still he trusted to the Shagara to keep him and his safe. Had Jemilha been right after all?

No. Acuyib had allowed him to live, that horrible night long ago, and to know what had happened to the al-Ma'aliq. How could any man worthy of being called a man live out his life without exacting payment for such evil?

"You are not just 'any man,' Azzad," said his wife's voice in his mind.

Fadhil was pacing again, back and forth along the precipice. "The hazziri we once used against the invading barbarians—"

"—are old," Haffiz finished for him. "And the men they were made for are dead these hundred years and more."

Azzad clenched his fists. "I don't want the people of this land to suffer, Fadhil."

"A noble sentiment," said Haffiz. "And I am reminded that when I reported all this to Abb Shagara, he gave me things for you." From his sash he produced a fistful of gold, silver, and jewels: necklace, armbands, rings. The late sunlight glossed the finery in red-gold. "Not to replace the ones you wear now, but to add to their protections."

"Abb Shagara is generous and wise," Azzad said. He accepted the gifts, and had put on the two rings and one armband when Fadhil suddenly leaped toward him and snatched the necklace from his fingers.

"What is this?" he gasped. "Azzad, get rid of those—hurry!" His fingers scrabbled at the armband. "Haffiz, what have you done?"

"Righted a great wrong," said Haffiz—and in a movement too swift for eyes to follow in the dimness, he stabbed a long, dark, needle-thin knife into Azzad's arm.

Azzad grunted, more with surprise than pain. The knife slid from his flesh, leaving only a single drop of blood to stain his sleeve. Haffiz stood immobile, the knife shining clean now in his hand, watching as Fadhil emptied his satchel of medicines onto the ground.

"Traitor!" Fadhil spat, searching frantically through the chaos of vials and packets and small glass bottles.

"*You* are the traitor," Haffiz replied calmly. "You dishonored yourself and the Shagara by selling your heritage to this gharribeh. He so corrupted you that you used your healing skills to help him mutilate—"

"They were his enemies, and thus my enemies." Fadhil squinted at the label on a bottle, then discarded it for another. "Tell me what you used on him. Tell me!"

"No."

Azzad regarded all this with a frown. It was but a pinprick, not even painful.

And then he realized that it should have been painful.

"He deserves to die," Haffiz stated.

"For what reason?" Fadhil cried. He grabbed for a little silk pouch, opened it, ripped Azzad's sleeve, and sprinkled whitish powder on the wound. Azzad could not believe that any pinprick so tiny could kill him— but he also knew how skilled were the Shagara.

"He brought new ways," Haffiz said, as if that were the sum and substance of it. "With his horses for riding and his enemies that are nothing to do with us, he is as deadly as a disease. But he will die, and when I am known to be his killer, I will become Abb Shagara and lead our people back to the true path."

"How did Meryem fail to discover your madness?" Azzad asked, and his voice to his own hearing was as an echo coming up from the valley far below.

"Madness?" His words came from blackening shadow. "Is it madness to kill you before the army of Sheyqa Nizzira comes—so that with you already dead, the land and the people will not suffer?"

Fadhil had chosen a vial from the litter on the ground, and forced it to Azzad's lips. "Drink. Quickly."

He gulped, and coughed at the sour taste. Surely this could not be happening. Not to him. Not now. Not after all he had been through and all he had done—

"As for Challa Meryem—she knew nothing of my thoughts or my plans.

None of them did. More fools," he added with a shrug. "She and Challa Ley-liah will be the first to admit their errors and accept me as Abb Shagara, or they will be the first to die."

Fadhil sprang to his feet and cuffed him across the face.

Haffiz staggered, tripped over the Jemilha's little castle of pebbles, smashed it beneath his boot heel. He caught his balance, then coughed and spat out blood. "Another perversion. Would you sin against all Shagara by murdering a fellow Haddiyat?"

Azzad was not sure if the world was darkening because of the poisoned knife or the gathering dusk. But when his friend knelt before him and took both his hands, he knew. Even in the darkness he saw his own death in Fad-hil's tear-filled eyes. Numbness had spread up his arm to his shoulder, across his back, and would soon find both his head and his heart. It occurred to him that the Mualeef boy would be finishing his book rather sooner than either of them had expected. Ayia, an interesting ending to an interesting life.

But it was not yet over, and there were things he must say.

"Even if Haffiz is correct," Azzad said slowly, "and Nizzira's army spares the people, my wife and children will not be spared. See them safe, Fadhil. Please."

"I will do it. After I kill Haffiz."

"No. Do not break your ancient laws. He matters nothing." He heard Haffiz suck in a breath at this insult. He wondered briefly why Haffiz was content to stand and watch Azzad die, then decided he must truly be mad, to think that killing a single man would solve all his problems, fulfill all his dreams, make him Abb Shagara. Fadhil was safe from him; Shagara tradi-tion would not allow him to kill another Haddiyat.

"Azzad—" Fadhil's voice was cloudy with tears.

"Take Jemilha and the children away. Now. Tonight. Take all the horses. Leave—" His lips felt cold and stiff. "Leave only fire behind you. Especially the maqtabba. They must not know the names of those I employ in Rimmal Madar."

"It will be done, al-Ma'aliq. I will make all appear as if everyone died in the fire."

As his mother and sisters and aunts and cousins had died. Perhaps it would work. If Fadhil left talishann enough, the Qoundi Ammar would be-lieve. He tried to say this, but his mouth was reluctant to form words. It didn't matter, anyway; Fadhil would know what to do.

But there was more he must say. He struggled, purposely biting his tongue to feel pain, refusing to be frightened when the response was sluggish and muted, and managed, "Children—tell them—"

"I will, Azzad. I will tell them how much you love them."

A long while seemed to pass. He seemed to hear the shrieking of a hawk somewhere above the trees. He tasted blood, coppery-sweet, flooding away the bitter medicine, and then he could taste nothing at all.

Now, at the last: "Jemilha."

"Yes, Azzad. I will tell her."

Ayia, she was never "just any woman," my Jemilha, he thought, wishing he could smile. The numbness that had claimed his lips reached his heart, and then, through the gathering darkness, his eyes as he looked down at the tiny lights that marked his home, where his children were, and Jemilha. Fadhil would see them safe.

The army of Rimmal Madar invaded, plundering and burning, putting all to the sword. From the coast they marched inland, where the terrified city of Hazganni surrendered rather than be destroyed. When Sheyqir Za'aid, Nizzira's son and leader of the army, learned that the trees around the city were the trees of Azzad al-Ma'aliq, he ordered them hacked down. With the Qoundi Ammar to control the land with sword and ax and fear, he declared it part of the realm of Rimmal Madar.

Haffiz had not been alone in his disaffection; six young Shagara who thought as he did, and as secretly, had stolen into the house in Sihabbah. Haddiyat all, armed with hazziri to cancel those set by Fadhil—as those made by Haffiz had unworked those worn by Azzad—they slaughtered the family within and set the house afire. When Fadhil, mourning over Azzad's newly dead body up on the mountainside, looked down to see the blaze, he struck Haffiz a blow that sent him tumbling over the cliff to his death in the night shadows below.

Fadhil ran down to Sihabbah, and spent his body's strength in fighting the fire beside the people of the town. The house went up in flames, and the stables. The rest of Sihabbah was spared.

At dawn, by the embers' glow, Fadhil saw Azzad carried down from the mountainside by six grieving women. Yaminna had discovered the corpse; Feyrah and Sabbah had washed and shrouded him. He was buried beside the noble Khamsin. Of Jemilha and the children, there was nothing identifiable to bury.

As the last clods of earth fell, Fadhil raised his eyes from the grave to the pasture, and caught sight of a tall young boy on horseback. There was nothing that could lift the darkness from his heart, but sight of the boy was like a distant glimmer that might yet shine. Fadhil rose painfully to his feet and waited for the rider to approach. Together he and Alessid left Sihabbah.

— FERRHAN MUALEEF, *Deeds of Il-Kadiri*, 654

Il-Nazzari

631-698

Let me tell you of him.

Orphaned through treachery at the age of fourteen, taken to live with the Shagara who had repeatedly saved his father's life, it would be natural to assume that he would spend his life in obscurity, hiding from his enemies in the desert.

Instead, he became the ancestor of empresses.

By Acuyib, the Wonderful and Strange, that which follows is the truth.

—RAFFIQ MURAH, *Deeds of Il-Nazzari*, 701

11

A long and bitter journey it was from Sihabbah. Alessid spent much of it unable to see clearly for the tears that came to his eyes no matter how he fought them. Ayia, he was a man now and should be past childish weeping. But weep he did—though only at night, when Fadhil couldn't see him in the moondark wasteland.

They rested during the hottest part of each day and rode on at dusk, stopping at dawn to graze and water the horses. Of all that had belonged to the al-Ma'aliq in Sihabbah, only the horses were left—those, and Azzad's rings. Fadhil had shown them to Alessid, offered them silently in an outstretched palm. He shook his head sharply, refusing them.

He refused everything about his father now. He had to. Azzad al-Ma'aliq had been a fool—and Alessid knew that to be like him, to admire him, to love him still, would make of Azzad's son an even greater fool.

He had always adored his father. He had wanted to be just like Azzad al-Ma'aliq: tall and handsome, always smiling, beloved by his family, cherished by his friends. Alessid, during near-sleepless afternoons and long, star-hazed nights, examined the events of his own scant fourteen years of life and determined that from now on he would work very hard to be as different from his father as possible.

I am alive, he would tell himself when the tears blurred his vision. *I am alive, and everyone else is dead. My Ab'ya is dead, because he was a fool.*

Everyone knew the story of how Azzad had been dallying with a mistress in the city of Dayira Azreyq when the al-Ma'aliq were massacred. He had survived by the Grace of Acuyib, not through his own cunning. It had happened differently for Alessid.

It happened again and again in his memory as he rode to the Shagara camp. Again, and again, and again . . .

Mother was greatly annoyed when Father and Fadhil did not return for dinner. Later, after everyone had gone up to bed, Alessid was awakened by the sound of footsteps in the hall. Thinking that his father had at last returned, Alessid went to his door—about to open it and warn that Mother was very angry. Then he realized there were far too many footsteps, and a voice he didn't know said, "Two more boys, and the two girls. The infant will be with the woman. Pay heed to their hazziri—we don't know what Fadhil made for them."

Geysh Dushann—again. But how had they entered past the protections? And how did they know Fadhil's name? Alessid ran to his balcony, flung open the carved wooden screens, and shinnied down the flowery trellis to the ground. Moonlight shone on the garden and the pastures beyond—but brighter was the red glow from his parents' windows. Before he could do more than blink, the glass burst and fire gushed outward like Chaydann's gloating laughter from a fissure in the earth.

Alessid sprinted for the door of Uncle Bazir's maqtabba. Within, he coughed on smoke gushing down from the upper floor. His mother, brothers, sisters— where was Father? Had he and Fadhil returned? Did they burn, too, in the inferno overhead?

Alessid heard more footsteps, and peered from behind the maqtabba door. Six men clattered down the stairs a mere jump ahead of the hungry flames.

"Ayia, we shouldn't have been so merciful," grumbled one man, "to kill them and all their servants before the fire took them. The walls have been silenced. No one would have heard them scream."

Another man snorted. "More merciful than the Geysh Dushann would be— or the soldiers of Sheyqa Nizzira." He paused to cough smoke from his throat. "Hurry. We must set the rest afire before we meet Haffiz at the boundary stone."

"Did we get them all? The biggest boy was wearing no hazziri that I could see."

It was then that Alessid knew that Addad, son of his mother's favorite maidservant, his friend and playmate all the fourteen years of their lives, had been mistaken for him and had died in his place. Their rooms were not so far from each other, a circumstance that had allowed for much midnight mischief in the past. Knuckling his eyes, Alessid slipped out the back door and looked upward. The whole top floor was burning. The roof above his parents' chambers fell in with a horrific crash. And just as al-Ma'aliq had died nearly twenty years ago, so al-Ma'aliq died tonight.

Alessid could see moving shadows through silk curtains on the ground floor.

He dragged a heavy wooden bench over to the doors, blocking them. Only then did he see the runes drawn over Fadhil's subtle and beautiful patterns, like smears of spoor marking a trespassing animal's usurped territory.

He ran back to the garden doors and to barricade them toppled two of his father's prized potted orange trees. For the kitchen door, he used a bench and a pile of large wooden toys the younger children had left in the yard—Zellim's painted wagon, Azzifa's rocking horse, Meryem's doll-cart. At the front of the house, he put his shoulder to the stone pedestal and bronze basin where guests washed their hands before entering the house. None of these barriers would hold for long, but he didn't need much time.

He ran for the stables. Mazzud and Annif, who slept above, surely should have awakened by now. So, in fact, should the whole of Sihabbah. Silencing the walls was one thing; disguising the sudden blaze of flames and the acrid smell of smoke was quite another. Alessid recalled his father's tales of how empty the streets of Dayira Azreyq had been, how he had seen no one but the royal guard. There had been no spells then, but there was magic here tonight. The assassins were not Geysh Dushann, and not of the al-Ammarizzad—and they had scrawled Shagara symbols on the walls and doors. Perhaps other symbols had been drawn on other doors and windows tonight, and the people of Sihabbah would not know what had happened until the estate burned to the ground.

Alessid heard horses screaming. The fire would spread, and the horses knew it. He kicked open doors and flung open stalls, and they fled at the gallop. He yelled for Mazzud, for Annif, for anyone at all. There was no reply. Last of all he freed his beloved Zaqia, pausing to bridle her before leaping up onto her back. He tried to rein her around into the streets of Sihabbah, thinking to alert the town to the danger. But she was having none of it; she reared once, whinnied, and her iron shoes struck sparks from the stable yard cobbles in her flight.

She finally slowed, responding at last to his hands and heels, in a forest clearing miles from Sihabbah. She had found others of the al-Ma'aliq herd—in their terror, they had jumped fences previously judged too high for them. Alessid spent a long time gathering strays, usually with only a few sharp whistles that alerted them to his presence. They seemed relieved to find him, and their stablemates, and by daybreak Alessid had rounded up almost sixty horses.

He had watched, hidden in the trees, as solemn women carried his father's body down from the mountain. He had seen Fadhil weeping as the grave was dug. He had been near to tears himself when Fadhil embraced him with cries of praise to Acuyib for sparing this one last al-Ma'aliq. The scenes played over and over in his memory as he rode farther and farther from Si-habbah. And Alessid ended each repeat of that terrible night with a curse and a vow. He would have vengeance—but not the pale imitation of it his father had exacted. Azzad had only hurt al-Ma'aliq enemies. Alessid would destroy them.

In the months that followed, Alessid became one of the Shagara; but for the darkness of his skin, so unlike their burnished golden complexions, no one would guess that he was not a true son of the tribe. A precocious adolescent, he came to emotional manhood without ever passing through youth. A year after losing his family, his body was just fifteen years old, his face had no beard, and his shoulders had not yet broadened. But the eyes that gazed unflinchingly at the world were those of a man grown, and grown older than the count of his birthdays.

Alessid knew all this about himself. With the example of a charming, thoughtless, carefree fool of a father behind him, a man who would not even have known how to analyze his own character—and would have seen no use for such analysis—Alessid ruthlessly subjected himself to scrutiny. Every motive, every emotion, every action and reaction, all were examined for signs of likeness to his father. And at fifteen, he was satisfied that there was nothing of Azzad al-Ma'aliq in him.

He knew that he had sacrificed charm along with self-ignorance. Smiles had departed when he rejected humor. The characteristics he despised in his father were the very same that had made Azzad capable of winning hearts. Even so, Alessid was sufficiently attractive to have won the most eligible girl in the Shagara tents: Mirzah, daughter of Challa Leyliah and her husband Razhid Harirri. And now that they were both fifteen, they were to be married.

Abb Shagara would preside over the ceremony. It would in all probability be his last official act. Though not yet forty, he looked and moved like a man twice that age. His chosen successor, who spent most of his time trying to hide his eagerness for authority, was a young man proud of his full black beard and abundant black hair, prouder still of his position in the tribe, and proudest of all of the name the Shagara had gained as breeders of horses. Alessid considered him a fool. But Alessid considered almost everyone a fool.

The exceptions were Chal Fadhil, Challa Meryem, Challa Leyliah, her husband Razhid Harirri, and their daughter, Alessid's bride. Yet even the three healers had not his total respect, for they remembered his father with affection and sadness, and spoke of him often. Alessid thought of him only with contempt, and talked about him not at all.

The other exception was Abb Shagara. When it was learned that the al-Ma'aliq had been murdered by apostate Shagara, everyone else cried out in horror. Grimly silent, Abb Shagara stared long and hard at Fadhil, then went to the private tent where he did his work. Two days later he emerged, exhausted by his labors—for though he was not yet forty, he had not been young for many years—and ordered every close friend and near relation of the renegades brought before him. To each of these people in turn he gave a weighty silver bowl, newly made, studded with lapis. And then he asked his questions.

Did you know of their plans?
Did you help them in any way?
Are there others who believe as they believe?
What are their names?

In this manner he discovered twelve who knew, four others who helped their friends without knowing what their friends were truly doing, and the names of six Shagara not present at the inquiry who secretly supported the rebels.

Alessid watched it all, part of him believing in Abb Shagara's method, part of him howling that Fadhil's hazziri had not saved his family, and still a third part knowing that it was no fault of Fadhil's, for the renegade Haddiyat had obliterated his work with their own. As the questions were asked, he sensed Meryem observe him closely, probably expecting rage or tears or cries of hatred or some other emotional display; he kept his feelings to himself, as his father had never bothered to do, and stood in silence at Fadhil's side. Meryem could worry about him as she pleased. As Challi Dawa'an, that was her function in life. His was to wait until he was older.

That same evening he was summoned to Abb Shagara's tent.

"Alessid. Take this." Fadhil gave him the silver bowl.

Abb Shagara, reclining on cushions, regarded Alessid narrowly. "Lie to me, boy. How old are you?"

He started to say "*Thirty-nine.*" What came out of his mouth was, "Fourteen."

"Does Khamsin still live?"

He tried to say "*Yes.*" What he said was, "No."

Abb Shagara poured from a pitcher of hot, sweet qawah. His fingers were shaking a little, and his face was haggard with weariness. "Alessid, do you believe that this hazzir can pry the truth out of even those most determined to tell lies?"

This time he didn't bother to attempt a lie. "Yes."

Fadhil took the bowl from his hands, and bowed to Abb Shagara.

"The guilty will be executed," said Abb Shagara. "Haddiyat or no, they deserve death for what they have helped to do. Those who assisted but did not understand will be watched by special hazziri until their loyalty is no longer in doubt. Does this satisfy you?"

"Yes," Alessid replied. But it was as well that the bowl was no longer in his hands, for what he was thinking was, "*No.*"

The reason his father had been a fool was that he had allowed himself to be distracted from the true work of his life by the pleasures life could offer. These had been given him in abundance: family, friends, wealth, influence. Jemilha el-Gallidh had given him children and the power that came with land and money. His time with the Shagara had given him an invaluable asset in friends—and their magic. But Azzad had stumbled blindly into all of them, as if the most potent hazzir for luck ever made had rested against his skin from birth.

Alessid saw the world very differently: not as a marvelous place in which one might discover unexpected joy at any moment, but as a place filled with things and people to be used.

Children were meant for marriage alliances. Wealth's power was meant to be hoarded until it would be spent most effectively. And brotherhood with the Shagara meant access to their magic, which was the greatest power of all.

Thus Alessid would marry Mirzah Shagara. They would have many daughters, who would marry men of strength and authority; they would also have many sons, who would bring kinship with important tribes. One of these sons might be Haddiyat—possibly even becoming Abb Shagara in time—and Alessid hoped this would be so. What such sons did not produce in grandchildren would be more than compensated for by their magic.

On the night of his wedding, he dressed in a new white wool robe and donned the two rings that would be his only jewelry until Abb Shagara placed the marriage hazziri on his wrists, he did not think as any other young man would about the night to come. He did not think of his bride's sweet young body, or the wealth of her soft black hair, or the best ways to please her. He thought about the results of this night, or a night in the near future, and wondered if he would sire a son first or a daughter.

His father's ring, the only keepsake of the al-Ma'aliq he possessed, glinted from his right hand. From his left glowed Bazir al-Gallidh's pearl, given by that noble man to Azzad and taken, like the topaz carved with a leaf, from his dead hand by Fadhil. Both had since become hazziri through the efforts of Fadhil. The pearl gave health, purity, and wisdom; the topaz was for wealth, long life, and fame. Alessid intended to make specific use of his health, wealth, and long life. Fame would come as it would; he cared nothing for it, except as it would provide confirmation of his destiny. Of wisdom he had no need. He was already wise enough at fifteen to reject his father's example—no, to set his father up before him as an example of how *not* to live his life. As for purity—pure was the purpose of his life's journey, and marrying Mirzah Shagara was its first step.

For the al-Ma'aliq, he would take final revenge on Sheyqa Nizzira.

For himself, he would take back what was his.

And he would take the Shagara and their magic with him.

On the night of his wedding, Alessid waited calmly inside his tent until dusk. At length Razhid Harirri shoved aside the tent flap. Alessid glanced up quickly from the book in his hands. The ceremony had begun.

Mirzah's father was dressed in a black robe and headcloth and carried a long knife in each hand. These blades he pointed threateningly at Alessid, who pushed past him out into the dusk. A dozen other men in dark clothes were there, also armed. After a few moments of turning this way and that, seeking a way out, Alessid capitulated. Mirzah's eldest brother, another Fadhil, tied his hands before him, and Razhid forced him to walk forward at the points of both knives at his back. A crowd of women assembled quickly—whistling, stamping their feet, and calling out ribald remarks on Alessid's youth, looks, and probable sexual prowess. He forbade himself to blush.

When they reached a newly made tent, woven of sand-pale wool and decorated with gifts of hazziri, Abb Shagara emerged from it, wearing a robe of embroidered golden silk.

"Who is this man?" he demanded.

Razhid replied, "He is called Alessid, from the tribe al-Ma'aliq. I think he will do for my daughter."

"For what reason?"

"He is a Believer in Acuyib's Glory. He is of an age with Mirzah. He is strong. He is rich in horses, though not in sheep or goats."

"*You* may think he will do for your daughter," scoffed Abb Shagara, "but what does her mother think?"

Leyliah came out of the tent, arrayed in all her finery—including a white silk scarf embroidered with snowflakes. She took a torch held out to her by Meryem and made a great show of inspecting the captive. "He seems acceptable," she said at last, and winked at Alessid.

"Will he please your daughter?"

"If he doesn't, I will have his head on a brass plate with his skewered balls for garnish," growled Razhid, expertly flourishing both knives.

The crowd applauded with whistles and more laughter. Abb Shagara held up a hand, and they settled down, anticipating the next act in this little drama.

"Bring your daughter," he ordered, and Leyliah clapped her hands twice, and Mirzah came forth. "Do you accept this man?"

Alessid, who had gone along with the absurd ritual so far out of respect for the Shagara, forgot his own part entirely when he saw his bride. Mirzah was a small girl, lightly made, with a pure golden skin and her father's subtle, heavy-lidded eyes. To Alessid, she had never looked older than twelve. But tonight her mother had dressed her in amber-colored silk embroidered in gold, and enough jewels to purchase the finest seaside mansion and all its lands besides. Covering her was a gigantic silver scarf, a transparent silken glimmer that covered her from head to knees, as if she walked within a cloud. Suddenly Alessid was minded of the *Lessons of Acuyib* about the essential mystery of Woman, veiled to Man until the moment of their joining. And that moment was suddenly too far off for his liking.

Someone in the crowd hooted, and everyone else laughed, and Alessid knew his reaction to her was on his face. Disturbed, bewildered, he told himself this was just Mirzah, familiar and, if not precisely beloved, then at least dear to him for the children they would have. He regained control of his expression and told himself he was a man, and it was only proper that a man look with desire on the wife he would sleep beside all the rest of his nights.

But he could not deny his sudden eagerness for this first night to begin, and not only because a son might come of it.

"Ayia, daughter," Razhid said, "I've brought you a husband. Look him over, and tell me if he is to your taste."

Advice both practical and indelicate was shouted from all around as Mirzah inspected him from behind the sheer silvery veil. He hoped he had never done anything to offend her—because she could legitimately retaliate now by telling her father she wanted to see Alessid stripped naked. And this was precisely what the women of the tribe were encouraging her to do.

The ceremony of taking a husband was a relic of a long ago time when Shagara fathers raided other tribes, brought the men to their daughters, and asked if they would suit. If a man was rejected, he was sent around to other tents where any unwed girl could claim him if she wished. If there were no takers at all, he was given food, water, and directions back to his own tribe's camp. Razhid Harirri had been famously wed to Leyliah in this manner—after choosing him, she had arranged for Abb Shagara to take him to every other woman in the tribe before finally coming to her tent, and then she pretended great reluctance in accepting him. He had entered into the teasing with zest, making a great show of pleading with each girl to take him as her husband, "For surely the last unwed girl Abb Shagara offers me to will be the ugliest, stupidest, least desirable of all!" Razhid and his wife shared a sense of humor that to Alessid was utterly incomprehensible. And as he stood there while Mirzah walked slowly around him, he was afraid that their daughter might similarly indulge herself.

There was a completely different ritual when Shagara married Shagara. Fadhil had argued for Alessid's right to this—an infinitely more dignified process—but Abb Shagara had sulked and complained that they hadn't had a real abduction marriage all year and *he* wanted to have some fun.

Mirzah seemed determined to provide him with it. As the women yelled demands to strip Alessid ("Make sure exactly what you're getting, girl!"), she circled him slowly, drawing out the moment. He stood frozen, a muscle in his jaw twitching, and flinched when a trailing edge of her scarf brushed his hand.

At last she stood in front of him, looking up at him through silver silk, and smiled just a little before turning to Abb Shagara. "I suppose he will do."

There were groans of disappointment and cheers of approval, and Abb Shagara waited them out before saying, "Then the man Alessid of the tribe al-Ma'aliq is accepted by Mirzah Shagara as husband. He shall live in her tent, and father her children, and become our brother. Do you agree to this, my people?"

None but shouts of approval now, and Alessid felt a soft, stirring warmth inside him. Something deep, and profound, and more exciting even than Mirzah's tantalizing glance at him from beneath her silvery veil. These people were his people now. They accepted him for his father's sake, yes, but now, after this year with them, also for his own.

Abb Shagara gestured, and Alessid remembered that now he was supposed to lift his bound hands. As he did so, Abb Shagara said, "Alessid al-Ma'aliq, you may choose to accept this marriage freely, and take the Shagara as your own tribe. Or you may resist, and be forced to wear hazziri to bind you to her and to us. Whichever you choose, never doubt that you are well and truly married to this girl, and the only means of separation is a divorce of her choosing, not yours. Shall you be free, or bound?"

"Free. I accept the Shagara as my own tribe, and Mirzah as my wife."

Abb Shagara untied his hands and replaced the ropes with armbands of his own crafting—one gold, one silver, both set with gems and carved with runes. Then he lifted the scarf from Mirzah's face, and once more Alessid was astonished by his reaction to this familiar girl. She had never been pretty before. She had never looked so happy before. Was it truly because she was marrying him? Women were a mystery, indeed.

Abb Shagara arranged the scarf across her shoulders, leaving her shining black hair uncovered, and fastened about her neck a gold hazzir on a short chain, also made by him. The he stood back, and gestured with both hands.

"Mirzah, here is your husband. Alessid, here is your wife. Acuyib be praised!" As the cheering swelled, he turned to Alessid and complained, "You could have put up a bit more fuss, you know. I was looking forward to some resistance. It's much more fun that way."

"Why should I resist what I have wanted this year and more?" Alessid asked, and took Mirzah's hand. *And wanting it more every moment*, he thought, and hoped his eyes were telling her so.

That night, very late, after the feasting and dancing and singing had quieted somewhat, he again took his bride's hand and led her to her new tent. Outside were wind chimes that rang sweetly in the cool wind: for happiness, for love, for many children. Inside were bright cushions, beautiful rugs, and an iron brazier for warmth in the winter night.

Mirzah removed her veil in a swirl of silk, and folded it carefully away in a small wooden chest. She stripped off the belt, rings, earrings, bracelets, necklaces, and hairpins that were the collected finery of all her unwed friends, and sorted them by owner for return in the morning. It was considered a good omen to lend jewelry to a bride, in the belief that her happiness rubbed off.

At last she stood before him in the dim glow of the coals, slim as a flame in her loosened amber dress, the hazzir glinting in the hollow of her throat.

"Ayia, husband?"

He looked her up and down, much as she had done to him—but without any sense of teasing her. Abruptly uneasy, he asked, "Would you have taken me if I had been stolen by your father from another tribe?"

"Oh, yes." A tiny smile quirked her full, soft lips. "But I would have asked to see you naked first." She untied the ribbons at her neck. "I would ask now, but virgin men are notoriously shy."

"And Shagara women are notoriously bold." He froze. "Who says I am virgin?"

"I do. And so does Fadhil."

He mentally cursed his father's old friend. But in mid-invective he was struck by a horrible thought. "Are you—your father told me you had never—"

"He did not lie, Alessid. My father never lies." Suddenly he saw that her fingers were trembling. "I could have, when I was fourteen. But then you came to us, and I decided that each of my children will not be only Shagara—though that is enough pride in itself—they will also be al-Ma'aliq, descended of powerful sheyqirs."

So he would be her first, as she would be his. He had a momentary twinge of nerves. What if he couldn't please her? In the next instant he relaxed, for if she was as inexperienced as he, she'd never know the difference.

Because of him, because she wanted her children to be al-Ma'aliq, she had refused to bear a child to prove she could do so, and perhaps provide a Haddiyat for the Shagara as well. He drew himself up proudly, knowing she valued him more than her own traditions.

But what if she were barren? What if she could not give him the sons and daughters he required? They could not divorce except by her declaration—and the onus would be on him, not her. That was how it was done with the Shagara; a woman who did not conceive within three years of marriage divorced her husband for infertility and married someone else. It held even for women of other tribes who wed Shagara men. What if—

There was only one way to find out.

At least she was as ambitious for their children as he was. They would make fine babies together, Shagara sons and daughters descended from shey-qirs. He had to believe that. He had to convince himself that she—

"Alessid," said Mirzah, "I know that you are often away elsewhere, even when you are standing before me. I don't mind it, not usually. But I do mind it very much when I am standing before you like *this*."

He looked, and saw. Abruptly—urgently—he wanted to find out if he and she could make babies together.

But within a few scant minutes, he forgot about babies completely.

"Good! Excellent! Now sweep to the left—the left, Hassam!—and attack!"

Alessid watched his "cavalry" maneuver their horses across the plain. They were far in advance of the main caravan of Shagara, on their way to the winter encampment. For more than a year, since before his marriage, Alessid had been drilling more and more youths his own age and slightly older in the techniques of armed, mounted warfare. This was all a secret from their elders.

In this generation, one of the marks of full manhood had become the acquisition of one's own horse. Alessid had come to the Shagara with his own mare, Zaqia, and fifty-six more horses besides; by the standards of the Shagara, he was insanely wealthy. Eventually he would be the one gifting young men with horses, and their loyalty would be to him.

Azzad al-Ma'aliq had always gelded the colts marked for sale. He warned buyers of fillies that as strong as they looked, they were too delicate to be bred to the native studs. *"Try it, and you'll end with a dead foal that has killed its mother."* Three times it had happened, and that had been enough to convince people that the al-Ma'aliq mares must not be bred. And so Azzad had kept total control of the supply.

Alessid had to admit that his father had been clever in this, at least. The Shagara and the Harirri were clever, too, following the same policy. The descendants of Khamsin and the Geysh Dushann stallions were kept separate from the huge draft horses, trained differently, and doled out to boys when they became men.

Now, as Alessid watched his troop sweep down on an imaginary foe, he stroked Zaqia's sleek neck and smiled. They knew the basics. Soon he would teach them more complex tactics. And their horses, trained for riding, would be trained for war.

"Alessid! Alessid!"

He turned in his saddle, scowling at the sight of a lone rider galloping toward him. A quick whistle broke the lines of cavalry into chaos that would disguise their maneuvers as a game of yaqbout—he only hoped someone would be quick about putting into play the stitched sheep bladder that served as a ball. Fortunately, the man riding toward him was not the observant sort regarding anything but medicine.

"Your wife has birthed the child!" shouted Nassayr.

Alessid gripped his saddle. Fadhil, Meryem, Leyliah—all had said Mirzah's time was another month distant. "She lives?"

"Of course—Chal Fadhil is with her. And the baby is fine—a strong son!"

"Acuyib be praised," he whispered, then heeled Zaqia around and galloped the four miles back to the main caravan.

Fadhil was just emerging from Leyliah's wagon. Alessid leaped down from Zaqia to embrace him. "Fadhil! I have a son!"

"Yes, and a second time yes." The healer grinned wearily. "Nassayr raced away to tell you before he knew there was more to tell. *Twin* sons, Alessid. A very good omen. Come and see."

Mirzah lay on piled rugs, her mother kneeling beside her. Leyliah smiled and held up two babies, one cradled in each arm.

"Beautiful," Alessid said, looking at his wife.

"Now I know why I could get no sleep," she replied with a sigh. "When one stopped kicking, the other started!"

"Have you named them yet?"

"Kemmal and Kammil," she replied. "'Beautiful' and 'perfect,' because that's exactly what they are. I hope you approve," she added—for courtesy, because the naming of a child was the mother's prerogative. He had wanted something a little more powerful, but was well-pleased with her choices. At least Mirzah had not followed her mother's suggestion; at least she had not named a son for Azzad.

"They're very fine names for very fine boys." He knelt down to inspect his sons, taking one into his arms. "Which one is this?"

"Kammil," said Leyliah. "You can tell by the white yarn around his wrist. We put yellow on Kemmal."

Staring first at one and then the other, he appreciated Leyliah's wisdom. The boys were as alike as two ears on a horse. All at once he began to laugh. The al-Ma'aliq dynasty had begun.

When he became a father for the first—and second—time, Alessid was ten moons older and two inches taller than when he married. He was eighteen when Mirzah bore Addad, and over the next eight years came Ra'abi, Jemilha, and Za'arifa.

When Kemmal and Kammil were fifteen years old, they were importantly married, one to a girl of the Harirri, the other to a girl of the Tallib. Two years later, Addad married Ka'arli, "Black Rose" of the Azwadh tribe and prize of her generation. With personal ties to the three most powerful tribes in the land, and the Shagara as his own kin, in the early spring of 649 Alessid received the sign from Acuyib for which he had been waiting for nineteen long, busy years.

— RAFFIQ MURAH, *Deeds of Il-Nazzari*, 701

12

Alessid had been expecting the summons to Abb Shagara's tent. Creating the impression that he was not expecting it, however, took some doing.

The normal course of his day was to rise at dawn, start the fire outside in the stone pit and set the water on to boil, then wake his wife. They shared a large mug of qawah together—outside, if the weather was fine, to watch the sunrise gild the desert and spark white off distant snow-covered mountains—then woke the children for the morning meal. After this, he went to greet his wife's parents, and he and Razhid tended and trained horses until noon. Another meal at his wife's tent, a brief rest, an hour spent listening to the children's lessons, and he was back with the horses until dusk. It was a calm, rational, productive, well-ordered life, and very little ever happened to disturb it—or the self-discipline with which he conducted it.

But today would be different. Today he must be readily available while appearing to be vitally busy. He lingered inside the tent until Mirzah chased him out. Rather than leave the vicinity, he spent a great deal of time inspecting the sand-colored wool for imaginary worn spots. He hauled out his best saddle and polished the silver hazziri, then did the same with the bridle. He scrubbed iron grills and pot hangers, cleaned ash from the firepit, and was in the middle of rebuilding the entire circle of stones when at last Abb Shagara's fourteen-year-old nephew came to him.

"Alessid," said Jefar, "if you have time, Abb Shagara asks for your presence in his tent. If you have time," he repeated diffidently.

Alessid was well aware that the new Abb Shagara had not phrased it that way. If anything, it had been a direct order—*"Bring Alessid to me instantly."* How he regretted the death of Meryem's wise and whimsical son. But the successor was the one he must deal with, and a haughtier man he could not imagine. Jefar, however, was a polite boy, deferential to his elders, and in awe of Alessid's horses, so on his lips brusque command became respectful request.

Quite deliberately, Alessid took his time. He washed his hands and face, donned a fresh robe, and told his eldest daughter that he might or might not be back for the noon meal. Ra'abi, twelve years old and in charge of her sisters when her mother was otherwise busy, looked up at him through long black lashes.

"Will you come hear our lessons? Jemilha and I have learned a new song."

"I wish very much to hear it, but I cannot promise to return in time. Why don't you sing it for Grandfather Razhid?"

"Because we want to sing for *you!*"

Alessid cleared his throat. Ra'abi was the most imperious of his girls, fretful for the day when she would rule her own tent. "I will try," he said. "Ayia, I cannot keep Abb Shagara waiting."

"You've washed and dressed, and that takes time, so you can't be in that much of a hurry—"

"Ra'abi, enough."

He was the only one who could quell her. She bent her head submissively—though her small fists clenched at her sides. "Yes, Ab'ya."

Alessid walked with Jefar through the encampment. Since last night, when Abb Harirri and Abb Azwadh had arrived with a dozen each of their strongest young men, the usual calm efficiency of the Shagara had been disturbed. Not by much; nothing much ever agitated the composure of these people, a thing Alessid found comforting. Perhaps it was the timelessness of the desert wastes around them that produced such peace. Or perhaps the word was *balance*—between the eternal dry wilderness and the undying hidden spring, between the winds that in winter lashed storms of cold rain and in summer stinging sand. This balance was not the precarious one he would have imagined. There was a space in which the Shagara and other wandering tribes existed, a space as unchanging as the land. They knew its dimensions, its dangers, every plant that could heal or kill, all the signs and signals of scents on the wind and colors in the evening sky. They altered nothing about its qualities and rhythms, knowing how to live with it and within it. And, Alessid reflected, when one did not worry about having to change the land every year to grow crops, and when one knew precisely what must be done to survive and even to thrive, the orderly round of life took on a tranquility of purpose. It was not a gentle serenity—life here was harsh and demanding—but the Shagara did not contend with the land. They were part of it, and to battle against it would be like battling themselves.

But the presence of Abb Harirri and Abb Azwadh had caused a stir. Alessid knew from the rumors brought to him by his wife that there was a battle coming, and as he entered Abb Shagara's tent and bowed, he hid his eagerness for the day.

Abb Harirri was the father of Mirzah's father Razhid; Abb Azwadh was the great-uncle of Alessid's son Addad's wife. Both men were in their vigorous sixties, lean and tough, their full beards only slightly grayed. They were men accustomed to command, not entreaty. Alessid greeted them as the kinsmen they were to him, and at Abb Shagara's gesture sat on a pile of carpets. He was never remiss in his respects toward the man; besides, he knew he could afford to be generous. He was well aware why the Harirri and Azwadh Fathers were here.

Young Jefar poured qawah for them all, handed round a small silver plate of delicacies, and retired to a corner of the tent. Although Abb Shagara's servitor was supposed to become invisible, with downcast eyes and deaf ears, Jefar was as alert as a stallion scenting new mares.

"Your wife is well, and all your children?" Abb Harirri asked politely.

"I thank you, yes," Alessid replied. "We hope for a son next year, to name Razhid for his grandfather." He turned to Abb Azwadh. "I hope that my son Addad causes happiness in the tent of the beauteous Black Rose."

"Ka'arli is with child, which is a great happiness for us all," Abb Azwadh said, but his smile was fleeting. He had more important matters on his mind.

Alessid, on the other hand, was completely delighted by the news. He showed it only with a slow nod, for it would be unseemly to gloat over this new link to the mighty Azwadh.

"And your horses?" Abb Azwadh went on. "All goes well with them?"

It was the next round in the usual courtesies—but Alessid knew this was not mere civility but the beginning of serious discussion. "Forty-two foals this year," he reported, "and thirty-eight now in training."

"And those fully educated but not yet claimed?"

"Twenty-six." There were in fact twenty-seven, but one of them was already privately bespoken by Jefar's father. From the corner of his eye he saw the boy's head jerk up, a blaze of joyous speculation in his dark eyes. An instant later he had resumed his self-effacing stance. Alessid was not surprised by his insight; Jefar was a clever, likable youth, and it was a pity Ra'abi was as yet too young to be considering him as a husband.

"Ayia," sighed Abb Harirri, "let us pace no more around the water hole, but slake our thirst. Alessid, the Harirri and the Azwadh would like to purchase as many horses as you can spare. You know that the tribes have moved to certain lands each season since time began. The Harirri winter lands are within two days of Hazganni. Closer than we are comfortable with, but there it is. Yet Sheyqir Za'aid al-Ammarizzad contends that we are too near, and—"

"There have been raids, and deaths," interrupted Abb Azwadh. "Our own winter camp is much farther from Hazganni, and yet our tents too have been burned and our people killed." He paused, and his mouth vanished between his beard and mustache as he bit both lips hard together.

"There will be vengeance, Abb Azwadh." Alessid spoke quietly.

"This is why we need your horses," said Abb Harirri. "Riders on the swiftest of them can stand guard, and come to warn us of impending raids. When we move camp, they can range out to patrol the trails ahead, and—"

"—and keep those cursed Qoundi Ammar from attacking our wagons!" Abb Azwadh exclaimed. "This happened to the Tallib while traveling to their winter camp—seventeen killed, five wagons destroyed—"

"Your son and his wife are safe, Alessid," Abb Harirri interposed smoothly. "In fact, I am told that Kammil led a group of young men on horseback to drive the raiders off."

Alessid nodded his gratitude for the reassurance, but what he was thinking was that Kammil had done exactly what Alessid needed him to do, as if they'd planned it together. A clever boy. "The raiders wanted to stop the Tallib where they were, so that they would go no farther?"

"That is the opinion of Abb Tallib. Otherwise, everyone would have been killed. Being the stubborn man he is, he buried his dead and continued on. But there have been no more raids. Kammil organized twenty young men of the tribe as sentries—"

"—which is where we got the idea to do the same," finished Abb Azwadh.

Better and better, thought Alessid, and sipped qawah.

Abb Shagara then spoke for the first time since Alessid had entered his tent. "I have told my fellow Fathers that as far as I am concerned, they may have these horses—and hazziri to go with them. We Shagara live far from any contact with the Qoundi Ammar. But just as we gave hazziri to the people along the coast to aid their fight against the northern barbarians long ago, so we must provide horses to the Harirri and Azwadh."

Careful to keep his voice very soft, Alessid asked, "And allow them to do our fighting for us against Sheyqir Za'aid?"

Abb Shagara stiffened.

"We can do more than post sentries to warn of attack."

"Ayia?" Abb Harirri leaned forward on his pile of carpets. "More?"

"Yes. More and better. We can do better than merely defending our people and lands."

Abb Azwadh set down his qawah and clenched both hands into fists.

Alessid had known since last night that the time was now. He knew what he would say and how he would say it—but to have the moment fluttering in his palm like a captured bird caused his heart to race and his breath to quicken. He paused, calmed himself, and began to speak.

"For too long this seventeenth son of Sheyqa Nizzira has lolled in Hazganni, claiming to rule while in truth he tyrannizes. He has taken village after village, town after town, with all their fields and pastures and riches, and nothing is ever enough. He demands taxes, with which he decorates more palaces in more gold and gems. Now he encroaches on the desert—not because he knows how to live here, or because his limited mind perceives anything of value here, but because the Harirri and the Azwadh and the Tabbor and the Tariq and the Tallib and the Shagara do not pay his taxes and bend their heads in the dust to him. I say that we of the Za'aba Izim never will pay either money or respect. I say his soldiers have taken for him all they are going to take. And I say further that it is time to take back what is ours."

He had them now, and he knew it. The idea that had come to him when he was but fourteen years old, during the long ride with Fadhil to the Shagara camp, had finally been expressed. It rested contented in his palm now, wings folded, and even sang to him, and he begged Acuyib for the words that would make its music sweet and powerful in the ears of these powerful men.

He looked at their eyes, and saw resistance only in the darkly narrowed gaze of Abb Shagara. But the others—they were hearing the song. And so he risked the other idea, an even sweeter one.

"And when I say 'ours,' I mean all the people of this region." Alessid saw their brows arch. They were not quite ready for this, not yet, but the timing was too propitious. "Abb Azwadh, your brother lives on the coast, watching over your trade. His wife comes from Hazganni. Abb Harirri, your mother's brother took a wife from Beit Za'ara, and one of their sons lives in Bayyid Qarhia. I was born in Sihabbah, where people still remember my family. We all have kin and friends in all parts of this land. They are like streams of blood that flow among all the villages and towns and camps. Sheyqir Za'aid has polluted many of these streams and filled many others in with sand. I say that it is time to purify."

Jefar had completely forgotten the restraint imposed by service to Abb Shagara. He was staring at Alessid with fire in his eyes and in his cheeks, and not even a scathing glance from his uncle could quench him.

"When I was a young boy," he went on, "I had an interest in growing things. I collected plants from the wide corners of this land, watching as they grew, discovering their properties. A thing I noticed is that it took very little effort to make them thrive. They knew their native soil—"

"Your father, I am told," observed Abb Harirri, "planted whole forests."

Alessid nodded, and for once in his life was pleased to acknowledge the man who had sired him. "He did, and it was wisely done. And it proves my point. Trees brought from Sihabbah grew happily in many places where such trees had not been known before . . . until the al-Ammarizzad destroyed them. They and their kind are *not* in their native soil. I say it is time to uproot them. And further, I say it is time to unite all tribes in a single purpose: the obliteration of the al-Ammarizzad from our country."

"For *your* vengeance," snapped Abb Shagara, no longer bothering to hide his scorn. "What was done to your family—"

"—was done by apostate Shagara," Alessid reminded him. "And yet— what drove them to it? They thought that by murdering the al-Ma'aliq, Sheyqir Za'aid would leave off his planned attack. They were wrong. It was thought that with control of Hazganni and a few other towns, Sheyqir Za'aid would leave off his conquests. This also was wrong. It has taken him nineteen years, but now he threatens even the desert. Anyone who thinks that the al-Ammarizzad will stop after a few tents and wagons have burned will be not just wrong, but dead."

Abb Azwadh stroked his gray-streaked beard. "Abb Shagara has mentioned that when the northern barbarians invaded a hundred and fifty years ago, the Shagara made hazziri for those who fought. Would it be possible—?"

"With respect," Alessid said, "it is not only hazziri we require. We must fight, and there is only one way to do it."

"On *their* terms—on horseback!" exclaimed Jefar from his corner.

"Out!" snarled his uncle. The boy fled the tent, and Abb Shagara continued, "What you are saying is abominable! I am as proud of the Shagara horses as any of us, and I know of at least a dozen hazziri that will protect in battle—but what you propose is—"

"—to cast out the usurper," Alessid interrupted, "and make of this land one nation, so no one can ever again do to us what the northern *or* the eastern barbarians have done."

"It would take time to organize a fighting force," mused Abb Harirri.

"Only as long as it takes for your young men to come here and be instructed." Alessid relished the way they all stared at him. "Come. I will show you."

He was further impressed by Jefar when he discovered that the boy had summoned as many members of the cavalry as he could find. Thirty-eight were already saddling their horses, and twenty-six more were hurrying to do the same. Jefar had taken it on himself to saddle Alessid's own Qishtan, only son of his much-mourned Zaqia. Alessid mounted, nodded his thanks to the boy, and gathered his troops. Desperately excited, ferociously proud that now the long, strict secrecy was ending, they responded with gratitude to his orders.

First, the smartly executed exercises in controlling their horses to behave as a single unit. Then the individual skills, showing the agility of horse and rider—and what a pair of hooves could do when they lashed out at an enemy, represented by bales of fodder. Finally, twenty men staged an assault against forty-four, and when the dust settled it was seen to be a victory for the smaller group.

By the time it was over, everyone in the Shagara camp and everyone who had come with Abb Harirri and Abb Azwadh had gathered to watch. When Alessid's horsemen came galloping back to the outskirts of the tents, the cheers were as loud as the thunder of hooves.

He had expected it, of course—so spectacular a display could not but produce delighted pride in his people. But he had not expected his own name to be chanted to the skies so even Acuyib must hear.

"All-ess-*eed!*"

As his father Azzad had been spared in Dayira Azreyq nearly forty years ago, so there was a reason Alessid lived when all his family had died. Azzad had failed in Acuyib's purpose. Alessid would not. He had these people with him, truly *with* him, praising his foresight and shouting his name.

"All-ess-*eed!*"

And there was nothing Abb Shagara could do about it. As Alessid led his cavalry into the small city of tents, Abb Shagara stood beside an awning, forgotten and furious. All other faces were elated: Abb Harirri and Abb Azwadh, parents who hadn't a clue what their sons had been up to, boys who clamored to join their elder brothers and cousins, unwed girls who looked on these warrior Shagara with astonished fascination. Even Mirzah could not hide her satisfaction, though she tried very hard to present a composed expression and conceal any unseemly pride. Only Abb Shagara, narrow-eyed and stiff-spined with anger, disapproved.

Abb Harirri and Abb Azwadh went to the guest tents without saying anything to Alessid. Leyliah attended her husband's kinsman, and Meryem escorted Abb Azwadh—who once, long ago, had thought to marry her. Alessid gave Qishtan over to Jefar's care. He had no wish to join his troops in celebrating their triumph among themselves as they unsaddled and walked and rubbed down their horses—for the achievement truly was theirs, and they would enjoy it more freely without him. He wished to be alone for a time away from everyone else, to provide ample opportunity for discussion before he began to answer any questions.

So he went to his wife's tent, where a question was waiting for him.

"Ayia, husband, I assume you wish your children to eat something hot for dinner and not starve, so may I—Jemilha, Za'arifa, you will *hush* while I talk to your father!—may I also assume there must be some very good reason why my firepit is half demolished?"

"Say rather that it is half finished, Mirzah."

"A pretty point of distinction," she retorted. "I suppose my father will allow us to borrow his fire to cook dinner. Go inside and hear the girls' lessons. Not that they'll make much sense, after the spectacle they just witnessed." And, to belie her sharpness, she leaned up in full view of anyone with eyes to look and kissed Alessid on the lips. "I am proud of you, husband."

"You will be prouder yet, wife." He stroked her cheek with one finger, a rare gesture of tenderness, and went inside the tent.

"I am less surprised than others that you've kept all this secret." Meryem nodded acceptance of the qawah Alessid served her but declined the candied fruit and nuts Mirzah offered. "The Shagara are, after all, accustomed to keeping their mouths shut."

"But for ten years?" Leyliah asked.

"Nearly seventeen," Alessid replied blandly. "At first I disguised my intent as lessons in the full extent of their horses' capabilities." He poured for Leyliah, then sat down on a small leather cushion usually occupied by one of the children. Tonight, the carpets and silk pillows were for their guests.

"A pity my son is not alive to see this," Meryem said. "He would have enjoyed it appallingly."

"And Fadhil," murmured Leyliah.

"I regret this, too—more deeply than I can say." Alessid sipped at his cup, then set it carefully on the low table. "I still miss them."

"And even more so now, when you have a fool for an Abb Shagara?" She eyed him shrewdly.

"How large is the company of horseman, husband?" Mirzah spoke blandly, from mere idle curiosity, it seemed. But Alessid appreciated the two things she accomplished: deflecting an uncomfortable topic of conversation and letting Leyliah know that Mirzah was ignorant of his work. A lie of omission to one's mother was as bad as a direct falsehood. Alessid understood that; he had never been able to lie to his own mother, Jemilha.

"At present, nearly a hundred, as you saw today."

Leyliah's gaze was as astute as Meryem's. "And the number trained to war, who no longer camp with the Shagara? This is something Abb Shagara has not yet considered, I think."

"He may be close to guessing, but he won't know for certain until I tell him."

"Neither will we," snapped Meryem, flinging her long, silver-black braid over her shoulder. "So speak up."

He repressed a smile. "Those who married into the Harirri, thirty-three. Five more than that with the Azwadh. Nineteen with the Tallib, twenty with the Tabbor, thirteen with the Tariq, and seventeen with the Ammal." After a slight pause, he finished, "And those within the Shagara, who are trained but do not speak of it, two hundred and eighty-six—not including those you watched today."

None of these three women ever revealed more of her thoughts or emotions than she wished. But as Alessid spoke the numbers, beautiful black eyes widened, and full lips parted, and golden skin flushed across high cheekbones—and Alessid realized all over again how supremely lovely Shagara women were.

"More than five hundred," he finished, and gave them time to recover by pretending to be absorbed in selecting the perfect honeyed fig.

"How—?" was all Leyliah seemed able to say.

"The Shagara know how to keep a secret," he answered calmly.

"And when—" Meryem paused for a large swallow of qawah to clear her throat. "When these others have instructed more young men—"

"I would guess the total would be about eight hundred," Alessid remarked. "A more than respectable force, if correctly used."

"How many does Sheyqir Za'aid have?"

"About a thousand in Hazganni. Thrice that spread around in the towns and villages."

"And you know this because—?"

"I keep my ears open."

"They believe us weak," Meryem said slowly. "It is insulting—a mere four thousand warriors, for a land this size."

"Yet they've held almost all of this country for seventeen years," Alessid pointed out. "And what has anyone done about it?"

"You've been doing something for seventeen years," Meryem said. "But you waited. It was not the training of men and horses that took so long, it was the uniting of the other tribes in outrage."

He said nothing. She searched his eyes for a time, then shook her head.

Again Mirzah spoke, again quite mildly. "Of course, some of those who own suitable horses will be too old to fight. For the good of the tribes they must give up their horses to younger men who can—" She glanced at the closed tent flap, distracted by a polite rattling of the wooden chime. "Enter," she called out, and to everyone's astonishment, Abb Harirri came into the tent. Mirzah sprang to her feet, welcoming her grandfather with an embrace.

"Child, you're looking more beautiful than ever. Leyliah, Challa Meryem, I swear to you that if I were not already married, I would carry one of you off to my tent. Or perhaps not, for how could I possibly make a decision to take one and not the other?"

The two women smiled, for, as time-honored as such extravagant compliments were, Abb Harirri truly meant what he said.

"No, I want no qawah or sweets, thank you. Abb Shagara gave me a dinner tonight that staggers me still. What I wish, if convenient, is a private talk with Alessid. With your permission, Mirzah?"

A few minutes later the two men were outside, walking through the soft spring night toward the thorn fences. Alessid waited for the older man to speak, but the words were a long while coming.

At last, when they were far from the tents, Abb Harirri said, "Tallibah is still without a child. I am afraid that she may have to divorce Kemmal."

Expecting conversation about the horses and the cavalry and Sheyqir Za'aid, it took Alessid a moment to rearrange his thoughts. When he did, he was both disappointed and pleased. Only the former was expressed to Abb Harirri, though.

The older man nodded. "I too am sorry, but what can be done? Our friendship is separate from our kinship, Alessid—I hope you know this—but for reasons both of affection and of family I had hoped . . ." He ended with a shrug. "But you understand."

"Yes."

"I will of course support you in everything that benefits the Harirri."

"My wife's father is Harirri, and my children are of that blood. Whatever I do, it will be with the Harirri in my mind."

"Then we understand each other." Abb Harirri stretched widely, his brown silk robe glinting by moonlight with a delicate tracery of gold embroidery. "Tomorrow will be a strenuous day, I think. Discussions begin early. I will retire now."

"Sururi annam," Alessid said, and watched him return to the tents. For himself, he walked for a while longer in the fragrant night, considering this new information.

Neither Kemmal nor Kammil had sired a child. Alessid now was certain that they never would. And whereas he wished they could have given him grandchildren, they were of even more use to him for what they had proven: that the Shagara blood was strong in his line. The twins' infertility was proof that Mirzah had borne two Haddiyat sons. When one of her daughters bore one as well, Alessid's position with the Shagara would be secured. It would mean that the bloodline ran true.

But he could not wait for his girls to grow up and marry and have sons—

and then wait for the sons to grow up and marry and be divorced. The time was now. He was thirty-three this summer. He had already waited nineteen years for his vengeance—the same amount of time Azzad al-Ma'aliq had waited. But Alessid had put those years to much better use than had his frivolous, charming father. Where Azzad had created an empire of trade, Alessid would create an Empire.

He walked slowly back to his wife's tent. A little ways from it, he encountered Meryem. He would have nodded a good night, but what he had just heard from Abb Harirri and what he would do and say on the morrow made him stop.

"Challa Meryem," he said formally, "I have just discovered that my two eldest sons are almost certainly Haddiyat. I think it might be time for me to learn precisely what this means."

She was silent for a long while. Then: "I think you are right, Alessid." And she led the way to her own tent, where she talked and he listened until dawn.

There were not quite enough horses. But when Alessid and seventy riders of the Shagara made their first raid against the Qoundi Ammar, thirty horses were captured—and thirty more men of the Za'aba Izim were mounted on stallions trained for war.

All during the spring, young men came to the Shagara camp. Mirzah had the great joy of having all three of her sons back in her tent, and with them came men of the Tallib, the Azwadh, and the Harirri. They were taught battle maneuvers, and all but a few returned to their tribes to teach the same to their kinsmen. Some stayed with the Shagar, to become their tribes' contribution to Alessid's force.

By midsummer, he had more than four hundred skilled riders at his personal command. And as these mounted warriors swept across the land, led by a man on a stallion the color of sun-gilt cream, Sheyqir Za'aid al-Ammarizzad began to hear of a Golden Wind. But he was not yet afraid.

— RAFFIQ MURAH, *Deeds of Il-Nazzari, 701*

13

It was a clear, bright summer's night when Alessid watched his son Addad, qabda'an now of his own hundred warriors, ride away to return to his wife's tent at the Azwadh camp. The twins, Kemmal and Kammil, stayed.

"You know now what you are," Alessid told his sons, who walked beside him through the sparse grassland where flocks grazed. Washed gray and silver by starshine, the shadows shifted with the intricacies of the breeze. "The first year, you did not suspect. The second year, perhaps you thought about it. But it is nearly the third year, and your wives have borne no children."

He paused beneath a wool awning set up for the comfort of those who watched the goats and sheep. All the herders were out gathering the animals for the move tomorrow to a more remote location, the better to evade Sheyqir Za'aid's soldiers. Two hundred of them had been reported at Ouaraqqa, the last town before the wastes began. Once all the Shagara wagons were safely distant ...

Seating himself on a firm leather cushion, he put aside his plans for his enemies in favor of his plans for his sons. He took out his waterskin and drank briefly, then passed it to them. Their faces were impassive, and entirely identical but for the tiny scar above Kammel's right eyebrow, memento of the only time he had ever fallen off a horse. Their skin was not quite as golden as Mirzah's, but they had inherited the subtle eyes of her father Razhid. For the rest, their long noses, long limbs, and wide mouths were al-Ma'aliq. Handsome youths, sought in marriage by many girls, had they not been Haddiyat, they would have fathered many children.

Had they loved their wives? Would they miss the girls they had married? He did not know. He guessed it might be painful for them if he asked. So he decided he would never ask.

"Neither of you has any aptitude for medicine, nor are you skilled in the crafting of hazziri. The best I ever saw either of you do was pound out a reasonably round pair of copper cups for your mother's birthday." He smiled a little, partly to show their lack of skill did not trouble him, partly to show his affection for them, and partly because Mirzah treasured those cups as if they had been set with jewels by Abb Shagara himself. Wobbly, comically dented, the talishann for *warmth* lopsided and clumsy, they had never functioned as intended—though now she knew this was not because her sons had no Haddiyat gift, only that they had no talent.

"Abb Shagara has told me he is waiting for the results of certain tests. We know what those results will be, you and I. The usual work of the Haddiyat is neither to your aptitude nor to your liking. So it may appear to you that your gift is no gift at all, and useless to the tribe. But I tell you now, my sons, you are absolutely essential to me."

Kemmal wrapped his arms around his knees and swayed slightly back and forth. Alessid recognized it as a habit of childhood when he was thinking very hard. "You want us to work hazziri of a special, particular kind, a kind that Abb Shagara would probably not approve."

"I do."

Kammil was nodding slowly. With the measured style of speech of the noblemen he descended from, he said, "This summer we have reviewed with the mouallimas the lessons of long ago. What we did not fully remember took us but a short time to relearn. They have taught us more, and more esoteric, knowledge. Give us leave, Ab'ya, to consult with each other for a day, and we will tell you what can be done and not done."

"You have that leave. Shall I tell you what I need, or will you be able to guess?"

Both young men smiled, and Alessid was content. They had grown in confidence and knowledge during their three years away from the Shagara, and now that they knew what they were, there was a new dignity and consciousness of worth. Whereas it had been difficult at first for him to meet them as men and not as his little boys, now he was glad he had chosen marriage for them instead of the other path.

The son of a Shagara mother with Haddiyat men in her line had two alternatives on reaching fourteen years of age: try to father a child on a Shagara girl who had chosen to give a baby to the tribe before she married (which many girls did), or wait another year and marry. If, after three years, no child had come of the marriage, the young man was divorced. There were formal tests to determine whether he was truly Haddiyat, but cases where infertility was the woman's fault were rare.

The advantage to the marriage option was that a bond was formed with another tribe, the young man saw something of the world outside the Shagara tents, and when he returned to them, he was still only eighteen years old, with another twenty or so years of service ahead of him. The disadvantage was, perhaps, that he spent three years hoping in vain for a child. But every son of a Shagara mother with Haddiyat men in her line knew from childhood that his future might not include offspring.

All Shagara children were taught to read and write by the age of seven. The boys learned how to work with metals and alloys and jewels and to craft simple hazziri for the Haddiyat to inscribe. Those who showed a gift for the forge, for design, or for cutting or setting gems were apprenticed to special mouallimas, whether they turned out to be Haddiyat or not. The ones who were gifted, however—these were the treasures of the Shagara. When magic was mated with craft, the result was not only true art but true power.

Alessid had no interest in art.

He sent his sons to help the herdsmen if help should be needed this night, and he returned to Mirzah's tent. The girls were asleep. Mirzah should have been packing for the move tomorrow. Instead, she huddled on a pile of rolled and rope-tied carpets, weeping in silence.

"Wife, what is this?" Alessid knelt beside her, and was astonished when she jerked away from his hand. "Mirzah, what's wrong?" She refused to look at him. "You must not cry. It's bad for the child."

Her head snapped up. "What about my *other* children?"

"Mirzah—" He rocked back on his heels. "Quickly, tell me, is something wrong with the girls?"

"Ayia! By Chaydann al-Mamnoua'a, you are a fool!" She gave him a look of pure venom. "A mother should not outlive her sons!"

Alessid stared at her.

"I suspected—perhaps I even knew—but Abb Shagara came to me this morning and—" She pounded her fists on her thighs. "He made it *real*, Alessid!"

"Real?" he echoed stupidly.

"He said the testing was finished, and my boys—" She choked. "He told me what an honor it was—how pleased I should be! Of course he'd say so—he's Haddiyat himself! He doesn't understand!"

It came to him then, as it had not even when looking his sons in the eyes. Handsome, strong, obedient sons . . . young men who would grow old swiftly, as Fadhil had, and die before the age of forty-five, as Fadhil had.

Among the Shagara, being Haddiyat was the greatest honor a man could know. For the women who had birthed them . . .

Compassion ached within him—an unfamiliar emotion. He sought to gather his wife into his embrace. She once more shook him off.

"When you are busy killing," she said in the coldest voice he had ever heard from her, "when you are taking back what the al-Ammarad stole, remember who it was who gave you the tools you will use until they are used up. Remember that they are *my* sons. *Mine.* Remember whose blood it is that made the blood they will bleed for you until they have no blood left."

For the first time in his life, Alessid went onto his knees before another human being; he bowed his head down to the carpet and whispered, "Forgive me."

Mirzah was silent a long time; he could feel her watching him. Then there was a murmur of thin silk as she got to her feet, and her voice came from very high over his head.

"Never."

He remained there, having abased himself to no purpose, until long after she had left her tent.

They rode out in the early evening, the wagons and the warriors. It was midsummer and very hot even at night, and a breeze blew up from the Barrens that could sear the skin on a man's face. It was a miserable time for travel, but travel they did, northeast toward the mountains.

At midnight, on the salt flats, at a crossroads only a desert dweller could have identified, the tribe divided. Fifty young men on swift horses stayed with the wagons to guard and warn. The rest went with Alessid: three hundred riders cloaked in pale desert colors, arrayed for battle, gleaming with hazziri, eager for the deaths of their enemies.

And as they parted from their parents and children and friends, the tribe began to chant. Alessid, having kissed his daughters—and bowed much lower to Mirzah than most men ever did, even to a woman, even to his own wife—rode to the head of the group and glanced back over his shoulder once when first he heard it. A tiny smile touched his mouth beneath the protective scarf over the lower half of his face. He showed no other reaction, and did not look back again. But he heard the chanting long after, and all the way to the village of Ouaraqqa:

"Ah-less-*eed!* Ah-less-*eed!* Ah-less-*eed!*"

His people were truly his. Though he had not been born one of them, he had taken their most prized daughter to wife and sired upon her three daughters and three sons, two of them Haddiyat. He had shown the Shagara a new strength in their most ancient ways. And he would soon give them power in this land equal to the power they had bestowed on him.

Self-critical, self-analytical, Alessid knew precisely why he was doing this. For himself, primarily—which caused him not the slightest shame. He did it to make sure the name al-Ma'aliq was not spoken in the same breath as *failure*, as *disgrace*. To regain what belonged to him. To provide for his sons and daughters a heritage unequaled in the history of this land. To give the death blow to Sheyqa Nizzira, who slumped in wheezing decay on the Moonrise Throne, watching with rheumy eyes as those who remained of her offspring who were still men plotted all around her.

To prove that, unlike his father Azzad, Alessid was not a fool.

He led his cavalry northward, glancing every so often at the toppled columns and shattered statues strewn over the hilltops. Long ago the Qarrik had been the conquerors here, building temples to their false gods in the towns from which they ruled—for a time, and not so very long a time at that. The people had rebelled, and the Qarrik, who had overreached themselves, had been vanquished. Then had come the Hrumman, fiercer and more war-like, thicker of muscle and more proficient at arms, marching across the land to take what the Qarrik had lost, reconstructing the shrines and reestablish-ing foreign rule. But in time the Hrumman had also been expelled. All that remained to mark the mastery here of either barbarian nation were a few fallen stones, a few headless statues.

So would the al-Ammarizzad fall, by Acuyib's Will. Alessid would be His right hand, and the Shagara would be the sword in Alessid's hand. But as much as he would use the Shagara and their magic—and his own sons—for his ends, in the same measure he felt bound to bring them to the promi-nence they deserved. What other people could do what they did? How dared anyone threaten them or the tribes allied to them?

A hundred and fifty years ago, other barbarians had come, this time from the north, and conquered—for a time even briefer than the Qarrik or Hrumman. The Shagara had been the key to their defeat. As he listened to the cadence of the hooves behind him, Alessid knew that representatives of all the Za'aba Izim rode with him, protecting the Shagara, who in turn protected them. It was a relationship as timeless as the wastes they lived in and as balanced. With their silence, the tribes defended the Shagara, who defended them against sickness, injury, and death. All Alessid had done was show them a new way of defense, necessary because his father had brought them new dangers by being a fool.

In many ways, he was doing this to apologize.

When the Qarrik and then the Hrumman and then the northern barbarians had been driven from the land, no one had thought to unite the tribes with the towns and form a true nation. No one had been given the vision given to Alessid by Acuyib: a united country, strong and safe and invulnerable.

It required the Shagara to accomplish it and, moreover, the Shagara in a position of prominence such as they had never before known. Alessid knew this must be so; Abb Shagara was of a different opinion. But, like all Haddiyat, Abb Shagara had grown rapidly old; he was thirty-seven and by the look of him would not reach forty. Though less than half Sheyqa Nizzira's age, he was just as feeble and even more inconsequential to events—as irrelevant as the ancient broken columns and demolished statues littering these hills.

On the third evening, twenty miles from the town of Ouaraqqa, Alessid halted his cavalry for a quick and early meal. They would don dark cloaks and ride again when darkness fell, and circle the garrison by midnight. The Haddiyat had been heroically busy these last months, creating things they had never before been asked to create, with splendid results. Every rider wore a special hazzir, made of silver for magical strength, set with hematite for protection in battle and garnet for protection from wounds, and inscribed with four owls that gave patience, watchfulness, wisdom, and—most importantly in this endeavor—the ability to see in the dark.

But the subtleties of belief among his warriors affected the hazziri in strange ways. Those who had absolute faith (the Shagara, of course, and some others of the Za'aba Izim) were protected against everything but their own reckless folly. And Alessid did not allow stupid men to ride with him, whether they trusted Haddiyat skills or not. In previous skirmishes—he did not delude himself that these were true battles—the hazziri had protected the uncertain to a lesser extent than those who believed. The openly skeptical had taken a few wounds, which had not promoted certitude in their hearts. So this time, when the hazziri were given out, he let it be known that these were merely for luck. The Shagara, who knew better, kept silent. Alessid's thought was that ignorance of the true power of these hazziri would prevent specific disbelief and therefore would protect even the men who doubted.

There was a kind of skewed logic to it, he supposed, smiling wryly as he ate his share of goat cheese and hard bread. If one didn't know exactly what one was supposed to believe in, one could not disbelieve it. Ayia, he would see this proved or disproved tonight.

Kemmal and Kammil approached on descendants of Khamsin. His heart swelled at the sight of his sons—tall and handsome and strong, qabda'ans of a hundred riders each, everything a father could wish. For a moment he felt kinship with his own father, knowing that Azzad's look of pride graced his own features now. And yet—

Pushing aside memory of Mirzah's tear-streaked face and icy blame, he addressed his young Haddiyat. "Kemmal will lead the Harirri up from the south. Kammil, take the Tallib down from the north. When you are in position—" He stopped, seeing them exchange glances and tiny smiles in the dimness. "What? Is there a problem? Have you questions?"

"No, Ab'ya," said Kammil. "It's only that we've been over this a dozen times."

"We know what to do," Kemmal assured him.

"Ayia, then—go and do it. Acuyib smile upon you, my sons."

"And on you, Ab'ya, always."

As they rode off to organize their troops, Alessid berated himself for unnecessary repetition of his orders. His men knew what they were doing. In truth, his faith in his warriors was as absolute as in his hazziri—but he wondered if perhaps he was a little nervous. This was no skirmish with isolated contingents of Qoundi Ammar far from any settlement; this was the first time Alessid had attempted to take an entire town.

Though he had never been to Ouaraqqa, it was familiar to those of the Shagara who conducted trade for the tribe. He had spoken at length with them and studied the maps they had drawn, so when he gazed upon the town from the top of a hill, it was as if he had already been there a dozen times. Twice the size of Sihabbah, it sprawled at the bottom of a gorge, on the eastern side of a mountain stream that during spring runoff became a torrent. Ancient ruins on the western bank bore mute witness to foreign fools who had built on the flat flood plain rather than the slopes. Part of Ouaraqqa was mud brick, part of it was wood, and some of it—most notably the water mill that ground grain to flour—had been built of toppled stone temples from across the stream. Alessid thought about that for a moment, and smiled; the people of this land had turned the possessions of former conquerors to their own use. He wondered what of Sheyqir Za'aid's he would employ once the al-Ammarizzad were gone the way of the Qarrik and Hrumman and the northern barbarians. He could think of nothing the al-Ammarad had established in this country but hatred—and indeed they had tried to destroy utterly the one thing about which he and his father Azzad were in accord: the wealth of trees.

But renewing that wealth would come later. Right now he must take Ouaraqqa.

Only starlight glinted off the stream, thin in midsummer. The mill was silent, the flocks were gone to high summer pasture, the winding streets were empty of townsfolk. Only the occasional Qoundi Ammar rode through on patrol. All this was reported to him by Jefar Shagara, who despite the objections of his uncle Abb Shagara had been given permission by his parents to accompany Alessid on this assault. He had been given his horse in advance of his fifteenth birthday—a four-year-old half-breed mare named Filfila for the peppery black-and-gray dapples that made her blend into the night shadows. There was no prouder warrior in Alessid's cavalry. Nor, with the exception of his own sons, one Alessid would do more to keep safe.

Accordingly, he received the boy's report and sent him to the rear of the company. Jefar was not happy, but neither was he skilled enough yet with a sword to join in the attack. Alessid stroked Qishtan's glossy cream-gold neck and waited for his sons' messengers. When they came, and told him the Tallib and Harirri were arrayed as ordered, Alessid touched the hazzir at his breast and roared the command to charge.

The Qoundi Ammar in their arrogance and their contempt for the people of this land believed that no one would dare attack a town they held for Sheyqir Za'aid and his exalted mother. Alessid knew with regret that this arrogance would change once this night was over, but he had chosen his target with this in mind. Ouaraqqa was important to its own people only as a prosperous market town, but to the military mind it was vital: It commanded the only pass through this part of the mountains. For this reason, it was garrisoned with a force of two hundred. With this place in his hands, Alessid could isolate the Sheyqir's warriors who patrolled the south. Without support, without a home position, they would be easy prey for the Tabbor, whose lands they occupied.

It was risky in some ways; Challa Meryem had warned him that once liberated, the Tabbor might withdraw from the larger campaign. But he had to have Ouaraqqa to deny Sheyqir Za'aid this pass, and so Ouaraqqa must be taken.

The Tallib, with Kammil as their qabda'an, swept down from the north along the watercourse. And as they did, Alessid led his own troops in from the east, crushing the town on two sides. The Qoundi Ammar were roused from their garrison—the four largest houses in the center of town, commandeered without compensation for the owners. But their horses were not only penned far from the soldiers' quarters, they were now galloping down the gorge—for, from the south, the Harirri with Kemmal leading them had freed two hundred pure white stallions trained for war.

"Slaughter," Kammil said afterward, with admirable succinctness. And it was true.

Alessid, inspecting the town by dawnlight, heard the cheers of Ouaraqqa's people and saw their grateful amazement that no one but Qoundi Ammar had been killed. His warriors had taken only minor wounds—and the ones who had were none of them Shagara. Moreover, they had separated townsfolk from enemy soldier as if they battled in full daylight. The most serious injury, in fact, was to a young Tallib skeptic who had not even been wearing his hazzir; he was knocked in the head by a low-swinging shop sign he hadn't seen in the dark. After he came back to consciousness and learned how few of his companions had been wounded in the fighting, he was a skeptic no longer.

Alessid accepted the invitation of the town elders to share their morning meal. As they lauded his courage, his skill, his daring, and his brilliance over strong qawah and the softest bread he had ever eaten, he knew that it would never be this easy again.

All that autumn and into the first month of winter, the Riders on the Golden Wind swept through the land Sheyqir Za'aid claimed for his mother, Nizzira. By the time he began to be afraid, it was too late to send for more soldiers from home; the sea had succumbed to storms, just as the Qoundi Ammar in town after town succumbed to the warriors of the Za'aba Izim.

Sheyqir Za'aid saw, as the new year began, that he had lost more than half his territory. The only lands still tight in his grip were the coast and the region around Hazganni. To this city he went, and he ordered four great towers to be built, and walls to link the towers. And in this way he fortified Hazganni as never before and felt himself safe until spring, when the seas calmed and he could apply to his mother for help. All the warriors left to him, he commanded to Hazganni.

On the day the walls of Hazganni were finished, Alessid rode into Sihabbah, the town of his birth, for the first time in twenty years. He had fled a boy and returned the savior of his people. It was there that he was first called Il-Nazzari, "Bringer of Victories."

Also in Sihabbah that spring he received from the women who had carried his father's murdered body down from the mountain a small silken pouch containing twenty-two pearls. He knew these gems; they had been part of his mother's bridal necklace. The women had picked them carefully from the charred remains of the House of al-Gallid. The moment he saw them was the first time anyone ever saw tears in his eyes.

By summer's end, the Haddiyat of the Shagara had made of these pearls earrings for Mirzah, Ra'abi, Jemilha, Za'arifa, and Mairid, the daughter born that summer. Two pearls remained, and these Alessid had placed on the chain of his hazzir, near his heart, in memory of his mother.

And, perhaps, his father.

— RAFFIQ MURAH, *Deeds of Il-Nazzari*, 701

14

All that remained was Hazganni.

Alessid remembered the city from his childhood: a cheerful maze of shops, houses, mansions, gardens, warehouses, and the huge central zouq where once he and his brother Bazir had escaped Fadhil's watchful eye for one whole delightful afternoon. The belting they had received that evening had been well worth the excitement. In the vast zoqalo, all manner of vendors sold a dizzying variety of merchandise: whole rainbows of bright silks and woven woolens, thread and yarn, buttons and lengths of embroidery, spices and candies, shoes and scarves and cloaks and gloves, pottery jars, brass plates, bronze bells, copper bowls, "silver" jewelry that was really tin, wooden toys . . .

There was also an array of "medical" specialists, hawking cures for the bald and the ugly, the sore and the lame, and every disease with which Chaydann al-Mamnoua'a had ever afflicted humankind. Bazir's favorite had been an old man in the very center of the zoqalo who sing-songed his skills while pacing back and forth on a garish carpet, a gruesome collection of clamps and pliers jingling from a chain around his neck as he rattled a tray of successfully yanked teeth. Alessid, gazing down at the city from the hills, smiled to think that perhaps that same old man would be there, exhibiting his souvenirs to other wide-eyed, deliciously horrified boys. The great zouq had been a magical place, and Alessid had loved the tangle of it, the smells, the noise, the swift brilliance of color and movement.

But he was told that the zoqalo was nearly empty now, nearly silent. The local vendors were all too terrified to set foot outside their own shops, if any. The towers and walls built at Sheyqir Za'aid's order kept folk from the countryside from freely entering the city with their wares. There was poverty within and without those walls. From a hilltop three miles from Hazganni, Alessid cursed Sheyqir Za'aid for the people's sake.

For his own, he damned the man for destroying the trees. Not because his father had either planted them himself or encouraged others to do so; not because without them there was no protection from the ever-hungry desert; not even because of his childhood memories of playing beneath those trees. The groves would have made cover enough for an army twice the size of Alessid's. Now there was nothing between him and Hazganni but miles of dead open country.

Turning his back on the city, he walked downhill to his tent. There, beside the fire, Jefar was brewing qawah for the qabda'ans. The warriors of the Za'aba Izim were consolidated now, over a thousand strong. They knew how to fight; every man had been in at least ten actions. Their horses—many of them pure white, captured from the Qoundi Annam—were fully trained to war. Alessid had kept them in their original groupings, one for each of the seven tribes. But they knew they must now become a single force, to take Hazganni.

Alessid stood apart for a few moments, surveying the qabda'ans. Despite having been divorced by their wives, Kemmal still led the Tallib and Kammil was qabda'an of the Harirri. Alessid's third son, Addad, was in no danger of being divorced; his wife was hugely pregnant, and the Azwadh followed the husband of their beloved Black Rose as if he had been born one of them. Alessid had blood ties to the Ammal, as well, for Mirzah's grandmother and great-grandmother had been of that tribe. The qabda'an of the Tabbor had wed Mirzah's close cousin. Only the Tariq had no intimate ties to Alessid. The Shagara themselves were, of course, Alessid's personal army.

Over a thousand, all told. Within Hazganni and patrolling its walls were more than twice that number.

Accepting the cup Jefar offered him, Alessid sat on a flat rock and addressed his qabda'ans. "Aqq'im, my esteemed brothers, we cannot storm the walls of this city. They will see us coming for miles, even at night with a dark moon. It seems to me there are two alternatives. Either we face them in open battle on the plain outside the city, or we destroy them from within."

They all knew that neither would be easy to accomplish. Why should the Qoundi Ammar come out to do battle, when all they need do was laugh atop the towers? And how could anyone get inside a city so tightly shut that not even a snake could slither inside unremarked?

"If we *could* get inside," mused Addad, "the people might aid us. Surely they know what we've done for others, what we hope to do for them."

"Grandson," said Razhid, "when Sheyqir Za'aid first came here, the people of Hazganni capitulated rather than fight for their city and their freedom. After nearly twenty years, can you think they would suddenly rise up?"

Addad sighed. "You're right, of course, Grandsire. But surely there must be some who would aid us."

"And how could we find them? Sneak someone inside and have him knock on doors asking if anyone would care to open the gates for us?" Razhid echoed his grandson's sigh. "There may be some, as you say, who would help us—but there will be many, many more who would gladly sell us to the Sheyqir."

Alessid nodded. "I don't think it's possible to get enough warriors secretly inside to make a difference. Yet how can we lure them out of their security into battle?"

"Do we have to?" asked Azadel Tabbor, a fiercely bearded man whose shoulder muscles bulged beneath his robes. "Could we not starve them out?"

Alessid raised a hand as if to ward off such an occurrence. "The people of the city would be burying each other long before the Sheyqir feels even the slightest pang of hunger. Our enemies are the soldiers of the Qoundi Annam, not the forty thousand people of Hazganni."

"Al-Ma'aliq," said Kammil, giving his father the formal title rather than calling him *Ab'ya*, "may I point out that we have what the Sheyqir does not?"

"More horses?" Tabbor asked, frowning. "Finer warriors? A better commander?"

Kemmal nodded acknowledgment of the compliment to his father, then glanced at his twin. "Those, certainly," he agreed. "But I believe my brother has something else in mind."

Two days later, his eldest sons came to Alessid's tent and presented him with a plain wooden box. Inside, resting on black silk, was a simple rectangular plaque, three inches high and two wide, depicting an ibis in low relief. Inspecting it without touching it, Alessid listened to his sons explain.

"We reworked an existing piece," Kemmal began, "for as you know we're both terrible at design and crafting. Grandfather Razhid remembered that his grandfather had an ibis hazzir, for what purpose he didn't recall, and that it had been passed to youngest sons at their marriage."

"And now—?" Alessid prompted.

"Magic—both the silver and the bird. We set the sapphire eye to give dreams of loss. It was done in late morning, when it is most powerful."

Kemmal said, "And the onyxes were done at midnight. One stone on the breast for doubts, the other atop the head for terrifying dreams."

"Have you a plan for getting this to the Sheyqir? It is a magnificent piece, and he is greedy, like all of his kind, but suspicious. I can't just send it to him."

"There is among us one who volunteered to 'betray' our people," Kammil told him. "He will say it is out of concern for relatives inside Hazganni, but he will make it obvious enough that he is simply a coward terrified of the coming battle—"

"A nice impression for them to have of us!" Alessid approved. "Go on."

"This will be in his possession, but we haven't decided if it is a token of his good faith, stolen from someone important—perhaps yourself, Ab'ya—as a gift for the Sheyqir, or if it would be more subtle to make it a family treasure with which he is reluctant to part. He feels confident that he can make either work and can get it into the Sheyqir's hands."

"And who is this supposed traitor?"

The twins exchanged half-glances. "Jefar."

"Absolutely not."

"Ab'ya—"

"No." He stared at the hazzir for a time. "Should this reach the Sheyqir, will this frighten him enough?"

"Over time, yes."

"How much time?"

They traded looks again. Kammil answered, "Perhaps a month."

"We don't have a month." Alessid shut the box. "Make it more powerful."

"Ab'ya—" Kemmal bit his upper lip. "These are things the mouallimas caution against. We Haddiyat learn the sigils and the properties of the gems, but there are certain applications—"

"—that are not done," Alessid finished for him. "Do you see any mouallimas here? Do they ride with us, their swords ready to take Hazganni? Make it stronger, Kemmal."

"With respect, Ab'ya—"

"Acuyib give me patience! If a man's family is starving and a sheep is available to him and he knows how to slaughter it, he slaughters the damned sheep!"

"But if it is the only one left, his family will soon starve anyway." Kammil met his gaze squarely. "Should we work this hazzir to be more powerful—to do actual harm rather than merely suggesting certain things to the Sheyqir's mind—"

"Enough!" Alessid slapped his hands on his thighs. "I want this man frightened out of his wits. I want him sick with fear—in both his mind and his body. I want him plagued and tormented and leaping at the smallest shadow. Do you understand me? Either make this more powerful or think up something else."

"Yes, Ab'ya," they said together, and departed his tent.

Eight days later, on a fine, fair evening just before dusk, Alessid rode to a promontory overlooking Hazganni. The setting sun glowed behind him, turning his robe and his horse's cream-gold hide to molten sunlight. The soldiers on duty in the tower saw him at once. An alarm drum pounded, and the walls bristled silver with swords and spears.

Alessid watched. A stray bit of whimsy left somehow inside him observed that the city looked rather like a prickleback hunching to bristle its spines: silly and ineffectual against anything larger than a snake. There was a lesson in it, he mused—the little animal trusted too much to its defenses against a particular enemy and had not the wit even to realize that other enemies could be much more dangerous.

Too, he thought, the wayward amusement diverting him again, it was a clever snake that knew a mouthful of spines was avoidable. All it had to do was find a single slender gap in all those defenses, slither through it, and strike.

At length, in a voice honed by years of training his cavalry in the wide wilderness, he shouted, "Soldiers of the Qoundi Ammar! Tonight your sleep will bring you dreams of the future! We show you these visions in warning of what is to come!"

Behind him, out of the soldiers' sight, his men began to chant: "Ah-less-*eed*! Ah-less-*eed*! Ah-less-*eed*!"

He let the sound wash past him, flowing down the rise to surge against the city walls like the ocean few of them had ever seen. If there was laughter among the Qoundi Ammar, and he knew there would be, it was drowned in the rhythmic tide of his name.

He smiled and rode away.

That night, wrapped in black cloaks and protected by potent hazziri, Kemmal and Kammil walked down the hillside. Silent as shadows and as invisible, they worked with swift thoroughness. On each of the four towers and at the midpoint of each connecting wall, they wrote and drew. By midnight, Hazganni was encircled with Shagara magic, delineated in al-Maʿaliq blood.

The next evening, just at dusk, Alessid once more rode golden Qishtan down to the hillock. The response was the same, with soldiers scrambling to their posts, but this time someone threw an axe at him. He watched it thunk harmlessly to the ground far from where he sat his horse, and smiled.

"Soldiers of the Qoundi Ammar! Tonight every bond in the city will loosen! Listen while stones shift against their mortaring, and know that the walls of the al-Ammarizzad are beginning to topple!"

"Ah-less-*eed!* Ah-less-*eed!* Ah-less-*eed!*"

Over dinner that night, Razhid observed, "Our old friend Abb Shagara, may his soul find splendor with Acuyib, would have loved this. And Fadhil would have been appalled—or at least feel compelled to give the appearance of it before laughing himself out of breath."

Alessid poured more qawah for them both. "Ayia, if I didn't keep Abb Akkil Akkem Akkim Akkar strictly out of my thoughts as I bellow at the top of my lungs, I'd be laughing so hard I'd fall from my saddle. And think what an inspiring picture that would be!"

His wife's father eyed him. "Alessid, did you just make a joke?"

He thought for a moment, then smiled. "I believe I did."

"Don't worry, I won't tell anyone." After a wry grin, Razhid grew serious. "How are the boys feeling?"

"Fine. Is there a reason they shouldn't?"

"Surely you know what they're using to write with."

"Of course. I'm their commander."

"And their father! They worship you, Alessid. And they'll spend themselves for you," he warned, "completely and unselfishly."

"I know." He thought of Mirzah and refused to let her father see his pain.

When his sons returned very late that night, Alessid was waiting for them with strong wine, fresh fruit, and new-baked bread. "How many more nights can you do this?" he asked.

"As many as you require of us, Ab'ya."

But Kammil was almost too tired to lift the cup to his lips, and Kemmal didn't say anything at all. Razhid had been correct; they were spending themselves for him without thought to their health. If they returned to their mother's tent as wilted and pale as they were now, Mirzah would slit Alessid's throat.

And she wouldn't even wait until he was sleeping to do it.

"I think we will let the Qoundi Ammar wait before the next working," he said to his sons. "Wait, and wonder, and grumble about the Sheyqir—" He had been speaking almost at random, trusting his mind to come up with reasons convincing enough that would save his sons' pride, but now he smiled in genuine liking for the idea. "—and exhaust themselves inspecting every wall in Hazganni!"

Kemmal dutifully smiled back; Kammil dutifully protested, "We can continue as originally planned."

"I believe it would be better to wait a day." He said the words in such a way that they knew they were not to argue.

The next day while they slept, he took care of the restive elements among his cavalry. After a spring and summer of battles, every man was brashly convinced that he could defeat fifty Qoundi Ammar without breaking a sweat. They wanted to fight, and they wanted to do it *now*. Alessid appreciated and approved their zeal, but if all went as planned, they would do very little actual fighting for Hazganni. Where would all this energy go once they returned to their tents and the admiration of their people? It was a question that had been occupying his thoughts for quite some time.

That afternoon Alessid found a quiet place away from the camp and sat down to consider. His men would return to their tribes and renew the ancient balance of life in the wilderness: work, family, seasonal travel from one place to another. These places had been claimed by them forever; Sheyqir Za'aid had perturbed the natural equilibrium between the wasteland and its people, but had not Alessid done the same thing even while he was attempting to restore it? The men of the Za'aba Izim knew now how to make war to take back what was theirs; would they ever use these skills to take what was *not* theirs?

For one of the few times in his adult life he called up memories of his father, so that he could review his father's memories. Rimmal Madar; Dayira Azhreq; the lying, greedy sheyqas who, not content to throw out barbarian invaders, had taken what had belonged to the al-Ma'aliq and made it theirs. Or attempted to. The al-Ma'aliq lands had never truly belonged to the al-Ammarizzad, any more than Hazganni and all the other towns and fields and forests and mountains of this country would ever belong to them. In truth, he could think of only one place and one people belonging entirely to and with each other: the desert and the Za'aba Izim.

As he sat through the long hours of the night, gazing down at the city—and especially the ruined groves—it was with a slow and certain understanding that he discovered why.

The Seven Names, the desert. The tribes were the land's. They knew it, used it, cared for it. They knew the places where water, grazing, even fruit could be found; they hunted its animals and harvested its plants; they never lingered so long in one place as to deplete its resources. But how had it happened that the desert belonged as well to the Za'aba Izim? For Alessid knew it did; he had sensed it on some deeper level of his soul. It was not because they put walls around the desert, or drew adamant lines on maps, or defended it with their blood, or—

No. *That* was the reason. The blood. Especially the blood of the Shagara.

The sun and wind and water, the ground from which food grew—the herbs for medicine and the herbs for seasoning—all these things were within the Za'aba Izim and had been for uncounted lifetimes. Their bones and flesh and blood were made of the desert. In the Shagara, for reasons unknown and unknowable, that blood had turned into power.

The land itself had given them the means with which to protect and defend it. The land was theirs.

Not his. Not Alessid's. He knew that. He no more belonged to this country than it could ever belong to him. He had not given it enough.

Mother, father, sisters and brothers, friends—

But not *his* blood.

Not until now.

It was nearly dawn before he roused himself. In the dirt he drew a rough map. The mountains here, the coastline there, Hazganni and Sihabbah and Ouaraqqa and other towns marked by pebbles. To the south was the Barrens; to the west, fine grazing and growing land; to the east, more wastes and then the Ammarad; and to the north, the Ga'af Shammal and beyond it the barbarian domains. None of it was needed, none of it even coveted. But great swaths of it were there for the taking.

An army's purpose was to make war. Alessid had crafted an army that had defeated the best that Sheyqir Za'aid could field against him. This was not so remarkable as it appeared, as Meryem had pointed out.

"*The Qoundi Ammar have no homes here, no families, no sheep they have tended or fields they have plowed. But look at the Tabbor—initially reluctant to fight, until their lands were threatened. And then they fought like demons. The wonderment of it is that once their own interests were taken care of, they continued to fight to reclaim the lands of others. Do you see what you've done, Alessid?*"

He saw indeed. Where once Za'aba Izim and townsfolk had been almost strangers to each other, and the only bonds between them had been of language and trade, now they had begun to think of themselves as a single people, and all this land as theirs, together. It had not happened when the Qarrik invaded, nor the Hrumman, nor the northern barbarians from beyond the Ga'af Shammal. It had taken twenty years of Sheyqir Za'aid's rule to make it happen—and, Alessid knew without vainglory, the presence of one man strong enough to unite tribes and townsfolk against a common enemy. One man who taught them how to make war in a new and terrifyingly effective way.

He would win. He knew it as surely as he knew his father had not been capable of this. Victory was a honey-sweet thing, and the people had discovered its taste and liked it—but what happened when the enemy was gone? Proficient in war, the tribes might fall upon each other—definitely a thing to be avoided. But without practice, the skills of war would wither, and anyone with an army could invade this land again. The Qarrik had done it, and the Hrumman, and the northern barbarians, and the al-Ammarizzad.

"It will not happen again," he vowed quietly. "We will be strong."

After Hazganni was taken and Sheyqir Za'aid was dead, there would be a tense time while everyone waited for Sheyqa Nizzira's vengeance. Yet after that—? An army was necessary, but it was necessary to give an army something to do.

The first of the al-Ammarizzad had found a solution in Rimmal Madar. Deeply as Alessid despised the thought of borrowing ideas from his family's enemies, he had to admit it made sense. The majority of men who fought to protect their homeland did so because they wished their lives to be what they had been: settled, serene. These men would sheathe their swords without regret and go home. But those who had a real talent for armed conflict—ayia, these were the men that had been formed into the Qoundi Ammar. Azzad al-Ma'aliq's youthful ambition had been membership in this elite corps, and his reminiscences flooded Alessid's mind.

Neither time nor contemplation would reveal any other solution. Those of Alessid's army who wanted only to have done with war and go home, they would do so with his blessing and the gratitude of the Za'aba Izim. But those who enjoyed war—those who, he suddenly realized, found laughter in contemplation of battle, just as he did—those men he would keep.

He would ask Razhid to watch and listen and give him a list of names. And he looked at the map drawn in the dirt, and especially at the Ga'af Shammal and the rich lands to the north. Odd names they had: Granidiya, Trastemar, Qaysh. He wondered if he had not found something for his soldiers to do.

"Soldiers of the Qoundi Ammar! Tonight one wall of Hazganni will collapse! Tomorrow night, another wall—and then another, and another, until the towers are rubble and the city lies in ruins! You people of Hazganni who despise the Sheyqir, I do not ask you to rise up against him, for fighting is the work of warriors. My words are for the Qoundi Ammar. Those who do not wish to die, come out by dawn light and throw down your swords. By Acuyib's Glory, you have the word of Alessid al-Ma'aliq that you will not be harmed. All those who refuse this offer of life, prepare yourselves to die!"

"Ah-less-*eed!* Ah-less-*eed!* Ah-less-*eed!*"

That night he went with his sons to the walls of the city. Clothed in black—and careful not to be seen, for the hazziri were theirs, not his—he walked beside them down a ravine and out on the flatland. Once there had been green crops here, graceful palm trees, sturdy pines. Now: scrub grasses, dry and yellow amid the stumps and charred corpses of trees. What had Za'aid al-Ammarad been thinking? Alessid shook his head. The man was a fool, and deserved to die as a consequence of his folly.

He saw no glint of swords. A light burned in each tower, but he was willing to wager that Shagara magic had everyone in Hazganni busy shoring up walls. As they neared the city, sounds echoing off the buildings confirmed it: shouted orders, clattering wood beams, the hollow ring of hammered nails. He very nearly laughed aloud.

A disembodied whisper and a hand on his arm slowed his steps. The hazziri truly were remarkable; he could see Kemmal only as a vague shadow against the starlit hills. "Ditch," was all the young man said. Alessid nodded, and followed him cautiously downward, giving grudging acknowledgment to the cleverness of the Qoundi Ammar. At the bottom of the ditch were short, sharp stakes—made of wood, not steel that would gleam even by night, their angle and the dark smear of poison on their tips fatal to charging men and horses.

A brief climb, and they were at the wall. Alessid crouched low, watching as twin shadows drifted back and forth, back and forth. They had begged him to stay in the camp, but they needed a guard just in case, and who better than their own father, their commander? This reasoning had fooled neither of his sons. He wanted to be there, he wanted to witness this magic being conjured at his pleasure.

He knew they were drawing griffins and vultures in their own blood: retribution and death. He wasn't certain which other symbols they used, but he did know dozens of bloodstones were being wedged into the cracks between bricks. Collected from hazziri worn by Shagara and Harirri and Tallib, Ammal and Tariq and Azwadh and Tabbor, they had previously been worked for beneficial purposes: to stop bleeding, to protect against scorpions, to purify the blood, to assuage grief. Over the past days Kemmal and Kammil had changed them, charged them with new purpose.

Kemmal had told him, "Were there clouds, we could persuade them through the bloodstones, and there would be a tempest. The same with wind, which also responds to this stone. But because there are no clouds and no wind . . ."

"One does not mock Acuyib by attempting to raise storms in late summer," Kammil had added. "There is a balance to magic, a rhythm that intertwines with the world of which it is a part."

"All I require is the toppling of a wall," Alessid had assured them. "Nothing so gaudy as a storm."

He listened to the frantic midnight noise from within the city and watched the dark and silent suggestions of men move back and forth nearby. Not fifty feet from him was an iron door in the wall. He looked at it longingly, wondering if he should have sent someone to steal inside and poison the Sheyqir's well, or open the main gates for the army, or scatter hazziri around the barracks to unman the Qoundi Ammar, or—

No. It was better done this way, done with demonstrable magic. Everyone in the city would see that the wall had toppled without any visible attack.

At length he began to hear a low, silken hum. Frowning, he concentrated—and gave a start when he realized it was coming from his sons. Rising, falling, a tuneless song and a wordless chant, the sound soothed and stimulated all at once, and he was so intent upon it that the first he knew of the magic's effect was when the wall at his back quivered.

Alessid scrambled to his feet as dust-dry mortar sifted down on him. The twins had done their work too well—the wall was not supposed to topple until tomorrow. Again he felt a hand on his arm, and the shadow before him murmured, "It begins—but it will be slow."

"You're finished?"

"Yes, Ab'ya." Kammil's voice was distant, exhausted. Alessid put his hands where he thought his son's arm must be and held only empty air. The shadow had moved on.

They were back down at the bottom of the ditch, weaving their way through the wooden stakes, when they heard the footsteps. Kemmal and Kammil had not reported any patrols on the other nights of their working—another stupidity of a complacent, arrogant al-Ammarizzad. But footsteps there were, and Alessid froze, his sleeve a finger's breadth from poison. He was trapped here in the lethal forest, hideously exposed and utterly helpless.

He looked over his shoulder. A single man, bent nearly double under the weight of a huge sack, trod heavy-footed to the iron door. He lowered his burden to the ground, wiped his brow, and drank from a waterskin at his belt. Alessid's muscles began to ache with the strain of immobility and the thwarted urge to flee.

A few minutes passed. Then the door opened, silent on well-oiled hinges. A woman's shape was limned by light from the small candle she held. The man swung the sack over the threshold as she groped in a pocket of her dark cloak for a small pouch, which she handed to him. Food, Alessid thought. Only a woman buying food for her family or for sale. With the cessation of regular delivery from the countryside for almost a month, people acquired food however they could. He watched the man shake his head and try to give back the pouch and deduced that he was a relative, perhaps a brother or cousin, unwilling to accept payment for keeping this woman and her family alive. At least the Sheyqir's idiocy in not posting regular patrols allowed clandestine supplies to enter Hazganni. Perhaps some of the Qoundi Ammar were well-paid to ignore the traffic.

But the woman glanced over her shoulder nervously, as if worried she might be seen and caught. The man moved to close the iron door as she hunched over, grasping for a hold on the burlap. All at once she jerked convulsively, and pitched forward to sprawl across the sack.

The man stumbled, and cried out, and fell down dead, and five soldiers surged out the door, crimson cloaks swirling as the dreaded Qoundi Ammar spread out to search for other prey.

"That's two," a soldier said to his companion, "who'll not be defying the Sheyqir's orders."

"Did they think us so stupid that we would not be watching, even when we seem not to watch?" another chuckled.

Alessid could not even tell his sons, his twin shadows, to escape. He dared not utter a sound. He found that he *could* not utter a sound. Yet it was not fear but anger that closed his throat and thickened his tongue within his mouth and sheened his skin with sweat. He had been as stupid as the pair now lying dead on the ground. He had put too much faith in Shagara magic to keep each and every member of the Qoundi Ammar working at the walls all night in terror of their falling down tomorrow. Instead, his enemies would fall upon him—it would be only moments before their questing eyes turned to the ditch—and his dream would die with him. His purpose, his hope, his desire, his reason for being alive, all would be gone. And without him—

He saw then the danger of investing all vision, all power, in one man. One mortal, killable man.

Over the renewed shouts within the city and the calls of the soldiers to each other and the thud of their boots on the sun-baked soil, Alessid heard a hiss of pain. An instant later he felt someone take his hand and force upon his thumb a ring that felt slick and wet. The world became darker, and the starlit edges of the stakes and the ditch and the hills beyond blurred delicately. And he saw, quite clearly, Kammil standing beside him, no longer wearing the hazzir of agate and opal and silver that rendered him invisible. The young man's eyes were hazy with the lingering effects of his work, his face haggard, his shoulders sagging.

"Hurry—I'll distract them." His voice was scarcely a whisper.

"They'll kill you—" This from Kemmal, still a shadow.

"I'm already dead." He held out his arm, where the sleeve had been torn by a sharpened stake of poisoned wood.

Alessid never knew whether or not Kammil had grazed himself intentionally. It would be like him: a sacrifice to save father and brother, the act of a truly noble man. Alessid had time only to touch his son's face with a shadowy hand before Kammil ran back up the slope and called out derisively to the Qoundi Ammar.

Alessid and Kemmal escaped. They reached the hills, and the encampment, and Alessid's tent, and there Razhid was waiting. When he heard what had happened, he wept for his grandson, for in their shock and grief and exhaustion, his father and twin brother could not.

The wall fell.

Sheyqir Za'aid was slain by his own frightened and disaffected officials, who then surrendered the city to the mercy of Il-Nazzari.

Of the hundreds of Qoundi Ammar who had not managed to kill themselves for the shame of their defeat, Alessid selected ten and set the rest to replanting every single tree that Sheyqir Za'id had destroyed. When he was satisfied, he had them slaughtered. The ten, however, he sent back to Rimmal Madar. These were given hazziri to prevent them from taking their own lives because of their dishonor. Once in Dayira Azreyq, they said to Sheyqa Nizzira what Alessid had told them to say: that there was now a new, strong, united country in the world. Its name was Tza'ab Rih, for the searing, golden sand-laden storms that scoured its deserts, and for the army led by Il-Nazzari—whose true name was Alessid al-Ma'aliq, son of Azzad al-Ma'aliq.

When Nizzira raged and swore retaliation, the men told her the story of the fall of Hazganni.

Nizzira gave immediate, infuriated, inevitable orders to the qabda'ans of her army: Make ready a force sufficient to crush the al-Ma'aliq forever. The humiliated Qoundi Ammar agreed, eager to reestablish their honor. That night, the qabda'ans quietly and secretly came to a very different agreement: Enough soldiers and strength and substance had been spent on a land no one but the Sheyqa cared about. An hour before dawn, they sought out the only al-Ma'aliq remaining in Rimmal Madar in her well-protected obscurity, and they called upon her to leave her insignificant estate outside the city and become the new Sheyqa.

The precise circumstances of Nizzira al-Ammarizzad's death remain unknown.

Sheyqa Sayyida's first act was to declare that she and her progeny would henceforth be known as al-Ammarizzad al-Ma'aliq, in memory of her murdered forebears. Her second act was to send her eldest son to Hazganni on the fastest ship in the fleet.

Sheyqir Allim arrived two days before a magnificent springtime celebration at Hazganni and greeted Alessid as kinsman, conveying the heartfelt wish of his mother that the two nations live in peace, prosperity, and friendship, as befitted cousins bearing the same name and blood. To this, Alessid agreed—just as the qabda'ans of Rimmal Madar had hoped when they fixed on Sayyida as the only choice to take the Moonrise Throne.

Of the many gifts Sayyida's son brought with him, one became legendary in Tza'ab Rih: the elegant little diamond-studded crown given to Ammineh el-Ma'aliq by her grandfather and worn by her on the day she wed Nizzira's son. Saved by a loyal maidservant, given to Sayyida as a reminder of her mother, kept by her in secret, she sent it now to Alessid in token of their kinship. As it happened, this was the gift that pleased Alessid most of all.

The celebration was a gathering of representatives from every city, town, and village in the land, to witness and acknowledge the accession of the al-Ma'aliq. There was great rejoicing and feasting among the people from noon until sunset, and then the moment came. But when Alessid was summoned by the acclamations of the people into the great torchlit zocalo of Hazganni, he did not walk the flower-scattered path alone. Bareheaded, he was only the escort for his wife, in whose high-piled hair shone a delicate golden crown lavish with tiny diamonds. And that night Mirzah became Sheyqa of Tza'ab Rih.

The al-Ma'aliq left the celebrations at midnight. With Meryem and Leyliah and Razhid, the family paced in silent mourning to the place where Kammil lay buried beneath the wall he had helped to topple, securing the victory he had not lived to see.

— RAFFIQ MURAH, *Deeds of Il-Nazzari*, 701

15

"Aqq Allim, my friend!" Alessid rose to welcome his kinsman into his private maqtabba. "What brings you all the way here from Dayira Azreyq?"

Allim grinned. "The squalling of my newborn son. I swear to you, I was three days out to sea before the echoes faded and I could finally get some sleep." Tall and handsome like all the al-Ma'aliq men, he could have passed for the younger brother Alessid had named him. Only the cleft in his rounded chin was anomalous to their family, legacy of his late grandmother, Sheyqa Nizzira.

"My congratulations to his mother and to you—and to Oushta Sayyida. How fares she?"

Alessid served qawah with his own hands and settled with his cousin on piled pillows. He had two offices; this one inside the palace had a proper work table and chairs but also carpets and cushions to remind those who came here of his youth in the wilderness. The other maqtabba was a tent in the palace's vast gardens, where he met with the Za'aba Izim. In it, there were no reminders of the city.

"The name of al-Ma'aliq was enough to conciliate the northern tribes," Allim said. "They trust us, as they did not trust Nizzira. I am glad to report that Rimmal Madar knows a peace such as has not been known within living memory."

"This pleases me greatly," Alessid replied, nodding. Sheyqa Sayyida was a shrewd woman; the qabda'ans had been thinking of the immediate problem of Tza'ab Rih when they invited her to succeed her grandmother, but Sayyida had much more to offer with her al-Ma'aliq heritage. Peace with Alessid, to be sure—that was what the qabda'ans had wanted, and they got it. But there was peace with mettlesome northern tribes as well. Now both Rimmal

Madar and Tza'ab Rih were free of disputes, free to thrive. Trade had doubled and tripled in the last two years, and everyone was growing very rich.

Allim sipped his qawah and suggested, "I would imagine you find the al-Ma'aliq name almost as helpful as my mother does? True, here it does not have the same long history as in Rimmal Madar, but your father was greatly loved, and his memory is yet green."

Alessid made the required smile and nod: the former for the pun on his father's nickname, the latter for the compliment. Allim then hesitated, as if about to lead into the topic he had come across the sea to discuss. But Alessid wanted to hear more about Rimmal Madar first—because he had a very good idea of what Sayyida had sent Allim to ask.

So he diverted the conversation by saying, "But have I heard something about your mother's kin?"

Allim grimaced. "Chaydann al-Mamnoua'a has afflicted my mother with twenty-nine pestilences who are most unfortunately related to her by blood. I would not honor them with the term *kin*."

Of the fifty offspring of Nizzira al-Ammarizzad, children and grandchildren, one sat on the Moonrise Throne. Sixteen were dead of various causes: war against the northern tribes, illness, accident, suicide—including poetic Reihan. The others who had been with Reihan lived in seclusion far from the court. That left twenty-nine relatives of Sheyqa Sayyida to plague her.

"My own mother is a gentle, quiet woman," Allim continued, "who wishes only to tend her family and her country in peace."

"Admirable." Though it was of course a bald-faced lie; Sayyida would not have survived to inherit the Moonrise Throne had she been gentle and quiet.

"In fact—"

Ayia, here it was.

"—deeply as my mother loves my father, she often laments that he is not the kind of man who can rule a family the size of ours." Another grimace. "Three of my brothers married al-Ammarizzad. They are quite despicably prolific."

Sayyida had used those marriages to ensure her own survival in the years before her grandmother's death. Presumably the time was not yet propitious for divorces, or perhaps the young men had grown fond of the ladies and Sayyida did not wish to make her sons unhappy and therefore dangerous. Alessid understood perfectly, however, that because the Sheyqa was without daughters of her own, daughters-in-law were the only candidates for the succession until granddaughters came of age. Another al-Ammarizzad ruling Rimmal Madar? Unthinkable. And unnecessary.

"With so many to be ruled," mused Alessid, "it would be troublesome for even the cleverest man. More qawah?"

"Thank you. My mother," Allim persisted, "to be quite frank, envies you your daughters."

"And she wants to marry one of her sons to one of them, so that her grandchildren are doubly al-Ma'aliq—and have Tza'ab Rih doubly for an ally."

Allim's jaw dropped a little. Alessid smiled.

"Ayia, my friend and brother, it was not so very hard to guess. Sayyida is an astute woman. It is as well that you have no sisters, for I have no sons to send—one of them was divorced and no woman wants another woman's leavings. My other son is happily married, with two children, and I would have every Azwadh in the country at my throat were I even to hint at a divorce from their adored Black Rose."

Allim had recovered and said feelingly, for he had met the lady on a previous visit, "Any man who asked a divorce of Ka'arli Azwadh would be too stupid to find his own nose in a mirror."

"Besides this, Oushta Sayyida requires an intelligent young woman who can keep her informed."

"That is precisely her thinking. Would you consider it?"

Alessid pretended to do so, from politeness. At length he shook his head. "Ra'abi is the only one of an age to marry. Jemilha is but thirteen, Za'arifa ten, and Mairid only two. But I believe that even Ra'abi is too young to leave her home and marry a man she has never met and live in a place strange to her."

"My brother Zaqir would of course come to Hazganni, so that she may see him before any betrothal is contemplated." Blandly, he added, "It may be advisable for him to linger here. . .perhaps for several years."

Alessid nodded with equal composure. Sayyida had waited many patient years to become Sheyqa of Rimmal Madar; all her sons presumably also knew how to wait. Allim, however, seemed determined to make sure one of his brothers did his waiting a long, long way from home.

"Zaqir is the youngest," Allim went on, "and—though our mother pretends otherwise—quite her favorite."

A tidy way of saying that Sayyida was already disposed to look upon this son's daughters more favorably than the others.

Alessid mused, "I would actually consider sending her to Rimmal Madar, much as I would miss her—" He hid a grin as Allim's eyebrows twitched. "—but for one thing. The Sheyqa Mirzah is Shagara. Though special leave was given for my sons and daughters to be called by my own name, they remain Shagara in all that matters." Especially in the matter of the daughters who might bear Haddiyat sons. He had not the slightest intention of gifting his dear cousin, friend, and fellow al-Ma'aliq Sayyida with Shagara magic in the form of one of Ra'abi's sons. "In that tribe, it is the men who marry outside the tents, not the women."

"I am aware of this oddity," Allim answered. "But as an exception has been made in the name they bear, surely a similar exception—"

Alessid shook his head. "I am sorry, but this is impossible. I greatly desire an even closer connection with Rimmal Madar. But my wife would divorce me if I sent him one of our daughters."

"Divorce? Surely not! You have made her Sheyqa of Tza'ab Rih!"

"A task at which she excels. But she would be just as happy returning to her tent, and her family, and the ways of the Shagara."

Allim set down his cup. "So if this marriage is to occur, Zaqir must come to live in Tza'ab Rih." He actually managed to sound reluctant.

"Yes. And his children would be called al-Ma'aliq—*without* the al-Ammarizzad."

Allim's lips quirked in amusement, and it was Acuyib's honest truth that came from his lips as he said, "He would not mind. He loathed our late unlamented grandmother even more than I did. Ayia, when I return home, I will tell my mother all this—and Zaqir, too. I think they will agree. The Sheyqa desires this marriage."

Alessid nodded. He knew that Sayyida had in fact told Allim not to return without a firm commitment: The sons of Azzad's agents in Rimmal Madar were now working for Alessid.

"Aqq Alessid, you have not asked what kind of man Zaqir is, or whether he would suit Ra'abi." Allim's eyes had narrowed slightly, but there was a gleam of humor in them—as if he knew very well that Alessid already possessed more, and more intimate, information about his brother Zaqir than did their own mother.

Alessid pretended to consider. "She will not be shy about stating her views. If he believes talking is important in a woman, he is either extremely wise or an absolute idiot. If the former, Ra'abi would admire him. If the latter—" He grinned suddenly. "—she would most likely slay him."

"Ah. I begin to wish I was not myself married."

Alessid smiled. "More qawah?"

"Would that we marry off the other girls so easily—and so exaltedly," Alessid told his wife that evening.

Mirzah made no answer. She had put Mairid to bed and now sat on a couch upholstered in sky-blue silk, a basket of mending at her feet and one of Jemilha's tunics in her lap. Alessid watched her needle skim in and out of the soft green fabric, taking almost invisible stitches with the speed of long practice.

Perhaps Sayyida had pretended to be a sweet, gentle, useless woman who preferred to sit, and sew, and ignore the larger world. Mirzah would never have done so, not even to ensure her own survival. Shagara women did not pretend meek deference. Earlier, Mirzah had described the arrival of the forty Tallib women whose turn it was to guest in the palace and her plans for their stay. Each tribe was invited to send their most important women for a month in spring or autumn, when the weather was most pleasant and it was easiest to travel. The visits were Mirzah's idea, as were the small gatherings at which the women of Hazganni met and talked with the women of the tribes—and found that despite differences in their everyday lives they had much in common. Mirzah's next project would be to take groups out to a special encampment the Azwadh had volunteered to raise near the city, so that women who lived in houses could see how their sisters lived in tents.

The forging of a united country was not accomplished solely through the fellowship of men in war. Eventually there would be hundreds of marriages among tribes and townsfolk, and by the time the grandchildren were born, the people of Tza'ab Rih would think of themselves as *one* people, not many.

He watched Mirzah's needle glide through Jemilha's tunic, and he knew he had not only a wife but a true Sheyqa.

Still . . .

"Why don't you have the servants do that?"

Her shoulders, covered by a white silk robe and draped in a flame-colored scarf, lifted in a shrug. She kept on with her sewing.

"For nearly two years you have been Sheyqa, and yet you do your own mending. Mirzah, my wife, not only are there servants to do it for you, but it truly need not be done at all. Jemilha and all the girls can have as many new clothes as they wish when their old ones wear out."

"This is her favorite. I can hardly get her to wear anything else. And it's not worn out. The fabric is perfectly good. She merely tore a hole in it, climbing a tree."

Since coming to live at the palace, none of the girls could be kept out of the trees. Alessid understood. He'd spent his childhood leading his little brothers up every tree in Sihabbah, much to their mother's anxiety. Jemilha, though, had a special reason for risking scrapes and bruises: She wanted the best possible view of everything, so she could draw its likeness. From the first moment pen and ink were set before her, she had scorned making letters for the more complex delights of making pictures.

"She could climb a hundred trees and tear a hundred holes in a hundred tunics, and—"

"That she may do," Mirzah interrupted, her fierceness startling him. "You may call me Sheyqa of Tza'ab Rih, and we may live in this echoing great cavern with a hundred people waiting on us hand and foot—but if I want to mend my daughter's favorite clothes myself with my own sovereign hands, then by Acuyib I *will*!"

"You miss your own tent," he said.

Another shrug, and another silence, and another series of fine stitches.

"I understand, Mirzah." He was not overly fond of living in a palace, either, except for what it represented. And he had spent much time, effort, and money changing what it represented. Workers had spent half a year gutting it of Sheyqir Za'aid's atrocities. Most were merely ugly: tapestries of garish and improbable flowers, dreadful furniture with not an inch left uncarved. Some were truly ridiculous: the Sheyqir's own crimson porcelain commode, which had small braziers on either side so the royal member would not be chilled and a cushiony velvet seat so that the royal rump would not be chafed. A few of Za'aid's decorations were appallingly obscene: Alessid didn't like to think about the lewd paintings in the bedchamber. The seaside estate had been even worse. Mirzah had ordered the disgusting playground of the al-Ammarizzad emptied from cellars to roof tiles, and given it to her brother Fadhil to be turned into a dawa'an sheymma staffed with Shagara healers. For this alone, Tza'ab Rih praised their Sheyqa's name.

"I do understand," he repeated, and she looked up from sewing long enough to give him a skeptical frown. "Come, leave that. I have something to show you."

"I'm not finished."

"Finish tomorrow. Jemilha can live for a day without her favorite tunic, and climb trees wearing something else. Come."

He led her through the family's quarters, down a flight of stairs, and along a stone corridor to a large double door. The wood was carved with an intricate tree that disguised the juncture. On the left panel was a lion; on the right, a griffin. Both beasts wore crowns.

He saw that she comprehended the symbols at once. The lion that was his own name. the griffin that had become his personal icon, and the tree of life that was the Shagara.

"These will be your rooms," he told her. "I had hoped to have them ready for your birthday, to surprise you—but I think tonight you need to see them."

"My rooms now are perfectly adequate."

"Mirzah, don't be so stubborn!" He opened the doors and heard her catch her breath. All the gaudy, tasteless al-Ammarizzad ornamentation had been removed. The entry hall was a soothing square of green tile floor and white walls and four rounded archways, with an intricacy of gilded plaster-work molding that spelled out excerpts from *The Lessons of Acuyib* dealing with family joys.

"To the right are your reception chambers," Alessid told his wife. "To the left, your private rooms. And straight ahead—"

He guided her toward the far portal. Beyond a carved folding screen was an indoor garden, but without plants. Instead, artisans had created a cool, inviting haven of rich color and gentle sound. From a central fountain water chirruped into a shallow square pool tiled in a whirl of blues. The raised edge was green, as were the floors and the walls as high as Alessid's knees; a winding maze of gleaming trellises rose ten feet high, dappled with flowers. Above this the tiles were blue again, darker and darker as they rose to the ceiling: a deep sapphire dome misted with tiny silver stars. From the dome's apex depended delicate silver hazziri on nearly invisible chains that chimed counterpoint to the fountain. An arching alcove in the north wall contained a carpet, a real one, of blue and green and rose, matching pillows, and a small recessed shelf for a lamp and books.

"This, too, is yours," Alessid said softly.

Mirzah glanced up at him. "Mine?"

"Yes—and any guests you care to share it with." He slipped an arm around her waist and drew her toward the softly carpeted alcove. "I was hoping to be the first. . . ."

She froze beside him. "No. There will be no more daughters to sell off in marriage—and no more Haddiyat sons that I will outlive."

He touched her cheek, trying to soothe her. She jerked her head away. Telling himself to be patient, he began, "Kammel's death—"

"—came too soon, even for one of his kind. How long will his brother live? Shall I go on having babies to replace the sons I will lose?" Her voice rose, her words quickened. "I'm young enough still. How many do you want, husband? How many sons and daughters does the al-Ma'aliq require?"

"Mirzah, you don't mean this."

"I mean it with every bone in my body, Alessid."

"Ayia," he said coldly, "then I will trouble you no more. There are other beds, after all."

"Ayia," she responded in the same tone, "and should I learn that you have lain down in one, I will divorce you as is my right and take my children back to the Shagara tents."

Alessid al-Ma'aliq was not accustomed to being thwarted; still less was he familiar with being threatened. For a full minute he simply failed to react.

In that time his wife turned on her heel and left the ever-blooming garden he had created for her delight. He heard the soft whisper of her slippers on the tiles. The opening and closing of the doors. The mindless chatter of the fountain and the maddening tinkle of the hazziri. He looked around at the shining tiles—a mimicry of living things and glinting stars, a chill illusion.

To the unreality, he said, "Does she think I do not grieve?"

He left the cold tile garden and never set foot in it again.

Ra'abi el-Ma'aliq and Zaqir al-Ammarizzad el-Ma'aliq duly met, and genuinely liked each other despite the promptings of their parents' ambitions. She was pleased by his looks, his manners, his elegance, his education—and his deference to her greater position here in Tza'ab Rih while never behaving as anything less than the sheyqir he had been born. For his part, he was pleased that not only was she as lovely as his brother Allim had said, and as clever, but her words were as interesting as they were abundant. In 654 they were wed, and a year later she bore a son. Mirzah wept when she was told the child was a boy, but by the time she went to see him her eyes were dry and she was smiling.

Mirzah remained Alessid's Sheyqa, capable and conscientious, but she was no longer his wife. He was discreet about his infrequent pleasures. He might have taken an official concubine, of course, but as deeply as Mirzah had injured him, he would not injure her dignity by putting another woman in the palace. Indeed, he never took a woman inside its walls. Instead, when he traveled Tza'ab Rih—which he did often, showing himself to the people and familiarizing himself with their lives and problems—he invariably chose a young widow who never afterward remembered who her lover had been. Kemmal had been most obliging.

The young man had explained himself to his father on the night he offered the talishann. "I understand my mother's pain. I understand the guilt she feels. Because of her, I am gifted with that which makes me honored among the Shagara, that which allows me to do what other men cannot. But because of her, I will never father a child, and I will be dead at an age when other men are not even old."

"You may understand, but I do not. Other women have borne Haddiyat sons—Meryem, Leyliah—"

"She suffered greatly, losing Kammil so young," Kemmal murmured. "Forgive me, Ab'ya, but I think I may be the only one who knows what she feels. He was my twin brother, as close to me as my own thoughts."

Stung, Alessid said, "He was my son, too."

"I do not think she ever allowed herself to acknowledge that Kammil or Addad or I might be Haddiyat—just as she does not speak of it regarding her brother Fadhil. But now she cannot escape the knowledge."

"You mean to say that if she could be guaranteed only daughters—"

"Yes. Only watch her with Mairid. The joy of a girl-child is unencumbered." Kemmal paused a moment, then said, "I know that you cherish my mother. I know you would prefer to be her husband rather than another woman's lover. To go from woman to woman reminds you too much of your own father, and the tales told of—"

"Be silent!"

"Forgive me, Ab'ya. All I would add is that for your own health, you should not be emulating Sa'ahid the Chaste, content to chant *The Lessons* every night until dawn."

And then he had presented his father with appropriate hazziri and in-structions as to how they worked.

With Ra'abi happily married to Zaqir, Jemilha was next. She chose Ka'ateb Tallib from the young men presented as suitable. Her sister Za'arifa, barely fourteen, decided at the wedding that Ka'ateb's younger brother was the man for her and made the next year unbearable with her impatience.

There was never any further question about where his daughters' hus-bands would live. Not only were the girls Shagara, who therefore did not leave the tribe, but one did not marry a son into the family of the Sheyqa of Tza'ab Rih and then negate the advantage by keeping him and her in the desert. The young men were their families' conduits to influence, and they all knew it.

The day after Za'arifa's marriage, a delegation from Ga'af Shammal begged audience with Alessid. Invited to the wedding for courtesy's sake, they made the long journey for curiosity's sake and were dazzled by all they saw. In the audience hall they came straight out with it: they wished to be-come part of Tza'ab Rih.

Their unmannerly directness offended Mirzah. Standing at her side where she sat in the plain wooden chair she insisted on, scorning the silver throne left here by the al-Ammarad, Alessid felt her fingers claw stiffly into his wrist, and placed his hand over hers in warning.

She spoke before he could draw breath. "You are independent of any ruler. You have ever been so."

"Yes, great Sheyqa," said the al-Arroun who headed the delegation. "And have paid for it in our blood. When the Qarrik came, and the Hrumman, and the barbarians from Granidiya and elsewhere—ayia, we survived them all, but we are weary. We must waste the time and strength of our young men to guard the northern border when they ought to be adding to our wealth by crafting goods and tilling fields and tending sheep."

Living could be dangerous in Ga'af Shammal. Raiding barbarians sacked towns and stole livestock. They did not attempt to take the land, only to take from its people the fruits of it and their labors.

"You have an army, glorious Sheyqa," al-Arroun continued, "mounted on strong horses."

"Ayia, I do," Mirzah told him. "And you propose what, precisely?"

Alessid bowed his head to her, saying, "Your permission, Sheyqa?"

Compressing her lips, she nodded briefly. He was always scrupulously polite about the fiction that she ruled Tza'ab Rih's exterior as well as interior affairs. He knew she hated him for it.

"We are not just neighbors but kinsmen, if I am not mistaken," he said. "There is more than one al-Arroun in the al-Gallidh line of my mother, is there not?"

"Perhaps another marriage can be arranged," Mirzah said cuttingly. "We have one or two daughters yet unwed, do we not, husband?"

Alessid forced a noncommittal smile onto his face. Mirzah seemed to care less and less about the manners she showed *him*.

Al-Arroun's eyes—dark green, legacy no doubt of some invading barbarian ancestor he was ashamed to acknowledge—had rounded like dinner plates with the prospect of alliance with the al-Ma'aliq. "It would not need that," he said hastily, "to bind our loyalty. We have all of us talked long and worriedly about this. There are those who dislike the prospect of becoming part of your realm—no insult to Your Highnesses intended. But they dislike even more seeing their houses burned and their work destroyed and their sons carrying swords. If it is agreeable to you, we would welcome you as our Sheyqa."

And so it was that Mirzah went to Ga'af Shammal, and met her new people, and set with her own hands the boundary stones that marked the borders. Alessid and five hundred of his cavalry went with her, and two hundred laborers to construct barracks in ten different locations, and ten Haddiyat of the Shagara to work the runes and icons that would seal the safety of Tza'ab Rih on this new borderland.

Some weeks after their return to their palace in Hazganni, a curious incident occurred. The chattering fountain in the chambers Alessid had created for Mirzah, and which she never used or even visited, suddenly stopped working. This was due, said the annoyed Master of the Household, to little Sheyqir Zakim, youngest of Alessid's grandsons. An energetic toddler, he was into everything and usually able to get himself out of it. This time, however, he had decided to bathe his puppy in the shallow fountain pool, and the resulting combination of soap, fur, and a brush that shed most of its bristles had proved fatal to the delicate mechanism. The trouble was that the specifications had been lost, and the artisan who had designed the fountain was long dead. The waters would never play in the same fashion as before.

"Don't distress yourself," Alessid reassured him. "It doesn't really matter exactly how the water dribbles, does it?"

"But, al-Ma'aliq, there is the commission!" When Alessid looked a question at him, he went on, "From Sheyqa Ra'abi, to make for her husband's exalted mother a book of pictures showing the whole of the palace. It is for the anniversary of the Sheyqa's ascent to the Moonrise Throne, and it must be finished, it must!" He paced the carpets of Alessid's maqtabba and fretted as if the fountain had deliberately betrayed him. "Al-Ma'aliq, I appeal to you!"

Alessid knew who must be doing the drawings: Mirzah's brother Fadhil. He was Haddiyat like the man he had been named for, and at forty-two years old, Acuyib had been kind to him: His age showed not in stiffened joints or wrinkled skin but only in the pure white of his hair and a slight impairment of his hearing. Otherwise, he looked nearly the same as on that long-ago day when he had taken Alessid to Mirzah's tent to be married. Still, Alessid could not help but contrast Fadhil's age with his own vigorous prime, though he was only a year the younger. In the spring of last year Fadhil had given over governance of the seaside dawa'an sheymma to a younger healer, retiring not to his tribe's tents but to his sister's palace. And in his comparative idleness—there were always sniffles and scrapes and strains and sprains to be treated among the hundreds living here—he had learned from Jemilha how to draw.

She was very good. He was even better. Her work was careful and deliberate. His was instinctive, as if the pen and ink had been waiting for him and him alone. Discovery of this new talent so late in his life was a delightful surprise, and he had taken the likenesses of all the family, illustrated books for the children, and begun a series of landscape studies. He was the natural choice to prepare this very personal gift for Sheyqa Sayyida.

Fadhil laughed when Alessid told him of the Master's anguish. "I was saving all the fountains for last, you know," he confided as he opened the leather case containing his drawings. "Water at play is difficult. I'd almost rather draw each grain of sand in a storm! But I think I recall enough of how that one danced."

The illustrations were exquisite. Every leaf on every tree; each smooth cobble in the courtyards; all the delicate shadows and radiant light caught like an indrawn breath of delight on paper.

The drawing of pictures was not a Shagara art. Indeed, such impulses had always found expression in abstract pattern and ornamentation rather than faithful depiction of scenes or people. Signs and symbols, and the graceful script of *The Lessons*, these things were common decoration in the homes of Tza'ab Rih. Leyliah had considered this and in typical fashion had decided why it was so.

"If it is not small and portable, the Seven Names have no use for it," she told Alessid. "Look at that huge leather book my son is assembling! Can you imagine every family lugging something like that from camp to camp, adding to it, creating others through the generations? No, such things are for people who settle in towns, and have money to pay for them, and leisure to contemplate them, and don't have to pack them up and carry them!"

"But—"

"Yes, I know," she said before Alessid could fully form the thought, let alone voice it. "My answer to *that* is that in the distant past all the Names in this land—not just the Seven remaining in the desert, but all of them, Alessid—everyone lived according to the old ways. Some of them decided to stay in one place or another, and that was how Sihabbah and Hazganni and all the other towns were established. But people obviously retained the habits of travel, even though they traveled no longer. Besides, there is the question of materials. Parchment can be written on and scraped clean over and over—and Acuyib knows there are enough sheep and goats to provide it. But paper? Hideously expensive." She eyed him with the sudden sparkle of a smile that made her look half her age. "Fadhil is lucky that his sister is so very rich that when he makes a mistake or is dissatisfied with his work, he has only to rip the paper up or toss it in the fire."

Recalling his days of schooling—the tedium of having to scrape his faulty script off a parchment page so he could correct his mistakes was equal to the embarrassment of knowing that the action brayed his errors—Alessid was pleased all over again that he had made so wise a trade agreement with the barbarian realm of Qaysh. An enviable land, Qaysh was so lushly forested that trees could heedlessly be harvested for the production of paper.

A few days after Fadhil started on his depictions of the various fountains, he came to dinner one night with a bandage around his hand. "I was in my rooms, sharpening the pen to get the finer lines right, and the knife slipped," he explained. "I'm afraid I bled all over the drawing of that fountain in the tiled garden. But don't worry, I made another."

"I shall be interested to see it," Mirzah said at once, with a poisonously sweet sidelong glance at Alessid. "I've forgotten how many years it's been since I was in that part of the palace."

The next morning it was discovered that the broken fountain had sprung back to life. But the morning after that it was silent and still once more. No one noticed, except for the Master of the Household and the workers he shouted at—for Fadhil had unexpectedly died during the night.

Mirzah refused to leave her chambers. Alessid knew she mourned not just her brother but her remaining Haddiyat son, even though Kemmal was still alive and well and strong. Impatient with her obstinate determination to suffer, Alessid left her to it. She could accomplish her goal much better without him.

The morning after Fadhil's death, Leyliah prepared to take her son's body back to the desert. She invited Alessid to help her sort through Fadhil's possessions for remembrances to distribute among those he loved.

"I don't know why it happened," she fretted, folding and refolding tunics, shirts, trousers. "He was always well, wasn't he? A healthy little boy, and even as he grew older it never seemed as though he was growing old."

Alessid busied himself packing books that would be added to his own libraries—for the Shagara did not haul books from camp to camp any more than they did big leatherbound folders of artwork. He said nothing to Leyliah, but he was thinking that with the death of her adored son, she seemed all at once to have grown old.

"Something hidden," she went on broodingly, "something without symptoms . . . such things are not unknown, of course, but I wish I knew . . . I wish I had been here with him . . ."

He glanced around, astonished to hear tears in her voice. But she was dry-eyed, self-disciplined as always. He wished Mirzah could summon up the same control. Ra'abi had told him that her weeping was the worried talk of the palace.

To Leyliah he murmured, "It was very quick, I was told. A servant had brought qawah only moments before and hadn't even reached the stairs before she met a messenger in the hallway." What he didn't mention was that however swiftly death had come upon Fadhil, it had not been painless. The messenger, receiving no answer to his knock, had debated a moment whether or not to enter. A cry and a clatter from within decided him. Sprawled before the blazing hearth was Fadhil, already dead, an expression of appalling agony on his face. *"And the oddest thing, al-Ma'aliq—I didn't like to talk of this, either, not in front of his mother and the Sheyqa, but—*" The messenger twisted his fingers together. "*Both his hands were reaching toward the fire—like claws, as a heat-maddened man would grope his way toward water in the desert.*"

Why there had been a fire in the hearth in late summer was obvious to Alessid now. There were scraps of paper in the grate. Fadhil had been cleaning out his sketches, tossing into the flames those he didn't like or couldn't use. As Leyliah went through her son's jewelry coffer, Alessid crouched down and picked up the few remaining bits of scorched paper. A horse's head and part of the neck, the windblown mane much drawn-over, as if he couldn't get it quite right. The flow of a curtain drawn again and again, each one different, as if recording the shift of the breeze against the silk. The first tiled tiers of a fountain pool, which Alessid reluctantly recognized, a few stray droplets caught gleaming, the paper discolored by some brownish stain. A man's and a woman's clasped hands, with the beginning of a verse from *The Lessons* scrawled below ("*Let the woman and the man live with and for each other—*"). Alessid could not help but note the tenderness of that drawing, and wondered all at once if Fadhil had ever loved a woman. If he had ever regretted not having a child.

"What are those?" Leyliah asked.

She was standing right beside him, and only a lifetime of self-control prevented him from flinching his startlement. He showed her the little handful of half-burned drawings. "He was talented," he murmured. "Very talented."

"Yes." She glanced through them, lingering over the partial depiction of the fountain. Plucking it from his fingers, she said, "This must be the one he spoiled by bleeding on it. I must look through the finished pieces, to see if he managed to do a fair drawing for Sheyqa Sayyida."

She turned away, the blood-stained drawing still in her hand, and opened the leather book. Muttering something about better light, she swung the book around on the table, and put her back to him. Only when her shoulders began to tremble did he understand. He tossed the remnants of Fadhil's art back onto the hearth and let himself silently out of the room.

With her surviving children well married—all but Mairid, and Kemmal who had long been divorced—the Sheqya Mirzah applied herself more and more to governance of a realm that now stretched from the Barrens to the sea. Al-Ma'aliq turned his own attentions to study of the barbarian lands, for he wished to increase trade and make Tza'ab Rih even wealthier.

Qaysh, for example, was a land north of Ga'af Shammal, known to al-Ma'aliq primarily for its fine paper. Ruled since the departure of the Hrumman by the "Iron Kings" (for their name, do'Ferro, meant iron in the barbarian language), the land lay along the coast of the Ma'ashatar, the great western ocean. Blessed by Acuyib with abundance in fish, vines, forests, and grain, the people of Qaysh lived an easy, pleasant life—the kind of settled life that allowed what Leyliah had called the leisure for contemplation.

Al-Ma'aliq soon learned, though, that such leisure also made for political friction and personal mischief, which on occasion were one and the same thing.

— RAFFIQ MURAH, *Deeds of Il-Nazzari*, 701

16

"No, Jefar. I will see no one," Alessid snapped. "I will not receive people I don't know, who have the impertinence to come here— uninvited!—during a time of mourning. How you can even suggest it is beyond my comprehension."

The younger man bowed nearly double. "Forgive me, al-Ma'aliq."

Alessid was instantly ashamed of himself. His own sorrow for the death of Meryem Shagara was deep; Jefar was hurting, too, for he had recently lost his young wife in childbed. So Alessid gave him words rarely thought, let alone spoken. "I am sorry, my friend. That was selfish of me."

Jefar straightened up, gesturing away Alessid's concern. "The apology must be mine, al-Ma'aliq, for disturbing you. But what I have heard, together with what little this man has told me, made me believe you would wish to see him."

"Who is he?" Alessid rose from the paper-strewn table where he had spent the last futile hour trying to lose his grief in work. Meryem, one of the mainstays of his life—and one of the few who still remembered his father, Azzad. It irked him that this latter thought occurred to him over and over again. "What does he want?"

"He calls himself Baron Zandro do'Gortova, an emissary from Count Garza do'Joharra."

"Oh. A barbarian."

"Ayia, yes," Jefar replied casually, "but with a tale to tell of King Orturro of Qaysh, and—"

Interest sparked. "The one with the daughter?"

"Yes." Jefar paused. "The intriguing thing is that I have had a report from a border garrison that an emissary from the King of Qaysh crossed into Tza'ab Rih a day behind this man who would speak for Count do'Joharra."

Alessid paced the carpet for a few moments, then turned to Jefar with a smile. "Then the rumors are true, and the girl is with child."

"So it would seem, al-Ma'aliq." Jefar had a golden Shagara face of the type that would only grow more handsome as he entered his thirties and forties, but his eyes at that moment might have been those of a naughty little boy contemplating mischief with unholy glee. "Qaysh and Joharra are evenly matched, they say."

"The reason for the proposed marriage alliance. Precisely. I think I would very much enjoy meeting these barbarians, don't you?"

Orturro do'Ferro da'Qaysh, a man in his late prime, had occupied the throne of his ancestors for eight years. Depending on which faction one listened to, he was energetic, self-confident, and resolute, or restless, arrogant, and stubborn. Denied by his late father nothing but that which he wanted most—power—he had come to kingship at the age of forty determined to exercise the full scope of royal privilege, especially when it came to the right of taxation. Decrees flowed from the palace at Ferro, and what flowed back was money—in torrents. With it, he established a court such as Qaysh had never before seen. To this court at Ferro had come Count Garza do'Joharra, who ruled an independent realm of his own. Approximately the king's age, having just buried his third wife, Count Garza presented himself as a suitor for the hand of Orturro's daughter. He was still very handsome; she was ambitious for an important marriage; her father understood quite thoroughly that he could not best Joharra on the battlefield, so he might as well face facts. Matters progressed to the satisfaction of all—until Count Garza's only daughter, Nadaline, arrived in Qaysh ten days before the celebration of her father's fourth wedding.

It was said that King Orturro had been so instantaneously smitten that the fabulous pearl-and-garnet necklace he had intended as his daughter's wedding present had graced Nadaline's lovely throat within hours of her arrival. Everybody was furious, nobody was speaking to anybody else, and not only had the marriage been canceled, but all parties had withdrawn to their best-defended strongholds to prepare for a war neither could win.

"Ayia, one would not think it compassionate," Alessid mused, "to find so much amusement in other people's calamities."

"I think, al-Ma'aliq, that Acuyib has a most elegant sense of humor."

"I agree. Allow these men to present themselves—one at a time, and each without knowing the other is here. This is possible?" he asked, knowing it was.

"Of course," Jefar answered. "The one from Qaysh has been here three days, the one from Joharra less than one—both in strict isolation. They're not happy about it." He shook his head sadly, dark eyes dancing.

"In a few days, then, they will be most desperate to be cheered up."

Jefar bowed again, shoulders shaking now with repressed mirth. "Al-Ma'aliq is wise and perceptive."

"Al-Ma'aliq is wondering how he will keep from laughing himself silly."

Four mornings later Alessid entered the tent in his garden. Garbed in a white silk robe with an embroidered white-on-white gauze cloak over it, an elaborate hazzir gleaming from his breast and the rings that had been his father's and great-uncle's on his hands, he arranged himself on carpets and pillows to receive the ambassador. He had not ordered refreshments; those who believed in Acuyib's Glory did not eat or drink with barbarians. In fact, everything about this reception would purposely emphasize the differences between the people of Tza'ab Rih and those who had once thought to conquer them. It was as luscious as the taste of wine-soaked pears on a sweltering day, that now the northern barbarians had come not to conquer but to beg. For Alessid had a very good notion of why both the King of Qaysh and the Count do'Joharra, so evenly matched in military terms and so enraged with each other, had sent their men to him.

The tent flap parted, and Raffiq Murah entered and bowed. He was a plump little man with a scholarly air, sent to court some years ago by his father to acquire some polish. As the scope of Tza'ab Rih's affairs widened, Alessid had been delighted to discover that Raffiq had an ear for languages and a tongue that could work its way around barbarian speech. Its written form was as ugly to the eye as its words were to the ear, all angles and sharp points; a language, spoken or written, ought to flow like water.

"Stand here beside me, Raffiq, and do not give me only his words, but your thoughts on their meaning."

"Al-Ma'aliq honors me."

Jefar brought in the ambassador. A big, brawny-chested man with a high color staining his broad cheeks, he had to duck far beneath the opened flap, which caused him to bow sooner and lower than he intended. This upset him, and Alessid almost smiled to see it. But what interested him most in these first moments was that the man wore a most curious assemblage of clothing. The bright red shirt had flamboyant, billowing sleeves, not buttoned at throat and wrists like an honest man's but tied with fluttering ribbons stiff with gold embroidery. The sleeveless woolen garment that went over it was bright green and likewise embroidered in gold; it was closed with laces to the waist, where it was cut sharply back to fall from hips to the tops of high black boots. An immodest garment, showing everything a man possessed, for, oddest of all, he wore trousers such as women wore beneath work tunics. The trousers were made of leather. Alessid blinked once, thinking that he must be mad to wear such things in this climate, and nodded permission for Jefar to speak.

"Al-Ma'aliq, I present to your notice Don Pederro do'Praca, nephew and ambassador of King Orturro do'Ferro da'Qaysh."

Hearing his name, the man bowed and spoke. Raffiq translated. "My noble uncle King Orturro greets His Excellency with all good will and friendship, in the Name of the Mother and the Son."

Alessid replied, "Al-Ma'aliq recognizes the emissary of King Orturro of Qaysh, and welcomes him to Tza'ab Rih in the Name of Acuyib of the Great Tent, may the brilliance of His Glory be made known to all those pitiable souls currently living in darkness."

When this was translated, Don Pederro's thick brows quirked in faint annoyance at the implication, but his voice was smooth as he expressed his wishes for the continued health and happiness of Alessid and his family. Alessid answered in kind. There were more pleasantries, indicating that the barbarian had at least a modicum of manners, but Alessid was amused to note that the ambassador's cheeks were redder than ever, and sweat had appeared on his brow. At length, Alessid did the correct thing and told Raffiq to ask Don Pederro the purpose of his visit.

There followed a protracted tale of insulted pride and outraged honor. Many times Raffiq had to beg the man to slow down. Alessid easily picked the ripest bits: if Nadaline do'Joharra was pregnant, and it was by no means certain that she was, it was none of King Orturro's doing; Orturro's own daughter was inconsolably insulted by Count Garza's repudiation and abandonment of her mere days before their wedding; the crimes against Qaysh were obvious and required immediate redress.

"The King of Qaysh is confident that his friend the King of Tza'ab Rih—I must add for myself, al-Ma'aliq, that the insult to the Sheyqa be forgiven, for this man comes from a place that cannot work its collective mind around the notion of a woman as head of state."

"No matter. Go on."

"The King of Qaysh knows that Your Highness will readily understand that an insult to one royal master is a challenge to all and must not be allowed to stand," Raffiq concluded, stifling a sigh of sheer gratitude as the ambassador at last fell silent. Alessid traded amused glances with Jefar. "Finally—again, I ask forgiveness on my own behalf, al-Ma'aliq, this man has the manners of a goat—he says that the King of Qaysh is certain that his request will be given a favorable reply."

"Oh, he is, is he?" Alessid kept his face and voice as bland as milk. "And what do *you* think?"

"I believe he has been told to return with a favorable reply or not to return at all."

"I agree." Alessid reclined on his pillows. "Ayia, his story is most entertaining, but he's lying when he says the girl might not be pregnant. She is, and by the king. *Don't* tell him that!" he added quickly as Raffiq opened his mouth. "Tell him that I am—ayia, what am I, Jefar?"

"Stunned, al-Ma'aliq. And perhaps sympathetic, as the father of daughters?"

"Oh, absolutely. I am stunned and sympathetic, and I will consider seriously the King's request. Now get him out of here. He looks as if he'll collapse any moment. Leather, in this heat!"

That afternoon the scene was repeated with the emissary from Count Garza do'Joharra. Baron do'Gortova was introduced, sweating even more profusely than Don Pederro, for his clothes were entirely of yellow wool, lushly embroidered in silver, and he wore a large black felt hat with two purple plumes that sagged limply in the heat. The pleasantries exchanged were the same; the tale of insulted pride and outraged honor was the same (though from the opposite perspective, and Nadaline was definitely pregnant); the request that ended the recital and Alessid's promise to consider the matter were also the same.

When the Baron had departed, Alessid lay back on his pillows and laughed himself silly. "Two furious women wanting vengeance on their lovers, two furious fathers wanting the other's balls on a stick, and two armies preparing for a war neither can win! Acuyib is more than good to us, Jefar!"

Two mornings later, to Don Pederro of Qaysh, Alessid said: "I am shocked and appalled by the tale you have told me. After much thought, I have decided to honor your request. In twelve days' time, my men will cross the border. I shall expect your master's troops to leave whatever strongholds they now occupy and proceed to a suitable place for battle. Be assured that I will send enough men to make certain of a great victory."

That same afternoon, to Baron do'Gortova of Joharra, Alessid said: "I am shocked and appalled by the tale you have told me. After much thought, I have decided to honor your request. In twelve days' time, my men will cross the border. I shall expect your master's troops to leave whatever strongholds they now occupy and proceed to a suitable place for battle. Be assured that I will send enough men to make certain of a great victory."

It was only the literal truth.

In due course the mounted troops of Tza'ab Rih rode north to a river valley, a most suitable place for battle, whereon were assembled the opposing forces of the King of Qaysh and the Count do'Joharra. Messages were sent to both camps suggesting certain tactics—to which they readily agreed. Then battle was joined, each side expecting the Tza'ab to enter on its behalf. The Riders on the Golden Wind split into two sections. One, led by Alessid al-Ma'aliq, annihilated the Qayshi; the other, led by Jefar Shagara, massacred the Joharrans. It was indeed a great victory.

And thus was the conquest of the rich barbarians lands begun, and the Empire of Tza'ab Rih established.

Twenty days after the battle, King Orturro do'Ferro da'Qaysh was found in a fishing village, ludicrously attempting to blend in with the local folk by living in a cottage. Jefar remarked that he might have gotten away with it longer had he not been paying for food with coins bearing his own likeness. The king was brought before Alessid, where he blustered and raved for a brief but amusing time before being given a choice of prisons: up a tower or down a dungeon. He chose the former and was led away. Ra'abi was then declared Queen of Qaysh—the title was familiar to the populace, even if power vested in the hands of a woman was not. But none objected, for all understood that her mother's land of Tza'ab Rih and her husband's mother's land of Rimmal Madar lurked behind her.

Sheyqa Sayyida was vastly pleased that Zaqir had become a king, but she was a little disappointed when Alessid gently corrected the mistake: Zaqir was the Queen's husband. No matter what the local custom, both title and authority would reside in Ra'abi. He didn't mention that after long consultation with Leyliah, he had decided that the people of Qaysh would simply have to get used to the idea that royal descent came through the female line. It was the female who produced Haddiyat sons—and no al-Ma'aliq ruler should be without one.

"People accustomed to kings will grumble," Leyliah warned.

Alessid shrugged. "Their opinions do not concern me."

"They should! You're letting them keep their religion—"

"A ridiculous faith."

"—their customs—"

"Including their incredibly impractical clothing."

"Alessid, *will* you allow me to finish!" she snapped. "They'll retain their lands and livelihoods as long as they're loyal—but consider the shock all this must be to them. I think it would be best if you let it be put about that Ra'abi is merely a figurehead, and the real power rests with Zaqir."

"That," he said, "would be a lie. The real power rests with *me*."

Thus at the age of twenty-three Ra'abi became a Queen, and took a new name: al-Qaysh al-Ma'aliq. She and Zaqir and their children traveled north to the palace at Ferro, which also received a new name. *Ferro* was too much like *ferrha*; Ra'abi declared herself unwilling to inhabit a bakery and so called her residence Il-Kadirat, honoring the name by which her grandfather Azzad was known among the people of Tza'ab Rih. It was an excellent and appropriate choice, for the palace rose in vine-covered stone in the midst of a lush valley, framed by forested hills and carpeted in wildflowers, and was green the year round.

That next spring Alessid took Mirzah with him on a ceremonial visit to Il-Kadirat. The people ought to see the great Sheyqa, who at forty-five was yet a handsome woman with great presence. She impressed them with her poise and dignity, but for warmth and charm they looked to Mairid. Ten years old, lively and quick and already bidding to be a spectacular beauty, Mairid was Alessid's favorite of his children. It pleased him to see that she was Qaysh's favorite as well.

The people, in truth, were genuinely welcoming. Alessid had given them the right to live their lives much as they had always done, including the practice of their Mother and Son religion. Their fear that Tza'ab Rih would bleed Qaysh dry was shown to be unfounded when Ra'abi canceled all of King Orturro's taxes. She levied only one to replace them: a yearly payment assessed of every man, woman, and child who did not profess belief in Acuyib's

Glory. Compared to what they had paid Orturro to support his ostentations, this tax was as nothing.

It helped when Mairid, instructed by Mirzah, announced to her sister's court that out of her own inheritance, *she* would pay the tax this year for every girl her own age in Qaysh. Naturally they loved her. And when in gratitude one of the noblemen gave her a pearl the size of a hen's egg, Alessid allowed her to keep it.

"You spoil her," Mirzah said that evening.

They were private in the chambers Ra'abi had readied for them—cool and luxurious, with windows half open to the breeze that rustled the pines. At home, windows were guarded by intricate wooden grilles; here, fine silk mesh screened out the insects, and of these there were an overabundance. Alessid heard his wife's words as he inspected bubbles in the window glass, intrigued and annoyed in equal measure by the way the flaws distorted the outside world. Imperfection always displeased him, but he had to admit that the strange shapes seen through the curvatures, especially the flickering of torches in the garden, might be considered pretty. It was a concept that abruptly disturbed him. It felt like something his father might have thought. Over his shoulder, he said, "Mairid is the last of my children. I intend to delight in her."

"There are always the grandchildren."

"But Mairid is *mine*." He paused an instant, and then with calculated coldness asked, "She *is* mine, is she not?"

Mirzah gasped.

"Ayia, of course she is," he went on. "She has my eyes, my cheekbones, my mouth—and my intelligence. She'll make a fine Empress."

"'*Empress*'?"

He turned to her then, relishing the shock in her eyes. "Didn't you know? Our son Addad is a fine man, but he lacks vision." Or, rather, he thought suddenly, Addad would see things through the distorting flaws in the glass, not as they were but as he imagined them to be—as they looked prettiest and most interesting. "The other girls will have their own lands—or hadn't I told you yet that Granidiya and Pracanza and Joharra will one day be a part of the Empire? I'm only waiting until Jemilha and Za'arifa are old enough to hold a country in their hands."

"Why?" The silver of her necklaces and earrings shivered with her rage. "Why must you always have more? More land, more wealth, more women—"

"I care nothing for land, except as it nourishes my people. Wealth is useful for the same reason. As for women, I defy you to find even one who claims to have enjoyed my favor."

"You haven't slept solitary all these years!"

"Prove it," he said. "Prove it, and divorce me—and see if your daughters wish to return with you to the Shagara tents, when I can give them kingdoms."

"Take care lest those in the Shagara tents come to *you*, as they did to your father!" She gave him a sleek smile: *I know things that even the great al-Ma'aliq does not!* "There are many who agree with those who exiled themselves years ago rather than countenance the perversion of Shagara ways."

"A few malcontents—"

"More than you know! And remember that they succeeded in killing your father where the mighty Geysh Dushann failed! You have used everyone, *everyone*—the Shagara, my daughters, my sons—without pity, without conscience—you're not the man your father was!"

"Acuyib be praised for it," he retorted.

"Chaydann al-Mamnoua'a be *blamed* for it! Azzad never used the people he loved! But you—you don't love anyone at all, *unless* they can be of use to you!" Tears streaked her face, aging her. "And it *kills*, Alessid—being of use to you *kills*."

He turned and left her, shutting the door behind him. He leaned against the carved wood, listening to the sound of her weeping. Long ago, he remembered, he had returned to her tent to find her crying over their Haddiyat sons. Her tears had moved him then. Not now. He wondered when he had stopped caring for his wife, and after a few moments' thought decided it had happened just now, tonight. Today he had been proud of her as she met the people of Qaysh; he had watched with pleasure as they admired her mature and dignified beauty; he had smiled when she smiled on accepting flowers from little girls. Not his wife for years now, she was an able Sheyqa, and that had been enough to retain his love.

It was no longer enough.

Mirzah was the mother of his children—surely he ought to love her still for that. But what was she, truly, other than a woman who used to be his wife, who had given him children in the past, whose function was to appear at his side and smile? He respected her as a Sheyqa, but he no longer loved her as a woman. Perhaps she was right about him. Perhaps he only loved where there was usefulness to his ambitions.

No. He loved his children unreservedly. Each time he passed the place where Kammil had died beneath the walls of Hazganni, he nearly wept anew.

Kammil had died being of use to him.

Alessid was not Azzad. Why should he regret this? He was alive, and he would make his children rulers of vast lands. What had charming, foolish Azzad done to match that?

After a brief and entirely satisfactory little war, Za'arifa became Queen of Granidiya. Two years later, King Joaono do'Trastemar was deposed and killed, and Jemilha became Queen of Ibrayanza. Yet even watching what happened to its neighbors, the land of Joharra resisted conquest by the Riders on the Golden Wind. This was a curious circumstance, for its army had been wiped out and Count Garza killed. But Nadaline yet lived, and her son as well, in the fastness of a mountain castle said to resemble the ancient al-Ma'aliq lands in Rimmal Madar, and loyalty to the girl and her baby was comparable to that of the people for the al-Ma'aliq. Alessid reluctantly respected this and decided the easier lands would be added to his empire first before he turned his attention to Joharra once and for all.

There was plenty to do in organizing the three countries already acquired. Tza'ab Rih flourished, as did his family. There were four grandsons and seven granddaughters to help Alessid celebrate his fifty-fifth birthday. He loved all of them—but part of his heart was reserved for the children his beloved Mairid would have one day. She was nearly sixteen, and it was time she married. He had kept her with him too long, cherishing her too much to relinquish her.

The day after his birthday banquet, he called her into the great tent in the gardens. He had done the same with her sisters to announce the names of the men from whom they would select their husbands. Ra'abi, Jemilha, and Za'arifa had all dressed in their finest, jingling with hazziri and swirling with silks, aware of the importance of the occasion even though it was private between each girl and her father. Mairid arrived in a plain work tunic and trousers, barefoot and bareheaded, filthy from working in the herb garden.

"I know what you want to say, Ab'ya," she told him before he could do more than open his mouth. "But I've already chosen my husband."

"Ayia?" was all he could manage.

"Ayia," she agreed, smiling. "Jefar."

"Jefar!" Alessid sat up straight on his piled cushions. "He's twice your age!"

"If that's your only objection—"

"It is not!" he roared.

She picked dirt from beneath her nails. "I can't think of a single reason why I shouldn't marry him. And I really don't want to hear any that you make up for the occasion. Should you forbid me, I'll simply take him into my bed. If you don't want a scandal, Ab'ya, for all of Hazganni to tittle over the way they did over that silly Nadaline girl, then you'd better let me marry him without making a fuss."

"You won't be taking anyone anywhere if you're locked in your rooms," he said darkly. "And I find it difficult to imagine how you could become pregnant if Jefar is posted to a garrison in Ga'af Shammal."

"Don't be silly, Ab'ya," she scolded, smiling. "You need him here. Don't you want to know why he'd make a good husband for an Empress?"

"No!"

"He's beloved of our people. He's Shagara—and we al-Ma'aliq need a link in this generation, after the Harirri and Azwadh and Tallib marriages. He's smart, and he's watched you govern all these years, just as I have, so it isn't as if I'd have to teach him anything. He's a brilliant war leader—having proved that at your side time and again—and the troops trust and love him. Just as important, the barbarians in the north have been defeated by him personally, so they'll know not to make trouble." She paused, and for the first time a powerful emotion shone in her eyes. "And I love him."

Alessid felt the air leave his lungs in a rush. She had thought it all through, like the Empress she would one day be—but she was also a young girl in love. He had never denied her anything, but he had to deny her this. Because it hurt him to do so, his voice was rough as he said, "Your feelings have nothing to do with it. You will not marry Jefar Shagara."

Suddenly she was no future Empress. Her jaw jutted, her eyes ignited, and her fists balled at her sides. "I *will* marry him! You can't stop me!" And with that she ran out of the tent.

Alessid jumped up and followed her. "Mairid!" he shouted, aware that it was undignified to be racing through the gardens after his wayward daughter. The workers were trying not to stare. "Mairid!"

She vanished into the stables. Cursing, he went after her, and in the noise and bustle of a hundred splendid horses and their grooms and trainers, he lost her. Grabbing a grizzled veteran of the war against Za'aid al-Ammarizzad, he demanded to know where Sheyqa Mairid had gone. The old man dropped the saddle in his arms, trembling with nerves at this furious aspect of the usually self-possessed al-Ma'aliq. Nothing came out of the aged veteran's mouth but panicky mumblings. Alessid abandoned him and strode along the alley between stalls. Beneath lofty rafters, magnificent stallions and noble mares looked curiously at him, many of them with Khamsin's eyes. He reached the last stalls, where Mairid's favorite filly, munching contentedly on oats, glanced around curiously when Alessid began a string of lurid curses.

Pushing through the back door into the sunlight, Alessid swore anew as he saw a slight figure on horseback galloping across the small paddock toward a fence. She had gone into the stables only to snatch a bridle from the tack room. Tempted to do the same and follow her, Alessid abruptly recalled days in his childhood when he had behaved exactly as Mairid did now. Frustrated, angry, unhappy, or simply bored, how often had he leaped onto a horse and ridden out of Sihabbah, putting speed and wind between him and his troubles?

He had done the same on that horrible night when his father and mother and sisters and brother had died. Escape—was there truly such a thing?

She was like him, his Mairid. She would return when she was ready. She would flee into the croplands, and then the forested hills, but eventually the horse would tire, and she would be back by nightfall. It wasn't like when he was a boy, and his mother worried about the Geysh Dushann. There were no such dangers in Tza'ab Rih, especially not to its ruler's favorite daughter.

Mairid did not come back by nightfall. Alessid worried, but told himself that a night spent sleeping on the hard ground wouldn't do her any harm. She would have sense enough to return home when morning came.

But morning did not come. Instead there blew in from the Barrens to the south a thick, choking wind, laden not with fine white-gold sand but with heavy black grit, thick and sticky. To go outside was madness, yet the daily life of Hazganni demanded that people indeed go outside—bundled in cloaks and veiled in silk and scarcely able to see.

Jefar Shagara went outside, draped from head to foot, his horse protected by thin silk over eyes and nostrils. Alessid waited for him to return with Mairid. He sat in his maqtabba, listening to the whining dark wind, his gaze shifting slowly from lamp to glowing lamp by which he was supposed to be tending the business of his Empire.

At last a servant came in. "Al-Ma'aliq, they're back."

Alessid went to the windows that overlooked the courtyard, but of course they were tightly shuttered. Even had they been open he would have seen nothing for the obscuring dirt. He stared grimly at the bubble-distorted glass and the carved screens beyond it, and said, "Send her to her rooms. Let no one see her but the servant who draws her bath and brings her food. If she is hurt, send her grandmother Leyliah to her. But no one else. And she is not to leave her chambers for three days."

The dark wind died down that night. Windows were gratefully opened to fresh air. Brooms wore out sweeping streets and zoqalos free of dirt. And everyone prayed to Acuyib for a swift rain to wash Hazganni clean.

When Mairid did not emerge from her rooms after the prescribed three days, Alessid surmised she was sulking. She was willful and stubborn, but so was he. Still, he called into his presence the servant who brought her food and water.

"What does she say when you leave her meals at her door?"

"Nothing, al-Ma'aliq. She has not come to the door to accept the food herself. The plates are left outside, and only the water is taken in."

Scorning him by starving herself was the action of a spoiled child. Mirzah was right; he had given Mairid her own way for too long. But when the fourth day passed and no one saw her, his anger was such that he went upstairs to her rooms and flung open the door, bellowing her name.

She lay on the flowered carpet, a frail little figure in a white nightrobe soaked with sweat and stained with vomit.

When Leyliah saw her—tucked up in bed, mumbling with fever—she turned white to the lips.

Alessid, who sat at his daughter's side holding her hand, felt his heart stop. "What?" he rasped. "What is this?"

"I cannot be sure," Leyliah whispered, suddenly looking every one of her seventy-four years.

Mirzah, seated on the other side of the bed, wrung out another cool rag and bathed Mairid's brow. "No, Mother. You *are* sure. Tell us."

Sinking into a chair, the old woman drew in a shaky breath. "Shagara legend tells of a burning dark wind that killed hundreds of our people."

"When their tents fell on them in the storm," Alessid reasoned.

"No. It was a disease. Hundreds died—the very old and the very young at first, then—"

"But some survived it."

Leyliah would not look at him. "Of every ten, four died."

"Mairid will live."

"Alessid—"

"She will *live*." He stared Leyliah down. "Summon Kemmal. He will make hazziri for his sister. She will live."

A spark of hope shone in Leyliah's beautiful eyes. "In that time long ago, there were no Haddiyat—" She stopped, and wonderment spread over her face. "Of the Shagara who survived, within a generation—"

"Then it's not inevitably fatal. Mairid will live." He looked at Mirzah. She nodded slightly. For that scant moment, they were in complete harmony.

"Yes. She will live." Mirzah's lips tightened as if to hold back other words, but within a moment they escaped, cold and bitter. "Al-Ma'aliq has decreed it."

At first the illness was confined to the poorer quarters, and people who tended animals, and those who worked in the fields. Not everyone took sick of having been outside, but there was no pattern to immunity. And soon the disease spread, and with it fear as more and more died.

The initial fever was followed by violent purging, as if the body tried desperately to rid itself of sickness. But this only weakened the victim, so that when the fever returned there was no defense. The tongue turned black, and death followed within hours.

Shagara healers were overwhelmed. Alessid sent to their summer encampment for others, but the disease had struck in the wilderness, too. The Haddiyat forsook their usual fine craftsmanship to make hundreds of crude hazziri, and after a time the specific combination of gems, metals, and talishann was discovered that could see a victim through the disease—although the work of some was more effective than the work of others.

But this took many weeks, and all the while people were dying.

— RAFFIQ MURAH, *Deeds of Il-Nazzari*, 701

17

He did not leave her bedside. He paid no heed to Leyliah, who urged him to eat, to sleep, to guard his own health. Mirzah came and went. She brought news that others were suffering among the family. The whole of Tza'ab Rih was in mourning for the Black Rose. Alessid felt a vague sort of pity. But he was too preoccupied with Mairid, too intent on her every breath and movement, to allow himself to think that soon he might be grieving. The disease ran its course; those who could not withstand it died, and those who were strong and blessed by Acuyib survived. By the twentieth day after the dark and stifling wind swept into Hazganni, no new cases were being reported.

Yet Mairid lay in her bed, fevered and insensible—not dead, praise be to Acuyib, but not recovering, either.

"It is interesting," Mirzah said one afternoon, while she bathed Mairid's parched and fevered skin, "that it took this to teach you how much you can love."

Too weary to contend with her, he said nothing.

"Then again," Mirzah went on, "if Mairid dies, she is of no use to you."

"Be silent."

"Who did you have in mind for her? One of the Tabbors?"

With sudden passion: "She can wed the King of Ghillas if she pleases—if only she will live."

"Careful. She might have heard that."

He glared at her over their daughter's frail body. "Get out."

"When I am finished here."

"Now."

She ignored him, and completed her task, and eventually rose and dried her hands. "Alessid, summon Jefar to her."

He felt something akin to hatred. Jefar, who had ridden out in the dark wind and stayed as well and healthy as ever. Jefar, whom his daughter loved.

It was bitter for Alessid to see Mairid's head turn feebly toward the sound of Jefar's voice. To see her dry lips curve ever-so-slightly in a smile when Jefar took her hand. To see the helpless agony in Jefar's eyes as he looked upon her fever-wasted face. To know himself supplanted, defeated. A bitter well from which he was compelled to drink deep. He watched them for a time, and then, when he saw in Mairid's eyes that she was lucid, clasped his own hands around theirs and said, "I betroth you, Mairid my daughter and Jefar my friend."

It had always been enough to be loved by those few whose love he desired. Now, to watch his daughter turn her eyes to another man, loving him more, Alessid knew there was more to love than *being* loved. And in proving his for Mairid, he had lost her. But surely, surely there was someone in whose eyes he would see it returned in full unchanging measure, someone in whose heart he would always be first.

His people. Yes. He had created a nation out of nothing. They knew it; they revered him; they loved him without reservation. When Mairid recovered and her marriage to Jefar Shagara was celebrated, their cheers were for Alessid as the bridal party walked through the streets of Hazganni. They cried out his name. It was release from worry and sorrow after the long months of sickness and death, but it was also love for him. For *him*. He had made them great. He would make them greater still. And he knew how he intended to do it.

Countess Nadaline do'Joharra had resisted Tza'ab Rih since the first Riders on the Golden Wind had destroyed her father and the father of her child. Barricaded in her mountain fortress with those who remained of her father's warriors—added to those who rallied to her from Qaysh, Granidiya, and Ibrayanza, the conquered lands—she had spent these years raising her son and keeping mostly to herself. Many years later, however, with the boy nearly a man and by all reports an accomplished youth beloved of his people, she had become an irritant. And Alessid was determined to take Joharra once and for all.

"How could we have let it come to this?" Mairid asked on the day word came that the army of Joharra had retaken five important villages from the Tza'ab. "Why wasn't she killed years ago, and her son with her?"

Alessid shrugged, and resettled himself on carpets in his garden tent. "I had other things to do."

"Ab'ya, it's time to give our attention to Joharra," she replied firmly. "This Countess Nadaline must be dealt with. And especially her son—for he can claim both Joharra *and* Qaysh."

"So your sister Ra'abi has been complaining to you, has she?"

"Having heard nothing from you on the subject, naturally the Queen of Qaysh is concerned." Brisk and efficient, she proceeded to detail options. As Alessid listened, he congratulated himself on choosing her to rule when he was dead. She knew what she wanted and how to plan most effectively to get it; tenacity was an excellent trait in a ruler. In the years since her marriage to Jefar she had borne two daughters and three sons, one of whom might be Haddiyat. The years had proven that all her sisters had birthed gifted Shagara males. It was very likely Mairid had done the same. But they would have to wait a while to find out—likely until after Alessid was dead.

But he was not dead yet. And Mairid was not so clever as she thought she was. He could still teach her a thing or two.

"All very interesting," he interrupted suddenly, winning a frown from her lovely brow. "But you forget an asset we have which the Joharrans do not."

"I've already described a plan for using hazziri—"

"I am thinking of something more subtle than magic."

"Which is?"

To her great and obvious frustration, he only smiled.

Later, alone with his thoughts in his maqtabba, he wrote a private letter to his cousin Sheyqa Kerrima of Rimmal Madar—who had succeeded to her mother Sayyida's Moonrise Throne earlier this year. What he proposed was not a thing Mairid would have considered. Nor Ra'abi, nor even her husband Zaqir, Kerrima's brother. But Alessid had thought of it, and that was why he ruled an Empire.

A few months after the delivery of the letter, Alessid had his reply. Countess Nadaline do'Joharra was dead, her son in exile, and all of Joharra firmly in the possession of Alessid's granddaughter Za'avedra the Younger, eldest child of Queen Za'avedra of Ibrayanza. Though it should have been one of Ra'abi's daughters, the only one available was but six years old. Thus it was that Joharra finally came into the Empire of Tza'ab Rih.

A little while thereafter, Alessid received in secret a strange and grim young tribesman from the east. He did not bow to the al-Ma'aliq, but the al-Ma'aliq didn't much mind. Sheyqa Mairid did mind; she frowned but said nothing.

"You allowed the son to escape," Alessid said.

"No, we did not, for the son was not in Joharra. Had he been, he would not have escaped."

"Nonetheless, Ra'amon do'Joharra yet lives." Alessid paused, relishing the moment. "As my father yet lived."

The Geysh Dushann tensed visibly, but only for an instant. "It was Acuyib's Will."

"Ayia?"

Reluctantly, his dark skin even darker with the rush of blood to his face, the Geysh Dushann replied, "As our kinswoman the great and noble Sheyqa Kerrima has said it, Azzad al-Ma'aliq lived, by Acuyib's Grace, that in time our enmity might be abolished in this favor to you."

Indignant, Mairid broke in, "Is that what she called it? A 'favor'?"

There was an impression of grinding teeth; the man was yet very young. "Reparation, then, for the attempts on your father's life."

Alessid nodded. "It is enough. Or, rather, it is not enough, but it will do. You and your tribe are no longer my enemies. I will so inform the Shagara, so that for the first time in almost seventy years your people may go to them for healing."

The Geysh Dushann was silent for a moment, and Alessid thought he might have stumbled upon a little wisdom. But then he burst out, "Which will not bring back my grandfather, or my father's brother, or any of those who died in those years from the enmity of the Shagara and the lack of that healing."

"As it will not bring back my father, my mother, my five brothers and two sisters," Alessid retorted. "We make our bargains based on the past, but we construct them so that the future will be better—or so we may hope." This was more for Mairid's benefit than that of the Geysh Dushann, but Alessid did not glance at his daughter to make sure she got the point. Eyeing the young man coldly, he commanded, "Declare to me, Ammarad."

The words blistered the proud lips speaking them, but they were said. "You and your tribe are no longer our enemies."

"Nor is the Empire of Tza'ab Rih."

More acid, but spewed out more swiftly so as to be rid of it. "Nor is the Empire of Tza'ab Rih." And he ended the oath by touching first his brow and then his heart.

Satisfied, Alessid asked, "So. How was it accomplished?"

For the first time, the Geysh Dushann looked smug and confident in what Alessid deduced must be the way of his kind. But his voice was bland as he remarked, "There is a family of artisans who make tiles. Very beautiful tiles. When these Grijalva came to redecorate the lady's bath, they were given . . . assistance. The tiles of a bath can be very slippery, and the waters thereupon . . ." He arched his brows delicately. ". . .treacherous in other ways."

"I trust no one else will experience the same accident?" Meaning, of course, that it should never be discovered as anything other than an accident.

"No one, al-Ma'aliq."

Alessid nodded and dismissed the assassin. Alone once more with his daughter, he said, "So you see, we did not require Shagara magic after all."

"Ayia," she sighed, removing the ornamental coronet that invariably gave her a headache, "but any contact with the Geysh Dushann is dangerous."

"As it happens, I agree. But this was the simplest way, and it solved two problems. I wish to leave you an empire as free of the past as I can make it."

"Yet the bargains we make based on the past—Grandsire Azzad's, yours, mine—are the foundations of what we do in the future. So there is no real freedom from the past, is there? Countess Nadaline is dead, the enmity of the Geysh Dushann is canceled, but—" She sat straighter, gaze narrowing. "The boy. Nothing was said of where he was, only of where he was not."

"So you caught that, too. Still . . . how much of a future can he possibly have?"

"None, if he intrudes upon my notice."

Alessid smiled to himself. "Go now, and say nothing of this. You will rule after me, so it was necessary for you to know the truth of what happened to Countess Nadaline. But to everyone else it must be a fortuitous accident."

When she was gone, he took out paper and pen to write another letter to his cousin Sheyqa Kerrima. He would send it with a fine young gelding and a gorgeous leather saddle from Sihabbah, jingling with golden Shagara hazziri.

Not the blooded kind, of course. Not the kind that really *worked*. One never knew when the past, in the form of al-Ammarizzad greed, might intrude once more upon his notice.

Leyliah Shagara was as beautiful in her old age as she had been when a girl. At eighty-six, her skin was a marvel of dusk-gold softness, and her hair was pure silver without a hint of yellowing, and her lustrous dark eyes saw as clear and straight as ever. She had outlived her husband, two Haddiyat sons, three daughters, six grandchildren, four great-grandchildren, and all the friends of her youth. She was the only one left besides Alessid who person-ally remembered Azzad al-Ma'aliq—one of the four men she had loved and the one she had mourned longest, for he had been the first to die. But in Alessid's opinion, Razhid and Fadhil and Abb Akkil were worthier of her sorrow than Azzad.

It was Leyliah, however, who pointed out what should have been obvi-ous to him: that Mairid's son Qamar, even in childhood, was Azzad all over again. At first Alessid rejected the notion. How could he love so thoroughly anyone who was so thoroughly a copy of his father? But when he looked with his heart, he saw the charm, the grace, the cheerful mischief, the enchant-ment of presence and smile. It was so easy to see Azzad as he must have been in boyhood, with his big dark eyes and laughing face and the ability to whee-dle anything he liked out of anyone he pleased. Yet even knowing this, fully aware that he was being wheedled, Alessid indulged the boy. The love be-tween them had nothing to do with favors asked or bestowed. Qamar loved him, even on the rare occasions when Alessid said *No*.

All the grandchildren spent at least a year living with the Shagara. Those who also had ties to the other tribes of the Za'aba Izim lived with them for a time as well, to affix the relationship as well as to teach the younglings about their heritage in the desert. The year Qamar spent with the Shagara was the loneliest of Alessid's long life.

The boy returned much taller but no more obedient than when he had left. Leyliah, in whose tent he had lived, reported him hopeless at every craft but one: that of horses. Alessid shrugged and smiled, and gave Qamar a splendid colt to train as his own. The horse loved him as devotedly as every-one else—to the extent of escaping his grooms and mounting the stairs to Qamar's chambers one evening when lessons had kept the boy from him for two whole days.

Thereafter, every few days Qamar spent the night sleeping in Shayir's stall. And every so often, Alessid joined him. He refused to concede to Mirzah that a bed of straw and blankets was not as beneficial to his aging bones as a feather mattress and silken quilts; indeed, he refused to acknowl-edge his years and did not even feel them when he was with Qamar.

They talked, and read books aloud by lamplight, and curried Shayir until he shone like golden fire. And then Qamar would sprawl on the straw, and Alessid would curl next to him and watch him sleep until sleep overcame him, too. He had never been so perfectly happy in all his life.

But when Leyliah had returned from the Shagara camp with Qamar, she had also brought words of warning. The Abb Shagara who had deplored Alessid's use of magic in war was long dead, as was his successor, but the new one thought like the old—and the cancellation of enmity between the Shagara and the Geysh Dushann, done without even consulting Abb Shagara, turned the leader's thoughts in grim directions. Leyliah had explained the necessity and the wisdom of it: that now no one in Tza'ab Rih need fear the assassins, that they had made recompense for the attacks against the al-Ma'aliq, that Joharra was now ruled by a Queen whose mother was a Shagara.

Abb Shagara had not been impressed.

"But neither does he encourage open rebellion," Leyliah concluded. "Though I must caution you, Alessid, that I believe this is more due to respect for my age than for your power. It is not right, but it is true."

"Then you shall have to live forever, ayia?" Alessid answered smiling, and went off to ride with his grandson.

Joharra did not stay quiet for long. Za'avedra the Younger ruled the land as her mother ruled Ibrayanza: lightly, unobtrusively. The people kept their homes, their farms, their shops, and their religion. But they also kept their pride alive, that they alone had resisted the Riders on the Golden Wind for so long. And they especially kept their hopes of return to independence, personified in the young man who, though bastard, could lay claim to two thrones.

Ra'amon do'Joharra was living in Cazdeyya, a mountainous land north of Joharra across the marshy river valley claimed by a family called do'Barradda. Alessid had no use for either piece of territory. He knew how far his influence could spread. He had established his borders and set up garrisons to guard them. Keeping the peace certainly gave his warriors enough to do.

Peace was the last thing on the minds of the Joharrans who attacked their own city in the autumn of 683. Ra'amon was not with them. Indeed, he later claimed he had no knowledge of what they did in his name. This was likely, as Cazdeyya was often isolated from the rest of the world by heavy winter snow and the occasional earthquake that rendered the roads impassable. Whether Ra'amon knew of it or not, however, the attack progressed—and succeeded. Queen Za'avedra, her husband, and their three-year-old son were captured and put to the sword. Joharra was no longer of the Empire of Tza'ab Rih.

This state lasted exactly as long as it took for the combined armies of Qaysh and Ibrayanza to reach Joharra. The siege and battles that ensued raped the surrounding countryside and nearly destroyed the city. But Joharra was at length retaken, and Alessid himself rode into its capital with its new Queen at his side: Za'avedra the Younger's sister, Dabirra. Eighteen years old, mother of two sons, Dabirra was determined not to make any of the mistakes she perceived her sister had made. It was only by direct order that she was restrained from reviving an ancient custom of the Hrummans who had once ruled this land: the taking of one life in every ten as punishment for a nation's crimes. Everyone knew who had given the command for mercy, and gratitude for Mairid's leniency was matched by real fear of Dabirra's wrath.

Alessid had come to Joharra with Mairid, Jefar, and three of their children. It was a pretty point of precedence, that entry into the city—Dabirra, after all, was now a Queen, but Mairid was the heir to the Empire. She let her cousin have her splendid day, following along last of all. For, as Mairid knew full well, once Dabirra and her husband and sons had passed beneath the war-shattered stone gates, all attention was on their future Empress. Alessid missed the spectacle, having ridden in front with Dabirra, but could imagine it. Beautiful Mairid, dignified gray-bearded Jefar; Rihana, sixteen and the image of her grandmother Mirzah at that age; Akkar, a scholarly fifteen and Mirzah's favorite; and nine-year-old Qamar, gleefully certain that all this commotion was for him and him alone.

"After all," he said to Alessid that evening, "was I not the very last one they saw? That makes me the one they waited all that while to see!" When Alessid laughed, stinging his grandson's pride, the boy sulked. "Ayia, you just wait! When I'm bigger, I'll make hazziri enough to show them all!"

And for the first time a chill settled on Alessid's heart when he looked at Qamar, because for the first time he began to understand the emotion that had crushed Mirzah's happiness.

Joharra soon settled under the iron grasp of Queen Dabirra and her husband. But she bore no more children, and her two sons were both Haddiyat.

When she died young, with no female heir, Alessid consulted Mairid regarding what was to be done.

Her answer was simple: give the people of Joharra what they wanted.

Her father stared at her. She laughed lightly and leaned over his worktable to tweak his white beard.

"How often have you seen Rihana these last few years? Not often. She fell in love when we first visited, Ab'ya."

"With a *barbarian*?"

"With Joharra. She will have it on any terms she can get. And I am of a mind to propose certain terms to her . . . and to Ra'amon do'Joharra. I think they will both agree."

Had he grown stupid in his old age? He understood none of this—most especially not the love of a half-Shagara girl for the mountains and forests and river valleys of a foreign country. An idea returned to him that in the last years he had been too busy to pursue: the relationship of people and place. Rihana belonged to Joharra, it seemed, through a process Alessid could not comprehend. Had her ancestors breathed its air? Had its water soothed their thirst? Had its soil yielded food for their tables?

He realized then that although he had lived with the Shagara for many years, had married a Shagara girl, and his dearest intimates were almost exclusively Shagara, he had never felt himself one of them. He had never really felt at home in the desert. He did not belong to that land, any more than it truly belonged to him. Was there too much of his mother in him, too much of Hazganni and Sihabbah—or, grim to consider, too much of his father and Rimmal Madar?

He did not understand it. Neither did he understand why Rihana agreed at once to marry a man she had never set eyes on for the sake of a land she had desired since first setting eyes on it. An emissary was sent to Cazdeyya, and Rihana moped and fretted for months before the reply returned. As preparations proceeded for this marriage Alessid would never comprehend, his granddaughter spent most of her time taking lessons from Raffiq Murah in how to speak her future husband's ugly language.

At seventeen years old, Qamar—who of course knew everything about everything—thought his sister a fool, and said so. His mother advised him to close his mouth and give thanks that not only had the matter been arranged to the satisfaction of all, but that Acuyib in His Wisdom had seen fit to move Ra'amon do'Joharra not only to change his name but his faith. He was as eager to return home to Joharra as Rihana was to make Joharra her home.

Alessid foresaw dreadful contention between them, despite the compromises each had willingly made for the sake of ambition. On the day Rihana departed for her new country and her new husband, he gave her a sealed letter, addressed to them both, to be opened the morning after the wedding. The contents were simple: a solemn reminder that peace and prosperity would come to Joharra not because of his name or her power but through a wise use of both. He urged the pair to let their mutual love of their land bind them to its service and recall always that their children would belong to Joharra and Tza'ab Rih in equal measure.

He did not write the words himself. In the last year or so, his hands had begun to stiffen and curl at the joints. Even lacking a single drop of Shagara blood in his veins, his fingers were as crooked as those of a rapidly aging Haddiyat. It was Qamar's slim, supple fingers that had written the letter. The boy added a touch of artistry to the solemn words, drawing talishann at each corner of the page, familiar to all who had ever bought a Shagara charm as a wedding gift: *happiness, fertility, love, fidelity.*

As Qamar waited for wax to melt so the letter could be sealed, he looked at his grandfather with eyes as large and sweetly innocent as a fawn's. Alessid knew exactly how much of this ingenuousness was a pose and how much was genuine: there was always a telltale quirk to Qamar's mouth when he was playing at an attitude. Alessid arched his brows, and the boy grinned suddenly, knowing he'd been caught yet again by a grandfather much smarter than he.

"Ayia, very well—I'll tell you," Qamar said. "What I don't understand is how Rihana's children can be half Tza'ab and half Joharran. It's one thing to be of two different tribes, like Challa Leyliah, or even two different countries, like you. I'm still trying to work out how Rihana can be so passionate about a place she doesn't even belong to, but that's another matter entirely. What I want to know is where her children's real loyalty will lie."

"It must be one or the other, you think?"

"Of course. I'm Tza'ab. An eighth part of me comes from Rimmal Madar, but it's been a very long time since Grandsire Azzad left, and I'm sure that even if I went there I wouldn't recognize any of it, or feel anything for it—not the way I did that year I lived with the Shagara."

"Recognize?" Alessid asked. "What does that mean to you?"

"I felt at home there." He shrugged elegant shoulders. "Maybe it was just hearing stories about it all my life, but maybe not. It just felt *right*, being there—as right as it does when I go to Sihabbah where your mother was born. Nothing tasted strange, the way it did when we went to Joharra."

"Tasted—" He regarded his grandson with astonishment. "That's it, you know. That truly is proof."

"Of what?"

"Do you remember, when Zaqir first came from Rimmal Madar to marry Ra'abi—"

The boy laughed. "Ab'ya, I wasn't born way back then!"

For a moment Alessid was startled. Such was his love for Qamar that it felt as if the boy had been in his life all of his life. "Someday you'll be an old man, too, and plagued with a pest of a grandson!" he scolded, but with a smile. "Ra'abi and Zaqir traveled the length and breadth of Tza'ab Rih, showing themselves to the people, getting to know them and the land. They were in one of the smaller villages beyond Sihabbah, dining with some people who had actually known my grandfather al-Gallidh. With the qawah and sweets at the end of the meal, nuts from their own groves were served. Zaqir swallowed exactly one of them—and began to choke to death."

Qamar's eyes could hardly get any bigger. "Why? Poison?"

"Don't be absurd, boy. Everyone ate from the same bowl, and no one else became sick. But if a Shagara healer had not been with them—Ra'abi was pregnant at the time, and taking no chances—Zaqir would have died. His throat swelled almost closed. He was from Rimmal Madar, where such nut trees are unknown."

A frown darkened the usual bright whimsy of Qamar's face. "If what you imply were true, then we ought to eat nothing that doesn't come from our native soil. I ate everything they put in front of me in Joharra, and so did everybody else, and nobody—"

"Zaqir's case was extreme. But let me tell you why this thought occurred to me."

He was only halfway through an explanation of how place and people belonged to each other when Qamar suddenly cried out in surprise and pain. Green wax had been melting all this time in its little glass bowl set in a bronze scaffold, gently heated by the small candle below it. But the candle had flickered and flared in an unruly draft. The luxurious feather quill Qamar had been twirling idly between his fingers had caught fire, burning his hand.

"It's all right, Ab'ya," he said at once. "It doesn't hurt—I was only startled. Here, let me set the seal, and then you can tell me the rest of your ideas."

"Leave it be," Alessid told him. "I'll call for a healer."

"No, it's nothing. I want to hear more." He didn't wince as he smoothed out the page, then folded it neatly so that the four corners met in the middle. He ran a singed and slightly bloody fingertip over the matrix of Alessid's personal seal, making sure there was no lingering wax to disfigure the impression. Green wax was poured, the seal was set, and the letter set aside.

Rihana and Ra'amon pleased each other very much. The people of Joharra were equally pleased. The man they considered their rightful ruler had returned. The woman he married had openly declared her love for their land and had all the power of the Empire of Tza'ab Rih behind her to keep them safe. His conversion to the Glory of Acuyib troubled them but little, for they saw it as an expediency. Joharra was worth a change in liturgy.

A few months after the marriage, Alessid received a letter from his granddaughter that confirmed everyone's wisdom, including his own. Love there was between Rihana and Ra'amon, and great joy; as far as each was concerned, no other man and no other woman existed in all the wide world; and she was already pregnant with their first child and hoping for a girl. Rihana praised everything from her new husband to her new Joharran-style clothes (their women dressed even more oddly than their men, imprisoning themselves in tight bodices and voluminous skirts). Alessid decided Mirzah ought to read it as well, and accordingly made his way to her apartments.

"With regret, al-Ma'aliq, the Empress is indisposed."

Alessid regarded his wife's maidservant, his eyes narrow and his lips taut. He had heard this same sentence a hundred times and more. He saw Mirzah only at official functions nowadays. She never even sat down to dinner with the family, preferring to stay in her rooms. He had indulged her even more disgracefully than he ever had Mairid or Qamar.

"Open the door."

"With regret, al-Ma'aliq—"

"Open it."

The woman's hands twisted. "I cannot," she whispered. "She has ordered whippings if—"

"Open the door or *I* will order your tongue cut out and your eyes burned blind," he snarled. He would never have done so, of course—not only was he disinclined to physical cruelty but terror was no way to rule an Empire. But the servant was already in such a state of nerves that she believed him. With a shiver, she opened the door she guarded, and he was admitted to the rooms of the Empress.

He had not been inside for years. This entrance was not the one that led to the fountain room with its tile garden; instead, he came in another way, by the portal from which she emerged in all her finery to receive ambassadors. There were servants here, too, and fear in their eyes at the sight of him. Alessid was more determined than ever to discover what was in his wife's rooms, that she so seldom and so unwillingly left them.

When he finally saw, he wished he had not.

Mirzah sat in the center of her bedchamber, on a priceless rug from Dayira Azreyq that had been a gift from the late Sheyqa Sayyida. She was filthy, her graying hair lank and unwashed, her body reeking, her robe stained with food. She was rocking slowly from side to side, humming as she stroked the yarn hair of seven dolls in their cradles, lulling them to sleep.

"She believes they are her babies," said a familiar voice behind Alessid. He turned to find Leyliah, suddenly bent and old, sorrow thickening her voice. "She calls them by their names . . ." She hesitated, then murmured, "And sometimes, the one that is usually Kemmal, she calls Qamar."

Alessid refused to feel. "How long has she been like this?"

"Until recently, it came rarely and went swiftly."

"How long this time? How long will she be like this?"

Leyliah shrugged. "Another day, or forever."

"Do something for her."

"There is nothing to be done."

"There must be!"

"Nothing, Alessid. It is not a thing a Shagara can heal—or the al-Ma'aliq can command."

He could not bear Mirzah's humming. He drew Leyliah into the outer chamber and kicked the door shut. "What happens when the people discover this?"

"They will not discover it. Her servants are few, loyal, and silent." She paused. "Qamar sits with her each day for a little while—she thinks sometimes that he is Azzad, when your father would visit the Shagara tents."

"But—you said that sometimes she—the doll—"

"Yes. Sometimes, when Qamar sits with her, she uses his name when she sings her children to sleep. He is very good about not being shocked by his grandmother's madness." She trembled briefly. "There, I have said it at last. My daughter is mad." And she covered her face with her hands and wept.

Alessid left his wife's rooms. He sat alone in his maqtabba for several days, and emerged at last to declare that the Empress, as befit a pious woman, had decided to spend the rest of her days in solitary devotion to Acuyib, praying for the happiness of the people of Tza'ab Rih. They revered her for this, sending tribute of the land's bounty: oranges, wine, silks and woolens, gems, candlesticks wrought of iron. Alessid thanked them in Mirzah's name and quietly distributed the gifts among the poor.

When Mirzah died, the whole Empire mourned. And when Leyliah followed her daughter into death a few months later, Abb Shagara himself came to take her body home to the desert.

He also came to speak his piece to Alessid. In the privacy of the great tent in the gardens, he confronted the al-Ma'aliq.

"It is you who drove Mirzah mad—your use of her sons and grandsons and the magic she gave them—you used them to make war."

Alessid said nothing.

"Be advised, al-Ma'aliq, that there are those among the Shagara who oppose you. While Leyliah lived, they kept silent. *I* kept silent. But now—"

"Now you will rebel?" He laughed without humor. "Look around you, Abb Shagara. The Za'aba Izim, the Qayshi, the Ibranyanzans, the Joharrans, the Granidiyans—half a million people look to me for law, protection, governance. Your handful of rebellious Shagara are nothing to me—magic or no magic."

"They are angry," he warned. "So am I."

"And so am *I*! You accuse me of misusing the Haddiyat—and yet they supported me like everyone else when I made Tza'ab Rih into a nation. No one denounced me then! Not when I was making the Shagara into the most powerful and revered tribe in all the country! And now you say it was I who caused the madness of my wife. Do you know, Abb Shagara, that many years ago she refused me her bed—me, her husband, father of her children—she denied me any more children, because she did not want any more Haddiyat sons. A Shagara woman bears Haddiyat proudly and rejoices in them. Mirzah did not. And because of it, she went mad. How can I be held responsible for this? I cannot. And you and your dissident Shagara know it."

"She—"

"Silence! Take your anger to the most obscure corner of my Empire and trouble me no more with it. Be assured that if I hear anything about dissension, I will treat the Shagara as I would treat any traitors to Tza'ab Rih."

Abb Shagara sucked in a breath. "You would not dare!"

"Would I not? Get out!"

A year or so later, he heard that Abb Shagara had died. Not that he was Abb Shagara when it happened, He had renounced the honor, a thing that had never been done before, and with a score of like-minded cousins, both male and female, set out to find a new home. He died along the way. The rest of the group established a small community, no one knew exactly where. They sent word back to the Shagara tents that they were safe, and anyone who wished to join them could come back with the messenger. Some did, finding the prospect of solitude and study appealing.

The men among them, some Haddiyat and some not, were dedicated to the preservation of the ancient traditions. The women, all of whom had Haddiyat in their lines, declared themselves unwilling to see their sons ride off to war—or their gifted sons craft hazziri for death and destruction rather than to help people.

"And how," Alessid mocked, "can they possibly help anyone, living no one knows where?"

Qamar made a face. "One suspects they intend to help only themselves. Who cares about them, anyway? Come, Ab'ya, Shayir has sired a new foal, and you must tell me what you think."

That was how it was between them: Alessid spending himself as always in the work of ruling until Qamar beguiled him from the maqtabba or the audience chamber or the now threadbare tent in the garden. They were well-nigh inseparable, the man in his seventies and the boy not yet twenty. He could not help but recall what Leyliah had said: that Qamar had soothed his grandmother Mirzah with his resemblance to Azzad. And then he invariably recalled also that Mirzah had believed Qamar to be Haddiyat.

Nonsense. The woman had been mad.

Qamar was a scapegrace of the first order, with a hundred broken maidenheads and broken hearts already to his credit. If he had any sense of duty, it was well hidden. As for dedication—only in pursuit of pleasure. Even aware that he was a copy of Azzad, Alessid loved the boy. Perhaps, he thought, *because* Qamar was so like Azzad, the father Alessid had once adored.

It came Alessid's time to die, peacefully and without too much pain. There was time to finalize certain arrangements—to further endow the hospitals that had been Mirzah's pride, to distribute money among the poor, to order the planting of yet another small forest of trees. For each of his descendants he chose a small memento: a ring, a bracelet, a necklace, something to remember him by. In looking through the jewels given to him over a lifetime, he found the armbands given him the day he had wed Mirzah. *Love* and *fidelity*, *fertility* and *happiness*. His lip curled at the sight of the talishann carved into the metal, and he was about to toss both armbands from him when he remembered slim fingers drawing the same symbols on the corners of a letter. And a burning feather. And a thin smearing of blood.

"No," he whispered to himself. "No. Not Qamar."

"Al-Ma'aliq?" asked the servant who was helping him sort the jewels. "Is anything wrong?"

"Nothing," he said, and heard his voice quiver, and said more strongly, "Nothing."

To Qamar, who was the only one with him when he died—by Alessid's own order, as he felt death approach—he gave the chadarang service of carnelian and jasper long ago rescued from the ashes of the house in Sihabbah, and the topaz that had belonged to Azzad, and the pearl of Bazir al-Gallidh, and the hazzir from his own breast.

He watched through dimming eyes as the boy slipped the chain over his head. If Acuyib had been so cruel as to make Qamar what Alessid was terrified to admit he might be—

No. He would not die in uncertainty. He would believe, and it would be as he believed, for had not his belief created an Empire?

And thus was extinguished the light that was Alessid al-Ma'aliq, ruler of Tza'ab Rih. His daughter Mairid ruled wisely and well for many years. After her came her Khalila, and then Numah, and Qabileh, and Yazminia, in an unbroken line of succession, mother to daughter. The Empire flourished.

So too the Shagara—both those who remained with the tribe, and those who had splintered from it to dwell in their mountain fastness, no one quite knew where.

And so did Qamar flourish as well, although in the year after his grandfather's death it seemed to him that his life had been made a deliberate misery by his mother, who decreed that at twenty-one years old, it was time and past time for her wastrel son to learn the responsibilities of being a Sheyqir of Tza'ab Rih.

In brief, and to his horrified indignation, she made him join the army.

— RAFFIQ MURAH, *Deeds of Il-Nazzari*, 701

Il-Ma'anzuri

698-716

Let me tell you of him.

He was his mother's last child and third son, indulged by all from infancy. He knew his grandfather Alessid for the first twenty-one years of his life, and was much favored by him. Handsome and spendthrift, witty and aimless, he was the image, it was said, of his great-grandfather Azzad in that great man's youth.

No one could ever have guessed what he would become.

By Acuyib, the Wonderful and Strange, that which follows is the truth.

—HAZZIN AL-JOHARRA, *Deeds of Il-Ma'anzuri*, 813

18

Qamar al-Ma'aliq had never been so tired, hot, thirsty, and saddle sore
in his entire life. In point of fact, he had never been any of those
things before in the twenty-one pampered, privileged years of his existence.
Choked by dust, wilted by heat, aching in every bone from a solid month in
the saddle, he did not go to far as to curse his mother, but he did enquire
forlornly of Acuyib as to why, of all the ideas for his future the Empress
Mairid might have entertained, He had seen fit to put the army into her
exalted head.

Qamar felt it keenly that he should have been back in Hazganni, dallying with a lissome beauty, sipping cool wine as she sang for him or told him
how wonderful he was. The most wearying thing in his life should have been
the choice of which robe to wear of the hundreds in his closets.

Instead, his Shagara-gold skin was sun-blistered, and his clothes were
rank with sweat, and his last woman had been over a month ago, and he was
convinced that life was no longer worth living.

Yet live it he did, every miserable hour of the ride, every rock-prodded
minute of the nights in rough camp on this quick advance through the dry
summer brownness of Ga'af Shammal, northward to Joharra. He was part
of an expeditionary force sent in haste to the aid of his sister Rihana and her
husband, Ra'amon al-Joharra—whose former Cazdeyyan hosts had belatedly decided to take exception to the marriage.

This circumstance was prompted by two women. One was an obscure
peasant girl who had visions and heard voices that told her the Tza'ab must
be evicted from all lands that believed in the Mother and Son. The holy men
in the mountains of Cazdeyya, calling loudly upon their captive brethren in
the south, had spread her vile spewings like a disease. But no attention would
have been paid to the peasant if not for the princess. Cazdeyyan royalty had

a turn for religious extremes; Princess Baetrizia's grandfather had ended his days in a cave with a cat that spoke to him, or so he avowed, in the very voice of the Blessed Mother. In a quest for similar sanctity, Baetrizia had taken this peasant girl, Solanna Grijalva, into her household, where they prayed and fasted, sang and meditated, and emerged to exhort the King every hour of the day and night until he finally agreed to march against the Tza'ab.

Qamar found much to curse about the King of Cazdeyya, his fanatical daughter, and the simple-minded child who were all causing him so much misery. Why couldn't they practice their silly religion in their great gray mountains, and leave the peaceful south alone? Consensus was that Chaydann Il-Mamnoua'a had instilled in them these evil notions, and it was the duty of the Believers in Acuyib's glory to defend the green land against the invader. It was all yet another move in the vast game of chadarang that went on throughout eternity, for Chaydann forever refused to concede defeat in the conflict between death and life, darkness and light. Empress Mirzah's pious prayers were said to have kept the Empire at peace for years even after her death; now her grandson Qamar was one of the pawns in the renewed game.

Qamar did not hold to this view of life in general and the Cazdeyyan threat in particular. But when others expounded upon it, more or less lyrically as their rhetorical gifts allowed, he did not mention the days he had spent sitting with his grandmother in her room of seven cradles, answering to the name "Azzad" instead of his own.

Ayia, he did acknowledge, reluctantly, that he was nothing more than a pawn. An exalted one, to be sure, mounted on a fine horse and jingling with hazziri. But a pawn all the same, and in no way enjoying it.

His father, Jefar Shagara, was not too old to command the army in the field, but he had given over the position to Khalila's husband, Allil Azwadh. Someday, when Khalila was Empress, Allil would have authority over the Riders on the Golden Wind, and this was as good a time as any to get them used to him. Ten years Qamar's senior, and a cousin of the famous Black Rose, Allil was as ill-favored as Ka'arli had been beautiful—but he knew how to lead troops. He inspired them with his steely will, underwent the same privations as they did, and had not even brought with him the silken tent that was his right as commander. Had he done so, Qamar could at least have claimed a portion of its floor and a few of its pillows and slept in comfort. But Allil was tough-minded, wilderness-raised, and had no use for even the simplest luxury. Still less had he time for the complaints of his wife's little brother.

"I weary of listening to you, Qamar," growled Allil one evening. "Today you have plagued me. Tomorrow I want you out of my sight."

Qamar clapped his hands together with delight. "Excellent! You're sending me home!"

"No, I am sending you forward with the scouts. Do exactly as they say, cause no trouble, make no mistakes, and perhaps I will consider giving you back your horse."

"What?"

"Do you think a scout can gallop along, raising clouds of dust for the enemy to see? You go on foot, my fine Sheyqir."

The twelve scouts left before dawn, ranging in a wide arc ahead of the army. The positions of farms and villages were reported back to Allim, who then guided his troops in maneuvers that skirted any habitation. Qamar thought this ridiculous. If they happened upon anyone, they should simply kill him so he wouldn't be able to warn of the oncoming Tza'ab. Qamar supposed his sister's husband was attempting to live up to his name: Allim meant "gentle and patient." But as Qamar followed the experienced scouts into hills covered with scrub oak and dry brush, he wondered irritably why Allim couldn't have chosen to exercise gentleness and patience on Qamar instead of the enemy.

The saddle soreness of these last weeks was a horror to him and a totally unforeseen imposition. It turned out that riding a cavalry horse from dawn until dusk, day after strenuous day, was a rather different thing from executing pretty patterns around a riding ring, or galloping off into the hills for an hour or two, or ambling along city streets. That first morning as a scout, the aching in his buttocks and thighs competed with blisters on his heels and toes. By midafternoon, the blisters had won the victory. He couldn't even indulge in a satisfying moan of anguish; his fellow scouts would have gagged him, throttled him, or worse. They were singularly unimpressed by his status as a son of the Empress. Qamar knew why. His mother had given orders: no special treatment. Indeed, they should consider him as if he were nothing more than the lowliest youngest son of the humblest family in all of Tza'ab Rih.

Grandfather would have come to his defense, he told himself as he concentrated on not snapping twigs beneath his sore feet. Grandfather would never have allowed this to happen to him. Grandfather would have been appalled by the conditions his adored Qamar lived in, and the mockery visited upon him by the common soldiers, and—

The screeching of a hawk made his head jerk up, and for a moment he was stunned by the size of the creature, its wingspan half again as broad as his own shoulders. It cried out again and soared away into the silent sky.

He had spent time enough with the Shagara to know that birds did not scream and fly without reason. But he could see nothing that should not have been in the forest: oaks studded with green acorns, various kinds of undergrowth, a bird's nest high in one of the trees, perhaps the hawk's own. The good farmland was farther north; Qamar supposed people here gathered the acorns, but he didn't much care as long as they did their gathering some other day.

Qamar brushed against a large bush, its prickles sticking into his shirt, scraping his skin. By the time he freed himself, his left arm was throbbing. His skin itched. His hand began to go numb. He had crossed a small stream about an hour ago—if he could find it again, he could bathe the rash in its coolness. He looked about him, swaying with sudden dizziness.

"Here's another of them, Father."

At least, Qamar surmised that was the meaning; the boy spoke a mangle of syllables combining civilized speech and barbarian gabble. Raffiq Murah, who had almost finished his biography of Alessid al-Ma'aliq, had drawn up a list of useful words for all troops of Tza'ab Rih to learn. Qamar had thought this pointless. *Empty your hands* and *Be silent or die* were hardly calculated to persuade a pretty girl into bed. Ayia, but when had he ever needed anything but his face and his big, melting dark eyes?

He rather wished right now that his eyes could actually see something besides sparks and great foggy swirls. His thorn-pricked arm hung heavy and useless from his shoulder. He staggered a few steps and leaned against an oak tree. On his finger the ring that had belonged to Azzad al-Ma'aliq, tawny topaz carved with a leaf, seemed to pulse with the pounding of his blood against swollen flesh. Dimly he perceived he was about to be captured and all his possessions stolen—stupid to have worn the ring to war, and the pearl ring of his great-great-grandfather al-Gallidh, but he'd promised himself he'd never take them off—indeed, the swelling would make them impossible to remove . . .

Ayia, of all the silly things to think! These barbarians would simply cut off his fingers. But before or after they killed him?

Another, deeper voice: "Let's have a look at him." His accent was excruciating, but he was comprehensible. Qamar saw two shapes, one tall and one shorter, approach through the trees, and wondered blurrily if he would ever see home again.

"Eiha, poisoned," said the man. "Come, Raffael, help him."

An unknown time later, Qamar came back to consciousness with no memory of passing out. He was propped against a wall beside a doorway, a hard pillow at his back, his left arm and shoulder bare and tingling.

"Never touch fire nettles!" scolded a woman's voice, and he looked up to find a face framed in dark hair above him.

"Woman, into the house!"

That tone of voice, that curt a command, would have almost any woman in Tza'ab Rih lunging for the nearest blunt instrument. Qamar's mother, his sisters, his cousins would all have reached instantly for their belt knives. And thrown them most accurately, too.

Alone in the sunshine with the man who had saved his life—an odd thing for an enemy to do—Qamar took the cup the man proffered, and drank. "Thank you."

Evidently his pronunciation left much to be desired. It took the man a moment to stop frowning and nod his understanding. But then he frowned even more deeply. "Tza'ab. Your army, it moves."

Had Qamar the use of both hands, he would have applauded the brilliance of this insight. "Yes." There was no point in denying it.

The man sat on his heels, head tilted slightly to one side. "We know."

Qamar shrugged and blinked in surprise when his left shoulder moved just as usual, without pain or stiffness. He looked down at his arm: normal size, the topaz ring fitting his hand again, with only a pink flush on his skin and a few darker pinpricks of red to show he had been poisoned. "Are all your healers as skilled as this?"

"We know plants to use. Your land is desert, so you know nothing."

"Nothing at all," he agreed cheerfully. "Our own healers have different ways." He sat up straighter, glancing into the cottage. Humble but clean, replete with flowers—where had they found flowers in this dryness?—and more comfortable than anywhere he'd been in the last month. But he had to leave. "Ayia, my thanks again, but I must go." He pushed himself to his feet—and remembered that he hadn't the vaguest idea where he was.

"Your army," the man told him, pointing to the western hills.

Qamar gulped and nodded. Then, curiously: "You won't try to stop me?"

"Why? Your army, your Empire, your Acuyib—these are nothings."

That stung his pride. "You won't think that way when we've conquered your land!"

A sound that Qamar supposed was laughter rumbled from the man's throat. "Ours. Not yours. Never yours."

We'll see about that, Qamar thought.

His expression must have invited further comment. The man said, "The Mother gives, the Son protects. This is all, and you are nothing."

It took Qamar a moment to understand that he was speaking of religion. How unutterably uninspiring.

The wife returned then, with a little tin pot of salve for use this evening as instructed. She eyed Qamar with interest—though not entirely in the manner he was used to from women: she was more intrigued by his strangeness than his beauty. He thanked her politely and went on his way.

If he half-expected to be felled by an arrow in the back, he was disappointed. It seemed the man really had no interest in what went on in the world beyond his house. Qamar could empathize. He didn't want to be anywhere but at home, either.

He slept that night beneath a shrub carefully chosen for its distance from anything that looked even remotely like that bush of stinging nettles. Perhaps *sleep* was the wrong word. He dozed, jerked awake, dozed again, and finally rose before dawn no more rested than he'd been when he lay down.

"I want to go home," he told a small reddish-brown rodent that eyed him from a clump of twigs obscuring its nest. "I am a Sheyqir of Tza'ab Rih, and I do *not* belong in this Acuyib-forsaken wilderness!"

If he was being honest with himself, he would have to admit that he was no more impressed by this than the rodent. What irked him was that the creature obviously considered him no more of a threat than the insects that flitted past. He was nothing against which anything, man or beast, must defend his home.

His waterskin was empty, but he didn't dare fill it at any of the sluggish streams he crossed. That he had absolutely no idea where he was did not prevent him from putting one blistered foot in front of the other. That the most beloved grandson of Alessid al-Ma'aliq should be reduced to this gave him the energy of anger. Besides, he knew his cousin's men would be looking for him, and he was determined to greet them on his feet and not huddled like a coward beneath a tree. It wasn't his fault the damned shrub had attacked him.

It was well after noon before he limped toward a sentry tent on the outskirts of the Tza'ab camp. He was hungry, thirsty, hot, exhausted, and his arm was throbbing again. Within the hour he was with the healers, who exclaimed over the nettle wounds and the salve as they tended him. Their learned discussion of local plants and indigenous medicaments interested him not at all, and especially not compared to the cool water assuaging his dry throat and his sore feet.

"Can you describe the exact shape of the nettles?"

"Was there any smell? Sweet, sour, pungent—"

"What was the length of time between touch and pain?"

"Was the pain sharp like a knife or acidic like a poison—"

"—or burning, like a—like a—"

"Like a burn?" Qamar narrowed his gaze at the little knot of Shagara healers. "I don't remember, and I don't care. I want to see my sister's husband."

"This salve," one of them said, sniffing at the little clay pot. "Do you know what it's made of?"

"If I had only brought my apparatus!" another mourned. "I wish I was back in my own tent, with all my instruments—"

Qamar scowled. "And *I* wish I was back in Hazganni! My sister's husband Allim! Summon him *now*! And give me that damned stuff, my hand hurts."

Rubbing the smooth cream into his arm, he smelled things he could not identify, odd pungencies that repelled him. He didn't belong here; he had nearly been killed by this land. Yet the thorns that had poisoned him had been counteracted by plants that also grew here, and perhaps Ab'ya Alessid would have found meaning in that. Qamar simply knew that this land wanted him gone, and he was most willing to oblige.

He was still rubbing the cream into his wounds when Allim arrived—through no effort of the healers. Word had filtered up from the sentry all the way up through the various levels of qabda'ans to the Sheyqir himself that his wife's wayward brother had finally returned.

"Your secret presence here is no secret," Qamar said without preamble. "Even the most isolated family living in a shed I wouldn't wish on a dying rat knows we're here. And they also know where we are."

"Explain yourself," Allim ordered.

"Over a large plate of food and a very large jug of wine? Certainly. Lead on."

By the time Qamar had finished his recital—and his meal—Allim was compelled to agree that he had earned a second jug of wine. "It seems you have stumbled across valuable information, Qamar. If the Cazdeyyans know we are here, and they know where we are, we have two choices. First, we can attempt to be where they think we are not."

"That's not feasible. They know their own lands, Allim. And I swear, their land is against us—or at least what grows on it is, which amounts to the same thing."

Allim arched a brow, as if to enquire if Qamar truly thought his opinion was worth hearing. "Your reasons are not my reasons. In fact, I have no idea what you think you mean, but that matters not at all. I won't march far and fast to outmaneuver the barbarians. It would be too great a hardship on the men."

Qamar poured himself another measure of wine and said nothing.

"I have decided to pull these Cazdeyyans into battle as soon as possible. We will make no secret of our movements—"

"Not that they were secret before," Qamar muttered into his winecup.

"—but we will move in such a way and to such a place as will invite them to believe us vulnerable to attack. Which, of course, we will not be."

"Of course." He did not say it as if he knew what he was talking about; they both knew he didn't. But it seemed easier to agree with Allim, and besides, he wanted something. "May I have my horse back?"

"By Acuyib the Merciful, I wish I could lash you to the saddle and send you back to Hazganni! But the Empress would want an explanation of why I have failed to make a man of you, and I have no intention of failing." He smiled grimly. "I trust we understand each other."

"Perfectly." Qamar smiled his sweetest and most innocent smile, rose, bowed, and left the tent—taking the second wine jug with him.

As far as Qamar understood, the Tza'ab then marched to a place no commander in his right mind would have chosen for a battle and waited for the Cazdeyyans to catch up. The barbarians accepted the invitation to a seemingly easy victory and hurried to the place Allim had chosen. Personally, Qamar didn't see it—neither the apparent idiocy of the location nor the battle itself. If it had been his mother's hope that he would find himself in war, she was wrong. He found nothing. In fact, he lost his horse, his sword, and his breakfast.

He'd had much too much to drink the night before, of course. But that wasn't his fault: his arm was aching again, and the stench of the salve disgusted him past bearing. It had needed the best part of three winejugs before the pain was gone. Unfortunately, his balance went with it, and although he'd been aiming for his bedroll, he'd spent the night on the ground beside it. Dawn came hours earlier than it should have. The meal that came with it churned in his stomach, competing with the dreadful thud in his head. His arm hurt so much that it was scant wonder he couldn't cinch the saddle girth quite tightly enough, nor grip his sword as firmly as he ought. So none of it was really his fault.

But his mother was going to flay him alive all the same.

A qabda'an screamed the charge. The onslaught of Cazdeyyan warriors on their tough little horses came over a hill like an ocean wave of dappled brown hides and red-and-yellow tunics and flashing swords. Qamar was never sure when exactly it was that his own sword slipped from his fingers, or when the saddle lurched to one side and he fell off his horse. But all at once he was sprawled on the ground, and the wave broke open to avoid him as if he was an inconveniently placed rock. All around him was the same disgusting pungent odor that had nearly turned his stomach in the forester's hut. *Nearly* became *definitely*, and he curled onto his side and vomited.

This simply could not be happening to him. He kept telling himself that as the hoofbeats faded into the distance. He was Sheyqir Qamar al-Ma'aliq of Tza'ab Rih. Ayia, that didn't matter as much as the fact that he had never fallen off a horse in his life. His arm hurt and his head ached, his blistered feet felt swollen inside his boots, and he was lying in the dirt with his cheek in his own stinking sickness, and there was a new pain all at once in his thigh that he didn't understand. He began to wish he'd never been born.

"So much for your career as a soldier," a voice said some unknown amount of time later.

Qamar's body twitched fitfully, and his eyelids cracked open, and he saw one of his Shagara relations regarding him with sardonic brown eyes in a golden-skinned face.

"Whatever would your mother say?" the man went on.

Qamar considered it a genuine pity that he'd survived to eventually find out.

The man folded his arms across his chest, and Qamar saw the light shift on the hazziri around his neck. The stones were different from those he was used to seeing a healer wear. "Sheyqir Allim might have a pertinent word or two, as well."

Qamar squeezed his eyes shut. His arm and thigh no longer hurt, but he still felt slightly sick, and the repulsive barbarian smell seemed stuck inside his nostrils of its own explicit will, for there could not be anyone among the healers who used native plants. Perhaps they were treating enemy wounded in the dawa'an sheymma. The stink really was insupportable; he wondered how anyone not born in this cursed land could endure it.

A different voice made Qamar's eyes open in startlement. "Find out who this one is. The look of him is right, but perhaps he's a Tariq or Azwadh cousin who merely looks like one of us."

Empress Mairid had always maintained that her youngest son was in possession of a fairly good mind, even though he seldom chose to use it. He didn't intentionally use it now, but it worked all the same.

They didn't know who he was.

If nothing else about him, they ought to have recognized Azzad al-Ma'aliq's topaz ring, if not al-Gallidh's pearl.

These people were not Shagara healers.

No, they *were* Shagara—did not the first man have the eyes and golden skin, and had not the second man said *one of us?* Possibly they were healers—Qamar's lack of pain suggested it.

But they were not Shagara healers of Tza'ab Rih.

There was only one conclusion, and it didn't please him at all that his mother was right, and his mind had turned out to be a rather fine one after all, even when he wasn't trying to use it.

These people were the renegade Shagara who lived no one knew where and did no one knew what. Tza'ab Rih had not heard from them in years—ever since Ab'ya Alessid had rid the land of them most gladly.

Ayia, they were living in Cazdeyya, and they were practicing the traditional Shagara arts of healing and of hazziri, and Qamar had the dismal feeling that Tza'ab Rih was going to hear from them again, and in very unpleasant fashion, once they found out his name.

Or they might just kill him, the way those of their angry persuasion had killed his great-grandfather Azzad.

Qamar had indeed been captured by that faction of the Shagara who had long since vanished into the barbarian lands. They were healers, and they crafted hazziri, but things had changed in the long years since the first of them fled Tza'ab Rih.

For one thing, they had learned perforce the properties and uses of the plants now available to them and had adapted their magic accordingly, for the time-honored methods and formulas were useless in a country where none of the familiar herbs and flowers grew.

For another, they were too poor to work in gold and silver and costly gemstones. Their talishann were hammered into bronze, brass, and tin, decorated with humble agates and quartzes. They also used paper and various inks. But Qamar did not discover this for quite some time.

What had not changed was their loathing for anything to do with the al-Ma'aliq, whom they held responsible for what they saw as the perversion of Shagara magic that had caused their fathers and grandfathers to exile themselves rather than countenance it.

Qamar had no need to be told this. Being an honorable man, he at once proclaimed his own rank and ancestry, and any recounting of his story that asserts otherwise is a lie.

— HAZZIN AL-JOHARRA, *Deeds of Il-Ma'anzuri*, 813

19

He had absolutely no intention of telling them who he was.

The influence of the local language had changed pronunciation, shifted emphasis, and added words to the language spoken by these Shagara, but two generations had not been enough to alter their speech so much that Qamar could not understand and then begin to copy it. Those two generations, however, had also seen the loss of several things and the introduction of several more.

They had lost knowledge of the specifics of the al-Ma'aliq. Most specifically, the ring that had been Azzad's and then Alessid's and was now Qamar's. Gold, set with a dark tawny topaz carved with the family's leaf symbol, it would have proclaimed his real name to anyone in Tza'ab Rih. It meant nothing to these people; neither did the al-Gallidh pearl. And so he was able to give them a name they had already surmised might be his. To them he was Qamar Tariq, whose Shagara father and great-grandfather had married into that tribe. This explained his coloring. He gave silent thanks to Acuyib for not making him Haddiyat—for this came only through the female line, and all sons of Shagara women had Shagara as a last name (except for the al-Ma'aliq line, of course; this was another grudge these people had against his family, the replacement of their ancient name), and trying to explain being a Tariq and also gifted was not a thing he felt equal to attempting.

It was difficult for a naturally gregarious, relentlessly glib young man to be deprived of his most effective arsenal. Long accustomed to talking his way into or out of just about anything, he was canny enough to know that he must keep his mouth shut until he understood much, much more about these Shagara. This meant he had to listen.

He had never been very good at listening. Neither were these people inclined to give him much to hear. When they spoke to him, it was to give orders or to demand answers to their questions. He meekly followed the first and resisted the second for quite a while by pretending not to comprehend. By the time this gambit could no longer be reasonably employed, he had worked out a story. He'd always been good at that sort of thing, as well, but this was not a fabrication made up on the spot to wiggle out of a belting. This was for his life.

Qamar knew very well that if they found out who he really was, the best he could hope for was to be sold for ransom, either to the Tza'ab or the Caz-deyyans. Neither had much appeal. His mother would pay whatever was asked, but the humiliation of his capture and the manner in which his part in the battle had ended before it even began made him want to wrap his arms around his head and vanish into one of the dungeons these barbarians were so clever at building. As for the Cazdeyyans—should they be the ones to ransom him, they would either barter with his mother for an even larger ransom or kill him. His death was what he expected the Shagara here would prefer; poor as they obviously were, their loathing for anything al-Ma'aliq would demand his transport back to Joharra in an astonishing number of pieces.

His plan, such as it was, must be to regain his strength, learn everything he could, and then escape.

And so he listened, and when instinct told him they would accept his excuse of incomprehensible accents no longer, he answered their questions with what he felt was a rather ingenious story.

Yes, he was a soldier of the Tza'ab. A cavalry officer, in fact. No insignia of rank? Have a look at these hazziri. They did, covetous and trying to hide it—all that lovely gold and silver, and the gemstones! He was rather surprised that he still wore them, and his rings, but evidently the laws of the dawa'an sheymma still applied, and a patient's belongings were safe.

Separated from his troops during the battle, he told them, he had been wounded in the leg, and loss of blood had toppled him from his horse, and he then became nauseated with pain and weakness and heat. And that was when the Shagara had found him.

So far, so good. What had happened after the battle, they knew better than he. It was the part before that was a bit dodgy.

"Young to be an officer," one of the healers remarked. "Favorite of some sheyqa or sheyqir, are you?"

"Pretty thing like him? Of course," said another.

"When I joined the Riders, an al-Ma'aliq sheyqa gave me these," he said, quite truthfully, touching the hazziri at his breast and the one depending from his left earlobe. "That was the last time I saw her—or any al-Ma'aliq of Tza'ab Rih." This was also true; he hadn't seen his mother since that day, and all his cousins were al-Ma'aliq of Joharra, Granidiya, Ibrayanza, and Qaysh. He wasted no time or wit wondering if he'd ever see any al-Ma'aliq again. "I am loyal to my name, like all the Za'aba Izim." When they looked blank as he used the term, he said, "The Seven Names. The desert tribes. Surely you have not been so long from home that you've forgotten—"

"*This* is our home," snarled the oldest of the healers. "We are now part of this land, and it now belongs to us. And it will never become part of the Tza'ab Empire."

"Ayia," Qamar admitted, "they don't even know where you are."

"And it will stay so." The old man hesitated, and an odd, reluctant yearning glazed his dark eyes. "I would know what you might tell me of the tribe whose name we share." Qamar's surprise made him add, "My grandmother was wife to a Shagara, one of those who first came here. Her name was Omaryya Tariq."

Grandmother—? But suddenly Qamar realized that although this man looked old enough to be a grandfather himself, he was not. He never could be. He was Haddiyat and could not be more than 45 years old. Repressing a shudder of pity, he sifted through his brain for whatever he knew about the Tariq. "We remain in the desert, and live according to the traditional ways, making the usual yearly round of camps." This was pleasing to the healer. Taking his cue, Qamar went on, "And of course we never send any of our people to the court, and we marry mostly with the Tabbor and Ammal—never the al-Ma'aliq!" This the healer liked even better. "In fact, we stay aloof from the larger affairs of Tza'ab Rih, except to contribute the finest soldiers in all the army, as befits our Name." *Tariq* meant *conqueror.* Qamar wondered for a moment if he'd laid it on a bit thick, but the proud smile indicated otherwise. "So I can't imagine anything is much different since your grandmother left."

This was precisely what everyone wanted to hear. It was as if with all the changes they had been compelled to make, all the compromises, the difficult adjustment of staying in one place, the experimentation necessary to continue their arts in this land of strange and exotic plants, they needed to know that the life their grandparents had left behind remained just like the stories that had been told them about their ancestral home.

Qamar hid his amazement that they knew so little of the history of the last seventy or so years. Then again, they would not want their antecedents known to the local populace and so could not ask much about affairs back home—and the way the old man had declared that *this* was now their home held a certain defiance. The wicked ways of the al-Ma'aliq had exiled them. Very well; so be it. They were no longer of Tza'ab Rih.

But they remained Shagara. As Qamar rattled off pleasing little tales of how the Azwadh, the Tabbor, and the Ammal also remained faithful to the traditional ways—his audience was made up of healers who descended from those tribes—his gaze kept flickering to his supposed Tariq kinsman. White hair, lines, wrinkles; hands cruelly twisted by bone-fever; eyes dimming, muscles more feeble by the day ... yes, they were still Shagara.

And so, through his father, was he. The distinctive Shagara coloring Jefar had bequeathed meant these people had let Qamar live. These distant cousins might honor him because of their shared ancestry, but *honor* and *trust* were two different things. Once he was recovered enough from his leg wound to rise from his bed and explore the intricate, inconvenient maze of alleys and passages between the stone buildings of their fortress, he was never left alone. One or another golden-skinned, dark-eyed young man shadowed him at all times. He was diverted from the outer walls, not permitted near the innermost fortification. As a Shagara, he was allowed certain liberties. As a cavalry officer of Tza'ab Rih, he was prohibited from taking advantage of them.

Some eight or nine days after he had fully recovered, a hammering rain woke him in the middle of the night. Just as well that it had: Someone was in the tiny cubicle he had been assigned, someone who moved in whispers of wool clothing and bare feet on cold stone. This person had not reckoned on lightning flashes through the high, barred windows. Nor, truthfully, had Qamar. When the sudden, fleeting illumination showed him the long gown and hooded cloak and startled face of a girl, it also showed her a man sitting straight up in bed with a clay candlestick in his hand.

"Who are you?" Qamar demanded.

"Singularly unoriginal," she snapped as night devoured the room once more. An instant later came another crack of lightning, just enough to show her bringing a knife out of her skirt pocket. "I know how to use this," she warned.

"I don't doubt it." He used the darkness to scramble out of bed, and tripped over his own boots. Her stifled giggle infuriated him. "That was a mistake," he said, leaped to one side so she could not get a fix on his voice, tossed the candlestick toward a corner to further confuse her, and lunged for where he was sure she would be.

He grabbed empty air and lost his balance. Fetching up against a wall—hard, bruising his shoulder—he cursed and swung around. The room wasn't that big; there weren't that many places to go.

An abrupt rush of air and the faint squeal of a hinge told him she'd opened the door—which was always locked when he retired for the night—and gone back outside. More noise from the hinges, a stillness in the air—and a metallic rattle that meant she was about to lock him in.

He grabbed the bars of the grille set at head-height in the door and yanked.

A moment later he was on his backside on the uncarpeted floor, and brief lightning showed him wildly waving arms and a shocked face beneath hair the color of sand as she staggered into the room. By the time she landed on him, it was pitch black again.

He laughed and wrapped his arms around her. She was smart enough not to struggle; he was smart enough to pin her elbows to her sides so she couldn't get at him with that knife. Lying back flat on the flagstones, he tightened his grip.

"Not that I'm not perfectly charmed by your visit, qarassia," he said into her ear through a mouthful of her blonde hair, "but was all this stealth really necessary?"

She called him something unspeakably filthy in the barbarian language—Raffiq Murah's little translation guide hadn't included it, but it was a soldier's obligation to learn how to swear at the enemy in his own language.

"Acuyib preserve me, such a mouth!"

"Let go of me!"

"Tell me why you're here, and I might consider it."

"I'll scream!"

"If you haven't by now, you won't anytime soon. You're not supposed to be here."

"I had the key, didn't I?"

"Stolen or borrowed, it doesn't matter. Nobody makes a social call in the middle of a rotten night like this one. If your visit was legitimate, or even sanctioned, you wouldn't be sneaking about with no shoes on. Now, why are you here?"

"I—I wanted a look at you."

He smirked. "To judge for yourself whether or not I'm as handsome as rumors must have it?"

"To see if you're really Shagara, like they say you are."

"No, sorry, not good enough." It was increasingly apparent to him that it was a sweet, dainty little bundle he wasn't quite cuddling. Beneath the bulky skirt and heavy cloak—which was soaked with rain, and getting his night-shirt wet—he could discern a slim body with inspiring curves. "Why are you here?" he asked for a third time.

"I told you. Let me go before someone hears us."

"I've been rather hoping someone will. After all, *I'm* exactly where I'm supposed to be."

"If I tell you, will you let me go?"

"Perhaps. If I believe you."

She sighed, and relaxed atop him. He didn't make the mistake of easing his hold; he'd played too many games with too many mistresses to be fooled by that trick. There was a blaze of lightning, and the rain pounded down harder than ever outside, but it was the roll of thunder that made her muscles tense again.

"I wanted to know if you really are the one I've been seeing."

"I have absolutely no idea what you're talking about."

"I've *seen* you! How do you think they knew where to find you? I saw you, and—"

"They actually went looking? For *me*?" He paused as a thought occurred to him. "What's your name?"

"Solanna. Solanna Grijalva. And yes, I'm the person you think I am—which is more than can be said for you!"

He crowed with derisive laughter. "Nonsense, girl! Everyone knows that Solanna Grijalva is a child and quite mad with her visions—"

"I'm fully seventeen, and I'm not mad! I *saw* you," she repeated. "But I wanted to look at you with my own eyes, so I could be sure."

"And you chose the blackest hours of a rainy night to do it?"

"Eiha, you're the one who's mad! Do you think I have any more freedom within these walls than you do? Didn't you hear my name? *Grijalva!* The Shagara despise me as much as they do you!"

Qamar considered. Although it was quite nice, having an armful of girl again, the chill stone floor was not being kind to his backbone. He sat up, still holding her fast, but allowed her to turn so that she was seated between his thighs with her back pressed to his chest. Her head, he noted, fit just beneath his chin. "There, that's better. Why should they despise you? Religious disputes?"

"So you believe the story Princess Baetrizia put around, do you? She thinks my visions and voices are visitations by the Mother."

"And you did nothing to disabuse her of this notion, did you? Quite the rise, from humble peasant to confidant of royalty!"

"You know nothing about it!"

"The fact remains that you were a guest of the simple-minded Baetrizia for quite some time. How did you come to be a guest of the Shagara?"

"I'm here on purpose! Which is more than can be said for you!"

Ayia, she had him there. What puzzled him was why, if she was here in his room clandestinely, during all their conversation she had not troubled to lower her voice. Although he knew himself to be the only occupant of this particular floor (the third) of the building, and the clattering rain and rumbling thunder and occasional crash of lightning were admittedly very loud, surely someone ought to have heard their voices by now. "Did you drug or bribe your way in?"

"I don't know what you mean."

"Having nothing but your delightful self to offer—and you really don't seem that sort of girl—it must have been drugs."

Grudgingly, she said, "I have trouble sleeping sometimes. They're very good with medicines, you know. The Shagara won't fight, but they sent healers to tend our soldiers."

So that much at least of Shagara capabilities was generally known. Interesting, that the imperative to use their healing gifts in service to others remained so strong. He nodded, his lips tickled by her wildly curling hair. "You did come here on purpose, then. You want the Tza'ab out of your country, and you thought you could convince the Shagara to help you do it." By the way she stiffened—and not in response to thunder—and then sagged against him, he knew he was right. Smarter than a seventeen-year-old girl; his mother would be so proud. "You might as well explain all of it," he invited, "in as much detail as whatever you used on the guards will allow."

"Only about an hour," she confessed. "Eiha, what do you want to know?"

"That lazy old king of Cazdeyya not moving fast enough for you, I take it? And you know what the Shagara can do by way of potions and—and things." How much did she know? "Poor qarassia, aren't you aware of their history? They left my country because gr—greater men than they used Shagara knowledge in ways they didn't approve!" He'd almost said *great-grandfather*.

"And thus they hate you Tza'ab almost as much as we do. In the end, we'll make common cause and throw you out. You don't belong here!"

"The land belongs to us now. You might as well accept it."

"You don't belong here, and you never will! Just because your troops march all over a country doesn't mean you own it. Land belongs to the people who belong to it."

This notion sounded vaguely familiar. He was distracted from chasing it down inside his head by her sudden wriggle to get free. To his surprise—and hers, to judge by her gasp—he let her go.

"The rain has slacked," he said as he got to his feet in the darkness. "And it's been nearly an hour, hasn't it? You'd better lock me in. If you'll forgive me, I'll wait until you're outside before giving you back your knife."

"Whoever you are, you're certainly a fool. An open door, sleeping guards—and you ask to be locked up again!"

"An open door, sleeping guards, and an entire fortress filled with many, many more guards between me and freedom. How far do you think I'd get?"

"How did I get here?" she taunted.

"Ayia, you are here, so why don't you have that look at me that you say you want so much?" He went to the corner where he'd thrown the candlestick, not surprised to find it in pieces. The candle was still intact, and he groped on his bedside table for flint. "I warn you, I'm not looking my best. I need my hair trimmed by someone who actually knows how, and a nightshirt isn't the most flattering of garments." He struck her knife against the flint and the candlewick ignited. Turning toward the door, he smiled.

She caught her breath. He might have been pleased with the reaction but for the nature of her shock. "You—you're so young! And there are no scars—"

His brows arched. "The nature of your visions dismays me, qarassia. You saw a scarred old man and mistook him for me?"

"I only saw you lying there in the dirt," she snapped. "I didn't see your face that clearly."

"Yet you had an impression of age and scars? I must have looked even worse than I felt at the time!"

"You don't understand! Nobody ever understands!"

With her brown eyes flashing and her chin jutting out, she didn't look seventeen. More like five or six, and threatening an impressive tantrum. He had to laugh. She really was rather adorable. Not precisely pretty, not to his usual tastes, but the pale hair was intriguing, and he suspected she had an enchanting smile. Not that he was likely to see it anytime soon.

"I saw you *old*," she hissed. "I saw it just as I saw Ra'amon al-Joharra's death in battle! And it came true! I saw it last summer, and this summer he died!"

"Ra'amon is dead?" Qamar had no time to feel anything. A deep and angry voice echoed off the stone walls all the way to the third floor, bellowing about lazy stupid louts who got so drunk they passed out while on duty. Fresh lightning and an immediate thunderclap couldn't drown out his roars.

Solanna flinched so violently that she dropped the key. Qamar bent to retrieve it, pushed her through the door, and blew out the candle.

"Go on, hurry! But don't forget the lock!"

Swinging the door closed, he heard her fumbling attempts to insert and then turn the key. More lightning, more thunder—and the enraged voice almost shaking the walls as the abuse went on and on. But it seemed the guards were in no condition to appreciate the creativity of his invective; most of the yelling consisted of orders to wake up.

"He'll have to go for help," Qamar told the girl through the barred window. "If you're careful, you can slip out then. Will you lock the damned door and get out of here?"

She said nothing, but in the darkness he heard the clink of metal on stone on the floor within his room. He had to wait for the next flash of lightning to be sure. But it was indeed the key.

No one accosted him the next day to demand what had gone on in the middle of the night. Thus he assumed that Solanna had safely reached her own quarters, wherever they might be. Over the next few days, on his walks around the rain-grayed alleys, he looked for possible "guest" accommodations—or, better still, a glimpse of her—but had no luck.

As for the key—ayia, guards who got drunk on duty were also capable of losing keys. That was what got shouted the next morning, and Qamar was disinclined to correct the mistake.

He kept it in his left boot, and Solanna's knife in the right.

The building in which he was not quite a prisoner but not quite a guest was a narrow construction crammed against another building several stories taller. The entire fortress always smelled cold and harsh, for everything here was built of stone and iron. He missed the sweet fragrances of wooden floors and staircases polished with oils. But he supposed that this, like the stinking salve and the pungent herbs that flavored the food, was yet another example of working with what one had. The lowest floor was divided into treatment rooms and a dispensary; the second was a single large room with beds for recovering patients. The third floor's dozen little rooms were all equipped with barred windows and lockable doors. Qamar wondered if this had been the doing of the original builders or if the Shagara had turned this floor into a prison.

One morning the healer who had Tariq forebears was the one to unlock Qamar's door. After a silent walk downstairs, he was ushered into a room almost as small as the one he inhabited upstairs.

"Please sit."

He did so, in a comfortable wooden chair at a table laid out with paper, pens, and bottles of different colored inks. Smiling brightly, he asked, "Am I to write my own ransom note?"

"You may be worth more than money." From a pocket he drew a much-folded sheet of paper. "Copy these symbols using the green ink."

What in the Name of Acuyib the Inscrutable was going on here? During boyhood he had spent a year with his Shagara relatives, but having no talent for even the most rudimentary talishann he'd been perfectly happy tending and training the horses instead. His Haddiyat cousins were forever writing and rewriting the protections at the family residences, and a few times Qamar had been bored enough with his other pursuits to watch. None of the symbols on this page looked familiar at all.

Shrugging, he opened the bottle of green ink, noting that the stopper was carved of green moss agate into the shape of a rather pretty flower he didn't recognize. He dipped a pen and made his copy.

"Now write my name at the top. Zario Shagara."

Qamar glanced up. "That's unusual."

"It commemorates the Cazdeyyan nobleman who gave us this fortress. One Shagara male at a time, and only one, bears the name. Do you want me to spell it?"

"Please." He wrote as he was told. When he looked up, expecting further instructions, Zario was holding a small, thin-bladed knife.

"Your hand," he said.

Qamar stared at him.

"I need a few drops of your blood. Hold out your hand."

He very nearly blurted out "*No!*" They must think—they thought he was—but he wasn't, he couldn't possibly—

He tried to remember what most people knew about Shagara magic. He was wearing hazziri, so he had to know something, but how much?

"*Your great-grandfather Azzad didn't believe until it was demonstrated to him over and over again,*" his great-grandmother Leyliah had told him a long time ago. "*Ayia, a very stubborn man! Your grandfather Alessid, of course, was told directly when Abb Shagara thought it time to do so. And now I will tell you. It is not just the talishann, nor the skill of the maker, nor the metal, nor the stones that make hazziri potent. Neither is it only the particular combination of herbs or flowers or the amount of wine or water or vinegar in a medication that gives it the power to heal.*"

They thought him Shagara, and he was—but not *that* sort of Shagara. He was certain of it. So let Zario do whatever it was he would do, conduct whatever test this might be.

Qamar shrugged and held out his hand.

Zario didn't prick Qamar's finger. He drew a long, shallow scratch across his own palm. He watched the blood well up, a meditative and bitter smile curving his lips. Then he wiped the blade between his fingers and seized Qamar's hand and pricked his thumb. Before Qamar had time to cry out his surprise, Zario had squeezed drops of blood onto each of the six symbols and both words of his name.

"What do you—how *dare* you—" He looked from the smear of blood on his thumb to the Shagara's face—but blocking his gaze was the man's palm. His clean, whole, uninjured palm, without a mark on it.

"But I'm *not!*" he cried. "I'm not one of you—I'm not like you!"

The old man who was not really an old man eyed him with a certain grim satisfaction. "All evidence to the contrary," he said.

"No—it's not possible—" He cast about frantically for some excuse.

Some reason. Some escape. "It was your blood, not mine—your blood still on the blade—"

"Are you calling me a clumsy fool, boy? I've done the testing these twenty and more years. It's one of the privileges of bearing my name. There is only one of me, you see, and so only one person that the signs and the blood and the paper and the ink can touch."

Qamar staggered up from his chair, dimly heard it crash behind him, backed away from Zario's shrewd, pitiless gaze. "*No! I can't be one of you!*"

"Certain of that, are you? Left a fine little collection of bastards behind you in Tza'ab Rih, did you?" He snorted a laugh, then drew himself up and squared his shoulders and said in cold and formal tones, "Qamar Tariq, it is my honor to inform you that you have been blessed by Acuyib and have the right to use the name Shagara."

His first encounter with Solanna Grijalva came when both were guests, or prisoners, or perhaps both, at the Shagara fortress, from which he escaped with great cunning. It would be more than half a year before he saw her again. Little is known of that portion of his life, although rumors have gradually transformed over time to legends, none of which are true. The most repellent of these stories would have it that he slaughtered a dozen or more Shagara during his escape from the fortress, and spent the next autumn and winter carousing from town to town. Any recounting of his life and deeds that asserts these things is a lie.

— HAZZIN AL-JOHARRA, *Deeds of Il-Ma'anzuri*, 813

20

After having it proved to him that he was Haddiyat, that he would age quickly and painfully, that at not quite twenty-two his life was half over, he spent three days alone in his room at the Shagara fortress. The door was no longer locked. This was a good thing, for it took less time to open it when more wine was delivered, and speedy delivery was second only to generous quantity in Qamar's bloodshot eyes.

On the fourth day, no wine arrived. Downstairs Zario Shagara was waiting for him in the room where his blood had proved what he was. *It often happens like this,* Zario said. *Some cannot face the truth at first,* he said. *I remember once a boy only a bit younger than you broke into the dispensary and swallowed everything he could stuff into his mouth.*

Now, despite the passage of many weeks, Qamar was still unable to decide whether or not he envied that boy. The fact that he was yet alive argued in one direction; the fact that he was planning to go on drinking argued in the other.

The first choice, Zario said, *is acceptance or despair. But your next choice,* he said, *is one never given to any man before: Stay here and learn how best to use your gifts, or return to your own Shagara, with whom you would probably be more happy.*

Happy. Ayia, of a certainty—happy as a colt in clover.

It was a dim, rickety little tavern he sat in now, a short walk from the palace in Joharra. He wasn't quite drunk enough. The last weeks had refined his perceptions of how much wine it took to make him forgetful and how much rendered him oblivious. There were stages between tipsy and insensible he had never bothered to catalog before. At the moment, he was at that unfortunate point where nervous caution still existed. It was a somewhat delicate calculation, but the amount of wine left in the jug was sufficient to bring on just enough recklessness so he could accomplish his goal. He had only one, very carefully thought out while he was stone sober. Simple, really. He needed money.

His Shagara relations—by Acuyib the Incomprehensible, how he loathed having to acknowledge them as such, and especially the reason he must acknowledge them—had no money to give him. What they had given was food enough for three days and a horse. This was after they'd drugged him for an unknown number of days, and taken him on a journey to Acuyib didn't want to know where, and left him with a vicious headache and the food and the horse and instructions to ride south for two days and then east. Or perhaps it had been east for one day and then south. He'd been beyond caring.

He'd ridden sober back into territory controlled by Joharra. That had been his last piece of luck—the right choice of direction, not the sobriety.

Seated in a corner of a tavern in Joharra, Qamar poured a precise amount of wine into his cup and wasted a few moments picking little floating bits of debris from it. *Happy*. He would not go to the desert, to the Shagara, to waste precious years of his abbreviated life crouched at some mouallima's knee, memorizing talishann or pounding designs into silver or mixing up healing potions, and dripping his blood onto or into his work.

Neither would he stay with the other Shagara in their Cazdeyyan fortress. The studying would be the same, and the bleeding. But his tools would be paper and pen and ink and the strange plants of a realm that had already tried to kill him once with lethal thorns. Besides, being pent up inside stone walls in a land not his own was not the way he wanted to live. Happy? He would go insane.

Not that this wasn't an intriguing thought, for a little while. Empress Mirzah had been quite, quite mad. When Qamar thought of the afternoons spent with her as she tended her dolls and called him by his great-grandfather's name, he was both attracted and repulsed by the prospect. To live out his days not understanding or caring; to lose all awareness of reality . . . to be shut up someplace safe and private where he could shock no one . . .

Ayia, he was here, in this filthy little tavern not far from his cousins' palace, so he had made the choice not to go mad, at any rate. Now that he thought about it, he had made quite a few choices. To stay alive, to leave Cazdeyya, to retain his sanity—although what he planned to do this evening would not be considered entirely sane.

Halfway through the last measure of wine now. He could feel nervousness turning to excitement, and smiled. He was still in an alien land that had first tried to kill him by piercing his body with poisoned thorns and in essence had succeeded in killing him with the truth about what he was. But a transplanted piece of Tza'ab Rih was a few streets away, eminently exploitable. He did not know how to live, let alone thrive, in this country that was full of barbarian people and poisonous plants and all manner of hideous things. *Happy?* he thought again, with a muffled snort. *Here?* He could not go home, but at least he could have one last hour of sensing home things all around him.

He began to be grateful, grudgingly, that the Shagara had let him go. *It is not so much that we trust you not to try to find us again,* Zario had said, *and lead your army to us. You have no idea where you are, and will have even less idea of it by the time you ride away.*

Then why? Qamar demanded. *Why allow me to leave?*

We value honor, Zario said. *My grandfather exiled himself from his homeland because the honor of the Shagara had been compromised by the unspeakable crimes of Azzad al-Ma'aliq—who must have been a truly vile man, to have used his friend Fadhil in such a fashion, killing his enemies.*

He didn't kill them, he gelded them, Qamar said—and in a moment of sheer spite added, *He made them like you.*

And you, Zario had said without a twitch of an eyelash. *Alessid al-Ma'aliq was even more shameless, for he corrupted his own sons to his purposes. Many more departed from the Shagara tents in disgust after that. Indeed, it is a wonder any stayed at all. Perhaps all honor is lost to them. But not to us.*

Ayia, perhaps Zario's implication had been correct, and all honor was lost to Qamar. What he was about to do was scarcely praiseworthy. Not that he much cared.

He left a swallow of wine in the cup, not needing it. Rising, he stretched widely, not thinking about the supple play of muscle and how it felt to be young. What he still possessed, he would use. A strong body, a beautiful face, melting dark eyes, and the infallible charm he had inherited from Azzad al-Ma'aliq—who had *not* killed his enemies, no matter what the renegade Shagara believed. He had exacted revenge, just as Ab'ya Alessid had done. As Qamar made his way through the dark city streets toward the palace, he wondered if Alessid had seen it as vengeance—whether of Acuyib or Chaydann al-Mamnoua'a—that his beloved wife had gone mad.

But if there was one thing Qamar had decided without even having to think about it, it was that his mother would never ever learn that she too had birthed a Haddiyat son. Not that it would break Mairid, as it had broken Mirzah; he simply did not wish to see anyone ever look at him the way he had seen them look sometimes at Mairid's brother Kemmal, with sadness and pity.

The palace guards did not recognize him. He had not expected them to. During his one night and one day back in Joharra, he had neither trimmed his beard nor changed to more conventional clothing. Both would have cost money much better spent in the tavern, achieving this lovely, carefree courage.

They did recognize his topaz ring.

"Sheyqir! Your whole family has been frantic with worry for months!"

"Not so loud!" he begged, laughing, and flicked a casual finger against one of the hazziri dangling from the gates. He didn't know what this particular one signified, but that he could touch it at all meant the magic recognized him. There were similar protections in every palace he'd ever lived in, things that admitted family and kept doors locked for all others. "I'm a surprise for Queen Rihana's birthday. A little late, of course, but—what? What is it?" he demanded as the two men exchanged agonized glances.

"The Queen . . . she has joined her beloved husband, may Acuyib gather them both into His Arms."

Qamar felt his stomach lurch and the wine within it turn sour. Solanna Grijalva had said she'd seen Ra'amon's death, and it had turned out to be true that he had died. Qamar had heard it in the taverns. But Rihana— "How did this happen? When? How did she die?"

"Earlier in the summer, after word was brought that her noble lord had been slain in a skirmish with the Taqlis—"

"The what?"

"It's another barbarian country, Sheyqir, somewhere west of Cazdeyya."

"By Acuyib's Glory, do these damned nations breed while we're not looking? And what was Ra'amon doing so far north?" He shook his head. "Ayia, I will learn all of this later." After tonight, once he could afford it, he'd find a better class of tavern, where men conversed civilly with each other rather than muttering glumly into their wine. He would not be asking any al-Ma'aliq for information. He did not intend to see any of them at all. "I assume the family still lives in the same apartments? Excellent.

Thank you. And not a word to anyone! Please?" He gave them a subdued version of the cheery, conspiratorial smile he'd planned, and they nodded and bowed.

Having successfully passed the gates and their protective hazziri, he was assumed by the rest of the guards to have legitimate business within. His body remembered the saunter appropriate to, and his face effortlessly arranged itself into the proper expression of, a casually arrogant al-Ma'aliq sheyqir. As he neared the Queen's chambers, it was necessary to display his topaz ring once or twice more, but persuading the sentries to secrecy was so simple that it would have distressed him had he been the one these guards were guarding. Ayia, once they discovered what had happened tonight, they would be more cautious. They exclaimed at his presence, as the others had; they yielded to his authority, as the others had. It was a bitter amusement that these were the last orders he would ever give as a sheyqir of Tza'ab Rih. *Tell no one I am here. No one.*

This time of night, the family would be sleeping. He had no need of private chambers—though his bones whispered a plea to rest in a soft, silken bed again. The first whimperings of what would eventually become screams . . . had not the girl Solanna seen him old and scarred? It was in him: His own early decay and death were inside him. How long before the whimpers turned to gasps of pain, and then moans, and then—

A little of the wine-inspired recklessness seeped away. There was only one remedy for that, and the maqtabba was entirely adequate to his purpose. It took him very little time to denude the room of all the lesser gold and silver fittings—doorknobs, drawer-pulls, and the like. From one of those drawers he took a large drawstring pouch of money kept there for incidentals. He was al-Ma'aliq, and the Shagara working did not defend against him. There was no lock because none was needed. Others could not even slide this drawer open, but he could.

Praising his deceased cousin Rihana for being royal enough to scorn carrying money on her exalted person, he weighed the pouch in his hand. He untied the sash from his waist and spread it across the table, then quickly folded the coins and doorknobs and such into it, twisted it to secure his booty, and wrapped it once more around him. He paused to smile slightly, recalling that great-grandfather Azzad had carried the famous necklace of pearls this way, long ago, the only wealth he had saved of all the vast al-Ma'aliq fortunes.

At the maqtabba's door he hesitated, then returned to the desk. In the drawer that had held the money he left behind his grandfather Alessid's hazzir, the necklace that had kept him safe through dozens of battles. Whoever found it would know who had been here; what they might think about why he had left himself unprotected, he cared not.

He kept the two rings. He had promised himself he would never take them off. All the other hazziri—the earring, an armband, two silver discs sewn into the heels of his boots—these he had already sold. But the rings he would keep as long as he lived. They were reminders of who he had once been: al-Ma'aliq, al-Gallidh.

Qamar walked unchallenged out of the palace at Joharra. At just past midnight he was enjoying a tasty meal and a large jug of very good wine at a clean, refined tavern that specialized in traditional Tza'ab cooking. Tomorrow, he decided, on his way out of Joharra, he would take the time to find out exactly what had happened to Rihana and Ra'amon and who was in charge now. On reflection, he decided it was probably Allim, a seasoned war-leader who could take care of the incursions from Cazdeyya and—what had the guard called it? Taqit? Taqim? Qamar didn't have it in him to care, not tonight. Tonight, he cared only about getting very, very drunk.

He stayed drunk all through the autumn and winter.

He found a congenial seaside town and called himself Assado, and said he was from the newly established Tza'ab town of Shagarra in the southeast, which his atrocious accent and somewhat limited vocabulary seemed to confirm. No one ever discovered much more about him than his name. He kept to himself and his wine jars. Indeed, he had chosen the town for the potency of the imported wines in its dockside taverns. Once or twice someone saw him ambling drunkenly down the pier or along the beach, and several of the tavern girls had graced him with their favors, for he was a handsome youth—at first, anyway. As autumn became winter, and the wine did its work on his body as well as his mind, all that remained of his beauty was the large dark eyes with their extravagant lashes and a certain withered sweetness to his smile.

At about the same time his money was running out, there arrived in the seaport an old man and a young girl. No one in the dockside taverns had ever seen them before, and no one ever saw them again. Nor did they ever see again the youth who called himself Assado.

Something smooth and gentle was beneath his back, cradling his relaxed body. The quiet soothed him. His skin and hair felt soft and clean, and his muscles were loose, as if he'd just had a hot bath and a shave and a long rubdown with expensive oils, the sort of thing one expected when one was a sheyqir of Tza'ab Rih. There was a scent of green grass, a tang of sandalwood, accented with a subtle hint of a woman's perfume, and a taste on his lips of mint tea.

All in all, he felt quite blissful. He must remember to remember whatever tavern it was that served wine as good as this.

"Eiha, about time you woke up."

Head turning lazily, he sought the voice above him. Her face was indistinct, a pale oval framed in wildly curling fair hair, backlit by white-gold sunlight. The eyes were brown, nearly as dark as his own. He wished she would lean closer so he could see her more clearly, hoping her face was as fascinating as her voice—low and soft, the oddities of a barbarian accent attractively negated by the lilting rise and fall of the syllables. "So what's your name, qarassia?"

She sat on the bed beside his hip, facing him, hands folded and head cocked to one side. She wore something white with a dull sheen to it, no embroidery or decoration. He still couldn't quite focus on her face, but her voice told him she disapproved of him. "You still look dreadful. Better than before, but still—"

Whenever *before* was a total blank, it usually meant he'd been very, very naughty. Father would glower, Mother would glare, and Ab'ya Alessid would shake his head and turn away to hide a smile.

He realized that there was a lot of *before* that he couldn't remember. The days all blurred together—or, rather, the nights did, for he spent the daylight hours sleeping. Ayia, to be honest, he spent them insensible, sometimes in his rented bed, sometimes on the street, sometimes on the beach, sometimes in a back corner of whatever tavern he'd honored with his noble presence that evening. Never yet, though, had he woken in a bed like this one. He was stretched out on a fine, soft mattress with sheer white curtains languidly swagged around carved wooden posts. White velvet was under his back, and his head rested on a white silk pillow. The whole of it was rather cloudlike and quite lovely.

"Would you like something to drink?"

"By Acuyib, yes!" He struggled to sit up; a light, insistent hand on his chest pushed him back down.

"Not just yet. Here."

He slurped from the glass she held to his mouth, then spluttered. *Water?* "Take that goat piss away and bring me wine!"

"Look like a tavern maid, do I?"

"I can't be sure if I can't see you properly, can I?" He gave her his best big-melting-brown-eyes smile—the look was a good one on him, and he knew it. "Come closer, qarassia, so I can see your face. And if you'd be so kind, please tell me where I am."

"Can you manage to take a single breath without trying to use it to seduce someone?"

"I've no idea," he replied blithely. "Though I must admit I don't usually find myself in bed with women like you." Abruptly aware that he had been rude without meaning to be, he blinked up at her. He still couldn't quite see her features. "Forgive me, I really didn't intend that for an insult. I meant that it's so rare to exchange more than a few words with a woman in these circumstances."

"These are not those circumstances."

He arranged his face into a sulk. "Why not?" Squinting up at the face that slowly came into focus, he gave a snort of disappointment, because she was really rather plain. The dark eyes were lovely, and the masses of pale curling hair, but the rest . . . ayia, had he caught sight of her at a feast, he wouldn't have troubled even to find out her name.

But it came to him that he already knew it.

"You truly don't know where you are, do you? And before you begin worrying about it, you didn't succeed."

"At what?"

"Drinking yourself to death."

"So much I had already realized," he drawled. "For instance, this cannot be Acuyib's Glory. Aside from the fact that it's the last place I'd ever end up— again, forgive me—you aren't my idea of the sarhafiya *The Lessons* so confidently promise."

Solanna didn't seem offended. "If I understand correctly, I would imagine such beings keep well clear of dangerous boys like you."

"Dangerous! Me?"

A breath of breeze fluttered the white gauzy bed hangings. "Do you intend to stay a little boy for the rest of your life?"

"What fool wants to grow old?" And then he remembered what he had been drinking in order to forget. He remembered what he was.

"I can see where the prospect wouldn't attract you. But not for the reasons you're thinking."

"How do you know what I'm thinking?"

"Simple. You found out that if you live, you'll grow old. So will all the rest of us. What's so special about you? That it will happen more quickly? You spent all autumn and winter encouraging it to happen very quickly indeed. You don't want to grow old. You're very good at being young, and you've enjoyed it very much. Eiha, of course you're good at it—it's all you've ever been. But isn't that true of everyone?"

"I'm only twenty-three years old—and at forty I'll be dying!"

"There are choices, you know. You can choose to grow old, and die. You can refuse to grow old, and choose to die. Or you can die, but choose not to grow old. Stop frowning as if you don't understand me."

"All I understand is that there *is* no choice. I'm going to die." The misery of it was that he'd lost what it felt like to be young. He'd drunk and whored just as he'd always done, but the sensations of true youth were lost to him. Every time he thought they might have returned, he would remember the symbols and the name and the blood on the paper, and Zario's voice saying he was entitled to the name *Shagara*.

"Everyone dies. That is a truth. Here's another: You are what you are, and you will die sooner than you expected. But that's true of everyone, as well." She rose from the bed. "No one wants to, everyone does. King of Cazdeyya, peasant farmer in Ghillas, sheyqir of Tza'ab Rih. Whatever you were born, you will die just like everyone else. The only thing you can choose is how old you are when you die. There are people, you know, who are walking around with unlined faces and not a single gray hair who are already quite, quite dead inside."

True enough, he had to admit. His grandmother had been one of them.

"If you want to be like them, I will send in the biggest jug of wine I can locate, and you can go back to killing yourself. And you will die having been a little boy and an old man, with *nothing* in between."

"Dead is dead. Get out."

She bent her knees and her head, mockingly, and her white skirts sighed across the stone floor.

He waited a long time. She sent no wine to his room. At length he slept, and woke to candlelight, wondering if he'd dreamed the whole thing.

A little boy, an old man . . . and *nothing* in between.

"I do not belong here," he said aloud. "This country is not mine. These people are not mine."

"Next you'll be whining for your mother."

His limbs were sluggish, but his mind was not; he recognized Zario Shagara's voice. Struggling to prop himself on his elbows, he succeeded only in collapsing onto his back once more.

And he could not move his legs at all.

"Calm yourself," Zario told him. "Don't fight against the medicine— you'll only prolong your stay in bed. What all that wine did to your belly and bowels—it was days before the contamination cleared from your body. As for your brain . . ." He folded his arms across his chest, head tilting to one side. "You would know best about that, I suppose."

Qamar lay back on the white bed, closing his eyes to the sight of the old man who was not truly old. "Now you will tell me she had another vision that led you to me again."

"In fact, yes. Several of them. Including one that showed you in a palace of the al-Ma'aliq."

He snorted. "Prove it."

"She saw a table, and a drawer you opened without a key, and the bag you took from within. Green velvet, stamped in gold with the same leaf carved on your ring."

"Nonsense."

"And the necklace you left in its place. She was adamant that we find and retrieve you before you either killed yourself with wine or someone killed you for those rings. It amazes me that they're still on your hands, considering where you were living."

"*She* is the one who needs medication, something to cure outrageous fantasies. It remains, Zario, that I do not belong here. And I do want to go home."

"It was not just her visions that prompted us to find you." His eyes gleamed with malicious amusement. "It was the description that reached us of the young al-Ma'aliq sought by his frantic family—including mention of those rings." He smirked. "Imagine our shock—and our shame that we had not treated a sheyqir of Tza'ab Rih with all due ceremony! We had to have you back, if only to remedy our earlier oversight." But as Qamar opened his mouth to protest further, Zario pushed himself to his feet and said, "Enough for now. You do not belong here, that is true. But you will not be going home."

He left, and though it was not the austere third-floor room of Qamar's previous guesting here, it did lock.

This did not particularly impress him. Reaching for his boots, he slipped a hand inside the left one and smiled. The Shagara were indeed honorable people—they had left him his possessions, such as were left of them anyway, and had not even searched them.

Over the next few days as he rested and recovered his full strength—it seemed he was always doing that, these days, and it came to him that he would be doing it more and more as the years went on—he formulated and began implementing his plan. The key he possessed, the key to that other door, was useless in this one, of course. But locks could be persuaded, if one knew the right talishann. From his year in the desert tents he recalled some of them, though too imperfectly to be of use. He remembered a few more from watching Haddiyat rework the protections around the palace. He did have a good brain, when not befuddled with liquor. Yet it seemed during those days, and especially during the nights, when he lay restless and frustrated, that all he really remembered with any clarity were symbols for things that were of absolutely no use to him whatsoever. *Safety; clean water;* the *neverfall* used on shelving; *wash twice* sewn into the corners of his clothes when he was a child because, as his father avowed, he was surely the first place dirt went when looking for a new home . . . After thinking this, he spent a whole hour musing on an entirely new means of employing Shagara talents: tapestries. It was another kind of artwork impractical in the desert, for, like the huge folios of drawings on paper, who would wish to lug such bulky things around? His father's people were ruthlessly practical. The metals they worked all year, for instance, were made only in the winter camp, where the permanent forge was. Thinking of this, he saw in his mind the talishann for *touch-not*, which neatly discouraged both curious and careless hands and possible thieves. Yes, very practical, his ancestors.

But nothing was coming to him that he could use right now. He tried to recall the symbols for *freedom, liberty, unlock, unbind, open,* but none of them coalesced in his mind.

He remembered other talishann, though, the ones he had written on the corners of Ab'ya's letter to Rihana and Ra'amon. He recognized it now as the first time he'd used his Shagara blood. He was the only one who could connect the arrogant cruelty of Allim's rule, about which he had heard much in the taverns during the autumn and winter whether he wanted to hear it or not, with that letter. Ab'ya had urged them to serve the land, and Qamar himself had added *love* and *fertility* and *happiness* and *fidelity* to the paper that had known the touch of his blood, however briefly. Binding on Rihana and Ra'amon, it was useless on Allim.

But none of those signs would help him now.

And then one morning when he woke he had it, and he muffled laughter in his pillow.

The key was brass—not the most potent of metals, but at least it wasn't iron. First he honed the handle of a spoon by scraping it against the stone walls. When the end of it was thin enough, sharp enough, he used it like a pen to scratch the appropriate lines onto the grip of the key. It was flat, undecorated, and the relatively soft metal responded to the abrasion as iron would not have done. Blessing Acuyib for inspiring the Shagara to make this talishann a simple one of straight lines and no curves, he tried to remember how deeply the work ought to be carved into wind chimes or bowls or hazziri for maximum effect, but could not.

At length he told himself he would have to be satisfied. He used the end of the spoon to prick his little finger and smeared the blood on the sign engraved into the key and then all over the key itself. As he passed his finger over and over the brass, he was reminded of the days spent passing the spoon handle over and over the walls, and how the steady, rhythmic motion had formed a framework for his thoughts.

Or, more accurately, for certain words that he knew now truly had been spoken to him while he was awake, not while he was dreaming. He sucked gently on his finger to bring up just a bit more blood, and heard the words again.

You can choose to grow old, and die.

You can refuse to grow old, and choose to die.

Or you can die, but choose not to grow old.

Crossing the room from the white-draped bed to the door, he slid the key into the lock and began laughing softly to himself.

For there was another choice, one Solanna had not considered.

He turned the key in the lock—the key stained with his blood and bearing the talishann marked over the interior of every gate in every al-Ma'aliq palace, in combination with others that warned or made the gate exclusive to merchants or servants or guards, or in extreme cases halted anyone approaching it in their tracks. The lock caught, the door opened, and he strolled down a long hallway lit by brilliant spring sunshine, all the way down six flights of stairs and into a large chamber filled with desks and paper and pens and adolescent boys.

Smiling, he chose a desk at the back and sat down. And when the mouallima—a severe matron with a face like a sour plum—stalked up to demand what he thought he was doing, he replied, "My education is sadly lacking, I fear. Please, return to the lesson. I'm eager to catch up."

"What's your name? Who are you?"

"Qamar al-Ma'aliq," he said amiably. "Sheyqir of Tza'ab Rih."

And thus he made the choice that for all her talents Solanna had not envisioned.

I choose not to die.

He was an excellent student, diligent in his studies. In later years he said himself, with a smile, that his own mother would not have known him as he sat hour after hour, day after day, learning his craft. His teachers rejoiced in him, his fellow pupils delighted in his company, and he earned the love and respect of all the Shagara in their mountain fortress.

Any recounting of his life that asserts otherwise is a lie.

— HAZZIN AL-JOHARRA, *Deeds of Il-Ma'anzuri,* 813

21

"White is the color of purity, of chastity, of clarity, of sincerity, of energy, of harmony, of serenity, of spirituality . . ."

. . . of truthity and of protectiony and of meditationy and of sheer stark raving lunacy *if this old fool doesn't end the class soon!* Qamar didn't say it out loud, of course. The man had knowledge he wanted—needed—and in the last year, if he had not learned patience, then at least he had discovered endurance.

As the mouallima's voice droned on about the properties of white, Qamar dutifully made notes to be added to the sheets already plumping the tooled leather folder at his feet. He had six of these folders, bulging with pages on each of six subjects: Color, Flowers and Herbs, Ink, Paper, Talishann, and Al-Fansihirro.

As for the first, had anyone asked him back when he lived in Hazganni, he would have said there were eight colors that looked very good on him, and why should he bother with the rest? In fact, according to these Shagara, there were scores of colors, and all of them had names and influences and powers and meanings, and the slightest variation could mean the difference between health and illness, even life and death.

The lessons about plants he found simply loathsome. This country had tried to kill him with its poisoned thorns. That it had also healed him was neither here nor there. It did not like him. He returned the sentiment.

When it came to the formulation of inks, it transpired that he had a real flair for the work. He got lampblack ink right the first time, for instance—not easy to do, as the mouallima grudgingly admitted. While the rest of the class was busy chasing down smuts of soot (lampblack was lighter than air and gleefully floated anywhere it pleased), Qamar was adding hot water one drop at a time to his little bowl and mixing it with a finger until the lampblack dissolved (again, difficult, as the soot tended to float atop the water). Subsequent formulations with various roots, leaves, flowers, nutshells, and tree barks were equally simple for him to master. And he found that he rather enjoyed it. Satisfying, to be good at something again without having to try much at all.

Paper turned out to be rather more physical than he'd anticipated. It seemed students were required to learn not just its properties but how to make it, and in several different varieties, too. His notes on this subject were scanty technical descriptions of various processes; the width of the folder was due to the samples. His work did not compare favorably to that of the masters who tried to teach him. Perhaps he had difficulty overcoming a Tza'ab's ingrained horror of cutting down trees instead of planting them.

The masters of the craft were known as Qa'arta, which seemed to be an adaptation of a barbarian word for *paper*. Their work was as messy as tending dye vats and not nearly as colorful, as smelly as a tannery—almost—and surprisingly demanding physically. The slurry of soaked fibers from wood, cloth, lint, fishing nets, bits of hemp rope, and seemingly anything else they took it into their heads to add must be stirred in vats with great wooden spoons. The screened frames dipped into those vats could weigh so much it took two men to maneuver them. The presses that squeezed all the water from the pages must be screwed down as tightly as possible. And all had to be done with precision.

"Tilt the frame to gather the fibers, Qamar—*not* when removing it from the vat! You'll end up with all the slurry at one end and all the water at the other! Do it again."

"The sheet should peel off smoothly, Qamar, in a single piece—*not* in shreds! Do it again."

"The task was to produce paper, Qamar—*not* a piece of shelving! Do it again."

He sincerely hated papermaking class.

The memorization of seemingly thousands of talishann had a tendency to make his eyes cross. From the simple to the intricate, the mild to the dangerous, every stroke of the pen that formed the symbols demanded absolute concentration. Qamar's mother had once accused him of having the attention span of a flitwing drunk on Challa Leyliah's best stimulant tonic. Whole afternoons of copying and recopying and copying yet again the twists and turns of symbols that, if not perfectly formed, ended up as at best useless and at worst potentially lethal—ayia, more than once he was shocked from a doze by the rap of a willow switch across his shoulders.

It was the class taught by Zario that combined all the other subjects into the craft of the gifted Shagara male. Al-Fansihirro: art and magic.

"The thought you invest in your work will determine its success. The color of the ink is as vital as the paper. What you add to the ink intensifies your intent. The talishann must be perfect. Never think that a hasty sketch on a scrap of paper with whatever ink is to hand will function as you wish simply because you bleed onto it. What we do is an art, as truly as our lost brothers pound out their hazziri in metals."

This last sentiment occurred often in his lectures, and when it did he invariably looked at Qamar. Qamar looked right back, unblinking. His complete lack of knowledge about anything to do with the making of hazziri—despite the key carved with the talishann for *exit* he had used to open the locked door of his room—irked Zario. Something, anything, the slightest hint of vague rumors—Qamar was a total disappointment to him regarding the traditional arts of the Shagara and, Zario implied, a total waste of his valuable time. For although they could not refuse education to one of their kind, they all suspected he would take what he had learned back to Tza'ab Rih at the first opportunity and use it in the service of the Empire's ambitions exactly as his great-grandfather and grandfather had done.

Qamar did not disabuse them of this error. It amused him to see them grind their teeth as they imparted some arcane magical formula, some obscure piece of herbal lore. He knew they were thinking that they were facilitating the very thing their forebears had fled Tza'ab Rih to avoid. He did not tell them that he had no intention of returning home.

He had two reasons for this. First, no one among the Shagara had ever succeeded even in slowing the rapid ageing of a Haddiyat. This told him everything he needed to know about the state of magic and medicine in his country. They could not do what he was determined to do. He could have received much the same education in signs and symbols there as here, but the people inside this fortress had something his kinfolk did not: plants the desert-dwelling Shagara had never seen and did not know how to use. The tools were here. He knew it. Whether it happened in metal and gemstones or ink on paper, he was positive that somewhere in the compendium of tradition and experimentation lay his answers. This land that had tried to kill him would be his salvation. He *knew* it.

The second reason was just as personal, though it became a reason almost without his being aware of it. Solanna Grijalva had not returned to her own people. If she had her reasons for this, Qamar was unsuccessful in discovering them. Her original purpose—to convince the Shagara to come to the aid of those fighting the Tza'ab—had failed. They would never turn directly against their "lost brothers." Why she had lingered at the fortress, when she had had the vision that had sent her and Zario to the seaport, and why she stayed now that he had been rescued from himself, Qamar could not have said. Perhaps she found the mountain air beneficial to her health.

She stayed. Rather than work with the other women in the daily chores of the fortress, she became a teacher. Every child between the ages of four and ten was required to sit in a schoolroom five hours of every day, learning to read, write, and cipher, reciting long passages of *The Lessons*, listening to lectures about the history of all civilized and barbarian countries and especially about the history and beliefs of the Shagara. Solanna's residence here allowed a new subject to be taught: her language.

Naturally, he attended her classes. He was not the only adult to do so. The men and women who had dealings with the world outside the fortress already knew much about the local tongue, but within a few months Solanna had everyone speaking nothing else in her classroom.

That she used these lessons to disseminate *her* version of history amused Qamar endlessly. He never actually laughed aloud, but every time he smirked or smiled, she scowled at him and demanded to know *his* view of whatever event she claimed had taken place or whatever motive she ascribed to the Tza'ab.

And then they would argue.

One early evening in autumn—Solanna's classes were held after work had finished for the day but before the evening meal—she began the lesson by saying, in her own language, "The invading army that came northward from Tza'ab Rih was a blatant violation of all decency and honor—"

"Or it would have been," Qamar agreed, "if we hadn't been invited."

Solanna gave him a glower, and continued, "Count Garza do'Joharra and King Orturro do'Ferro da'Qaysh—"

"—were each so incredibly furious with the other that they committed the same act of desperation," Qamar said, "because they knew neither could best the other on the battlefield."

"—were betrayed by underlings who wished to seize power for themselves—"

"Eiha!" Qamar exclaimed, wide-eyed. "Was *that* why Orturro had Don Pederro's throat cut?" To the others in the class, he continued, "I was always told that when it was seen that the Tza'ab had won the battle—"

"By treachery!" Solanna snapped.

"—Orturro ordered his nephew's death. He'd acted as ambassador to Sheyqir Alessid, you see." Turning back to Solanna, he said, "But I never learned what happened to Baron do'Gortova, who acted as emissary for Count Garza."

Solanna did not reply. Another of the students said, "I think he killed himself, didn't he?"

"No," an older man corrected, "his wife was unable to live with the disgrace and poisoned him."

"I thought it was his daughter."

"I heard he went into exile in Merse."

"No, it was Ghillas. Or maybe Elleon."

"Eiha, enough!" Solanna cried. "The fact is that the baron was heard of no more. And the *fact* is that the Tza'ab took control of both regions. They set up puppet rulers—"

Qamar couldn't help it. Laughter rendered him breathless for a few moments, while Solanna glared and the other students wondered what was so funny. At last he managed, "I would dearly love to hear you call Ra'abi that to her face!"

"As I was about to say," she went on, tight-lipped, "all real power rested with the husband of the Empress because the Empress, of course, was incapable of governing. She was, in *fact*, entirely mad."

Qamar felt the smile freeze on his face.

"They will tell you, in Tza'ab Rih, that she withdrew from public life to devote herself to prayer. This is not true. She was of the Shagara tribe, like all of you, and her shame at the uses to which her people's knowledge had been put by her power-hungry husband was at last too much for her. She agreed with your ancestors, in *fact*, that Shagara gifts ought not to be used for evil purposes but for healing and protection and all the other things you're learning how to do. And it serves as a warning, I think, to adhere strictly to these ways and not allow yourselves to be corrupted. Remember always how the Empress, unable to bear the wickedness her husband accomplished with the help of the Shagara, in the end lost her sanity."

Qamar discovered he was on his feet, and trembling. "You will apologize."

"I will not. It's true." She met his gaze calmly. "I saw it."

Everyone in the fortress knew what she claimed to be. That she had located Qamar and brought him back proved it. Qamar himself, however, kept recalling their first encounter, when she'd been surprised that he was young and handsome, not old and scarred. He didn't care for her visions, frankly. It wasn't so much that he doubted that she had indeed seen his grandmother somehow; it was that she was so wrong about why it had happened.

But it wasn't something he could tell the truth about. He knew that, even as he drew breath to do so. All around him, staring with astonishment, sat a broad sampling of the population of the fortress, here to learn Solanna's language. Children, young women and men, older people wanting to keep their minds alert—and mothers. If he corrected Solanna's interpretation of his grandmother's . . . difficulty . . . he would have to admit that it was not the shame of seeing her heritage misused but the misery of having birthed Haddiyat sons. There had to be at least one woman in this classroom who would know exactly what that meant, who had felt the unique anguish of knowing a son would die early and in pain. And even if there were no such mothers here tonight, everyone knew everyone else in the fortress, and he would not be thanked for bringing up a subject no one ever discussed. The women had to feel it; of course they felt it, before schooling themselves to feel only pride in having given birth to so valuable a son who would maintain Shagara traditions for one generation more.

Solanna was watching him through narrowed eyes. "You had a comment to make, Qamar?"

"Yes," he said softly. "Empress Mirzah was an unhappy woman, but not for the reason you give. She . . . she very much disliked living in palaces. She missed the desert tents." It was the truth, just not all of it.

"How would *you* know how she lived or how she felt about it?"

He looked her straight in the eye, and in the language of Tza'ab Rih—and of the Shagara—said, "She was my grandmother. You will excuse me, I trust. Sururi annam," he added to the class in general and walked out.

By the time he reached his own quarters—a few twisting alleys off the big eastern courtyard, which the locals called a zoqallo—he was shaking again with anger. Acuyib curse the girl, what business did she have telling her distorted version of history? And how dare she compel him to the unspeakable vulgarity of reminding her who he was and why he knew much better than she what went on in the palaces of Tza'ab Rih? The class had watched with fascination or amusement or boredom as their varying natures prompted, but he'd sensed a flinch run through every one of them at the reminder that this charming young man who lived in their fortress and studied their ways and was a gifted Shagara male was, in fact, a sheyqir of Tza'ab Rih.

Climbing the stone stairs three at a time to his second-floor room, he slammed the door shut behind him and fell across his bed without bothering to light the candle. What was he doing here, anyway? He could be at home, lolling on silk pillows, nibbling wine-soaked pears, and his most worrisome thought would be deciding which woman to invite to his bed that night. He did not belong here. This country was not his.

He lit the bedside candle, then the three-armed branch on the desk by the window. The light would glow down into the alley. He picked up a sheaf of notes on the uses of flowering plants found above a certain altitude in the mountains, read five words, and threw it aside.

She wasn't coming, not to apologize or to continue the argument or even to rebuke him for being rude.

He opened the folder of notes from Zario Shagara's class and began sorting through to find the first page so he could begin copying his one- or two-word prompts into sentences that actually made sense. For a moment he thought he'd lost the sheets and cursed aloud.

She wasn't coming.

Not that he had any reason to expect her. Still, their discussions often continued as they walked through the fortress passageways, until he took the turning that led to the eastern zoqallo. He still didn't know exactly where she lived. And how she could possibly go home tonight and sleep after insulting him so appallingly, he really didn't know—

Qamar's eye and his whole mind were suddenly fixed on the single word written in very large letters on his page of notes from this morning.

WILL.

Zario had said something different when it came time for his usual cautions about blood being insufficient—and indeed completely inadequate—if the work had not been properly prepared.

"It is not the paper, nor the talishann written on it, nor the ink in which they are written, that secure the achievement of your goals. It is not even the addition of your own blood. None of these things can do what your own mind can do. You must *will* your work into being. You must believe that all these things so meticulously chosen shall combine at your bidding to do your will. *You* are the most powerful ingredient of any magic. Not just your blood, not just your knowledge, but your *will*."

Qamar heard the words echo in his head. This was not something a Shagara of Tza'ab Rih would have said. They were the conduits of magic. They crafted the hazziri or concocted the medicines and took justifiable pride in their work. But they were not *part* of the magic. They contributed nothing of themselves except their blood. They would not agree that one man's force of will could play even the smallest part in his creations.

Yet Zario Shagara, only two generations removed from the desert, had spoken of that very thing. Of *willing* one's work into being.

Qamar happened to agree. And for the first time, he began to think that he might truly belong here. So intent was he on this thought, and others that followed after it, that he did not hear the soft, tentative tapping at his door.

Nor the less gentle knocking that followed.

He did hear a woman's voice call out his name. He turned in his chair, wondering bemusedly why she was coming to visit him at this hour.

"Qamar—I'm sorry, all right?"

Frowning, he tried to think what she might be apologizing for.

"I shouldn't have said that about—about the Empress."

He remembered now. He stood, about to walk the ten paces to the door—it was a much larger room than the one he'd lived in before—when she spoke again.

"It's just—I forget sometimes that you weren't born here. That you're one of them."

He unlatched and hauled open the door. "Say that again."

"What?"

"What you just said. Repeat it."

"I'm sorry for what I—"

"No, not that, who cares about that? Say what you said just now."

"That you're one of them?"

"Exactly. I wasn't born here. I don't belong here. I'm one of them." He grinned at her befuddlement. "Don't you see? So were the Shagara when they first got here. Yet you wouldn't call them foreigners *now*, would you? Different from the rest of the populace, to be sure, but not outsiders, not anymore. You originally came here to get them to work with you against the Tza'ab. That's not something you do with people you don't trust."

"Thanks to your grandfather's example!" she retorted.

"Exactly!" he said again. Then he paused, and frowned down at her. "You admit that it happened the way I said it happened?"

"I said the invasion was unprovoked and dishonorable. I said nothing about the reasons why it happened."

Qamar laughed again. He could see things, too: long, contentious talks with this girl, arguing out the finest details and most obscure implications.

"I find nothing amusing about any of this."

"Of course you don't. I haven't explained it yet." Then he had to admit, "I'm not sure I understand much of it myself—yet."

Solanna regarded him as if suspecting that despite all the healing Zario had done and the precautionary talishann around his room, he'd deliberately plunged head-first into a wine vat and drunk his way out, with predictable effects on his reason.

Grinning at her, he went on, "Would it help if I told you that you were right? What you said about the Tza'ab not belonging here."

"You're admitting to *that*?"

"Of course. You were right. But what came next—you were wrong, and the Shagara here are the proof. They were strangers here once. Generations ago. In the time since, they've married and had children with local women and men, haven't they? Of course they have—names like 'Zario' and 'Evetta' confirm it."

"Just because their blood is mixed with—"

"You're not *seeing* it."

She stiffened with insult, aware that he had used that word deliberately. When he laughed again, she turned for the door.

"No, wait—you haven't heard—"

"I have heard more than enough. And I have *seen* more than enough as well!"

"Have you? More than me, wallowing in wine?"

And then something else occurred to him. She had seen him *old*. She had seen him with—what, lines on his face? White hair? She had said scars, but couldn't they just have been wrinkles? It didn't matter. She had seen him *old*.

Old!

It meant he would succeed. It had to mean that. It must meant he would grow old the way other men grew old, and if he didn't actually conquer death, then at least he and his kind would no longer have to die too young.

"Wallowing with your whores, you mean," she snapped. "You were disgusting, and I don't know why I bothered to bring you back here. Filthy from your hair to your toenails, and the ugliest thing I've ever seen."

With difficulty he dragged his attention away from his glorious new realization. What he saw in her eyes was just as glorious. He knew that the damage of that autumn and winter was long gone. Bloodshot eyes, puffy face, thickened body—ayia, he *had* been ugly. But he wasn't ugly now, and he knew it.

"Why *did* you bring me back here?" he asked softly. "And why do you stay?"

Her back was to him, and he spent the moments of her silence admiring the coil of pale hair at her nape and the way curling tendrils escaped down her neck.

"What else have you seen, Solanna?"

"Myself," she whispered, not facing him. "Here. As a young woman, as I am now, and—and as a very old woman. I know what it means. I will spend most if not all my life here." Turning, she gave an unconvincing shrug of indifference. "So it would be absurd to leave, wouldn't it, for I will only return again. Why put myself through the bother of the long journey to my home, when I already know—"

"It's farther to the seacoast, where I was, than it is to Cazdeyya," he pointed out. He was enjoying this far too much, he knew, but he owed her a few moments of discomfort. Time to bring in another contender for the dominant emotion in her eyes, he told himself. "Did you see anyone with you, when you were old? Did you see *me*, Solanna?"

The victor turned out to be fury. He hadn't expected that. She took the four steps separating them, slapped him full in the face, and was gone before he could do anything more than gasp.

That slap was most inconvenient to the rest of his evening. The impatient and at times fretful exploration of new and puzzling ideas was interrupted by a stinging pain every time he grinned or laughed when another suspicion became a certainty. He managed to work out quite a bit of it all the same, even while being reminded of another puzzle he had some very good ideas about how to solve. And each time he thought this, he grinned again, and laid a hand to his cheek.

What he had realized, and what became the foundation of his beliefs, was that his grandfather and great-grandfather had been correct about many things. For the thing briefly discussed with his grandsire Alessid years earlier burst into his mind, and he understood Acuyib's meaning.

Each people, he reasoned, belonged to its own land by virtue of oneness with the soil, the air, the water, the plants and animals, becoming a part of the land and sharing in the spiritual quality unique to a particular place. Before one could truly understand and work the magic of the land, it must be in one's blood, and one must understand it, learn its ways and moods and contours. This could take years, or generations. But it did happen, as Azzad al-Ma'aliq had come to belong to the land he served.

Kings, armies, empires—these things came and went, and they were irrelevant to the land. The round of the seasons, birth, growth, thriving, death, and rebirth—these things were the essentials. They were, as Alessid had reasoned, the balance of living in the place one knew and understood, of being part of a place and its elemental nature.

The relationship between this rich green land and its people was comparable to the correlation of the Za'ada Izim to the desert.

It remained for him to find that balance in a land new to the Tza'ab. For if his people were to endure in this new place, they must become part of the land itself.

Any recounting of the Diviner's life that attributes to him motives other than these is a lie.

— HAZZIN AL-JOHARRA, *Deeds of Il-Ma'anzuri,* 813

22

Over the next years Qamar discovered several things, not all of them to do with his newfound art.

He learned, for example, that a man could woo a woman with exasperation instead of exuberance, and manage it quite successfully, too.

He found out that his wife's visions of the present were spontaneous, but that to see future events required the burning of a complexity of herbs that sometimes worked and sometimes did not but that always left her helpless with exhaustion for a full day afterward. When he had refined enough of his ideas to share them with her—knowing that imprecision would only annoy her and leave him open to criticism—she commented that by this way of thinking, her susceptibility to the smoke of these herbs seemed just one more way the land provided for the people who belonged to it.

He agreed with her and added the observation to the notes he was assembling. For the most important thing of all that he discovered was that he must learn everything—*everything*—about this land before he could truly begin what he saw as the great work of his life. The work that would *mean* his life.

Upon their marriage, Qamar and Solanna were assigned three rooms on the second floor of a building overlooking the west zoqallo. It was a corner apartment, with the reception room and Qamar's study—which he persisted in calling the maqtabba—facing south, a coveted advantage; they were given the chambers only because Zario Shagara, just before he died, asked that his rooms should become theirs as his wedding gift to them. Their bedroom window had a clear view of the western mountains. It became their habit, on clear days, to sit and watch the sunset together. Qamar both loved and dreaded that little ritual. Each nightfall meant that soon he would be in bed with Solanna—but each also meant that another day had passed without his solving more than a tiny fraction of the puzzle.

They had also inherited all of Zario's books. These included volumes that were relics of the exile, made of parchment in thin, light leather covers, bound in the outdated method of sewing together the tops of the pages. These days books were assembled with the stitching on the left. It was a small, eccentric collection, mainly poetry, and included the collected works of Sheyqir Reihan al-Ammarizzad.

"It's easy to tell which poems he wrote before, and which after," Solanna remarked one night. He had been teaching her to read and write the more ceremonial version of his language, the style used in all poetry. "I expect you have no need to ask 'Before and after what?'"

"None at all." He did not look up from drawing acorns. A dozen types of oak trees grew in the foothills, and he was discovering that each had subtly different properties.

"Neither do you feel any remorse for what your great-grandfather did to him."

"None at all," he said again.

"Using Shagara magic to help him do it."

He set down his pen. He recognized that note in her voice, the one that meant she would pursue the topic until he answered in a way that either satisfied her or angered her so much that she left the room. "Would you like me to write him a letter of apology? He's dead. What happened is what happened. Nothing I can do, say, think, or feel can possibly make any difference."

"It might, if you knew what his kinswoman has it in mind to do."

Frowning, he stoppered his ink bottle—he would get no more work done this afternoon—and said, "What have you heard?"

"Miqelo returned from Joharra yesterday."

She put the book aside and began pushing hairpins back into the coil at her nape. It was a very hot summer day, one of the few each year when Qamar regretted the south-facing windows that were exposed to fierce sunlight from dawn to twilight. The heat rarely bothered him, but Solanna suffered terribly on days such as these. Not that she would countenance a change of clothing to the practical silks and tunics worn in Tza'ab Rih; that would be conceding to those she considered her enemies. Qamar never quite understood how she could love him, seeing as how he was technically her enemy—but he never said a word about it. His mother would have told him he was learning wisdom, and about time, too.

"What does Miqelo have to say?" he asked.

"That there is a new Sheyqa of Rimmal Madar."

"New? Kerrima is dead?"

"This winter. Someone called Nizhria sits on the Moonrise Throne now. A cousin of yours in some way, but I'm not sure how."

"Kerrima's younger sister. And before you say it, I am quite sure the death was not a natural one. They're worse than spiders, those al-Ammarizzad. They not only eat their own young, they devour anything they can find."

"I thought the name was al-Ma'aliq these days, not al-Ammarizzad?"

"Only part of it." He rose and went to the cupboard where fruit juice was kept cool by their daily summer ration of hoarded winter ice. "Considering the woman Nizhria's name recalls, I wouldn't be at all surprised if she gets rid of it. And, to be honest, it's been a very long time since any al-Ma'aliq set foot in Rimmal Madar. The people will have forgotten us, I think. If Kerrima, who was a good friend to my grandfather and my Aunt Ra'abi, did not die a natural death, then I suspect it was done by the faction at the palace more loyal to the al-Ammarizzad than to the al-Ma'aliq."

Solanna had finished repinning her hair, and now shook her head in amazement—an action that threatened to loosen the hairpins again. "How do you keep track of them all?" she asked, accepting the clay cup of juice he gave her. "No, never mind, it makes my head ache even to think about it. And it doesn't matter anyway. Nizhria has decided that our land was so easy for the Tza'ab to conquer, surely her armies will do even better. From what Miqelo heard of the talk in Joharra, they fear she may have it in mind to use us as a base for conquering Tza'ab Rih itself. Or it may be simply that she hates the idea of the Empress owning more land than she does."

Qamar hid a smile behind his cup. Solanna would never accept the notion that the Empress of Tza'ab Rih was her mother-in-law. "Has Nizhria taken into account that she could be fighting both the locals *and* the Tza'ab here?"

It turned out that she had. Qamar couldn't decide if the new Sheyqa was worthy or unworthy of the woman for whom she was named. Nizhria certainly had the acquisitive instincts, but she was also about as subtle as an avalanche.

She sent emissaries to absolutely everyone who had any stake at all in a prospective war. To Empress Mairid, she wrote that whatever troublesome resistance was still to be encountered in the conquered lands, her armies would help the Tza'ab make short work of it. To the nobles, in power or not, of these same conquered lands, she wrote that only her assistance could free them of their hated Tza'ab masters. To everyone she promised that the price of her support was nothing more than a trading outpost here and there for her merchants.

Nobody believed any of it.

"Not that she expects anyone to believe it," said Qamar as he poured qawah for Miqelo that evening. "But she'll have everyone eyeing everyone else, wondering who will join with her and who will not."

"And too suspicious of each other even to bring up the subject of an alliance," Solanna added, then shook her head in disgust. "Trading outposts!"

"You will excuse me, Qamar, I'm sure," Miqelo replied with a grimace, "when I say that we learned with the Tza'ab that once an army is here, it stays."

Qamar shrugged. "Yet it seems there are those in Taqlis and Ibrayanza, and even in Cazdeyya, who are willing to take a chance."

"Taqlis," Solanna mused, "is quite a long way from everyone else. They may think the Sheyqa won't bother coming that far."

"I think the Cazdeyyan nobles have this in mind as well," Miqelo agreed. "This lamb is excellent, Solanna, I've never tasted it dressed with mint before."

"An experiment," Qamar said, smiling. "When you or my other roving friends bring me samples, once I've done with them we use them for cooking—*after* testing them for poison, Miqelo, I promise! This isn't our mountain mint but another kind—Ibrayanzan. It's odd, you know, that in the desert there are at most two or three varieties of any one plant—as if they learned early on what they must do in order to survive and just kept doing it. But here—ayia, my friends bring back for me four types of daisy, or six different grasses, and all from the same hillside! I've cataloged seven different sorts of mint, for instance, and of those acorns you brought me last time, three were entirely new to me. It's—" He broke off suddenly as Solanna clapped her napkin to her mouth, her dark eyes sparkling merrily. "I'm doing it again, aren't I?" he sighed. "Your pardon, Miqelo, I'm afraid I become worse than boring sometimes. Please go on with your news."

Grinning, the merchant ladled more mint sauce over his plate of lamb.

"It's good to see a young man with a real purpose in life, Qamar. My son—eiha, if he ever had a thought, it would die of shock at finding itself in his of all brains!"

Qamar laughed and did not look at his wife. His real purpose in life . . . after twelve years of marriage, after watching him do his research and helping him with it, she still had no idea what his real purpose was. That was how he preferred it.

"So our people—some of them, anyway—want to ally with Rimmal Madar to throw out the Tza'ab," Miqelo continued. "I think it's possible that Sheyqir Allil would unbend his stiff neck and accept the Sheyqa's help to subdue the outlying regions of Joharra. They do keep him busy, you know."

"I never much liked him," said Qamar. "I can imagine what would happen if he even hinted at such a plan to the Empress."

"It's a pity he won't dare," Solanna said. "She'd be so outraged she'd throw him out. If that happened, at least the Joharrans wouldn't have to suffer any more."

"Ayia, but what would happen then?" Qamar grinned at her. "Joharra might get to like their new ruler, and then what would happen to the spirit of rebellion?"

She scowled her opinion of his teasing. "And what if Sheyqa Nizhria simply attacks and succeeds in gaining a foothold? Do we join with her against the Tza'ab, or join with the Tza'ab to throw out this new enemy? And where, finally, stand the Shagara?"

"Aloof, as always," Miqelo said firmly.

Qamar exchanged a glance with his wife. "More wine?" he asked their guest, and poured from the chilled flagon. He would have liked a taste of it himself, but since that last tavern night in the seaport—so long ago now!—he had not touched a drop. He had promised Solanna.

So much to learn. So much to codify. So much to organize into useful, useless, and possibilities to be investigated further.

Berries, for example. Mulberry for peace and protection, raspberry for protection and love, strawberry for love and luck. Blackberry brambles prevented the dead from rising as ghosts, but in combination with rowan and ivy warded off all other sorts of evil.

The plants and trees that grew here gave fascinating promise. So many of them were unknown in Tza'ab Rih. Qamar wished that the Shagara in his homeland had thought to study them before now. If nothing else—and there was a great deal else—there was help here for the pains of the bone-fever that afflicted Haddiyat, help in the form of the humble walnut. Yet the tree had another tantalizing association: it *expanded* things. Wealth, horizons, the mind, the emotions, the perceptions, the soul. . .and magic. Its use in inks was long established, but Qamar had from the first seen other ways of using the tree. Specifically, the wood. More specifically, to write on the wood. And finally, and most specifically, to *draw* on the wood of the walnut tree that expanded magic.

A few months after their marriage, when they were still telling each other things about their families and childhood homes, the sort of idle reminiscences sparked by a word or a scent, Qamar was describing the palace where he had grown up. Gardens, gravel paths through them, intricate mazes of shrubs or walls that led to cooling fountains—all the serene beauties he had so taken for granted.

"But the most beautiful garden and fountain were inside the palace itself. It was all made of tile—the grass underfoot, the trellises of climbing roses, the sky above them, darker and still darker blue until they reached the domed ceiling, sparkling with millions of stars. In the middle of the room was a fountain . . ."

"Made of water, I hope?" An instant later she exclaimed, "Qamar! Stop that, you'll burn your hand!"

Startled from his thoughts, he snatched his hand back from lighting a candlebranch with a twig and blew out the flame that had indeed come almost near enough to scorch his fingers. And as he felt the heat that had not quite burned him, two separate memories swirled together like different inks combining to make a new and different essence.

"Qamar?"

"Yes," he said mindlessly. "The fountain. It stopped working. There was a book of drawings, and he drew the fountain from memory, and it worked again—but then it didn't, and he was dead with burned paper in the hearth—"

"Meya dolcho," she said with a worried frown, "what are you talking about?"

So he explained it to her, the curious thing he had heard about from Ab'ya Alessid years after the fact. The fountain, the drawing spoiled by blood from a cut finger, the dead fountain and the dead artist and the dead ashes in the hearth.

Solanna stared wide-eyed as he spoke. "Do you think—no, it's not possible."

"Isn't it? Fadhil was burning the drawings he didn't like or couldn't use, including the one with his blood on it—the one that had reawakened the fountain."

"With a *picture?*"

"Why not? We do it with words and symbols, why not a literal depiction of the thing we wish to influence?"

Suddenly she gripped his arm. "Or the person," she whispered. "That's what you're thinking, isn't it? You could draw a person, and in such detail that it would look real, and—and—"

"And I could do to it whatever I pleased," he said slowly. "I can do it now, with a name and ink and the right talishann and my own blood—but those are mere curse-tablets, like the Hrumman used to make. Piles of them are found every so often where their temples used to be. But they were superstition, useless. Powerless. If a likeness could be made that looks absolutely real—"

"Stop. I will hear no more of this." And to emphasize her determination, she rose from the chair beside him and went into their reception room and stayed there the rest of the evening.

So she did not hear his other story, the one about burning his hand as he wrote the letter to Rihana and Ra'amon for Ab'ya. His blood had surely been on that paper commanding them to rule wisely and gently, to unite his name with her power for the benefit of Joharra. Had they not done just that? Even when logic suggested otherwise, they had found ways to combine their strengths and—

—and he had even playfully included talishann for *love* and *fidelity* and *fertility* and *happiness*, and they had known all of those things in abundant measure.

But Rihana and Ra'amon were both dead, and Allil was ruling unwisely and ungently on behalf of the next queen, who was years away from taking power herself—if Allil was willing to give it up, which Qamar very much doubted.

Neither did Solanna hear his further conclusion: if someone had thrown that letter into a fire or ripped it up, was it likely that Qamar would not be alive?

In all the years since that night, he had never spoken of those things again, except to ask a casual question of one of his teachers. What was done with old pages? Once a healing had been accomplished, what became of the paper used to accomplish it?

"Back into the slurry, of course, to be used again. We've always done that—ever since the first years here, when we didn't have mountains of paper to waste."

So the blood was diluted, not actually destroyed by fire or its substance ripped apart by tearing the fibers into which it had soaked.

No one knew. No one knew about drawings, and no one knew about destruction.

Qamar kept these things to himself.

The original Shagara magic, in the desert wastes, had been medicine—potions and unguents and dressings made with precision and care—and then the hazziri, made with Haddiyat blood. Here, the medicine still obtained, though with new and different plants replacing the old familiar ones. The hazziri were much the same as well, though the materials used had changed drastically. From gold, silver, and gems to tin and brass, the traditional arts had been translated as best they had been able. But these Shagara had added something no one in Tza'ab Rih had ever even dreamed of—and whatever isolated instances might have provided the clues, no one had put everything together.

Qamar had recognized the entirety of it. The vastness of the magic that no one else had ever guessed. The art of the healer added to the art of the talishann, with quickening blood to kindle the magic, could find its ultimate potency in *art*.

As he researched and learned and organized his findings, he realized that in hundreds of instances the Shagara here had adapted old formulas without fully understanding the additional significances of the indigenous plants. Solanna knew much of the lore her people had assembled over the years; in remote villages, lacking formally trained healers, most people learned at least the basics and usually rather more than the basics. And whereas every healer—Shagara or otherwise—knew that the poppy was used for sleep potions, Solanna told him that among her people, the white poppy brought the gift of consolation and the yellow, success. How such things had originated, no one knew. But Qamar made note of them all, and through the years had been indulged in his obsession by Miqelo and other friends who traveled for the Shagara, who brought back not just herbs and flowers but books.

In one thing he was stymied. He could not draw. There were people here who had talent and tried to teach him, but it was all quite hopeless. He didn't dare experiment. What if he had asked someone to draw one of the climbing roses in exact detail, only with summer flowers heavy on its canes, and then added his own talishann and blood—and what if the roses changed, right in front of everyone? Temptation gnawed at him to try it, but his wife's reaction to the little he'd shared with her cautioned otherwise.

He spent a great deal of time walking the hills near the fortress, not to collect specimens but to escape the noise and bustle that necessarily resulted when hundreds of people lived in such close proximity. He needed to think. He needed to make sense of what he had learned, what he had intuited, and what he suspected might be true. He could not act on any of it until he was sure. But there was always so much more to be discovered, so many things to compare and balance with each other.

One thing became clearer to him the more he considered it. To influence a *person*, that most wondrous and complex of Acuyib's creations, a drawing would have to be not just accurate to the last detail but done in colors. The rosy flush of cheeks and lips, the dapple of freckles across a nose, the highlights of red or gold or bronze in dark hair—all these things would have to be depicted. So it was fortunate that he had turned out to be good at mixing inks. He secured a small chamber one floor down from their living quarters, stocked it with the usual and the unusual for making ink, and put to use his ever-growing knowledge. Solanna called this room the Inkwell, more than pleased that her husband's experiments were not cluttering up her home.

Qamar spent many long hours fussing with various recipes, even though he knew that ink would never be able to capture the delicate coloring of a human face, however subtle the artist. There had to be an answer to the difficulty, and he must be the one to find it—for the rest of the Shagara could not learn that there was any difficulty at all.

Sheyqa Nizhria grew weary of waiting for replies to her letters. Her next action was to send proclamations to all parties. Those who accepted her, she would not annihilate. Those who defied her would be destroyed. These were her terms.

She received many replies this time. All of them defied her, sometimes in language that had never before been read aloud in the presence of a Sheyqa of Rimmal Madar.

The Empress of Tza'ab Rih sent no answer at all.

With the early spring, ships sailed. Landing on isolated shores, they offloaded thousands of the Sheyqa's warriors, including a large contingent of Qoundi Ammar and their magnificent white horses. When word of the invading forces reached Joharra, Cazdeyya, Elleon, Taqlis, and the new city-state of Shagarra, men who had been training all winter in anticipation of just this event began to march.

This was precisely what the Sheyqa wanted.

Miqelo and his son Tanielo returned early and shaken from their first expedition after the snowmelt. More than half the goods loaded onto pack animals for sale in towns and cities was still securely in place, and on seeing this the crafters groaned. There would be no profits this year from the rolls of paper or the pretty tin hazziri wind chimes, the lush woven woolens or the hundreds of bottles of medicine coveted by traditional physicians. Worse, there would be no sacks of fine grains, no bolts of new cloth, no citrus fruits or dried dates or figs. The only thing Miqelo brought back with him was news. None of it was good.

For the first time in years, Qamar began to feel himself an outsider. Not just gharribeh, foreign, but dangerous. He was Tza'ab. His wife was Cazdeyyan. It had taken a long, long time for the people here to greet them as equals in the zoqallos and streets, then to speak with them, and finally to invite them into their homes for afternoon qawah or a casual meal. Yet Qamar knew that he and Solanna were still looked upon as outsiders. So he was surprised when a girl came to the Inkwell and said she had a message for him. She was a pretty little thing, so much Shagara in her looks that she might have just ridden in with her parents from the winter encampment in the wastes of Tza'ab Rih.

"Please, Sheyqir, I am to say you must be as quick as you can, please. There is an assembly—at the Khoubri." Her eyes widened like those of a startled fawn at the array of flasks and bottles on the shelves, the tables cluttered by heating rings with iron bowls nestled in them, jars of glass stirring rods, stacks of paper, bundles of unused pens. "The Khoubri, please, Sheyqir," she said, as if worried that the oddities had made her forget to mention it.

"I shall be there at once. Thank you." He watched her run out the door and heard the clatter of her shoes on the stairs. A sound he would never hear his own daughter making. There would be no daughters, no sons.

Shrugging off the thought as something he could never afford to dwell on, he rinsed his ink-stained hands in a bowl of clean water and ran his wet fingers through his hair. He was thirty-eight this year, but other than a few strands of gray and some lines around his eyes from squinting at his books too much, his age rested lightly on him. Especially for a Haddiyat. He knew this wouldn't last much longer. He dreaded every winter morning, positive that he would wake to pain in his hands, his knees, his back. Not yet, praise Acuyib. But soon.

The Khoubri was one of the oddest features of a very odd fortress. Its name was its description, for it served as a bridge between the outer wall and the building that housed the unmarried guards. At the junction, the bridge descended in a series of steps that gave out onto a large room with no windows and only one other exit. The idea, Qamar supposed, was that enemies gaining the walls would be funneled through the passage, push each other into the open, and discover they had only two choices: go forward through the single door and down the stairs, or shove their way back across the bridge and try to find another way in. Swords and spears would be waiting for them at the bottom of the stairs, of course.

Whatever the case, the room turned out to be a good place for general meetings. A speaker could stand a step or two above, to be seen more easily. The echoes in the Khoubri were annoying, but after a while one learned to deal with that.

Qamar climbed the stairs and sidled along with his back to a wall. There was no place to sit and no time to wriggle himself a space, for Miqelo was already standing on the second step, holding up his hands for quiet.

"The Sheyqa of Rimmal Madar has a new weapon. It is called a ballisda, and it need not be brought in the ships. These things can be built here in a day or two. It is a mechanical arm that throws giant stones, burning pitch, anything at all either into or over any walls." He paused. "Even ours."

Snorts and a few shouts of laughter greeted this. Miqelo again raised his hands.

"Listen to me! I have seen for myself what these things did to the walls of Granidiya! Nearly the height of our own, nearly as thick, and blasted in places to rubble as if Chaydann al-Mamnoua'a had directed a bolt of lightning! I saw from the nearby hills, I watched the smoke still rising from the city, and the only reason I was not here yesterday is that my son disobeyed me, and ran down to the walls, and came back the next morning with the whole story. And it is as well that he did."

Tanielo came forward when his father beckoned. Tall and gangly, with golden Shagara skin, though his golden-brown hair proclaimed at least one local man or woman in his ancestry, he cleared his throat nervously. "She—the Sheyqa—her ships did not land near Shagarra alone. More of them sailed on to the shores of Ibrayanza and began the march northward. The others marched west, and they met at Granidiya and destroyed it. But before this, they laid waste to every town in their path. Those with walls, they attacked with the ballisdas. Those without, they simply attacked and burned. But here is the terrible thing. This army has now split in two again, with one section heading for the palace at Praca, where the Queen of Ibrayanza lives. It may be there now. But the other part is marching north, due north."

"For Joharra!" someone called out.

"No!" Tanielo cried. "No, not Joharra at all! They won't touch Joharra, not a handful of its soil! Sheyqir Allil is her ally, he gave them maps of the easiest routes, and—"

"Why would he do such a thing? Doesn't he understand?"

"He's not one of us—he was never one of us—"

"And what of our own people?" another man yelled. "I thought that soldiers were coming from Taqlis and even Elleon, and everyplace in between, to fight the Sheyqa's army!"

Miqelo waited until the cheers and shouts had faded a bit, then told them, "I'm sure that was their intent—until they saw what happened to Granidiya! There is no army to oppose her, there is no one who—"

The uproar and the outrage shivered the stones of the Khoubri. Qamar didn't hear most of it; he was staring at the wall opposite him, and in his imagination its blankness was overlaid with a map. Tza'ab Rih to the south; Ibrayanza just beyond the narrowing; Shagarra to the east. Joharra just north of Ibrayanza . . . but not in the path of an army marching due north. Toward Cazdeyya.

He pushed away from the wall and waded into the eddies of seated men, trying to be careful not to step on anyone but intent on joining Miqelo and Tanielo at the stairs. When he was halfway there, someone called out his name.

"Qamar! Why don't you tell us all about Sheyqa Nizhria al-Ammarizzad al-Ma'aliq!"

He stopped, and turned. "That, I am unable to do. But I believe I can tell you what she wants."

"Our lands! All of us dead!"

"No." He glanced around the Khoubri. "The last thing in the world that she wants is the death of a single Shagara."

He was, of course, correct.

They did not believe him for quite some time, not until reports began to trickle in about the route being taken by the Sheyqa's armies. The troops that subdued Ibrayanza stayed there. Joharra was never threatened, never even touched, and this was understood to be Sheyqir Allil's doing—that same Allil who had been Qamar's commander years and years earlier, and who had decided to buy off the armies of Rimmal Madar with maps and advice. That portion of the army marching north kept marching, with only occasional forays into total destruction along the way, just to educate the populace. They had a goal, and they wished to reach it by midsummer.

And when they did, all the arguments anyone in the fortress could muster could not persuade Qamar to abandon them to their inevitable fate. It took his wife's cooperation—though some have termed it "treachery"—and a sleeping potion to remove him from the fortress. Any recounting of his life that asserts otherwise is a lie.

— HAZZIN AL-JOHARRA, *Deeds of Il-Ma'anzuri*, 813

23

It was maddening, the question of how Sheyqa Nizhria had learned that there were Shagara within her grasp.

Qamar could only postulate that someone, or several someones, had been extremely curious and extremely clever. After Ra'abi's marriage to Za-quir al-Ammarizzad, his cousins and his friends had visited, and of course he had brought servants with him, any one of whom could have been gathering information. And of course there were the Geysh Dushann. They would not hesitate to share knowledge of the Shagara with those in Rimmal Madar who considered themselves more al-Ammarizzad than al-Ma'aliq.

But few had ever tried to learn *why* the Shagara were such renowned healers. Rare plants in the desert, ancient lore, talents given by Acuyib the Merciful—there were explanations enough. No one had ever connected the trinkets and jewelry, the wind chimes and charms, with the healing arts of the Shagara.

Qamar was certain that now someone had.

And when he learned that Sheyqir Reihan, the poetic son of Nizzira, had been the power behind Nizhria's seizure of the Moonrise Throne, he had a fairly good idea of whose curiosity and cleverness had made the right connections. Reihan's poetry had indeed changed after Azzad al-Ma'aliq had exacted his vengeance. For one thing, he became obsessed with the ring that had been placed onto his finger, which he had worn to the end of his life. Scholars had many pretty things to say about this "symbolism" within his poems. None of them guessed that when he wrote that he was unable to remove the ring from his hand, he wrote the literal truth.

It mattered nothing that Reihan could not possibly know the exact methods of the magic. Qamar guessed that he had guessed. And if not him, then someone else. All that mattered was that Sheyqa Nizhria, positioned by Reihan and now in possession of the Moonrise Throne, unable to lay hands on the Shagara of Tza'ab Rih, had targeted the Shagara within her reach. The Shagara of Cazdeyya.

"This is for you."

Qamar followed the mouallimo's gesture to a book lying on the table. A beautiful book, folio size, bound in plain dark green, it was so new that the scents of paper and leather and glue clung to it still. There was no tooling, there were no symbols stamped into the covers or the spine. The most remarkable thing about it was the lock: made of gold, so much more precious here than in Tza'ab Rih, delicately wrought and fitted with a small key.

"The paper is all of your making, of course," said the crafter, Miqelo's brother. "Solanna gave it to me when I asked. Eight different kinds, fifty pages each. I hope that will be enough."

"Enough? Enough for what?" He reached a reverent finger to stroke the cover. "Yberrio, what is this for?"

"The book, of course. The one you will write that preserves everything we are." He sat wearily in a cushioned chair, rubbing absently at his swollen fingers. "All that we have learned since we came here about the plants, flowers, herbs, trees—how to make ink and paper—eiha, the talishann, those are safe with our kinsmen in the desert. But you must finish the work you began years ago. And this is the book in which you will do it."

Qamar nodded slowly. "It has been decided, then."

"Yes. Perhaps tomorrow, certainly within the next few days. As soon as everyone is ready." He paused for a grim smile. "And even if they are not."

Qamar weighed the book in his hands, looking at it so he would not have to look at his friend. Yberrio was one of the unlucky ones; he was a year Qamar's junior and looked twenty years his senior. "You haven't asked if I'm certain that they will come for us," he said abruptly. "Everyone else has asked if I'm certain."

"Everyone else wants it all to go away. And you forget that I have a reason for believing that others do not. Even if I didn't trust you, I trust Solanna. She has no reason to lie. Not that you do, either. If all you'd wanted was to steal what we know, you could have done it and left years ago." Leaning back in his chair, he waited until Qamar met his gaze, and chuckled. "I was one of those guarding you, when you returned to us from the seaside. By Acuyib, how I hated you! Never once did you set foot inside either of the taverns. And on cold nights, after you'd finished late with your work, I could have used a nice cup of mulled wine."

"So could I," he admitted wistfully. "Were you one of those who made sure I'd think thrice before ever really wanting one again?"

"Ayia, that was Zario." Yberrio raked the graying hair from his brow and said, "You know the present one is resisting. Doesn't want to leave his parents."

"He has to come, and all the other Haddiyat boys with him."

"And their mothers."

So that even if Sheyqa Nizhria succeeded in taking the fortress, she would find no useful Shagara within it.

That the fortress was indeed her aim became clearer with every city ignored on the march northward. Small groups of her soldiers peeled off from the main force every so often to burn a few villages as a warning. When, at one night's camp halfway to Cazdeyya, a well was found to be poisoned, every human being within a day's ride was slaughtered. There were no more attempts to interfere with the advance of the Sheyqa's army.

"I keep wondering," Qamar said suddenly, "how much Allil has revealed."

"Does it matter?"

"Joharra has been spared," Qamar said. "Allil bought this with maps and advice, that much is obvious. But I wonder how much he told her about the Shagara of Tza'ab Rih. That they provided hazziri to my grandfather, Sheyqir Alessid, when your people would not."

"You mean that we shall be easy for them to take and use, whereas our kindred of the desert would not?"

"They would defend themselves with the arts. You will not. They would aid the Empress in any attack against invasion—but you will not."

It was a major point of contention. Some of the younger Shagara here wanted to abandon their principles and create hazziri for war. Their elders utterly forbade it. But the Sheyqa could not know this, and so she marched northward as quickly as she could, to take the one place that she was certain would win her everything.

Including Tza'ab Rih. Solanna had seen it. Not in the smoke that deliberately incited visions, but unexpectedly one morning while helping him sort herbs in the Inkwell. The crash of glass as she leaped from her chair and backed into a table had brought other people running in time to see the stark unreasoning terror on her face. Qamar carried her upstairs, grateful that these attacks of sight had been rare these last dozen and more years; nobody knew what that look in her eyes meant except him.

And, it turned out, Miqelo. Someone had mentioned to someone else that Solanna had been taken ill, and Miqelo had heard of it, and by sundown he was in their reception room asking with brutal directness exactly what she had seen.

"A map," Qamar had answered for her. "Not of this land, but of Tza'ab Rih. All the towns and cities, the desert, everything."

"Labeled in Tza'ab script, not ours," she added. "And I saw a hand, a woman's hand thick with rings, and one of them was of silver and carnelians."

"I don't see—"

Qamar interrupted with, "Each sheyqir my great-grandfather gelded was given a ring. Carnelians set in silver, with rows of tiny ants etched into the bands. You know the symbolism, of course."

"*Harvest*," said Miqelo. "*Izzad*. Whose ring, do you think? All of them are dead by now, of course, so the rings would be no longer binding—"

"Reihan's, at a guess. He worked to put her where she is. What's obvious is that Nizhria intends to use you Shagara against those of Tza'ab Rih. She can't hope to conquer that land without you. I will wager that her troops in Ibrayanza are even now scouting the best place to do battle against the Empress."

"But we will never help her. *Never.*"

Solanna, still very pale and shaken, said, "Do you know what that hand was doing? Stroking the map, like it was the naked skin of her lover. You can tell her *No* until the sun turns cold, and all she will do is laugh—and start killing your families until you cooperate. And the first hazziri that doesn't work precisely the way she orders it to work, she'll kill more."

"Her armies destroy without mercy. She's showing herself as ruthless as her great-great-grandmother," Qamar added. "And that, my friend, is ruthless indeed."

The Shagara here would not use Al-Fansihirro for war and destruction or even self-preservation. Qamar admired their adherence to their beliefs but deplored their stubbornness. What little he had seen of war, he hated; these people hadn't seen war in over eighty years. They didn't even paper the fortress walls with talishann drawn in appropriate ink. Once the paper was slashed or burned the protections would be nullified, and the men who had worked them would die. Paper was frangible; it made the Haddiyat vulnerable.

And so . . . this book he held in his hands. In it, he would record everything these Shagara knew of magic.

To do this in safety, he must find a haven. Solanna had sent messages to every Grijalva connection she could think of, but it had been many long years since they had seen or even heard of her. Only a few wrote back, and only one did not berate her for abandoning her people. This one letter, from an elderly aunt, told her that if she needed a place to go, there was a valley three days from the great river, a box canyon where no one lived because it was useless for farming or cutting lumber or indeed anything but hiding in. It was to this lonely place that Qamar, Solanna, all the Haddiyat boys under the age of fifteen, and their mothers were preparing to go.

At least, this was what they told everyone. Qamar was under no illusions about what would happen to any Shagara left alive in the fortress after Ni-zhria's ballisdas had demolished it and her troops had overrun it. When they talked—and they *would* talk, the Geysh Dushann would make certain of it—they must speak what they thought to be the truth.

The only person who knew where they would really go was Miqelo. Twenty-five years of roaming these lands, first with his father and now with his son, had made him a living map. He assured Qamar that there were several places he had in mind, and he would decide only when they were at least three days away from the fortress.

Qamar walked back through the zoqallos, the green leather book cradled to his chest. The Shagara were learning why their forebears in the desert traveled light. He walked past buildings where paper was made, and ink, schoolrooms and forges, storehouses and binderies and the healer's quarter—each little street and narrow alley was congested with people doing one of three things. They carried items that would be taken out of the fortress, or ones to be hidden in hopes that they would survive, or ones that must be destroyed rather than fall into the hands of the Sheyqa. Qamar could always tell when someone had been assigned to that task: Their faces were either grim with purpose or bleak with sorrow.

There were armfuls of paper to be dumped into the slurry, even though no new sheets would be made from them. Metal dies to be melted in the white-hot forges, never to stamp talishann into tin or brass again. Crates of glass bottles and ceramic flasks to be emptied outside the walls and the containers smashed, some containing medicines, others full of inks. Bins and baskets of herbs, flowers, leaves, all the tools this land had given to the healers, burned.

And books. Beautiful, precious books, some of them as old as the Shagara's time here, many more made and bound since. Qamar held to his chest an empty book, and vowed to Acuyib that he would fill it.

They left at dawn two days later. Three wagons laden with food and other supplies followed thirty-seven horses carrying fifty people—most of the boys were small and light, and so could double up on horseback. The women rode in and sometimes drove the wagons. Tanielo and Solanna led the way out the gates. Miqelo and Qamar left last.

Yberrio saw them off. "Miqelo, my brother, we will not meet again this side of Acuyib's Great Garden, but it had better be many long years before I welcome you there. As for him—" He glanced up at Qamar, then at his brother once more, fiercely. "Miqelo, make sure this man lives."

Qamar was still thinking about those words when they made a rough camp that evening. Saddle sore after so many years when riding was only an occasional recreation, he came close to breaking his vow and asking for a flask of wine. But all he drank was strong, bitter qawah, and for the first time in a long time considered what life had made of the youngest and favorite son of an Empress, a Sheyqir of Tza'ab Rih.

"How delightful to hear you laughing," Solanna said in sour tones as she sat down beside him at the small fire.

"Qarassia," he said, slipping an arm around her, "there is laughing, and then there is laughter. Just as there are women, but only one woman."

"Sometimes I wish I didn't understand you," she replied, nestling close to him.

He tilted his head to look her in the eyes. "You know what my name means in my language. I know the meaning of yours. I always found this significant." When her brows quirked, he told her, "The moon has no light of its own. By itself, it's all in darkness. It's the sun's light that makes the moon shine."

Solanna's eyes filled with tears. "Qamar—"

"Ayia, none of that," he whispered, pulling her nearer again. "I will finish the work, and you will help me. When all his family died by poison or the sword or fire, Azzad yet lived. When his father was betrayed and murdered and his mother and sisters and brothers burned alive, Alessid yet lived. I—"

"Azzad was spared to wreak vengeance," she said tightly, "so that the souls of his family could be at peace. Alessid—"

"—threw out the usurpers and built a nation so that his family could never be destroyed again," he finished for her. "Think who it was who saved the lives of Azzad and Alessid. Shagara. They have done the same for me. I am in their debt, and they have told me how I must repay it. But I have been given what my forefathers did not have. And it is this land that has given it to me, given me you." Pressing his mouth to her fragrant hair, he finished, "I would truly be lost in darkness without you."

Miqelo, his son Tanielo, and four young men who regularly guarded them on trading journeys: These were all that stood between the Shagara and anyone who wanted a look at what might be in their wagons. The women, some of whom had never been farther from the fortress than the riverbank, wept or fretted or rode in stoic silence as their characters prompted. The boys, resentful at first that they were not allowed to stay and fight the invaders, awoke to the unaccustomed freedom of travel and could barely be restrained from galloping off in all directions. Qamar and Tanielo spent a lot of time chasing after them.

On the fourth day—one day after the proposed day of decision about their destination—Miqelo approached Qamar and Solanna very early in the morning and asked them to walk with him for a way.

"The more I think about it, the less I like it," he said. "We all know what will happen to those we left at the fortress. We have with us the hope of the Shagara. Those boys must be protected at all costs."

"I recommend poppy syrup in their morning qawah," Solanna said. "It'll make it easier to throw them in the wagons."

"I've been tempted," he replied with a brief smile. "But it seems to me that we have two separate aims. First is to keep these boys and their mothers safe. The other is the work you must do, Qamar. I think we must divide our group in different directions."

It was decided that the women and boys would travel as far and as fast as possible, find a place to hide—though not the box canyon recommended by Solanna's aunt—and wait until it was safe to return to Cazdeyya. The guards and Tanielo would go with them. All of them, schooled by Solanna in the basics of the family, would call themselves "Grijalva."

"Our tile makers have gone to many places," she explained. "Some of them came home, some stayed. You will be refugees from the conflict, returning to our native villages for safety. They will take you in. Your Shagara coloring can be explained by a generation or so of marriages in foreign towns." But they were never to mention her name, for the letters she had written earlier in the year had yielded no help they could actually use.

That left Qamar, Solanna, Miqelo, and a woman named Leisha, who volunteered to assist Solanna, and her thirteen-year-old son, Nassim, to assist Qamar. Leisha was quite frank about her reasons: she was convinced that she and her son would have a much better chance of survival with Qamar.

"I think," she said, "that Miqelo will work very, very hard to be sure you are not found."

The fourth day was spent making arrangements. Wagons were unloaded, the goods sorted evenly, and packed again. By sundown all was complete, and Miqelo recommended that everyone sleep soundly, for the next days would be difficult.

Qamar sat cross-legged in the dirt beside a small cookfire, listening to the sounds of the camp settling. Familiar to him from his year in the desert, yet there were differences—primary among them being the rustle and slur of the tall pine trees. He reached over to stir the pot of qawah, pleased to find there was still some left for Miqelo, who came to talk with him every night before rolling himself in a blanket to sleep.

Solanna joined Qamar by the fire, kneeling at his side. She had abandoned long skirts, as most of the other women had done, for riding clothes: snug trousers beneath a tunic that fell to midthigh, cut almost like a workingman's smock. The outfit concealed all feminine curves, and she had concealed her hair within a scarf to protect it from the dust of the road. For all her blonde hair, she looked like a woman of Tza'ab Rih.

Miqelo crouched down on the other side of the fire, not looking at either of them. Qamar was about to offer hot qawah when all at once Miqelo tossed a little woolen pouch into the heart of the fire. His dark eyes fixed on Solanna's face with a piercing intensity. Smoke billowed up from the fire, as fragrant as it was stinging. Qamar coughed. Solanna gasped—and in doing so inhaled a full lungful of smoke.

"Forgive me," Miqelo said softly. "But I must know."

Belatedly, Qamar recognized the scents. Herbs, some spices to disguise the odor, scorched wool from the little bag Miqelo had stored them in. Only a few times through the years had he smelled this exact combination, and the recollection made him want to grab Miqelo by the throat.

Too late. Solanna was trembling beside him. He tried to put an arm around her but she shook him off, scuttled sideways, and began to rock back and forth as she stared blindly into the fire. No, not blindly, but what she saw was not the flames.

She did this rarely and unwillingly, because the future ought to be opaque to all but Acuyib in His Wisdom. Sight frightened her. It also compelled her—as it had when she had first come into his room on a rainy night long ago, to see if he was truly the one she had envisioned. That seeing, undertaken reluctantly at Princess Baeatrizia's plea, had been of him, but old and with scars on his face—or so she had said. He had come to believe they were only the lines and wrinkles of great age. Another time, she had taken pity on Miqelo's dying wife and tried to see whether or not he would be home in time to bid her farewell. She had not quite lied to her friend, saying that Miqelo would be at her side very soon. She had chosen not to mention that she had seen him beside a casket being lowered into the ground.

Her other seeings, those unaided by the herbs, were always spontaneous and always of that exact moment in some other location. The hand she had seen caressing a map, the hand wearing a ring of Shagara making that could only have been taken from the finger of a dead man, had been illuminated by the setting sun; the vision had come to her as dusk fell over the Shagara fortress. The seeing that had shown her Qamar himself, stealing from the maqtabba in Joharra, had come to her—as nearly as they could tell—at the precise moment he put his hand on the money drawer and opened it.

But these visions, the ones prompted by the smoke—they were always of the future. As she shivered and swayed with the smoke swirling around her, Qamar glared across the fire at Miqelo.

"I must know," the other man repeated.

"How kind of your brother Yberrio to anticipate your need," he snapped. "Did he prepare it himself, or have a healer do it? Ayia, did he remember to send along something to help her through the next day or two, as she returns to her right mind?"

"The hawk," Solanna whispered, arms wrapped around herself. "The hawk flies from the empty mountain—across the river—"

Miqelo leaned toward her, his face obscured by flames and smoke. "Who is still alive?" he demanded. "Tell me what the hawk sees—"

"Be silent!" Qamar snarled.

Solanna heard neither of them. "Tents . . . carpets . . . the river and the hill . . . the white horses and—and—"

"And what?" Miqelo urged.

"—the book, the book—by lantern light—the boy has come, he's finishing—"

"Qamar's book? What boy? A Shagara, to take and preserve the book? Do you see our success? Solanna, answer me!"

But her eyes rolled up in her head. Qamar caught her as she collapsed toward the fire, barely keeping her from the flames. Without another word he gathered her into his arms and rose, carrying her to the deeper darkness beneath the trees. There he held her until dawn, ignoring the sounds of bridles and harness as the others made ready to go separate ways. At length all was silent. Qamar cradled his unconscious wife against his chest and did not stir from his place beneath the trees.

The boy Nassim eventually called out very softly, "Sheyqir, Miqelo and the others have departed. If the lady is well enough, we ought to go. Sheyqir?"

He rose to his feet, still with Solanna in his arms—and almost stumbled as his stiff knees grated with pain. So it was beginning for him, he thought; he could not blame this on the cold, for it was high summer, nor on the damp, for it had not rained in a month. It was beginning.

"Where is Tanielo?" he asked.

"Waiting with the horses. The others—"

"I don't care about the others." So Miqelo had assigned his son to protect Qamar, had he? Unable to face him or Solanna after what he'd forced upon her with the fire and smoke? "Bring my horse. We cannot ride far today, but we must ride."

Tanielo was wise enough to stay as far as he could from Qamar. By midafternoon, his whole body aching now with the strain of holding Solanna secure in the saddle before him, Qamar was more than ready to call a halt. But this morning's sharp ache had warned him that from now on he would have to learn how to hide pain. So it was nearly twilight before he reined in and told Nassim to bring Tanielo to him.

"Your father was my friend," he said flatly. "I will treat you with the respect I would show to the son of a friend who has died. Because he is dead to me now, for what he did last night. Don't even *think* of doing the same. Do you understand me?"

"Yes, Qamar."

"Sheyqir. You will address me as Sheyqir. All of you will. Bring Leisha to me now, and tell Nassim to make camp."

Just after dark, Solanna woke. Qamar was still holding her, dozing at her side beneath a light blanket. That day they had climbed far enough so that the air was thinner, colder, sharper with the scent of pine. It reminded him of his journeys to Sihabbah.

"How much did I say aloud?"

Qamar jerked awake, arms tightening around her. "Don't worry about that now. You need to eat."

"Tomorrow morning," she murmured. "Water will do, tonight."

As he sat up and reached for the nearby jug of stream water, he said, "I can't believe Miqelo did that to you."

"It was wrong of him, but I understand it. Did I say anything?"

"Something about a hawk." He handed her the water jug and wished there was a fire nearby, so he could see her expression.

"Nothing else?"

"No."

"Good." She drank long and deep, then set the jug aside. "Miqelo wouldn't have liked it."

He waited. At length she pushed her tangled hair from her face and sighed.

"The Sheyqa's army was camped on a wide, flat plain. It was autumn—the trees were red-gold and the river was shrunken from its banks."

"White horses, you said."

"Yes. The—what did you call them? The Qoundi Ammar. Many tents, many flags. One tent especially, red with gold, on the highest ground, with carpets flung all around it, as if to spare someone actually touching the earth—"

"—with her exalted feet," he finished. "The Sheyqa's tent, then."

"Likely." She sipped more water. "There was another army, behind a hill to the north. Cazdeyyan, Ibrayanzan, Qayshi—but some were golden-skinned. Tza'ab, Shagara—" She shook her head. "There were no walls to be toppled. Only the plain, and the two armies. Thousands of men, thousands."

Again he waited. When he could bear it no longer, he asked, "What did you see by lantern light?"

Solanna gave a start of surprise. "Did I say that?"

He nodded. "And something about the book."

Her smile was weary and triumphant. "*Your* book, meya dolcho. I saw your book!"

Then she had seen success. He smiled back and kissed both her hands.

It was still high summer when they rode into a sanctuary that remains unlocated to this day. Miqelo Shagara had learned of it from his father, and he had told his son, and it was to this place that Tanielo guided the Diviner so that the great work might be accomplished.

Meantime, the armies of the Sheyqa of Rimmal Madar continued their assault on the land and its people. Towns and cities fell. Joharra remained untouched. The march northward to Cazdeyya was accomplished.

Some have said that Qamar hid himself and his wife and servants in the deepest reaches of the mountains out of fear. This is a lie, and any account of his life that asserts otherwise is false.

— HAZZIN AL-JOHARRA, *Deeds of Il-Ma'anzuri*, 813

24

Qamar was sure that it would not happen that autumn. The assembly of so many soldiers from so many places simply wasn't possible in so brief a time. It might be the next autumn, or the one after that. But it would not happen this year.

This did not mean he worked any less persistently at the task he now believed Acuyib meant for him to accomplish. And if it was destined that he do this thing, then it was also destined that, like his grandfather and great-grandfather before him, he would succeed. Solanna had seen it.

The pocket in the mountains where Tanielo guided them was inhabited only by sheep. But there were stone huts already built for the convenience and comfort of the shepherds when they came at irregular intervals to check on their flocks. Within these snug little shelters were sacks of flour, dried fruits, and other provisions. There was even a small garden planted with root vegetables that were evidently unappetizing to the native animals, for no fencing had been placed around it.

Qamar took the largest of these huts for his workroom. The second he and Solanna used as living quarters; the third, which contained the provisions and a cooking hearth, was gradually expanded over the summer to provide sleeping room for Leisha, Nissim, and Tanielo. Qamar tried to ignore the noise as a wall was knocked down and the stones rearranged to form a foundation for the wooden slats of the disassembled wagon. But sometimes he needed absolute quiet, and took a sheaf of notes, a pen, and a bottle of ordinary ink and walked up to the narrowest part of the tiny valley, where a spring rippled down the rocks to a small pool. Seating himself beside the stream that whispered into the valley, he would mark off what was essential, what was important, what could be included if there was room, and what could be eliminated without damaging the whole. As the summer went on, he had to become more ruthless in his editing. The notes made over a dozen and more years had been distilled into sharp summations of his classes, his talks with fellow Haddiyat, other books, and his own experimentations. But he did not possess the luxury of infinite pages within his green leather book. He must restrict the final text to what was vital.

It was occasionally maddening. It was always frustrating. And each evening when the light grew too dim for him to work outside in the fresh air, he had Tanielo move his table back indoors and light the lamps, so that he might work well into the night.

When they first arrived, there was a particular notch in the cliffs where the sun disappeared. As the days shortened and the sun vanished earlier and earlier, farther and farther north of that notch, Qamar counted the pages he had written that day and began to despair. He knew he would finish, for Solanna had seen it, but he was afraid he would not be able to include the finer details, the subtler points. He wanted to finish quickly, because he had it in mind to have Nissim begin making a copy as soon as possible. And after that, another copy, and another. It would keep them busy during the winter when snow would trap them inside the huts. As his knees twinged more severely and more often, he began to fear that as the nights turned colder, the ache would move into his fingers. He told himself that the stiffness in his back was due only to long days bent over the manuscript. And if he must squint to see into the distance, to mark the movement of the sun farther and farther from that notch, it was only eyestrain from reading too much.

There was no word from the larger world until the shepherds came to attend to their flocks. From these men there was no astonishment that someone else was living in their little valley, no anger that their supplies had been used. On the day Qamar and his little group had ridden in, Tanielo had pointed out a series of wind chimes fashioned out of tin hanging from sapling pines: hazziri. Qamar had renewed them, added to them, and in some cases improved upon them, to ward away thieves, wolves, and lions. So the shepherds, already familiar with Shagara magic, had no complaints. They were getting more Shagara magic for free.

From these shepherds Qamar learned that Sheyqa Nizhria controlled Ibrayanza. She controlled Shagara. She controlled the passes that led to Tza'ab Rih. She controlled half the length of the great river, and portions of Elleon. She did not control Joharra, nor yet all of Cazdeyya.

"But there's two reasons for that," the most talkative of the shepherds

told Qamar over an outdoor fire the evening they arrived. "That filhio do'—"
Breaking off, he bowed slightly to Solanna and Leisha. "Forgive me, ladies,
my mother would scrub my tongue with lye for my manners."

Another of the men grunted. "We don't spend much time around decent
women."

"Eiha," the first went on, "Sheyqir Allil, he's kept Joharra out of it by
keeping Joharra *in* it, if you see what I mean. His soldiers are wearing the
colors of Rimmal Madar. They only change back to their own shirts once the
Sheyqa's army has moved on. And then—surprise! The nicer bits of Ibrayanza and Shagarra are redrawn on the maps as part of Joharra. He's acting
for the Empress, of course, cursed be her name."

Tanielo asked quickly, "And Cazdeyya?"

A shrug. "The Sheyqa is about halfway up the great river, camped in a
huge red tent all hung about with gold and silk. Her feet never touch the bare
ground, they say, for all the carpets flung about."

"She's not in one of the palaces?" Leisha asked.

"You'd think there'd be enough to choose from, wouldn't you, that she
could live in one of them instead of a tent? But she's taken a vow of some sort,
to live as her soldiers do until she rules from Cazdeyya to Ibrayanza." He
snorted. "I've yet to hear that her soldiers dine off golden plates!"

"For myself," said the oldest of the shepherds as he politely poured out
qawah for them all, "I think she has a yearning to rule more toward the south,
if you see what I mean."

"That has always been my thought," said Qamar. He had given them
only his first name, and let them assume he was called Shagara just as Tanielo and Leisha and Nissim were. Ayia, how very astonished they would be
if they heard his full name—and how very dead they would make him within
moments of hearing it.

Solanna fidgeted for a moment, then said, "I know it is very silly of me
to ask, for we are an obscure family, but—have you heard anything, anything
at all, about anyone named Grijalva?"

"Never heard of them," said the talkative shepherd, at the same time as
the oldest was saying, "The tile makers?"

"Yes!" She rewarded him with her most ravishing smile. "Do you know
them?"

"Their work. But I'm sorry, I know nothing current about them."

Late that night, as Qamar made ready for bed in his workroom—having given their usual hut to the visiting shepherds, who after all had built it—he watched his wife brush out her hair and pondered how best to ask his questions. At last he shrugged and decided on the direct approach.

"You haven't seen any of your family in years and never felt the lack that I've ever been able to tell. Why ask about them tonight? Are you worried for your aunt?"

"Yes," she answered. "If the women and boys now calling themselves Grijalva had been caught and discovered to be what they truly are, wouldn't the Grijalva name have been connected with the news? That nothing has been heard about them means there's nothing to hear."

He hoped she was right. All this long summer he had been too preoccupied to worry much about the other Shagara. To learn that the mountain fortress had not yet fallen to the Sheyqa was incredible news. But they must be running out of food, and as clever as the Haddiyat were, they could not make bread out of a few talishann and a drop or two of blood. Those who had taken the Grijalva name could be halfway to Ghillas by now. He had to believe, with Solanna, that if no one was talking about them, there must be nothing to talk about.

The shepherds were with them for three days. They left with their flocks after slaughtering two fat lambs as additional thanks for the hazziri. Tanielo and Solanna rode with them down to the narrow neck of the valley, and Qamar waited until they were out of sight before seating himself at his worktable.

Even after so many years absence from his home and family, it came to him every so often how amused his parents would be to see him now. Everyone had always said he was Azzad al-Ma'aliq all over again: a capricious, charming wastrel. It was interesting to him that he seemed to have taken on certain aspects of Ab'ya Alessid's personality now: the single-minded dedication, the commitment to a goal.

It was odd, how purely personal, purely selfish acts had such unexpected consequences to the larger world. If Azzad had not taken his vengeance on Sheyqa Nizzira, the army of Rimmal Madar would not be in this land right now. The sequence was clear. Nizzira's obliteration of the al-Ma'aliq; Azzad's revenge for it; his death at the hands of the Shagara faction that did not approve of his actions; the conquest of lands that would become Tza'ab Rih by Rimmal Madar; Alessid's retaking of those lands using Shagara magic; the exile of still more who deplored what they saw as misuse of their arts; the

establishment of first a nation and then an empire; the jealousy of a rapacious new Sheyqa, named for the old one, that led to invasion.

Very little of it could be attributed to anything resembling a noble motive. And Qamar came to see it as a linkage of death. So many deaths: the
al-Ma'aliq, Nizzira's sons and grandsons; Azzad; the people caught in the
middle of Rimmal Madar's invasion; the soldiers of the Za'aba Izim who
died to establish Tza'ab Rih; the Shagara who had died on their way to this
land; more Tza'ab troops and more people here, killed in battles that created
the Empire; thousands who had died and would die before the Sheyqa was
defeated.

Death connected to death, death causing death. It was endless. Inescapable.

But he would bring an end to it. He would escape. And so would those
who heeded him.

He was the codifier the Shagara needed. He was the one who could
recognize all the separate parts of their magic and relate them each to all the
others. But more than that, he was an outsider who discerned the correlation
between the magic and the land. When he had first mentioned this idea,
casually and rather diffidently, to Zario, the startlement in the old man's face
had told him all he needed to know. The concept was alien enough, coming
from him. He never dared tell anyone that it had come first from Alessid
al-Ma'aliq.

Air, water, soil, and the plants that provided food and medicines. These
things became part of the people who lived in a particular place. An army
might invade and conquer; farmers and crafters and merchants and all the
different sorts of people who made up a thriving population might come and
settle; but a place did not belong to someone simply because his house was
built upon it. It was a mutual growing together, an entwining of water with
blood, soil with flesh. This country had almost killed him with poisoned
thorns, for he did not belong here—never mind that anyone foolish enough
to grasp those thorns was in danger of death. The point was that he hadn't
known *not* to touch. But medication concocted here had saved his life, and
with the poison and the cure he had in some way taken part of the land into
himself.

Curiously enough, the wine he had nearly succeeded in killing himself
with had not been the product of this country. He had never been able to
stand the slightly tarry taste of what no one with any perception at all would

term "vintages." He had gotten drunk night after night on wines imported from Tza'ab Rih. He supposed, looking back, that his own land had almost killed him, too. But the cure had come to him *here*, in the form of Solanna, whose ancestors had lived here forever, and Zario, a man whose magic originated in another country but who had learned to adapt as this land demanded. Solanna's sight had found him; Zario's paper and ink had combined with the talishann of the desert to heal him.

As Qamar sorted and wrote and made a hundred decisions each day about what was vital and what was not, the interrelation of land and people was always in his mind. The colors, for example. Surely there were just as many at home, but who had ever thought to delineate them in such fine detail? No one had ever needed to. Their symbolism had been contained in other things, things unavailable here. The plants and flowers and herbs—such an obvious connection, land to herbs to medicine or food to people. This was nothing new to him. But paper—ayia, paper was intriguing, both for its own properties and for what it had led him to discover about trees. He'd heard, now and then, that paper made from a particular kind of wood was better for certain magic. From the paper to the tree was a simple step. He was surprised no one had ever figured this out before.

That it had never been guessed that there could be a connection between realistic drawings and magic did not surprise him at all.

And the inks—they especially fascinated him, for he saw them as akin to blood. They were blood he could manipulate, change, cause to do what he desired. And mixing his own blood into them had produced astounding results.

But he had never told anyone about the new knowledge he was adding to the Shagara wisdom. They were traditionalists, these distant cousins of his. Adjusting mixtures to accommodate different plants, learning how to make paper and ink, these things they had done of necessity. Had the same things been available to them here that their forebears had known in the desert, they never would have made any discoveries at all. But the real clue to their conservatism was in their unfading hatred of Azzad and Alessid al-Ma'aliq for perverting Shagara ways. Change born of inescapable circumstances was one thing. Change for its own sake was quite another. They would not have been pleased, even if he had demonstrated the usefulness of his discoveries, simply because he was the one to have made them. Shagara he was, Haddiyat he was—but also al-Ma'aliq.

Besides, they must not know his ultimate aim. Not until he could prove it.

There were so many possibilities, so many combinations of symbols and influences, medical certainties and hidden meanings. This country had saved his life twice. It would do so again.

Qamar had settled into the rhythms of this tiny world. Leisha made sure the huts were clean, the bedding aired, the meals appetizing, the clothes washed. Tanielo gathered firewood, cared for the horses, brought water from the stream. Solanna worked sometimes with Leisha after she had read Qamar's work of the previous day for clarity, and she spent her afternoons tending the garden. Within days of their arrival she had planted vegetables that by the end of summer were almost ready to be eaten. Nissim helped everyone with everything, but his major duties were with Qamar. His tasks ranged from sharpening pens to serving as Qamar's extra memory regarding what information was in which sheaf of notes. The days melted together, each very like the last. Only the inexorable northward shift of the sun from that notch in the crags reminded him that he must hurry, hurry.

Tanielo was also responsible for catching small animals for the cookpot, and when Qamar had no need of Nissim, the boy learned the fine art of setting snares. Squirrels and rabbits soon avoided the area around the huts—no matter how tempting the above-ground vegetables were—and thus traps were laid down farther and farther away. One morning Qamar was waiting impatiently for the pair to return from checking the night's pickings, for he needed Nissim's help in finding a particular reference to verbena that the boy had located only the day before, when a hawk appeared in the southern sky. Qamar watched it circle slowly, then settle on a treetop to preen its wings.

"Qamar? Someone's coming."

He looked down the valley to where Solanna pointed.

"And he's jingling," she went on, wringing out a shirt and handing it to Leisha for the drying line.

"More like ringing, isn't it?" Leisha asked. "Bells."

Qamar didn't admit that he could not hear what they did. He didn't even admit it to himself, any more than he admitted that their eyes at a distance were much better than his. The rider was discernable to him only because of the bright yellow shirt he wore.

"Wait a moment—isn't that Miqelo?" Solanna shook her hands free of water and started down the rise to the stream. After another moment she raised her arm and waved and called out his name.

At the same moment he let out a shrill whistle. The hawk bolted down from its perch and circled him once, then settled onto Miqelo's outstretched arm. Squinting, Qamar could just make out the gift of a scrap of meat and the skillful hooding of the bird.

"I won't ask whether or not I'm welcome," Miqelo began abruptly as he dismounted, the hawk still on his arm. The jingling had come from the bells decorating the ties of the leather hood. "That doesn't matter. But why in Acuyib's Holy Name are you unguarded? Where is my son?"

"Collecting dinner," Solanna said. "And a good thing, too, with an extra mouth to feed. Whatever your news, Miqelo, and I suspect it cannot be good, you are always welcome for yourself."

He searched her face for a moment, then bowed his head. "Thank you. Leisha, I would not turn away from a very large cup of water."

Qamar stayed where he was at his worktable, silent, watchful. While Miqelo downed first one cup of water and then two, he began tidying his pages and stoppering his ink bottles. Whatever had brought Miqelo here, he knew there would be no more work done today.

After coaxing the hawk to settle on the top rail of the chair Leisha brought for him, Miqelo sat and pulled off his riding gloves. "It's quite a distance from the Cazdeyyan court in exile," he remarked. "I was given this bird by the king."

"In exchange for?" Qamar asked.

"She hunts while I'm on the road," he went on, ignoring the question. "Very convenient, having roast pigeon or sparrow every night—and someone to talk to. The king is Baetrizia's nephew, by the way. She sends greetings, Solanna, and hopes to see you again before very long."

"She was always very kind." Solanna set a cup of spiced qawah before Qamar. "The nephew would be Bertolio?"

"Pedreyo. He's leading the Cazdeyyans south right now."

Qamar turned to his wife. "It cannot be this year. We're not ready. *I'm* not ready."

"Eiha, it begins to look as though we'll have to be ready." She nodded at the hooded hawk.

Miqelo looked from one to the other of them, then caught his breath. "So you *did* see something that night!"

"I swear to you, Miqelo," Qamar told him through gritted teeth, "if you do that to her again—"

"Do you know what's happening out there?" the older man cried. "Constant, pointless, tawdry little brawls from Ibrayanza to Elleon and all places between—eiha, except for Joharra, of course! Sheyqir Allil sits in the palace and redraws his maps to include pieces of other lands, but tells the Empress that she'd better send an army soon or there'll be nothing left to be Empress of! Yes, they're marching, the Tza'ab—"

"My mother is not such a fool!"

"Possibly not, but what does that matter when her sisters and nieces reach back to their desert blood connections and create their own armies? Azwadh, Tariq, Tallib—they come north to ride with the Queen of Qaysh, or Shagarra, or Ibrayanza—"

"Cazdeyya will join with them?" Leisha asked. "Against our common enemy?"

"Which enemy we have in common depends on who you hate more, the Sheyqa or the Tza'ab." Miqelo leaned forward in his chair, so vehemently that it rocked, disturbing the hawk. She unfurled one wing to keep her balance, then settled again. "Did you see the armies, Solanna? Could you tell who was fighting on whose side?"

Slowly she shook her head. "I saw the Sheyqa's tents and the white horses that Qamar tells me are the special privilege of her personal cavalry, the Qoundi Ammar. On the other side of the hill were our people—and, yes, there were Tza'ab among them. And Shagara. But whether they were the soldiers of the Empress, or those belonging to Ibrayanza or Qaysh, I don't know."

"But the battle itself—did you see it? Do you know who will win?"

"No," Qamar answered for her. "And she will not look again, Miqelo," he warned. "If it is this autumn, and not next, then I will manage. But there will be only one copy, and that's not nearly enough—" He broke off, frowning. "The fortress. Does it stand?"

"A few walls of it, yes."

Briefly he closed his eyes. After a moment he whispered, "How many dead?"

"Almost all. It turns out the Sheyqa's troops did not need their ballisdas. All they required was enough time to dig beneath the walls. And even then they did not need to go very far. When their tunnels began to fill with water, they used poisons that seeped back into the wells. There were very few wounds for the healers to treat, Qamar. Almost everyone was poisoned."

"Those who survived?"

"Told to create the magic required by the Sheyqa, or die. They died." He hesitated. "But not before torturing them revealed there were others who had left the fortress."

"Geysh Dushann," Qamar murmured.

"What?"

"A special group of assassins, kin of the al-Ammarizzad. The poison used by Sheyqa Nizzira on the al-Ma'aliq was of their making, or so Azzad always understood. They tried many, many times to kill him, but no one succeeded—until you Shagara," he finished bitterly.

Miqelo stiffened. "Not everyone agreed with what happened—"

"It doesn't matter. The poison released into the groundwater seeped into the wells. That was Geysh Dushann." He laughed without mirth. "Just like before!"

"Only now it is not the al-Ma'aliq but the Shagara—"

"Vengeance!" Qamar pushed himself to his feet, fists clenched. "That's how it all started, don't you see that? Over and over and over, people killing, ordering others killed, people dying in battle or when their towns burn—"

"Qamar," Solanna asked in a soft voice, "are you saying Azzad al-Ma'aliq was wrong to avenge the slaughter of his entire family?"

"Ayia, the chain reaches farther back than that. Nizzira hated the al-Ma'aliq for their power, for being beloved of the people. They hated her family for seizing the Moonrise Throne based on lies—claiming the al-Ammarizzad were responsible for what al-Ma'aliq warriors did, when the barbarians were thrown out of Rimmal Madar. Yes, *barbarians*—the same thing the Tza'ab call *you!*" He began to pace. "A chain I termed it, and a chain it is. Iron chains, fetters, shackles—every generation forging more links, and doing it willingly! Death following death following death—by Acuyib, does it never stop? Does the ground have to be soaked in blood before it stops?"

Words came to him then, with such suddenness that it made him breathless, unable to speak. So many words, crowding his mind, demanding to be written. No one but Solanna noticed it, because Tanielo and Nissim had returned, and the young man recognized his father and ran to greet him. But Qamar knew that Solanna saw it in his face, in his eyes. He could sense her watching him as he turned away, wrapped his arms around his ribs, shook his head as if to clear it of the words.

He made no excuses, simply walked away from them all into his workroom and lit all the lamps. He had left blank the first few pages of the green leather book, believing that once he was finished he would write an introduction to guide students through what followed. He had believed wrongly. It was not an introduction but a justification, an argument addressed to everyone, not just the Shagara.

It took him all night to write it. In the morning, Solanna brought him heated wine and made him drink it.

"It will help you sleep, and sleep is what you need after all that," she told him, gesturing to the tightly filled pages. "Don't quarrel with me, Qamar. You may not be unconscious, the way it happens to me, but you have seen things, and you need sleep and quiet just as I always do."

He felt himself stagger as she helped him into their stone shelter and had to admit she was right. After so long an abstinence, the wine hit him like a sandstorm in the desert. He slept all that day and into the next. And when he woke, it didn't particularly surprise him that for the first time, he felt old.

Solanna was sitting beside their bed when he finally woke. In her lap was the green book. As his gaze met hers, he saw that there were tears in her eyes.

"Azzad and Alessid—they truly believed these things that you have written here?"

"Yes."

"About land and people, and—"

"The ideas are theirs. I put words to them."

"As you have done with the knowledge of both Shagara tribes." She paused. "This has been inside you all these years?"

"I think so, yes." He propped himself on an elbow, biting back a groan of pain as every bone in his body protested movement. "Waiting for light," he added, and reached for her hand.

The wisdom of my great-great grandfather Azzad al-Ma'aliq was to bring green to the land of Tza'ab Rih. Thus the name by which he is known: Il-Kadiri. It was his thought, guided by Acuyib, to care for and enrich the land that had saved his life and given him family, friends, wealth, knowledge. His was the first impulse: to give to the land.

The life of my grandfather Alessid al-Ma'aliq was spent in winning back that which had been taken away, not only from him but from the people of Tza'ab Rih. Thus the name by which he is known: Il-Nazzari. But even beyond the victories, Acuyib guided his thoughts as He had guided Azzad's, and the results may be seen even today in the groves, originally planted by Azzad, restored by Alessid. More, he ordered gardens also, places of beauty and peace where all the people might walk at their leisure and contemplate the small victories in the never-ending chadarang game that pits Acuyib against Chaydann al-Mamnoua'a, green against red, living soil against dead sand. The replanting of Azzad's trees and the planting of gardens accomplished by Alessid, this was the second impulse: to replenish the land.

For Alessid understood the mutual hallowing of the land and the people. He had glimpsed the balance that must obtain between them. He knew that when that balance is overset, when the sanctity of either is polluted, all life becomes anxiety and conflict. And when this happens, Acuyib sorrows in His Realm of Splendor. And Chaydann al-Mamnoua'a laughs.

A further thought, guided by Acuyib, completes the understanding: that the sanctity must be achieved with blood. The rivers and wells, the soil and the plants that grow therefrom, the air, the very rhythm of the seasons: these things fill and hallow each generation until the land and the people are as one.

This is the yearning that caused Azzad to enrich the land with green. This is the craving that caused Alessid to replenish the land as symbol of his victory over those who would destroy it and its people. It is for further generations, bred and born of the land, drinking of its waters and nourished by its bounty, breathing its air and taking unto themselves the awareness of a place from leaf to fruit to dying leaf, to possess that which must first possess them.

To those who would conquer, be warned: there is no belonging, not until the third or fourth or perhaps even fifth generation, not until the blood had been changed, claimed, hallowed.

You must give. If you come only to take, you will lose.

Thus it was during those last anxious days in the mountains that Acuyib guided Qamar's thoughts, and he understood, and wrote swiftly of that understanding in the book we revere as the Kita'ab. The original, written in his own hand, has long been lost. The first copies of the original have vanished as well. But the words remain, and by their truths he became known as Il-Ma'anzuri, The Divinely Aided. More simply, The Diviner.

The greatest of these truths that came to him is this: The blood hallows the land.

This means that when a barbarian land is sanctified with blood, when the previously corrupt and wicked waters run red, the land is changed, the waters are changed, and forever after they belong to those whose blood was spilled in consecration.

For as the Diviner wrote: There is no belonging, not even unto the fourth and fifth generation, until the land has been changed, claimed, and hallowed by blood.

This is the Diviner's message. Any accounting of his life that asserts otherwise is a lie.

— HAZZIN AL-JOHARRA, *Deeds of Il-Ma'anzuri*, 813

25

It was as Solanna had seen it.

The army of tents and carpets, white horses and red banners, encamped on the floodplain. The red and gold of autumn trees. The second army behind a hill to the north, made up of Tza'ab and Cazdeyyan, Ibrayanzan, Qayshi, Andaluz, even Joharran. For Sheyqir Allil had at last realized his mistake and sent his troops to join the fight against Rimmal Madar. Or so he said. But whether they had been ordered there by their commander or came of their own accord, the Joharrans were indeed present.

The Sheyqa's forces now included many who, having learned what it was to be conquered, joined with her rather than be slaughtered. Some probably hoped that this would earn them the right to be left alone; others, that they might even enlarge what they owned, as Allil had done. All of them were afraid. It was their fear that Solanna proposed to exploit.

"Letters," she told her husband as they left their little valley and rode south. "You can send them letters, permeated with magic, that would—"

"No. I'm sorry, qarassia, but I cannot."

"But you don't have to harm them—just make them afraid. Didn't your uncles suggest that very thing to your grandfather? Didn't they offer to make hazziri to terrify the al-Ammarad?"

"They did, but he decided otherwise."

"Eiha, it sounds to me like a very good way to accomplish—"

"No, Solanna."

"It isn't as if you were making them ill, or physically hurting them, causing them pain—it would only be to enhance what they already feel, the fear and tension they *must* be feeling, to be in the army of the Sheyqa. We know their names," she coaxed. "All that need happen is that they touch the letters—"

He shook his head.

"Would your mother hesitate?"

It was the first time she had ever acknowledged that his mother and the Empress of Tza'ab Rih were one and the same woman, but he had no inclination to exclaim upon it now. "If the Shagara could choose to die rather than betray their beliefs, I cannot dishonor them."

"But this is different! You'd be using their knowledge to *stop* people from fighting!"

"A meticulous distinction," he admitted. "I will think about it."

They rode on in silence for a little while. Then she said, "I know where your thoughts take you, Qamar. Even if their qabda'ans are taken ill, the soldiers will fight anyway—and die. But if they withdraw—or try to—"

"The Sheyqa, and especially her Qoundi Ammar, will kill them. There are so many reasons not to do as you suggest. But in the end there is only one that matters. How could I have made this book, and then do this? How could I write these things, and then use them to kill? Because people will die, Solanna, we both know it. I cannot shame those Shagara who sacrificed their lives to keep us safe."

She had said nothing more about it, not during all the long journey to the broad plain where the two armies would meet.

Miqelo's hawk, gift from the King of Cazdeyya, soared sometimes overhead, and to Qamar it was yet another sign from Acuyib. He had rarely believed in such things before, but now it seemed that every turn of his head, every thought that occurred to him, held in it something of destiny. It seemed a hundred years ago that Challa Leyliah had told him the story Azzad had told about a hawk in the desert—ayia, how Ab'ya Alessid had rolled his eyes, and reminded her that the tale had grown more and more elaborate through the years about the hawk that had warned him about the gazelle and led him through the desert to the Shagara. Eventually the tale came to be that the hawk had alighted on his shoulder and guided him with cries and flapping wings to the rockslide; eventually, too, the very same hawk had flown ahead of him and Khamsin, dropping a feather here and there to make sure he reached the Shagara camp.

Qamar knew that this hawk was the very same one Solanna had seen flying over the opposing armies. And after they reached the hills above the plain, and Miqelo had found acquaintances among the Cazdeyyans, Qamar knew on the afternoon he saw the hawk flying overhead once more that the eve of battle had come.

He sought the shelter of a thicket of willow trees, private as the Sheyqa's own tent. He sat in the dirt with a single lamp beside him, his whole collection of inks in a case that formed a desk of sorts, the green book open atop it. So beautiful a binding, plain and yet luxurious, worthy of the unique papers within. He could only hope that the words were as beautiful, as valuable.

He leafed through the book, all the way to the back where he had tucked a few loose pages. They were one of his more interesting papers, made after much thought and careful collection of ingredients. The cypress in particular had been difficult to obtain; he owed it to Miqelo, of course, who had collected such fascinating things for him on his travels. Cypress, which local lore connected with longevity. Comfort. Health. Youthfulness. The immortal Soul.

He closed the book, set it aside. Opening the case of inks, he trailed his fingertips across the stoppers of each. They were as crucial as the paper. The colors, the composition—dragon's blood for power, vervain for enchantment, fern for magic, lavender for luck, yellow poppy for success . . . Qamar contemplated the largest bottle, full of black ink, and heard across the years Zario's voice: *"For wisdom and control, resilience and discipline. And although it is the most emphatic of colors, it has this curious quality: Black is the color that hides your thoughts and motives from others."*

More esoteric was the inclusion of fir bark, which symbolized time. But the commonest ingredients, white heather and acorns, were the most powerfully ambitious. Ground to powder, carefully mixed, each signified immortality.

Qamar was overreaching himself, he knew. There was in all likelihood a very good reason why no Shagara had ever sought to create the results he intended from these papers and inks, these talishann and his own blood. But whenever he thought about the first pages of that book, written in a controlled frenzy, he actually felt humbled: his selfish impulse of so many years ago, his determination to live, had turned out to have a greater purpose. The life he wanted so much was meant to be spent enlightening the peoples of two separate lands. Acuyib had shown him how to make the killings cease. And to do it, he must live. This was what he had been preparing for, this was why he was destined to succeed. Solanna had seen him old. He would succeed.

"Qamar? What in the world are you doing down here?"

The curtain of willow branches rustled opened, and Miqelo sidled in, an expression both worried and whimsical on his face.

"Not as grand as the Sheyqa's tent, but just as useful," Qamar said, smiling. "And much prettier, don't you think? Wonderful inside, but I'd imagine that from the outside it looks rather like a lantern with a green beaded shade."

The older man crouched down on the other side of the lamp. "We've caught a spy."

"Really? Whose?"

"I'm not sure *he* knows," Miqelo admitted. "Of course, that's not particularly unusual around here, is it?"

"I would think that their Mother and Son are conferring with our Acuyib, trying to sort out whose believers are in which army."

"And where their loyalties truly lie."

"Are we interested in this spy, or he merely a curiosity?"

"He says he's Grijalva."

Qamar sat up straighter, eyes wide. "Have you told Solanna?"

"I thought I'd bring him here first. In case he says things she might not wish to hear."

About her family, her home, her people who ought to have been at home making their beautiful painted tiles, who might be fighting on the wrong side tomorrow. Nodding, he said, "That was thoughtfully done."

Miqelo stood, swept aside branches, and called softly, "Tanielo!" Then he took up a position beside and slightly behind where Qamar sat: guarding him. His brother Yberrio's words whispered with the movement of leaves. *"Make sure this man lives."*

There was nothing about the young man to connect him in feature with Solanna except for the wild curling of his hair. A considerable nose, a very long jaw, a rather too-wide mouth—not a handsome face at all. Moreover, the eyes were of a color Qamar had rarely seen before: they were blue. Startlingly so, with the long black eyelashes and dark skin, those eyes met his without defiance, anxiety, fear, or indeed anything one might have expected to see in the eyes of a captured spy. Instead, as he took in Qamar's face with one coldly appraising stare, an emotion more familiar to Qamar tightened the thin lips. He had seen it a thousand times: the resentment of a conspicuously homely man for a conspicuously beautiful one.

Qamar addressed him in his own language, fully aware that his accent would mark him as one who had learned from a resident of Grijalva lands. "A pleasant evening, is it not? You seem to have strayed a bit."

A shrug of skinny shoulders. But the expected surprise flashed across his face as he recognized the accent.

"My friend says you call yourself a Grijalva. But I think there must be something of Ghillas in your background, eiha?"

There was open astonishment in the blue eyes now. "My grandmother's grandmother," he said, then looked just as startled that he'd actually responded to the question.

"And her name was Ysabielle, wasn't it?"

His jaw dropped open.

Qamar smiled. "I've been interested in the Grijalva family for quite some time. From Ysabielle came blue eyes in some, fair hair in others. Have you a first name?"

"J-Jaqiano," he stammered. "But how did you—?"

"The art of the Grijalva tiles is known to me—as it is to everyone with an eye for beauty. Please, sit down. I cannot offer you a chair, but the ground is soft enough."

The young man dropped as if his knees had suddenly given out, and then hastily arranged long limbs in a more dignified position. "You know my name—what's yours?"

"Qamar."

"If you're a soldier of the Tza'ab, where's your armor?"

"What makes you think I'm a soldier of the Tza'ab?"

"Your name. Your skin."

"But haven't we just established that while your name is Cazdeyyan, your eyes are not? There are Tza'ab and Tza'ab—just as there are Joharrans and Joharrans, these days. Perhaps the one thing we can agree upon is that there is only one type when it comes to Rimmal Madar." He paused. "Or perhaps I should say one type with three variations."

"Three—?"

"The regular soldiers. The elite cavalry. The assassins."

Jaqiano was silent for a moment. Then: "You know too much about them not to be camped with them, ready to fight for them tomorrow."

"Too much? Not nearly enough. But that doesn't matter." Nothing else had mattered the instant Miqelo had said *Grijalva*. "Tell me, Jaqiano—did you lose your sketchbook?"

And he nearly laughed aloud when shock scrawled itself across the young face.

Jaqiano Grijalva was precisely what Qamar had hoped he was. What he had known he would be from the instant he heard the name. Since the night he had spent writing, writing, he had felt the touch of Acuyib at his elbow, urging him gently onward. He had been mistaken about which autumn would be the decisive one. He had not been mistaken that Acuyib would provide.

The Grijalva craft was tilemaking. Wherever clay deposits were found, there also were Grijalva workshops. Some of them mixed clay to the correct consistency; others blended glazes; the women had charge of forming the tiles, and the men oversaw the kilns. At his age, Jaqiano would have been taught the basics of all of it. But Qamar had made a guess that was not truly a guess when he asked about the sketchbook. Jaqiano's long-boned, sensitive hands showed no scars from burns, as a kiln worker would have, but there were stains of a dozen different colors on his fingers. They were days from any workshops, and yet his fingers were stained. Qamar had hoped, and he had been right. The colors were paint, and Jaqiano was an artist.

Moreover, he was the son and grandson of artists, and proud of it. "We'd just won the commission to make the tiles for the new palace at Shagarra," he told Qamar. "But while we were there to plan it and take the dimensions, the Sheyqa came, and we were stranded, my father and I. It took us all spring to find any kind of armed resistance we could join—"

"I can well imagine. More qawah?" He poured from the pitcher Tanielo had brought. "So you found an army. Whose?"

"No one's. At first there were only about fifty of us, then twice that, and then we found another group—they were from Qaysh—it was all very tangled, and everyone argued about where to go, except then we happened upon a troop of real soldiers from Andaluz. And now we're here, and there are thousands of us!"

"We are on the same side, you know," Qamar said.

"Are we? Who do *you* hate most?"

Qamar understood very well what he meant. The Sheyqa Nizhria was at the top of the list; once she was defeated, the Tza'ab would be next. And then the peoples of this land would all fall upon each other, and lay waste whatever they touched. He could stop this. He could show them how futile it all was. He *would* do it. Solanna had seen him old; he would succeed.

"Do you draw patterns or scenes?" Both figured in Grijalva tiles, designs and landscapes.

Bewildered by the abrupt change of subject, Jaqiano took a moment to reply. When he did, it was with pride bordering on arrogance. "I can do all of it, and more besides. I've been sketching the soldiers—"

"—and they encouraged you to do their individual portraits to take home," Qamar murmured, "or to send home, just in case. Which is a thing nobody talks about, of course."

"How did you know that? How do you know *any* of this?"

"If I told you that it's necessary, all of it is necessary, you wouldn't understand. So you have learned how to draw the human face and form. Are you any good?" He asked the question only for effect. He already knew the boy was talented. He would not be here otherwise. Acuyib had provided.

"If I had my sketchbook, I'd show you. The sentries took it. I was only making the drawings for—"

Qamar waited, hiding a smile. At length, when the boy said nothing more, he finished for him, "For the grand great tile wall that will tell the story of victory over the Sheyqa. You *are* ambitious. Tanielo!" he called. "Find the guards who found this young man, and restore to him his sketchbook!"

"At once, Sh—Qamar," he amended hastily, for as adamant as Qamar had been about his title before, now he had given even stricter instructions that no one call him anything but his name.

Turning his attention back to the boy, he asked, "Do you mix your own glazes? Or perhaps the inks for your drawings?"

"I am an *artist*. There's no more imagination goes into mixing colors than there is in boiling water."

"I think you may be wrong about that." He opened the case of inks and pulled out a bottle. "Have you ever seen this color, for instance? Or this?"

The boy was indeed an artist. His blue eyes lit with longing at the diversity of inks, and his fingers actually reached for them before he remembered they were not his. Not *yet* his, Qamar thought. Not quite yet.

"You may be interested in the recipes, Jaqiano, for when you create your depiction of victory."

"Not just that—not just a single scene. I'll do a whole wall, as you said, but it will be the whole battle, a series of images, each tile moving seamlessly into the next."

Qamar remembered the beautiful garden of tiles his grandfather had ordered and the fountain that had not worked, and then had worked, and then had died once again. And the Haddiyat who had died in agony with the burning of a page.

Jaqiano mistook his silence for skepticism. "I can do it," he stated. "I *will* do it."

"I haven't a single doubt that you will. But perhaps you will oblige me, do me a great favor." He gave the boy a self-deprecating smile, a shrug. "Before you return to your fellow soldiers, would you be so kind . . . ?"

The portrait looked exactly like him. Not that he had expected anything else, but still—it was an extraordinary experience, looking into one's own face. Nothing like a mirror, he discovered: when he felt his own brows arch and his own eyes widen with surprise, the portrait did not respond as a reflection would. And all the tiny flaws that inevitably distorted glass were not to be found here. It was his perfect face he saw. *Perfect.*

Jaqiano watched him react, a smug grin spreading across his face. He had reason for his arrogance. Each subtle black line that delineated face and body was a stroke of brilliance. Delicate washes of ink defined golden skin and dark eyes, the flush of blood in cheeks and lips, the threads of silver in black hair, the shadows that marked the bones of his face. These were Qamar's eyes, dark and beautiful; these were his shoulders, his hands, down to the tiny scar left by a burning feather so many years ago. Down to the topaz leaf ring and the al-Gallidh pearl.

Yet there was more to the artist's self-satisfaction than pride in his own skill. It was as if this young man with the not-quite-ugly face had, in replicating the beauty of another, taken some of that beauty unto himself. The perfection of this portrait could not exist without him. He could rightly claim a share in that perfection.

Equally fine was the rendering of Qamar's plain white tunic, the brown trousers of lightweight wool. Feeling their softness against his body, he was convinced that a fingertip touched to their likenesses would feel just as soft. The gleam of polished leather boots was also taken from life, but the sash around his waist—white with green and glittering gold stripes—was entirely of Jaqiano's doing, suggested by Qamar and interpreted by imagination.

There was no background to the portrait, not even the suggestion of the willow leaves that sheltered him. Only darkness. In all the long hours of the night that it had taken to complete the picture, the lamplight had not wavered, providing a steady soft glow. The work contained time, for it had taken time to make—yet there was no sense of time within it, no specific shadows that would mean morning or afternoon or evening.

Qamar stared at himself, and after the first shock, he realized he looked much older than he'd expected. He didn't remember these lines radiating out from the corners of his eyes, the furrows of determination crossing his forehead. It was still a beautiful face, just not in the way he recalled it.

They were both exhausted, of course. Qamar poured out the last cold cups of qawah, and they sat with the picture lying atop the closed case of inks, looking at it in silence as they drank.

At last Qamar said, "You have done me a greater service than you can ever understand."

Jaqiano glanced briefly at him, but seemed incapable of taking his gaze from his own work for more than a few moments. "Doing this . . . it was different from all the others. Your inks are supple enough that the lines nearly draw themselves with the pen. And the colors blend almost without effort."

Recognizing the craving, Qamar smiled. "I have need of them yet, but once the battle is won, come back and I'll give them to you. Poor enough payment for such work, but—"

"I accept," he interrupted. "All of them? The whole case of inks?"

"All of them." He set aside his cup and stretched. "And now I think you had best return to your people. Some sleep before dawn would not be a bad thing. Again, I thank you. And—Jaqiano, do try not to get yourself killed, won't you? You're worth far more than your ability to wield a spear."

A blush stained the boy's cheeks. "I'm not very good in battle, it's true," he confessed, low-voiced. "The first time I was in a fight, I—"

Qamar lifted a hand to stop him. "*I* fell off my horse and threw up. You can't have done anything worse than that!" They traded grins, and Qamar finished, "Go, and give my compliments to your father—and to your mother, when you see her again, on having birthed such a son as you."

"You won't forget about the inks?"

"I won't forget."

When he was alone, Qamar unstoppered several bottles and picked up a fresh pen. With the portrait flat atop the green book, he began designing the border. Talishann after talishann, elegant and potent, gradually framing one side, then two, then three. He kept glancing into his own eyes, and smiling. He took up a finer pen and traced barely visible symbols into the subtle shadows on his clothing, entwined them in the lines of his sash. Only a little while until dawn, only a little while before he would be able to fulfill the mission with which Acuyib had entrusted him, for which he alone had the daring and ambition—

He shook off the momentary dizziness and dipped his pen once more in black ink. Another talishann, and another, along the bottom of the portrait now, adding one to each side so that soon they would meet in the middle and only one would be left, the one he would seal with his blood. Connected through the flowing lines of interwoven symbols, through the fibers of the paper saturated with inks forming his own image—

Perhaps it was the magic, awakening. He would sense the power, feel it, of course he would—he was kindling magic such as no Shagara had ever dared do before, no wonder he was growing dizzy—but in a few moments he would feel other things, he would feel younger, the aches in his fingers and knees gone, and the gray would vanish from his hair and all the lines from his face, not that any of that was important, not really, not compared to the work he would use these coming years to accomplish—his selfishness had ended up having a greater purpose, just as Azzad's and Alessid's individual desires had resulted in so much that they had not envisioned—they had changed their worlds, and he would do the same, only he would not have to kill anyone to do it—people would live, they would understand, they would spend their lives in peace, and surely his desire for more years than his kind could expect was a small thing to exchange for what he would tell them, what he would make them understand—

The breath was rasping in his throat. The edges of his vision were turning black, black as the ink staining his fingers, he couldn't find the little knife he'd intended to use to prick up drops of his blood and so he used the sharp point of the pen—dug it into his thumb—squinted to see that crimson dripped thick onto the last talishann the one that meant life—

He thought he heard Solanna's voice, through the screen of willow branches he could no longer see, and tried to call out to her that it was all right, everything would be perfect from now on, they would have years and years together, that she was right and he would grow old and there would be lines on his face.

His lips would not move. His head would not turn. He felt a great wrenching pain, heard a shrieking as of a furious storm, and knew nothing more.

She sat with the green book on her knees and the portrait of her husband smooth and beautiful atop it. Nissim had told her what most of the talishann meant. She had looked up the others in the book. She had taken all day to do it. With the battle raging over the hill, a battle for which she cared not at all, she had nothing else to do.

Which of the Tza'ab had betrayed the Sheyqa, which had stayed loyal to the Empress, and which had decided to fight on the side of their new land, she did not know. Which Joharrans and Cazdeyyans and Qayshi and Shagarrans and all the confused clutter of soldiers had fought with or against or for each other, she did not know. She was certain nobody else knew, either. Those who survived would tell whatever tale would allow their continued survival. They would go home and brag about their courage, their cleverness. Someone would end up taking the credit. It didn't matter. They would all go on fighting each other until someone emerged who was strong enough to make them stop.

Qamar had thought to do that. She had read it in the first few pages of the book.

> *Each people belongs to its own land by virtue of oneness with the air they breathe, the water they drink, the soil that grows their food. Over the generations the land hallows their blood. Their blood spilled in its defense hallows the land. And when this has happened, they are the land's, and the land is theirs. No one may come to claim it who is not willing to live on and with and for it, to take it into his blood and be willing to give that blood back in its defense.*
>
> *So you must understand the madness, the fatal madness, of believing that to stand in a field means you own that field. That to build a palace on a hill means you own that hill. That to construct a bridge across a river means you own that river. It is not until the field and the hill and the river own you that balance is achieved.*
>
> *How futile it is, how fatal, to make war for land that is not your own.*

"Solanna? I've found the boy."

Miqelo's voice made her glance around. It was growing dark now. She had been staring at her husband's face for many hours. Perhaps the battle was over. Probably it was. She didn't care. "And?"

"He was coming here anyway. Qamar promised him the inks."

"Did he." She looked down at the case that she had repacked, all the bottles with their carved stone stoppers nestled neatly together, the extra loose papers folded atop them. "Take them. He can have them."

"Perhaps you might want to talk to him. He's a Grijalva, after all."

"Yes, you already said. It may be that he and I shall meet one day. But not this day, Miqelo. I've changed my mind. Not this day."

She returned her gaze to her husband's beautiful face as Miqelo came inside the green canopy of willow leaves and picked up the inks, took them away to give to the young Grijalva who had all unknowing helped Qamar do this incredible, insane thing. Not the thing he had intended, of course. But it had happened all the same.

"Did you think you could stop a war?" she asked the portrait. "Did you truly think that? Did you think that if you showed them what was possible—" Her gaze flickered to the talishann so finely drawn, so thick around the borders of the page. *Life. Youth. Health. Strength.* A dozen more, repeated again and again, signs that originated with the Shagara in his desert homeland and variations discovered by the Shagara in their mountain fortress. The scents of the paper and the inks were still discernable, some of them still pungent. Many of them he had learned from his fellow Haddiyat. Some of them . . . some of them he had learned from her.

"Did you think," she resumed softly, "to show them the power of this land? And that they could not hope to conquer it, but only to become in time a part of it? That, Acuyib and Claydann and their great game aside, it is the Mother who gives, and the Son who defends?"

She saw her hand tremble slightly as a fingertip traced one of the talishann. There was the faintest tinge of dark crimson to the ink, telling her that this had been the last, the one drawn with his blood. *Life.*

Eiha, he lived. Just not in the way he'd intended.

A perfect likeness, his inks on his paper, though drawn by a hand not his own; sealed with Shagara symbols and Shagara blood. *Youth. Health. Time. Strength. Safety. Permanence. Life.* Woods and herbs and flowers and water had intensified the meanings of the talishann, amplified the potency of his blood. The magic had done what he had insisted it do, in the only way it could.

Just not in the way he'd intended.

Opening the book, she used a knife to slit the inside back cover. She wasted another moment looking at the portrait, then slid a protective sheet of paper across it and carefully slid both pages between the leather and the wooden backing. She would glue it closed later. It would be safe enough for now.

He would be safe enough. For now.

She closed the book, locked it, and slipped the small golden key into her pocket. Rising, she held the book to her breast with one hand and took up the dead lamp in the other. Nothing was left behind as she emerged from the willow tree and went to find Miqelo, to tell him she was ready to leave.

He waited for her beside their horses. In the darkness campfires sparked here and there on the hillsides. There was no moon.

"You still haven't said where Qamar went," he reminded her. "Or when he'll come back."

She held the book tighter. *He never left*, was the truthful answer. What she said was, "In his own time, I suppose. Come, Miqelo, I want to be far away from here by morning."

The Sheyqa's army was defeated.

The Sheyqa escaped, only to die when her ship was attacked by pirates from Diettro Mareia. Some say she threw herself into the sea rather than suffer the dishonor of capture, but others assert that her own qabda'ans murdered her and tossed her body overboard. A niece who had stayed loyal in her heart to her al-Ma'aliq origins became Sheyqa of Rimmal Madar, and her line has occupied the Moonrise Throne ever since.

The fate of Solanna Grijalva al-Ma'aliq is unclear. She may have returned to her Grijalva relations. She may have been killed after the battle or died on the journey home. There is a curious letter in the archives at Hazganni, dated two years after the battle and sent from Ibrayanza, claiming kinship with her husband's niece, the Empress Za'avedra, and asking for documents guaranteeing safe passage across the border into Tza'ab Rih for herself and her son. But this is undoubtedly a forgery.

Il-Ma'anzuri, having left the seven brief, brilliant pages of the Kita'ab to enlighten his people, chose to emulate his pious grandmother, Empress Mirzah, and spent the rest of his days in solitary devotions, and he was never seen again.

And so I have told you of him, and any telling of his life that differs in any respect from this one is a lie.

— HAZZIN AL-JOHARRA, *Deeds of Il-Ma'anzuri*, 813

AUTHOR'S NOTE

Basically, you see, it's very strange sometimes, the way books get written. Even now I recall perfectly receiving a fax at the Athens Gate Hotel in Athens, Greece. The gist of it was that my agent wanted to know if I'd be interested in doing a book with two of his other clients, Jennifer Roberson and Alis Rasmussen. So, the three of us being friends anyway, we agreed and in January of 1994 met at Jennifer's house in Phoenix, Arizona. (You may imagine the profundity of Alis' joy at sitting outside in shorts and a t-shirt, soaking up winter sunshine; her home was in Pennsylvania back then.) As we worked (and we did work, honest!), we sparked ideas off each other in ways that had never happened to any of us before and had ourselves a fine, creative, splendid time, and a lot of fun.

Not to put too fine a point on it, though, once we were off on the 1996 book tour, we were all flummoxed by the insinuations (and more than insinuations sometimes) that three women couldn't possibly work together on a book without multiple catfights. Drastic drops in ambient room temperature followed these interview questions—I can remember the first time it happened, when I sort of sat there with my jaw flapping open, Alis' eyes widened to approximately the size of teacups, and Jennifer's posture became that of a soldier on parade. (Some people "get their backs up" as the saying goes; Jennifer's spine becomes a ramrod.) How and what we answered, I've forgotten. Essentially, the implication was that nobody thought three women could work together on a project, especially one of this size and scope, without behaving like peevish children rather than professionals who admire and respect each other's work. Is it cantankerous of me to wonder if that sort of question would be asked of three male writers who wrote a book together?

Looking back, there is one shocking thing about that book. As presented in that original fax, the concept of *The Golden Key* was "about 50,000 words each." Clearly, this was ridiculous; the thing ended up being 337,000 words long. And I accounted for about 105,000 of them. Now, many people are skeptical that mine could be the shortest section, but I am occasionally capable of restraint. Kind of.

It's documented in the faxes we exchanged even before the Phoenix meeting (yes, faxes; not emails), that prior to working out the ideas and plotlines, we were determined that the book would give the readers the experience they expected from our solo novels. Should a reader come to *The Golden Key* as a Rawn, Roberson, or Elliott fan (or, most desirably, of course, a fan of all three!), we wanted to provide the feel of our individual work while ensuring that the story flowed as seamlessly as possible from section to section. Surely this sort of thing is impossible without knowing, understanding, and liking each other and each other's work?

Many years have gone by, but I've finally finished *The Diviner*. Yattering on about what happened betweentimes is fairly pointless; all I can do is apologize for taking so long. It had its start with questions we all had about where the Grijalva gift came from. Right before *The Golden Key* was published, I was traveling in Morocco, a land so amazingly beautiful that I wanted to use it as a backdrop. I add that whereas the best of Tza'ab Rih originates in Morocco, the politics, history, and religion of the former are the products of my imagination. Simply put, it ain't real—but my job is to make it feel real. Having received a Bachelor's in History from Scripps College, I worry sometimes that the distinguished professors who tried to make of me a scholar would cringe at the use to which I've put my education. Apologies to them, too.

Special thanks to Darcey (for linguistic advice which I then skewed to my own purposes—this is the difference between a Scholar and a Novelist). So too I need to thank Gordon Crabbe; Russ Galen; Laurie Rawn; B.J. Doty and Primus St. John; Rodney, James, and Jeane Relleve Caveness, Ph.D.; Teresa Taylor; Lee and Barbara Johnson; Jay and Sonia Busby.